About the Authors

Karen Booth is a Midwestern girl transplanted in the South, raised on '80s music and repeated readings of *Forever* by Judy Blume. When she's not writing about dreamy fictional men and the women who test them, she's in the garden, obsessing over college basketball, or spending time with her husband, college-age kids, and bratty cat.

Sarah M. Anderson won RT Reviewer's Choice 2012 Desire of the Year for *A Man of Privilege*. *The Nanny Plan* was a 2016 *RITA*® winner for Contemporary Romance: Short. Find out more about Sarah's love of cowboys at sarahmanderson.com

Cindy Myers became one of the most popular people in eighth grade when she and her best friend wrote a torrid historical romance and passed the manuscript around among friends. Fame was short-lived, alas; the English teacher confiscated the manuscript. Since then, Cindy has written more than fifty published novels. Her historical and contemporary romances and women's fiction have garnered praise from reviewers and readers alike.

D1634933

Seduction in the Snow

KAREN BOOTH

SARAH M. ANDERSON

CINDI MYERS

MILLS & BOON

First Published in Great Britain 2022
By Mills & Boon, an imprint of HarperCollins*Publishers* Ltd
1 London Bridge Street, London, SE1 9GF

www.harpercollins.co.uk

HarperCollins*Publishers*
1st Floor, Watermarque Building,
Ringsend Road, Dublin 4, Ireland

SEDUCTION IN THE SNOW © 2022 Harlequin Enterprises ULC.

Snowed In with a Billionaire © 2017 Harlequin Enterprises ULC.
A Beaumont Christmas Wedding © 2014 Sarah M. Anderson
Cold Conspiracy © 2019 Cynthia Myers

Special thanks and acknowledgement are given to Karen Booth for her contribution to the *Secrets of the A-List* series.

ISBN: 978-0-263-31801-2

SNOWED IN WITH
A BILLIONAIRE

KAREN BOOTH

One

Joy McKinley hated to lie to anyone, especially someone as sweet as her fellow bakery worker, Natalie. But she had no choice.

"This is me. On the right. Don't bother pulling into the driveway. It's tough to back out. Cars whiz around that turn so fast." Snow was coming down like crazy now. By all accounts, they were in for one heck of a storm.

"Cute house." Natalie peered through the window at the rustic cabin Joy had driven past every day on her way up the mountain. Her blond curls poked out from underneath her gray-and-white-striped knit hat. It had a giant pom-pom on top. "You make enough at the bakery to live here by yourself?"

If Natalie knew where Joy was really staying, her eyes would have popped out of her head. This house wasn't nice enough to be the shed behind the one she was currently living in. "It's really not that nice. It's a total fixer-upper on the inside. And it's just until I decide whether or not I'm staying in Vail long-term."

Every fib out of Joy's mouth, however small, ate at her. That was the reason she'd kept to herself since coming to Vail—it was easier to live covertly if you never had to speak to anyone about the details of your life. It made for a solitary existence though, one that was starting to chew a hole through Joy's sanity and sense of self, especially now that Christmas was almost here. Unfortunately, lies and lone-wolfing were the best ways to keep her cover, and keep it she must.

Natalie's car quaked and rumbled as it idled, but at least it was still spitting out heat. December in Colorado was no joke. Although Joy had grown up in Ohio and had lived through her fair share of bitter cold winters, she'd lost much of her immunity to chilly temperatures while living in LA and Santa Barbara over the last few years.

"Which way are you leaning? Staying or going?" Natalie asked.

"I'm not sure. I need to weigh my options, find a permanent place to live. Let me know if you hear of anyone who needs a roommate. I'd love to share the rent with someone."

"I'll definitely ask around. We'd hate to lose you at the bakery. I love working with you."

"That's so sweet of you to say. I love working with you, too." Joy nodded eagerly. Those words were the truth. Still, her pulse was starting to thunder in her ears. What if the real owner of this house came outside, wondering what a strange car was doing idling out front? What if they suddenly came home? The thought put her too close to the edge, a place she'd spent the last several months. Someday she would get settled. Someday she wouldn't have to be a nomad.

"Just so you know, I'm not trying to guilt you into staying. Seems like you're pretty overqualified to work there."

"I'm really not overqualified. Pastries and baking are just as much work as French or Italian cuisine." Those were Joy's specialties, but if she started talking about food, she'd never get out of the car, and she was already tempting fate by sitting there. Needing to force the issue, she pulled the handle and opened her car door. "I should go. I'm beat from today and you should really get home before the snow gets any worse."

Natalie leaned across the seat and looked up at Joy. "Do you want me to talk to my brother about helping you with your car? He works cheap if I tell him it's a favor to me."

Even cheap is too expensive for me. "It's nice of you to offer. I'll let you know. Thanks so much for the ride. I'll see you at work tomorrow."

Of course, I have no clue how I'm going to get there, but I'll worry about that later.

"If the bakery stays open in this storm. I'd check in with Bonnie later tonight before you go to bed. She'll tell you what the contingency plan is based on the forecast."

"Thanks. I'll do that." Joy dawdled on her way to the mailbox, pretending to fumble with her bag, then stood with her hand on the pull, waving at Natalie. As soon as she was out of view, Joy pulled back her hand. Knowing her luck, she'd get saddled with federal mail tampering charges.

Joy waited another moment, standing perfectly still as snow fell all around her, collecting on her shoulders and her nose. As soon as she was certain Natalie was long gone, she doubled back to the end of the street and started her long walk up the hill to the sprawling luxurious mountain estate of her former employers, Harrison and Mariella Marshall. Landing the job as head chef at the Marshalls' estate in Santa Barbara, California, had been a dream come true. Now she was enduring a bizarre bad dream, one in which her surroundings were still luxe and of the Marshall variety, but the reality was decidedly less shiny.

Harrison Marshall, one of the world's original celebrity chefs, owned a global culinary empire. Working for him was the ultimate foot in the door when it came to being a chef. Unfortunately, Harrison had been in a near-fatal car accident soon after Joy began working for him. In the aftermath, Harrison's family unraveled, especially his wife, Mariella. She used Joy as a verbal punching bag, launching unprovoked tirades about things as minor as what type of table salt to use. One day, Mariella pushed too hard, and Joy quit. With little money and zero prospects, she walked away from the best job she'd ever had.

Only empathy from Mariella's son Rafe had saved her, and it was a temporary fix. He'd given her the keys to the Vail house, saying she was okay to stay until mid-January, when his siblings would likely come to ski. It was such a beautiful home, her stay was a respite, of sorts, but she still needed to work, and the only employment she'd found was at the bakery downtown. It was money and that was all that mattered.

Normally, Joy would be driving her beat-up car home from the bakery at this time of day, rocking forward and back in the driver's seat and praying it would make it all the way to the top. Not today. The cantankerous piece of junk had decided not to start that morning. This was after she'd just spent the only significant chunk of money she had, nearly six hundred dollars, on fixing it. She would've been better off abandoning the car and keeping that money for a deposit on an apartment. The clock was ticking on that front. Mid-January would be here before she knew it.

She'd considered borrowing one of the three cars in the Marshalls' five-car garage, all of which had to cost more money than she could make in five years. As someone who was supposed to be laying low, driving around town in a showstopper of a vehicle was a recipe for attracting too much attention. She'd attempted to borrow one of the family's bicycles, but she only made it partway down the icy driveway before nearly wiping out. At that point, out of options and on the verge of being late for a job she absolutely needed, she'd decided to spend her last available cash on a taxi. Hence the ride home from Natalie.

The storm seemed to be gaining momentum now. The fluffy fat flakes from earlier were turning to icy pellets. The wind was blowing like crazy, howling between the trees and rustling snow from the branches in dramatic swirls. With a deluge of frozen precipitation pummeling her face, she had to squint in order to see. Joy tugged her scarf up around her ears and over her mouth. It was hard work to scale the hill, and she was breaking out into a sweat, even in the freezing temperatures. The high down in Vail that day had only been twenty-eight degrees. She got off work from the bakery at 3:00 p.m. each day, and it was nearly five now. The sun had set. The brittle night air grated against her cheeks; it worked its way into her bones. Colorado was beautiful, but Joy wasn't sure she was cut out for being a snow bunny long-term. She would've done anything at that moment for a margarita and a beach.

She dug the toes of her boots into the compacted snow, trudging away, careful to stay as far to the side of the road as possible. So much snow had fallen over the last few weeks that waist-high banks lined both sides of the street. She zipped her jacket up around her face and focused on what was waiting for her when she reached the top. She visualized the unbelievable bed she'd been sleeping in every night, the fluffy king-sized pillow-top in Mariella's daughter's room. Climbing in and sinking into that luxurious mattress, swishing her bare feet against the fine sheets, was pure heaven. It was her reward for surviving every day. It was also her safe place, a place where she didn't allow herself to become mired in negative thoughts or worries about where she would go next or what she was going to do in terms of building a future. Yes, she was living a borrowed life right now, and a clandestinely borrowed one at that, but she had to be thankful for what she had. A roof over her head and a warm place to sleep were at the top of the list of her blessings.

The incline was getting steeper. She hitched her bag up on her shoulder. Her breaths came faster, icy air slicing through her lungs. Everything was freezing—her feet, her thighs, her fingers, and especially her cheeks. She started to shake from the cold. *Think of the bed. Think of the bed.* Just then a soft glow came from around the bend. Light bounced off the snowbanks and the snow-covered branches of the dense stands of trees all around her. The light became brighter. It swept from side to side. But it was the strangest thing. There was no noise. She'd typically hear a car by now. And then came a recognizable sound—the crunch of tires over snow.

The black car came into view, up at the very top of the hill. She inched closer to the side of the road to be safe. She waved her hand to make sure the driver saw her, and he seemed to, slowly moving to the center of the road. She looked down at her feet for an instant and the next thing she knew, the car was skidding across a patch of ice, drifting closer to the opposite side. She could see his exact trajectory. He was going to go into the ditch. The car turned sharply. An overcorrection. The back end fishtailed. The car slid sideways. The tires crunched against the snow again. The driver had slammed on the brakes. But it kept going. Coming right for her. *Run.* That was all she could think. But which way? Up seemed like the only answer. Her feet slipped. She fell forward, clawing at the snow with her hands, scrambling out of the way. The headlights blinded her. The car barreled at her. She righted herself and scrambled. Not enough time. She did the only thing she could do. She dove into a snowbank.

Cold shot through her entire body, like a tidal wave fueled by adrenaline. She took a sharp breath, her lungs filled with unbelievable iciness. Her throat tightened. She couldn't breathe. Snow was everywhere. Like she'd jumped into the deepest part of the ocean and was surrounded by icebergs. She flailed about, all arms and legs, struggling to stand. She couldn't get a foothold. There was no solid ground. Only snow to breathe and swallow. Did people drown in snowbanks? She was about to find out. Leave it to her to be the first person to accomplish such a feat. As she struggled with her arms, trying to push herself up, something grabbed her leg. *Oh, God. A bear.*

It was full-on panic—flailing, fighting and kicking. She screamed at the top of her lungs and managed to roll to her back. Whatever had her in its clutches was pulling on her now. She dug her hands into the snow, trying to stop her progress, but the beast was too strong for her. She couldn't fight it off. She was going to get eaten by a bear. Now she wished she was back to drowning in the snow.

With a thump, her butt landed on hard ground. The bear let go. She kicked and screamed. A dark figure loomed over her. It was lit from behind. *Wait a minute.* If this was a bear, he had very nice shoulders and an awfully nice head of hair.

"Are you okay?" the figure asked, desperately. "Give me your hand."

Joy was finally able to sit up, but she couldn't stand. She was still gathering her wits. She stared at the figure. A man. It was a man. Behind him was a car. *The* car. The lights beamed across the road. The man in the car had pulled her out of the snowbank. It was all starting to come together. He crouched down in front of her, grasping her shoulder.

"Are you okay?" he asked again. "Are you hurt? Can you hear me?"

She wasn't merely disoriented when her eyes were able to focus and he came into sharper view. For a second she thought she might be dead. *Wow. He's handsome. He's like a fairy-tale prince.* A real one, with thick dark hair that held a perfect wave. His eyes were icy blue. He even had a dimple in his chin.

That was it. She was dead.

The handsome prince dug in his pocket and pulled out a phone. "I'm calling an ambulance. You must be in shock."

Joy instinctively grabbed his wrist. "No. No. I'm fine." She took a deep breath and as the air fully filled her lungs, she realized she was not dead. Plus, her hand had landed on firm man. A real man. "I'm so sorry. I just… I didn't know what to do and it was my first instinct to jump into the snow. I'm sure that seems crazy."

"Do you think you're okay to stand up?"

"Probably." She nodded. As soon as she was on her feet, she saw that she had not been crazy to leap into the snow. The rear end of his car had stopped just shy of the bank. "Wow. I could have been hit."

"I'm so sorry. I ran into a patch of ice and lost control of the car. Sometimes these precision vehicles do what you want them to and sometimes they don't." The handsome prince had a very deep voice, rich and authoritative. He was probably really good at telling people what to do. He was tall. And good God, now that she could see his face in its entirety, she couldn't help but notice that he was unbearably handsome. He was all high cheekbones and full lips. A strong jaw and brow line. There was nothing soft about him. Everything was defined. He wore a black wool coat and black leather gloves. "Do you mind if I ask what in the world you were doing out here walking alongside the road in the dark?"

Oh, yeah. That. "Hiking."

"Hiking? In those boots?" He pointed at her feet, which were clad in her brown leather boots with the chunky heel. They were surprisingly comfortable and made her butt look damn good in jeans. She didn't wear them at work, though. She donned the chef's clogs that were currently in her bag for the long hours on her feet.

"Yeah, I know. I guess I'm just a slave to fashion." She tittered nervously.

He narrowed his focus on her, his eyebrows drawing together so tightly they nearly touched. "Okay. Well, I don't think it's a good idea for you to finish your hike. Why don't you let me drive you home?"

Home? *Oh, no.* That would never work. Her home was the Marshalls' home and absolutely no one was supposed to know she was there. For all she knew, this guy was a friend of the Marshalls. They not only knew a lot of people, most people knew of them. "I'm fine. Really." She waved him off.

He shook his head. "No way. You are not fine. You should see yourself right now. Your hair and your makeup." He drew a circle in the air in front of her face. "Plus, I'm not entirely sure you didn't hit your head. I'm driving you home. If my mother were still alive, she'd be horrified if she found out that I was anything less than a perfect gentleman."

Oh, sure. Bring your dead mother into it. "No, really…"

"No. Really. I insist. Either that or I call an ambulance for you. You're not walking home."

Joy blew out a breath and knew it was time to relent. If they got to the top of the hill and he said a peep about the Marshalls, she'd have to come up with a quick excuse. In the meantime, at least with Prince Charming around, she was fairly sure she wasn't in danger of being arrested. "Okay. Sure. That'd be nice."

Alex stepped ahead of the mystery woman and opened the passenger door for her. "I can turn on the heated seat for you in a moment." He took care when closing the door. He still wasn't convinced she wasn't in shock. He was certainly disoriented. One minute he was out for a drive, trying to blow off some work-related steam, and the next thing he knew, his car was sliding down a mountain and he nearly hit a woman. The scene that followed, the epic panic in the snowbank, was like something out of a movie. He could hardly believe what he'd witnessed.

He climbed inside and glanced over at her. She was using the visor mirror to wipe away the smudges of makeup beneath her eyes and smooth her hair.

"I wasn't trying to say you needed to primp."

"You were right. I'm a disaster."

Even though her hair had looked like it had been through a tornado, he couldn't imagine her ever looking bad. In the soft light coming from the mirror, only in profile, she still stole his breath. She was a classic beauty, like something out of an old Technicolor movie—creamy complexion, lively flush on her cheeks. Her now-tidier hair was long, rolling past her shoulders in gentle waves.

"If this is your version of a disaster, I'd love to see what you look like when you're going out."

She turned, sizing him up with her soulful brown eyes.

He reached out his hand. "Seems like introductions are in order. I'm Alex. Well, Alexander if you want the long version. Alexander Townsend."

She swiped off her fluffy mitten and placed her hand in his. "Nice to meet you, Alexander Townsend, although if this is your way of picking up women, I suggest you get a new technique."

Alex laughed. Beautiful and witty. It was his lucky day. "And your name?"

She flipped the visor up, tugging her mitten back on. "Joy."

"Nice to meet you, Joy. Just Joy or is there more to it?"

"Baker."

"You aren't a Denver Baker, are you?"

"Excuse me?"

"The Denver Bakers. I'm very good friends with Patrick. He and I both graduated from Columbia the same year." The look on her face said that she was not a member of the Baker family from Denver. "I'm guessing no?"

She shrugged. "Sorry. I don't know them."

"Ah. Well. Thought I'd ask. Where are you from, Joy Baker?"

She cleared her throat. "Santa Barbara."

"I'm from Chicago. Not nearly as picturesque as coastal California, but it's home."

"Sounds nice."

This conversation didn't seem to be going anywhere. Probably best to move along. "Where can I take you?"

"Do you know this road well?"

"Clearly, I don't."

She pointed up the hill. "It's at the top. Just drive and I'll show you."

He followed her directions, the headlights casting golden beams across the silver snow. That bit of friendly back-and-forth had been pleasant enough, but reality was sinking in. He could have killed her. For all he knew, she was injured. Bleeding internally? Head trauma? All possible. The thought set him doubly on edge. His protective side came out with all women, sometimes to his own detriment. It was a product of his childhood, years of his father mistreating his mother, and Alex having to be the buffer. He had to remind himself that he hardly knew Joy. There was no reason to protect her any more than any other stranger.

But there was reason to worry. With his money, and

his family name, he had been the frequent target of unscrupulous people. The most notable of which had been his former fiancée, and although that was a chapter of his life best left closed, it did make him wary of people and their intentions.

"It's up here. On the left. You can just pull up to the gate and I'll get out."

He crested the hill and the vista opened up, almost as if they were perched on top of the world. It was all vast blue-black sky and stars up here; the house Joy had pointed to a showpiece that seemed to go on forever. His shoulders lightened. He had no need to worry about her intentions. Joy, from the look of things, had more than enough of her own resources.

He pulled closer to the gate and rolled down his window. "Code?"

"Oh, no. It's fine. I'll just get out right here. You can go now."

Alex didn't know what to say. It wasn't like he saw himself as God's gift to women, but he was certainly not accustomed to getting the swift brush-off. Usually, women enjoyed being in his company. And it wasn't like he'd asked her out. This was a ride up the driveway. "I promise I won't memorize it. I work in finance, but I'm actually horrible with numbers. Well, small ones at least." He laughed quietly at his own joke, but she didn't. *Idiot.*

"I just… I don't know that I should let you in."

He nodded, trying to understand what sort of vibe he was giving off that made her so uneasy. Part of him wanted to tell her that he was the most trustworthy guy imaginable when it came to women, always a perfect gentleman, but what kind of guy says that? Someone who's the exact opposite, that's who. The trouble was, he wasn't entirely certain she was okay after her swan dive into the snowbank. "I don't want to bring up my mom again, but can't a guy at least drive you to the door? That driveway has to be at least a five-minute walk. Probably ten in those boots. Which are completely inappropriate for hiking, by the way. I can't believe you got in a single step before you wiped out."

"If you'll stop criticizing my footwear choices, I'll let you drive me up."

"Deal."

"The code is 6274."

He punched in the numbers and the tall wrought iron gate pulled back behind a towering stone pillar topped with a craftsman light fixture. The car crept ahead, but with this much power under the hood, he was careful not to gun it. The house was impressive as they approached, with tall windows peeking out from under at least a dozen gables, supported by honed timber trusses. The roof was blanketed in snow, the exterior clad in cedar shakes and trim. This gorgeous mountain lodge could likely sleep twenty people comfortably.

"Beautiful home you have here. It reminds me of my place in Switzerland. Of course, the skiing over there is better, but I wanted a quick getaway this Christmas, so my house in Vail seemed like the right choice."

"Oh. Um. This isn't my house. It belongs to friends of mine."

"Who are your friends? Maybe I know them."

"Uh. The Santiago family? They're letting me stay here for a while." Her voice was a bit shaky and unsure. Maybe she really had been hurt in the fall.

"Hmm. I don't know them. You're staying here by yourself?"

"Well, yes. Wanted some time to myself. Life gets crazy." Joy collected her things and opened her car door. "Thank you, again." She turned back to him only this time, there was a momentary connection difficult to ignore.

"Of course. It's the least I can do." Something about this wasn't right. "Hey. Is it okay if we exchange numbers? I want you to be able to call me if you aren't feeling well."

She pressed her lips together like she was trying to escape a deeply uncomfortable situation. "How about I just take your number?"

Fair enough. "Sure thing." He rattled off the digits and she put it into her phone, or at least he thought she did.

With that, she climbed out, closed her door, and scaled the grand sweep of stone stairs leading up to the front porch. Joy was tall, her legs long and lithe, but she looked tiny compared to the massive wood double door. She keyed her way in and as soon as she disappeared inside, he put the car into Reverse and backed up. Her sweet fragrance lingered—an aroma like spun sugar. It'd been months since he'd been on a date with a woman, and even just a few minutes with Joy was going to haunt him. He had a sense she was holding back or hiding something.

Hopefully, it wasn't that she'd been hurt in the accident.

Two

Joy flipped the dead bolt and collapsed against the door. That had been entirely too close a call. When Rafe Marshall, Mariella's son, had said she could stay in the house, he'd been explicit about one thing—no one could know she was there. His mother would kill him if she found out he'd given sanctuary to someone who'd dared to quit her employ, and the Marshalls knew a lot of people in Vail. A lot of very wealthy, powerful people. People like Alex.

Thank goodness she'd been quick enough to say that the house belonged to the Santiago family. Santiago was Mariella Marshall's maiden name, and luckily did not ring a bell with Alex. Joy despised these little white lies, but she was deeply concerned about her future in the culinary world. Mariella Marshall could kill her entire career, everything she'd worked so hard for, with one or two well-placed phone calls.

Joy raced to the window and pulled back the heavy gold tapestry drape, peeking outside. The red of Alex's taillights glowed in the dark as his car cleared the gate. As soon as the wrought iron barrier completed its trip back across the driveway, she felt as though she could breathe. He was gone. Unbelievably hot Prince Charming had flown the coop. And that was a good thing, however disappointing it might seem. She'd been lonely since she'd come to Colorado. She hadn't had a single in-person conversation that hadn't revolved around working at the bakery. Some time with a personable, good-looking man would have been welcome. It would have been wonderful, actually.

Not for you, she reminded herself as she dropped her bag, traveled down the hall, and walked upstairs to the bedroom she'd been staying in. Rich guys were just asking for trouble. She'd met her fair share working in the restaurant world. Whether it was wealthy owners, investors or customers, men with money were too accustomed to getting whatever they wanted, when they wanted it. Joy was too bullheaded to ever put up with that.

If anything, having a man make demands sent Joy running in the opposite direction. Case in point, her hometown ex-boyfriend. He hadn't had money, but he'd always had control. Getting away from him had been a harrowing experience. It still wasn't over. Money and her car were obstacles, but he was the big reason she couldn't go home at Christmas. There were no secrets in her small town. He always found out when she returned, and then he'd start circling in on her. It was best to stay away, however sad and lonely it made her to not be with her family.

Joy removed her work clothes, turned on the shower

and stepped inside, closing the glass door behind her. The spray was the ideal temperature, with the perfect amount of water pressure to soothe her aching muscles. Baking was hard work, physically exhausting, possibly even more so than being a chef. Taking a mile-long hike up a mountain and ultimately landing in a snowbank had been a less-than-ideal way to end her day. She felt every bit of it.

Even though this house had unlimited hot water, she decided she couldn't spend her entire evening in the shower. She climbed out, curled her toes into the plush bath mat, and wrapped herself up in the fluffy white towel. Everything in this house was the finest quality. Every element was chosen with an eye for luxury and comfort, and she would've been lying if she'd said that she didn't appreciate every second of it.

Mariella's daughter Elana's bathroom was a perfect example—marble-topped vanity with custom cherry cabinetry, a shower with a waterfall head and shimmery glass tile. There was even a towel warmer. Joy didn't use it often. It was more of a treat, which was a silly notion, but Joy didn't want to get too accustomed to this life. She wouldn't have it for long.

She grabbed her robe from the hook and towel-dried her hair, studying herself in the mirror. Some days it was a necessary reminder of who she was and what she was. She was Joy McKinley, a hardworking girl from Ohio. She did not come from a house like this, nor would she live in a house like this. Pipe dreams didn't get anyone anywhere. Hard work did. She most definitely was *not* Joy Baker, invited guest of the Marshall family and woman perfectly at home staying by herself in a sprawling estate. She'd only let Alex believe those things because she was covering her tracks and he was nothing more than an acquaintance. A ridiculously sexy one, but a stranger nonetheless.

The security system control panel on the bathroom wall dinged. Joy jumped. Someone was at the door. Her pulse took off in a sprint. Anyone who arrived on her doorstep had already passed through the gate. Had someone from the Marshall family arrived without their key? Had Mariella Marshall invited friends to stay here, leaving Joy to explain herself and hightail it out of there? She jabbed the button for the security camera. Alex came into view in pixelated black and white. Relief washed over her, followed by a jolt of excitement. But why was he back?

"Hello?" she asked into the intercom.

"Hi. It's Alex. From before. The car? The hill?" He was so adorable, talking into the doorbell instead of looking up at the security camera.

"Yes. I remember."

"I got halfway home and I had to turn around. Are you sure you're okay?"

She waited to answer. She really wanted to invite him in. She wanted to have a real conversation. If he didn't want to talk, she could just stare at him for a while or maybe she could convince him that a brief make-out session with a stranger was totally normal. "I feel fine. I think."

"See? That's a problem. I think I should call 911. This could be serious."

"No. Please don't do that."

"Can you come to the door and talk to me?"

He was the most insistent man she'd been around in a long time. "Fine. I'm coming." Down the stairs she thundered. She opened the door but quickly remembered she was wearing a bathrobe and nothing else, and stopped herself from flinging it wide open. She greeted him by poking her head out through the narrow opening. "I'm fine." The soft amber glow from the porch lights made him even more movie star handsome. It was going to hurt to tell him to go away.

"It doesn't seem like you should be by yourself right now," he said.

"I told you I'm fine." Except that she wasn't entirely sure she was. Her neck still felt tight, even after that long shower, and she had a headache brewing.

He pursed his lips and looked down at the ground for a moment. "I think you should see a doctor."

"That's not necessary. I just need to get some sleep."

"Are you positive you didn't hit your head? If you have a head injury, it could be a bad idea to go to sleep."

Good God, he was persistent. "It was snow. Nothing hard to hit my head on."

He moved his face closer to hers, studying her. The breath hitched in her throat. He had a really sexy mouth. Totally worth kissing. What if they ended up having that make-out session after all? "It seems like your pupils are pretty dilated."

"I don't even know what to say to that. It's not like I can see my own eyes right now. Nor do I even know what it means if they are, in fact, dilated."

"Can I please come in for a moment? I promise I'm not wielding an axe."

She sighed and opened the door wider, the brutally cold air rushing in behind him. The snow was coming down even harder now, which she hadn't thought possible. "Have you ever noticed that murderers don't carry an axe, they wield it?"

"It just occurred to me that I shouldn't have used axe-murderer terminology. I'm sorry. I swear I'm a good guy." His smile was extra convincing. Alex wasn't a threat, although she might pass out from how blindingly perfect his mouth was.

Joy couldn't imagine finding a reason to put Alex off, even when logic said she should. That smile had done something to her. It had left a chink in her armor. "Please. Come in. You must be freezing. It's horrible out there."

He shook snow from his hair and stomped his boots on the foyer rug. "Yeah, the forecast isn't looking good." His eyes dipped south, then returned to her face. "It's much nicer in here."

A vaguely familiar tingle zipped through her. Was he flirting with her? Was Prince Charming making the moves? A breath of cold air crossed her shoulders and she realized then that the top of her robe had gaped quite significantly. It wasn't a full-on wardrobe malfunction, but it wasn't far off. She quickly covered up and re-cinched the tie. Embarrassment covered her from head to toe.

"Can I make you a cup of tea?" She wasn't sure what else to offer the man who'd showed up at her door again.

"That would be great, but I was hoping we could call my doctor together. I'll feel a lot better about things if you just talk to him."

"So I don't have to go anywhere?"

"Nope. You can do this from the comfort of your own home."

My own home. If only. "Okay. Do you want to have a seat in the living room while I run upstairs and get dressed?"

"You don't have to change on my account. I think you look pretty amazing just as you are."

There it was again—that flirtatious lilt to his voice. Or maybe he was just one of those men whose every comment came off with an edge of innuendo. Regardless of whether he was trying hard or not, she had a deep desire to comb her fingers through his hair, if only to learn whether it was as thick as it looked. It'd been more than a year since she'd been with a man, and that one had been a deeply disappointing kisser—weak lips and a hesitant tongue. If a man was going to kiss her, she wanted him to go for it. Send a message. Alex looked like he could knock a woman off her heels with a single kiss. And here they were, all alone in this big beautiful house, she in a near state of undress.

"You're sweet, but I think it would be best if I was wearing something that more closely resembled clothes. I'll be right back."

She turned and darted up the stairs, mumbling to herself, "What in the hell are you doing? Why did you let him inside? That was really, really dumb. We're going to call his doctor? At night? How weird is that?"

Learning firsthand how adept Alex was at talking her into something, she needed to remain on her toes. She also needed to remain calm and allow him to leave of his own accord. Making a stink was a good way to arouse suspicion, and she didn't want to give him any reason to decide she was acting strangely or quite possibly didn't belong in this house. For all she knew, he'd call the police. Surely a guy as thorough and conscientious as Alex wouldn't even hesitate to turn her in if he thought she wasn't on the up-and-up. She had to do her best to appear to belong here. She had to make things seem as normal as possible, then hope he would leave so she could return to her sad, but relatively safe existence where she still got to sleep in an amazing bed.

Dressed in far less revealing pajama pants, tank top and hoodie, Joy hurried back downstairs. As she turned the corner for the living room, she saw the glow and heard the crackle of a fire in the hearth. She hadn't bargained on Alex making himself at home. "Oh. You built a fire."

"Well, yeah. Look at it out there." He tossed his head toward the long wall of the living room, where the windows soared to the top of the cathedral ceiling and stood in single file like soldiers. The night sky was a midnight blue, dotted with fat, glowing snowflakes. "That's half the point of having a mountain house. To build a roaring fire when it's snowing."

Except that building a fire created a wisp of smoke that trailed from the chimney, letting anyone who might happen to drive by know that someone was staying there. Sure, it was a long shot, but if that person knew the Marshalls and decided to stop by or call Mariella to ask how long she'd be in town? That would be very bad. She not only didn't make a habit of lighting the wood-burning fireplaces, she'd been careful to use as few lights as possible. "Um. Sure. It's very nice."

"I thought so." He plopped down on one of two sprawling sectional couches, each covered in plush tapestry fabric in shades of taupe and rust. He pulled out his phone. "Come. Sit. We'll call the doctor." He patted the sofa cushion right next to him.

This was officially the strangest situation Joy had ever been in, but she'd be lying if she'd said she didn't want to sit close to him without a car's center console between them. "Okay." She carefully took the seat next to him. It was impossible not to fixate on his warm and masculine smell, or just how big his hands were as he cradled the phone.

The screen came to life, showing a tiny picture of the two of them in the bottom corner. She couldn't help but notice that they looked cute together, even when he was dressed nicely in a black sweater and jeans while she was in her PJs. "A video call?"

"Well, yeah. He's probably going to want to see you. I figured this is easier."

Another face popped onto the screen, a face so familiar that Joy had to blink several times to be certain she was seeing who she was seeing. *Holy crap.* This was no regular doctor. This was Dr. David, the doctor who made a living on the TV talk show circuit. He was the guy every network called when there was a big health scare and people needed someone impossibly good-looking to talk them off the ledge. "Alex? Are you seriously calling me from Vail? Shouldn't you be hitting the slopes?" Dr. David asked.

Oh, great. Alex isn't just a guy with a super expensive car and a house in Switzerland. He's on a first-name basis with celebrities. What world am I living in, anyway?

Alex laughed. "I've been doing some of that, but I was calling because I have a friend who might have hit her head. I was hoping you could talk to her."

He tilted the phone in Joy's direction, and she had no choice but to wave and say, "Hi. I'm the friend. I'm Joy."

"Hello, Joy. I'm Dr. David."

Well, duh. Another wave of embarrassment hit her. She was sure his first question was going to be why her cheeks were flaming red. "Hi, Dr. David." She did her best to pass it off as if she chatted with ridiculously famous people every day.

"Tell me what's going on," he said.

Joy glanced over at Alex. He looked so uncertain and worried, it made it hard to know what to say. He was concerned about her. That was why he'd come back. This revelation was sweet, but dangerous. Joy needed to be invisible right now, not attracting attention.

Alex listened as Joy told the story of the near-accident. With every word out of her mouth, he felt exponentially guiltier. She'd really, truly been in harm's way and it had all been his fault. He quite literally could have killed her. He could have ended the life of this beautiful woman. The weight of that sat squarely on his shoulders. Call it his biggest fear, but ever since he'd been a kid, he'd worried about making a choice that would lead to an irreversible mistake. If he hadn't decided to go for a drive, Joy wouldn't have ended up in the snowbank.

As reluctant as she'd seemed to accept help, he would have to insist on whatever Dr. David's orders were. No ifs, ands, or buts.

Dr. David was nodding and writing down some notes. "Okay, well, it sounds to me like you're going to be okay. It doesn't sound like you've sustained any kind of serious injury."

Joy sighed and her shoulders dropped in relief. "Oh, good. Thank you."

"That being said, you should not be alone over the next 24 hours. If something crops up, you'll need help to get to the nearest medical center."

Now Joy didn't seem quite so happy. "I'm staying by

myself right now, but it's not a big deal. You said it yourself. It sounds like I haven't sustained any real injury."

"But I can't be certain of that without examining you myself. I think it's best if Alex stays with you if his schedule allows."

The ramifications of that sank in quickly, but Alex knew David was right. She shouldn't be alone. Just to be on the safe side. He would never forgive himself if something bad happened to her. "I'm on vacation, so I have nowhere else I need to be. I'm happy to do it."

"We're supposed to get a lot of snow tonight," Joy pled. "You could get stuck here."

Again, this was not the sort of reaction Alex was used to. Most women did everything they could to spend time with him. It wasn't a boastful bit of information; it was merely the truth. "That's quite literally the last thing I'm worried about right now."

"I'm sure you two can work it out," David said. "Call me at this time tomorrow and let me know how the patient is doing. And Alex, if you need anything in the middle of the night, don't hesitate to call. I'll have my phone right by the bed."

"Thanks so much. You're a real lifesaver," Alex replied. "We'll call you tomorrow." With that, he ended the call.

Joy sat back on the couch and wrapped her arms around herself. "I'm fine. Really, I am."

"I know. I know. I still think we have to play it safe."

She twisted her lips and tucked her leg under herself.

"We could play cards. Or watch TV. Or talk. You must get lonely living in this big house by yourself." It occurred to him then that he'd assumed that since she was alone, she'd always be alone. "Oh, wait. Do you have someone coming to stay with you? For the holidays? A boyfriend? A husband?"

She cocked an eyebrow at him. "Is that your way of asking if I'm taken?"

He wasn't convinced it had been a bad approach. He shrugged and kicked off his shoes. Might as well make himself comfortable. "Well? Are you?"

"No. I'm not. I'm too focused on my career for a man right now anyway."

Judging by the generosity of the friends who were letting her stay in their house, Joy must have a pretty big and successful career. "What do you do? No. Wait. Let me guess." He studied her face, trying to keep his eyes from drifting to her other pleasing features like the graceful slope of her neck, her long legs. She was definitely serious. Focused. But she also had this girl-next-door vibe that was not only super sexy, it wasn't entirely congruous with being a bigwig. "Entrepreneur. You started some company that went through the roof. Organic cosmetics or maybe yoga wear?"

She shook her head. "You couldn't be more off base if you tried."

"Well, you're definitely a huge success, whatever it is that you do. That's pretty obvious."

"I wouldn't say I'm a huge success, but I get by."

She was modest. He liked that. Most people in his circles were eager to rattle off their pedigree and accomplishments, whether they'd worked hard for them or not. Joy was a lovely change of pace. "Oh, come on. You're spending time in this huge house all by yourself. You obviously have some very successful friends, and in my experience, successful people attract other successful people. Plus, you just have that air about you."

She narrowed her skeptical eyes. "That air?"

Alex let out a frustrated sigh. He wasn't doing particularly well for himself. Nothing he said seemed to be clicking. "You seem very comfortable here in a home like this, that's all. That's a sign of someone who's had some success."

Joy pulled her leg up and set her foot on the edge of the couch. Her toes were painted a deep red that made his pulse race. She was certainly a beguiling creature. She rested her chin on her knee and cast a thoughtful look at him. "What about you? What does Alex Townsend do?"

Part of him wanted to ignore her reply and circle back to her. She hadn't really answered his question. She might have an even greater sense of humility than he'd realized. Or perhaps there was stress and strain involved with her occupation, and now that it was the holidays, she simply wanted a break, a concept with which he was intimately familiar. After all, she was staying in this big house all by herself at Christmas. If anything said, "I need to be alone," it was that. "I work in finance. Investments. It's my family's business, but I'm running it right now. It's not the most thrilling career, but it's what my family has always done."

"Are you close with your family?"

"I'm very close with my brothers. We all work together. My dad retired last year and put me in charge, but he's not doing a very good job of being a retired person."

"Has to keep his nose in everything?"

It was a constant point of friction, the most difficult part of Alex's day. As the oldest Townsend son, he'd always been heir apparent to Townsend & Associates Investments. He'd looked forward to the day when his father would finally step aside and let Alex take the reins.

Unfortunately, his dad second-guessed him constantly, especially now that Alex was putting his own stamp on the company and changing things, making their operation more modern and more equitable among the employees. "Yeah. You could say that. I keep hoping it'll get better. It's only been a little more than a year since I took over."

"Sometimes parents can be overbearing. Mine were not happy when I decided to go to culinary school."

"So you're a chef? I wasn't that off base."

"You're were pretty off base." She nodded. "At the moment, my focus is baking."

"Hold on a second. You're Joy Baker, the baker?" He couldn't hold back his grin. There was something extremely adorable about this revelation.

"Yes, although I'm not sure why that is so funny. I'm classically trained. Cooking is my passion. My grandmother instilled that in me."

"I'm sorry. I wasn't trying to make light of it."

"Well, it's important to me."

Alex was again having a hard time not smiling. He loved her fire, and how nice it must be to have a family connection to a career that didn't involve money and was rather related to something homey or creative. "So if it's so important, why didn't you parents approve?" She averted her eyes, and Alex fought his first inclination, which was to think that a woman was hiding something when she looked away. It had become a habit, one he was desperate to be rid of. He wanted to trust. He truly did.

"They thought I'd never make enough money, which isn't exactly wrong. It isn't always a high-paying line of work. But I'm not in it for the money. I'm in it because I love doing it."

Joy was a breath of fresh air. He had to admire her bravery. She'd gone against her parents' wishes to pursue her passion, and she'd clearly done very well for herself. He wished he felt so strongly about something. "I think that's fantastic. It's very impressive."

"You know, you didn't say anything about your mom. What does she do?"

It felt as though the air around him had gone flat, which was too bad considering how sparkling their conversation had just been. "She passed away when I was in college." Even years later, the guilt over not being there when his mother died was immense. She'd suffered greatly and Alex had been hundreds of miles away in New York.

"I'm so sorry."

The pity in Joy's voice was a mixed blessing. It was genuine, and he appreciated that more than anything. So much in his life no longer felt real, not since Sharon had betrayed his love with lies. But he also didn't want Joy to feel sorry for him. He wanted her to see him as strong and capable, not weak or vulnerable. "Tell me more about your parents. What do they do?"

Joy closed her eyes for a moment. "You know, maybe this is a conversation best left for another time. I'm feeling pretty tired. I should probably head up to bed."

Was that deflection? Or was she truly tired? Alex couldn't arrive at a conclusion. *Stop with the paranoia.* She'd been through a lot tonight, all of it set in motion when he'd lost control of his car. "I hope you don't have a headache."

She shook her head and got up from the couch. "No. I feel fine. Truly. I'm just tired."

"Okay. Sure. Where do you want me to sleep tonight? I can crash on the couch if that's best."

"Don't be silly. There are a bunch of bedrooms upstairs. You can stay in the first one on the left in the hall upstairs. I'm two doors down from that."

She'd been sure to leave some space between them, which Alex had to respect. He was a strange man staying in her house. It would set any woman on edge. "Thank you. I appreciate that. I'm also wondering if it would be all right for me to move my car into the garage. No telling how much snow we'll get tonight."

"Oh. Of course. The door is to the left after you walk through the entry. I believe one of the bays is empty."

"Thank you so much. Good night."

"Sleep well." With that, Joy left him to his own devices.

Alex found the garage with little trouble and opened the door. The wind had picked up considerably, and the snow was already drifting in the driveway. There were three or four inches on the ground, and although his Bugatti had a lot of firepower, it wasn't a huge fan of the snow. It took a bit of convincing to get it into the garage. He grabbed his gym bag from the back seat. At least he'd have clean underwear and some toiletries.

He shook off the cold when he got back inside. He wasn't sure he'd ever gotten himself into a more bizarre situation. He couldn't bring himself to be upset about it, however perilously close the incident with the car had come to hurting her. At least he had a temporary interruption to his very dull and lonely Christmas vacation.

Still, there was something about Joy that wasn't quite right, and that worried him. However much he hated walking around with his defenses up, he couldn't be the guy who could be fooled more than once. In his position, with a vast personal fortune and a professional reputation to maintain, he had to be leery of everyone. The one time he hadn't been careful, it had nearly destroyed him. If the unthinkable had happened and he'd married Sharon, his former fiancée, the woman who duped him into thinking not only that she loved him, but that they didn't need a prenuptial agreement, his face would've eventually been splashed all over the cover of tabloid magazines. Half of his money would've been gone.

Alex trailed through the foyer and back into the living room, dialing the number for Paul, the Townsend & Associates Investments staff investigator. His primary duties for the firm involved due diligence on potential mergers and acquisitions, but he was especially good at digging up skeletons. He'd been at the company for a long time, since Alex was a teenager. Alex's entire family trusted Paul implicitly. In some ways, Paul was like a dad figure to Alex. Alex could speak openly with him and have a real discussion without it turning into a referendum on Alex's style of leadership.

"Aren't you supposed to be on vacation?" Paul asked when he answered.

Alex walked to the far side of the room. He didn't want Joy to overhear him. "I am on vacation. And I'm enjoying myself. But I want you to check into something for me."

"Something or *someone*?"

Paul was a smart man. No question about that. "Someone. A woman."

"Oh, boy," Paul said. "I hope you aren't putting yourself into a delicate situation again."

Alex closed his eyes and blew out a breath through his nose. Paul had every right to be wary. He'd suspected something about Sharon from the moment he'd met her. He'd kept it to himself for quite a while, but when it got close to the wedding day, Paul had taken the initiative and started digging. What he found was a trail of lies. Alex had let his heart cloud the issue when it had come to Sharon, and he'd come close to paying for it dearly.

"It's not exactly a neat and tidy situation. I met a woman tonight, but only because I hit a patch of ice and nearly ran into her with my car. I'm at her house right now. I just want to make sure there aren't any surprises I should know about. She's lovely. I'd like to ask her out, maybe take her to dinner. But there's also something about her that seems off. I'm not quite sure what it is."

A few moments of silence played out on Paul's end of the line, and Alex knew he was thinking, hard. "Off in what way? I don't want you to be unduly paranoid because of Sharon. The vast majority of people are mostly honest."

"Mostly?"

"We all tell little lies. The question is how little."

Indeed. "Do you think you should look into it?"

"It can't hurt. What's her name?"

"It's Joy Baker. She's from Santa Barbara."

"California, I take it."

"That's what I assumed."

"Can you tell me anything about her family? Does she own any businesses?"

"I'm afraid I don't know anything about her family other than she's not related to the Bakers in Denver. And oddly enough, Joy Baker is a baker."

Once again, Paul was dead quiet on the other end of the line. "Okay. Got it. I'll look into her and give you a call tomorrow."

Three

Joy climbed into the bed she'd been fantasizing about during her trudge up the hill. It was just as heavenly as it had been the night before, and the night before that. This bedroom was gorgeous, and it wasn't even the master bedroom. Joy couldn't stomach the idea of taking Mariella and Harrison Marshall's room. She was already pushing things far enough.

She'd instead chosen their daughter Elana's room, with its beautiful cherry wood sleigh bed and richly colored tapestry carpet in shades of gold, cream and taupe. There was a gas fireplace in the corner of the room, lit with the simple flick of a switch. The flames would probably cast a golden glow and warm the entire room, but Joy was too nervous to turn it on. Windows spanned one wall overlooking the back of the property, which had a stunning view of the seemingly never-ending mountain vista. Being in this bed felt like being on top of the world.

The snow was still coming down. Joy picked up her phone and pulled up the weather app. They were predicting an unusually heavy snowfall overnight. It took a lot of snow to shut things down in this part of Colorado, but the reality was that the Marshall estate was at the very top of the mountain. Even if life was normal down in town, it would take a while for plows to make their way up here. Rafe had told her as much when he'd given her the keys to the house.

Bad weather or not, there was no way she'd be able to get to work tomorrow. Not with Alex and his 24-hour timeline, courtesy of Dr. David. She still couldn't believe she'd practically met a celebrity while she was wearing her pajamas. The Marshalls had lots of famous friends, some just as well-known as Dr. David, but she'd certainly never had a conversation with any of them.

She dialed the number for her boss at the bakery. "Hey there," Bonnie answered. "I take it you're calling to chat about this lovely bout we're having with Mother Nature?"

Joy smiled and sat back against the pillows. "In part, yes. But even if the weather cooperates, I don't think I can come in tomorrow. I had a small accident when I came home and the doctor wants me to rest for 24 hours. I'm sorry if that leaves you in the lurch. I think you know how much I hate to miss work. I love working at the bakery." *And I don't want to jeopardize my job.*

"I hope it's nothing serious."

"The doctor doesn't think so, but he's not entirely sure I didn't hit my head. That's why he wants me to lay low."

"What in the world happened?"

Oh, nothing. Just a super handsome man flew down

a mountain and almost killed me. "I slipped and fell. Stupid snow."

Bonnie clucked her tongue as if she was scolding Joy. "Ouch. Well, I wouldn't worry about work tomorrow anyway. I'm not sure we'll be able to open on time, and even then, I'm not sure we'll have any customers. This storm is supposed to be pretty bad. I think it's best you stay inside and recuperate. We'll see you on Thursday if all is back to normal."

Joy breathed a huge sigh of relief. Bonnie was a wonderful boss. After Mariella Marshall, this was one life change Joy was glad for. "Thank you so much. I really appreciate it. I'll be in touch. Stay safe."

"You, too."

Joy hung up and settled back in bed, her mind zeroing in on her other problem—Alex. It would've been so nice to stay up and chat with him, but he asked too many questions. It took a lot of effort to think about the ramifications of every answer she gave, and she knew it made her come off as someone who was hiding something. She didn't want to be that person. She was horrible at being that person, but such was the situation she'd gotten herself into.

Part of her wished she never would've given him a fake last name. It set a bad precedent, and she'd done a ridiculously bad job with it, to boot. *Baker? Seriously?* It was the first thing that had come to mind, a perfect illustration of how ill-equipped she was to go around the world being anyone other than herself. Luckily—or unluckily, depending on how you looked at it—she would only know Alex for a short time. Twenty-four hours. He'd never have to know she'd fibbed a few times. It certainly wasn't hurting anyone.

Despite her inability to lie for hours at a time, she would've liked to have talked to Alex more and at least find out about him. She was a naturally curious person, and he'd been almost as dismissive of her questions as she'd been of his. He hadn't made a big deal of his occupation, but if his car was any indication, he had to be an important guy... She didn't like the idea of snooping, but maybe one internet search wasn't too nosy. He *was* sleeping in the same house as her, after all.

She pulled up the web browser on her phone and typed in Alexander Townsend, Chicago, Illinois. As the results came back, it quickly dawned on Joy that she was in over her head. He wasn't merely Alexander Townsend. He was Alexander Townsend III. Joy had never been acquainted with someone with roman numerals after their name. Ever. Judging by the bio and photos that came up, her hunch about Alex being somebody had been absolutely correct.

The Townsends were one of the wealthiest families in Chicago and had resided there for decades. They were old money personified—houses all over the world, expensive vacations, lots of heavy political ties and famous friends. As she scrolled through the stories about Alex though, she learned that he was generating his own new money. He was responsible for taking Townsend & Associates Investments to a whole new level of success. According to several business publications, he was doing so with aplomb. Good for him.

Joy clicked on Images and she was glad no one was watching her while she did this. She got all tingly and hot-faced just from seeing pictures of him. She needed to have her head examined—it wasn't as if she hadn't just had the chance to look at him as much as she liked.

Most of the photographs were from big social events and fund-raisers, the theater, fancy dinners. He was in a suit in many of them, a tux in a few, always dashing and impeccably dressed. With every suit came a stunning woman on his arm. After a while, it became her mission to find a picture of him without a woman, but all she could find was his corporate head shot and a few of him leaving or arriving at his office.

Alex's parade of women was ready for the covers of magazines. They were ripe for the society pages or the red carpet—gorgeous hair and makeup, flawless designer gowns, long legs and perfect skin. None of these women, Joy was quite certain, was a baker from Ohio. She might have enjoyed her conversation with Alex, she might have liked riding in his car, she'd had a few minutes of fun with the fantasy of kissing him, but between these photos and her phone call with Dr. David, Joy knew one thing for certain—Alexander Townsend III was 100 percent out of her league.

They weren't even playing the same game.

Her number one job tomorrow, after assessing the road conditions and passing the 24-hour mark, was getting Alex out of this house. Joy knew rich people. She'd worked for too many to not understand precisely how they operated. They stuck together. If Alex found out she didn't really belong here, he'd call the police before she'd even have time to sputter out the long, drawn-out truth. She had to clean her mind of sexy thoughts about him and get rid of him. As to how she was supposed to sleep with this information fresh in her mind, she had no idea. She only knew that she was stuck in this room for now.

The trouble was, she couldn't relax. She liked Alex, but letting him into the house had left her exposed. She was vulnerable, and she didn't like it. Living on the brink did that to a person. If you spent enough days worrying about money or food or shelter, you eventually became territorial. You'd cling to every good thing you could find. She knew this house wasn't hers, and it certainly wasn't home, but it was all she had right now.

Her car was a piece of junk and a money pit. It had left her with eleven dollars in the bank. She had a job, but she wasn't sure she could afford to stay in Vail. And to make things especially heartbreaking, it was Christmas.

Embarrassment over quitting her job with the Marshalls was part of the reason she couldn't go home for the holidays. She couldn't admit to her parents that she'd not only failed, but her failure had been an implosion of her own making. They'd had enough reservations over her culinary career. She didn't need to add fuel to the fire. Her mother had always voiced the loudest concerns. She'd seen her own mother struggle to make ends meet, and she didn't want that life for her daughter. Joy understood, completely, but it didn't change the fact that her grandmother had lit a fire in her that would never go out. Everything about cooking appealed to Joy—the creativity, the connection to family, the sights and smells, the ability to bring pleasure to someone's life. There was absolutely nothing better than having someone eat your food and express their approval.

The other reason for not going home loomed like a dark cloud—her ex, Ben. Her parents had protested Joy's decision to attend culinary school, but Ben had flown into a rage. He'd never liked any sign of Joy improving her lot in life. He liked her best when she was down, when she was at a disadvantage. Of course, she'd enrolled anyway, because she couldn't bear the thought of *not* cooking, and she wanted to do it well.

She'd worked hard in the school kitchens and studied on nights and on the weekends. She'd been determined to prove to everyone that she could not only be extraordinary at cooking, she could make a life for herself—a big life without worries about money. An important life where people knew her name and regarded her work with high esteem. But as every day went by, and Joy became more immersed in her studies, it became clearer that Ben would not be a part of her life moving forward. He was too controlling. He didn't want what was best for her. Her parents saw it. Her friends saw it. Joy saw it, too, but it had taken a lot of nerve to sever that cord.

His response had been exactly what she'd expected— first rage, putting his fist through a wall. Then he begged her to change her mind, kneeling before her and clutching her hands. She'd cried her eyes out, wishing she could help him but knowing she couldn't. Then, finally, the anger came again, but it was different the second time, hate filled and spiteful. He'd called her trash. He'd said no one would ever love her. He'd said he would never leave her alone.

A judge had granted a restraining order eventually, but it did little good. Ben still drove by the house all the time. Joy would take pictures. She would call the police. Her dad would go out on the front stoop and yell. But in the end, Ben would only ever get a slap on the wrist. Ben had too many buddies in the police department. As soon as she was done with culinary school, she got out of Ohio. She went straight to Los Angeles and took her first job. She didn't look back. She knew Ben wouldn't follow her outside of his little bubble, but that didn't mean he was gone for good. Every holiday, he'd start stalking her parents' house. Hence, another Christmas alone. Someday she'd be able to afford to fly her parents to see her, but that day wasn't coming anytime soon.

Still unable to sleep, Joy got up to go to the bathroom. When she stepped back into her bedroom, there was a knock at the door.

"Joy? Are you okay in there?"

What the hell? Was he out in the hallway listening? Joy did not like overprotective guys. She could take care of herself. "Yeah. I'm fine. Getting a drink of water."

"Okay. I'm sorry. I was just on my way to bed. Good night."

"Good night." Joy headed back to her own bed, knowing what she had to do, even though she dreaded it. Tomorrow, she would thank sweet, handsome Alex Townsend. She'd probably employ her talents and make him a nice breakfast. He had been exceedingly kind to spend the night with her, all because he was worried about her head injury. Then, as soon as the twenty-four hours were up, sexy or not, Alex Townsend needed to go.

She didn't want some guy watching her every move when she was living in a house that wasn't hers, no matter how much he might be Joy's idea of Prince Charming.

Alex woke to the rich, heavenly smell of coffee and sat up straight in bed. He could muster great enthusiasm for his morning hit of caffeine, and knowing that Joy was downstairs making it only added to the appeal. If they were snowed in, he hoped she'd lose that skittish edge. He hoped Paul wasn't going to call him and tell him he needed to hightail it out of there.

Alex climbed out of bed. Outside, there was much

more than a blanket of snow on the ground. It looked as though there'd been an avalanche overnight, leaving behind endless billowing drifts. Alex pulled on the basketball shorts he had in his gym bag.

A few steps into the living room, and he caught a glimpse of Joy in the adjoining open-plan kitchen. His feet felt like they were in cement. He wasn't entirely sure he was, in fact, breathing. She was wearing an off-the-shoulder top that showed off the graceful stretch of her neck and just enough skin to paint a white-hot picture in his head, one that might require visual confirmation at some point. Her glossy brown hair was gathered to one side in a loose and sexy ponytail. She was pulling out a mixing bowl and some other items from the kitchen drawers, doing the most benign of tasks, and yet he couldn't have found her more enchanting if he tried.

"Too bad you don't have a housekeeper here to do that," he quipped, forcing himself to walk with a normal gait.

Joy shook her head and continued working. "I'm perfectly capable of doing this myself. No housekeeper needed."

He liked how independent she was. "I can see that."

"Coffee's on."

"I could smell it all the way upstairs. It's the only thing that could get me out of bed." *That, and the idea that you might be downstairs.* "That mattress is quite comfortable." He watched as Joy stood on tiptoes in fluffy pink slippers, plucking a coffee mug from the cabinet. She smiled when she handed it to him, but there was something about her this morning, again—that edge that left him feeling unsettled. He decided to shake it off and filled his mug from the carafe. He took a sip. It was strong and full-bodied, just how he liked it. "Delicious."

"No cream or sugar?"

He leaned back against the counter. "No way. I avoid that stuff at all costs. I've grown to like black coffee."

Joy visibly shuddered. She scrunched up her adorable nose. "Yuck."

"I'm guessing you don't take your coffee that way."

"Absolutely not. I will die without cream and sugar. And since I will die without coffee in the morning, it's necessary to have all three on hand at all times."

Alex made a mental note that if he ever got to make her a cup of coffee at his place, he would be sure to follow her rules. Making beautiful women happy was one of his favorite pastimes, mostly because it almost always paid off. "Have you checked on the weather at all?"

She nodded at the big-screen TV in the living room, which was on, but the sound was muted. "The storm is tapering off. We're just supposed to get flurries for the rest of the day, but it's going to take a while for everyone to dig out. We got almost two feet of snow."

"Wow." There was his answer—he would definitely be spending the day with her. How did he get so damn lucky? He'd nearly run over a gorgeous, smart, highly successful young woman. Hopefully one without a single skeleton in her closet, or at least nothing of huge consequence.

"I'm sorry you're stuck here in this house with me. I'm sure you have more important things to be doing."

Was his work more important? Technically, yes. But more appealing? Definitely not. "You know, I think a day off is going to be really good for me. I don't take nearly enough downtime."

"Workaholic?"

The last year at Townsend & Associates Investments had been absolutely brutal, but the workload was entirely of Alex's making. He'd been waiting for years to put his own stamp on the company and stop taking orders from his father. He could see now that he might have been overzealous, but he wasn't going to dwell on it. His hard work had paid almost immediate dividends. The money was rolling in and the world of finance was taking notice. Still, Alex had recognized two things over the course of the last twelve months—he never would've been able to work the way he had if he'd been married or had a serious girlfriend, and second, it was already getting old. If he didn't make a change, he'd burn out before his thirty-fifth birthday. "Something like that."

"Yeah. I can relate. I'm always working. But I love it." The wall oven next to the range top beeped. "Oh. Oven's preheated. I'd better get to work on breakfast."

"I hope you aren't going to any trouble. I don't normally eat before lunch."

True horror crossed Joy's face. "Didn't your mom ever tell you it's the most important meal of the day?"

Alex's mom had told him lots of things, but not that. In fact, the question of whether or not to eat breakfast had been answered when he was a young kid. His mother was a morning drinker and he couldn't bear to be around it. So he usually kept to his room until it was time to leave for school. But he wasn't about to share that with Joy. He never spoke of it to anyone, not even his brothers. "Sorry. No."

"Well, you haven't had my scones. I promise you will change your stance on breakfast." She measured out flour, added a sprinkle of salt, and unwrapped a stick of butter, cutting it into small cubes, then scraped that from a cutting board into the bowl.

Alex took a seat at one of the barstools across the kitchen island and watched intently. She was so comfortable and at ease in the kitchen, humming to herself as she worked. This was not a woman with a treacherous past. He was fairly certain of that. "Now what are you doing?"

She had pulled out a fork and was mashing the mixture in the bowl. "Cutting in the butter. You want it in tiny pieces the size of a baby pea. That makes a flaky scone."

"I take it this was part of your classical training?"

"I took a few baking classes, yes. A good chef has to be well versed in everything." She turned and fetched a bottle of milk from the fridge. She added a splash to the bowl and mixed with the fork again.

"You don't measure much. I thought baking was like science."

"Cakes and cookies, yes. Bread and other baked goods are more like art and science mixed together. You need to learn what to look for. You don't want the dough to be too sticky or too dry. With scones, you don't want to overmix. With bread, it's almost the opposite."

"Interesting." He took another sip of his coffee. He enjoyed being with Joy even when she was hesitant to answer his questions, but the times when she was chatty were certainly more fun and interesting.

"I'm sure this is boring to you." She picked up a glass jar that had been sitting with her other baking ingredients. "How do you feel about dried cranberries?"

"Honestly? I never really thought about them enough

to have a feeling one way or the other. But I like fruit, so sure."

"Good. Because I love them." She grinned and shook a handful onto the cutting board, chopped them roughly, then added them to the mix. She then pushed everything aside, sprinkled some flour on the counter and dumped out the dough.

"Now what are you doing?"

She picked up a rolling pin and shook it at him. "Please tell me you know what this is for."

"Depends on your personal preferences in the bedroom."

A smile played at the corner of her lips, making everything below his waist go taut. Finally, he was acting like his normal semi-witty self, not the idiot who asked questions she didn't feel like answering.

"I'm not much for pain," she replied, working on the dough. It was impossible not to stare at her shoulders while she worked. The display was poetry in motion.

"A bigger fan of pleasure?" He took a sip of coffee, happy he managed not to choke on it. Things were escalating, and he liked this new direction.

"Definitely." She cut the dough into triangles, transferred them to a baking sheet, brushed them with cream and sprinkled them with sugar.

"The triumphant return of your good friends, cream and sugar."

"Not a return, Alex. They are a fixture." She smiled, even more effortlessly this time, then put the pan into the oven and set a timer.

Damn, he liked hearing her say his name. Her voice was so sweet and soft. It was hard not to wonder what it might be like to have her moan it in his ear. *Down, boy.*

Normally, the thought of being stuck in a house with nowhere to go would bother him greatly, but not today. He had nowhere he needed to be, nobody he wanted to see, except Joy.

"So tell me why you're here alone in this big house at the holidays. Why not go home to Santa Barbara?"

She busied herself with cleaning up the counters and putting dishes into the dishwasher. "Why aren't you going home to Chicago? You told me yourself that you're close with your family."

There she was again, trying to flip the conversation so they ended up talking about him. Did the modesty she'd shown him last night when talking about her career cover all aspects of her life? Was she simply one of those people who didn't want to talk about herself? "I asked you first."

"I'm not sure you want to hear this. We hardly know each other."

"You can tell me anything. I'm a good listener. I promise."

She sighed, then nodded in resignation. "It's difficult for me to go home. I have an ex-boyfriend who's bad news. If he hears I'm around, he starts looking for me. It's easier if I just stay away." She seemed embarrassed, almost ashamed, and that made him feel horrible about having pushed the issue.

"I'm so sorry. I had no idea it was something so serious."

"It's okay. We all have our stories, don't we? It's not a happy subject. And it's the holidays. This should be a happy time."

Alex had to respect her plea for privacy. "I'm not at home for Christmas because I needed a break from my father and his wife, if that makes you feel any better. They're insufferable. My brothers are both off partying in the Caribbean. Call me old-fashioned, but I want snow at Christmas. I grew up in Chicago. I don't know any other way."

"I'm with you. I have to have snow, too, or it just doesn't seem right."

"I'm not a meteorologist or anything, but I'm guessing you don't get much snow in Santa Barbara."

She shrugged it off. "Oh. Of course. You know. Lots of winter getaways with my parents when I was younger." The timer buzzed. Joy stepped over to the oven and removed the sheet pan. She carefully moved the scones to a plate, then presented them to Alex. The smells that filled the kitchen were unbelievable—warm, sweet, and comforting.

He took a scone from the plate, opened his mouth, but stopped shy of taking a bite. "Wait a second. I don't know if I'm ready for this. What if you end up ruining me for all other scones? Then what?"

Joy brought two small plates and a stack of napkins, then took the seat next to him. "I can't be responsible for other people's shortcomings. If I blow your mind, I blow your mind. Not my fault."

All Alex could think was that his mind was already blown by Joy. He still didn't know what to make of her. She was so down-to-earth for someone who'd been born with a silver spoon in her mouth. Perhaps her decision to pursue her passion had helped to ground her. Or perhaps it was whatever had happened with her ex, a situation he couldn't dare let himself think about too much, lest his temper flare.

"Here goes nothing." His teeth sank into the flaky

pastry. As soon as he got a taste of the slightly sweet treat, he was a goner. It was buttery and rich, but light as a cloud. "Oh, my God. I have never had a scone that good. Not even in England."

She took a bite herself and dabbed at the corners of her lips with the napkin. "Told you so. I don't like to brag, but the customers down at the bakery are always raving about them."

"Customers at what bakery?" He pointed around the kitchen. "You practically have a bakery right here."

Joy coughed, almost like she was choking. Alex patted her back, then hopped up to fill a water glass. "Are you okay?"

Tears were misting her eyes. "Yeah. Just went down the wrong way." She took several long drinks of the water and slapped her hand against her chest.

"Better?"

"Much."

"So what bakery? Do you have your own bakery in town? I thought you were just visiting."

Joy cast her sights away, probably getting ready to be modest again. "I've been working out of the bakery in town. I'm working on a cookbook and it's good to do your research and recipe development when there are people around to test out your work. It's much better than eating it all yourself. I'd be the size of a water buffalo if I ate scones all day long."

"So you have writing aspirations. Sounds like being a chef goes well beyond just cooking for you."

"Definitely. I'm not the sort of person who sits around all day long. I'd like to have my own empire at some point. A little empire, I guess."

"Why would it have to be little? You could definitely

have your own TV show. You're more than beautiful enough to be on camera." Funny thing was, he didn't know her very well, but he could already see her doing those things.

Joy Baker didn't seem like the type of woman who failed at anything.

Four

Joy was taken aback by Alex's supportiveness. Sure, she'd had a lot of people appreciate her work, but very few acted as though her greatest aspirations, her biggest pie-in-the-sky dreams, might come true. And he thought she was beautiful? Alex was not only accustomed to beauty, he was apparently a big fan, judging by the photos she'd seen last night. The weight of the compliment did not go unnoticed. "Thank you. That means a lot to me. Truly."

"Good. I'm glad." He looked right at her, for long enough that she could feel their connection all the way down to her toes. His eyes were so breathtaking, the most vivid shade of sky blue. It wasn't easy to sustain a direct hit, but what delicious pleasure it was to stand firm and take it anyway. It left her feeling as though she was in the presence of greatness, and that was a wonderful sensation.

"You know, I'm sorry I knocked on your door last night," he continued. "I didn't mean to intrude. I just happened to come up the stairs for bed and I heard you up and about. This house is so quiet, it's hard not to hear."

So he hadn't been eavesdropping or checking up on her—he'd been concerned. She needed to stop being so silly. Every guy was not Ben. Alex wasn't even close. Hell, he'd expressed more enthusiasm for her dreams and pursuits in the last five minutes than her ex had been capable of showing in a lifetime. "Please. Don't worry about it. I'm thankful you were worried enough about me to stay the night. Most guys would not do that."

"The way I see it, I'm spending my day with a gorgeous future celebrity chef. I definitely won't get bored or go hungry. I'm not exactly suffering here." He picked up his coffee mug and took a sip, delivering a clever look that left her breathless. Alexander Townsend was supremely confident in everything he did. Probably why he was so tempting to spend time with. He set down his mug and raised his arm, giving his armpit a whiff. "Although you might be suffering soon, unless I throw in some laundry. I had some gym clothes in my car, but that's about it."

She hadn't considered that. "My friend's son has a whole closet full of clothes in your room. You're about the same build." She knew she'd made a mistake as soon as the words left her mouth. What was she doing? Offering to loan out Luc Marshall's clothes?

"Do you think he would mind?"

What was she supposed to say to that? "Of course not. He's a really good guy." He wasn't really. He was nice enough, but would he loan his clothes to a stranger? Joy doubted it, but she couldn't renege on the offer now.

"Any port in a storm, right?"

Joy glanced out the window. The sky was still gray and unsettled. "I'd say this weather definitely qualifies."

"Lead the way then."

With every step up the stairs with Alex, Joy's pulse began to pick up. She liked Alex. She liked him a lot. He'd been incredibly kind to her, and even when she'd worried that he might be getting nosy, she'd learned that he was being nothing of the sort. Did he like her the same way? And if he was interested, would they have a chance to pursue anything? She didn't know how long it would take a plow to get up to their house and clear the driveway, but Rafe had made it sound as though it might take a day if the weather was bad. At the very least, she hoped she'd get a parting kiss. She needed more happy remembrances of nice guys. There hadn't been nearly enough.

Now that they were alone in Luc's room, she had to admit that she was more than a bit curious about Alex and what his demeanor might be like in a romantic situation. He had this very smooth veneer, but there was an underlying wit that had her intrigued. He also had a tender and sweet side. After all, what man comes back in a snowstorm to check on a woman he hardly knows? So the question was, where did the passion lie inside Alexander Townsend? And how much was there? What would his kiss be like? Soft and polite? Or would he skip right to the white-hot part, where things became frantic, hands were everywhere, and clothes started disappearing?

Alex came up behind her and put his hands on her shoulders. "Ready?" He stepped around her and made his way to the closet. His touch was gone entirely too soon, but he left behind a lasting heat, like he'd branded her. She couldn't help but notice that the bed was rumpled, bedding piled up in a heap. There was something so intimate about the sight, it sent flickers of electricity along Joy's spine. Did the sheets still hold his warmth? Did they smell like him? A very big part of her wanted to experience the fantasy of being with Alex, have him take off her clothes and pull her down onto the mattress…put his manly hands all over her and give her the ultimate snow day.

Alex flipped on the closet light and stepped inside. Joy followed. The walls were lined on three sides with hanging clothes and rows of shelves topped with neatly folded garments. A round, tufted leather ottoman sat in the middle of the room. Why anyone needed so many clothes in a vacation home was beyond Joy. Plus, she had to wonder about the logistics. What did Luc do if he was getting dressed in Santa Barbara and remembered that his favorite shirt actually lived in Vail? Maybe he had two or three of everything.

"What do you think you need?" Joy watched as Alex perused the findings.

"Just a pair of jeans and a sweater for now." He glanced back over his shoulder at her, flashing her a sly look. "I sleep in the nude, so I don't need any pajamas."

Between that and the rolling pin remark in the kitchen—was Alex leaving her a trail of sexual bread crumbs? Did he want her the way she wanted him? And if so, who would be the first to give in, break the ice, and just kiss the other person? "It looks like the sweaters are there on the shelves. It looks like the jeans are hanging next to them." She sat on the ottoman, trying not to think about the fact that if Mariella Marshall could see her right now, Joy would never again work in the culinary world. Mariella was just that vindictive.

Joy instead tried to soak up the moment, being in this luxe setting with Alex. This was as close as she'd ever come to winning the lottery.

He pulled a chocolate brown sweater from the shelf and checked the label. "One hundred percent cashmere. Good. I can't stand wool. And it's a quality maker as well. This should work." Alex whipped off his T-shirt and tossed it onto the ottoman. It landed right next to her.

Joy swallowed hard, staring at the garment, preparing herself to look while her brain was telling her she was an idiot if she didn't hurry up. She planted her hand on the ottoman and crossed her legs, eying him as he threaded the sweater over his head. Wow. Alex was…built. Much more so than any other man she'd been fortunate enough to see without his shirt. She didn't need to touch him to know he was firm, but damn if her palms weren't itching to conduct a thorough inspection. He was solid. His pecs were defined, his abs a ladder of muscle. She wasn't about to tear her eyes away, but then he poked his arms into the sleeves and tugged down the hem. The heavenly vision disappeared far too fast. But she'd seen enough to know she wanted an eyeful a second time. And a third.

He looked down at her. "Well?"

Joy was finding it hard to breathe. "It's nice. That color is nice on you." That part was true. The warm brown was the perfect counterpoint to his steely blue eyes. It was like they were meant to go together. Fire and ice.

"It's a little snug in the shoulders."

"Yeah. You're a lot more muscular than I had guessed." She had definitely underestimated his build as compared to Luc.

"You guessed?" He cocked an eyebrow at her.

Her face flamed with heat. "Of course I did. You needed clothes and I was just thinking that the guy whose clothes you're borrowing is tall. Like you. And he's, you know…" She drew a line in the air to match the angle of his shoulders, hoping this would somehow illustrate her point and make her seem less hopelessly distracted by his beautiful body. "He's broad like you, too. But he's not anywhere near as, you know, built."

"So I could take him in a fight. That's what you're telling me." He winked and laughed. "Kidding."

You could take me in a fight. I would hardly fight at all. What had happened since she'd walked into this closet? She was struggling to keep up.

Alex pulled a pair of jeans from the shelf and she quickly realized what was coming next. She wanted to stay, but she didn't. Whatever shred of prim and proper resided in her body was telling her to clamp her eyes shut or get out of there. She popped up from the otto-man. "I'll let you finish on your own. You don't need me here." The next logical step was to walk right out of that closet. But her feet apparently wanted to stay for the show because they wouldn't move. Perhaps they'd cut a deal with her eyes.

He undid the button on his own jeans and stepped out of them. "I'm not shy, if that's what you're worried about."

Yeah, I'm beginning to understand that. "I'm not worried about anything."

Except that she was worried this was all a ruse. That it wasn't real. She didn't belong in this house or in this world or with this man. Hell, he didn't even know her real name.

He zipped open his gym bag and pulled out a pair of

black boxers. Her feet were just going to have to cooperate with her exit strategy. She pivoted on her heels and stared at one wall of Luc's clothes, everything hanging so neatly, so perfectly. There had to be tens of thousands of dollars of clothing in here, just waiting for the odd weekend when its owner would show up, but that excess wasn't enough of a distraction from Alex. It was impossible not to wonder about his state of undress. Just thinking about it made her body temperature spike a few degrees.

"It's okay to look now. I'm not naked anymore."

She turned back, but her face felt as though she'd just had a steam facial. "Oh. Okay. I just wanted you to have your privacy."

"I don't know you particularly well, but you seem on edge." He stepped into Luc's jeans, and she stole a look at his legs, which were as much a marvel as the other parts of him she'd been privy to—solid, with uncommon curves and contours. Somewhere there had to be a block of marble waiting to be carved into his likeness. If any man should eventually become a statue, it was Alex. "I hope it's not me. I hope I'm not making you uncomfortable."

"No. You're not. I'm fine. I've always been wound a little tight." The chronic worrier. If she ever got to a point in her life where she didn't have a care in the world, she had no doubt she could come up with new concerns. It was just the way her brain was wired.

He straightened the pockets of the jeans by stuffing his hands inside, then folded up his own clothes. "All better. I'll probably take a shower later."

A shower. Sounds nice. "Oh, sure."

He clamped his hand on her shoulder and gently kneaded. She was still in her PJs, not wearing a bra.

The heat of his hand sent a sizzle through her body that made her nipples tighten. Her shoulders caved in, if only to hide her body's response to him.

"You sure you're okay?" His voice was so deep and rich, it only made it harder to stay wedged in reality.

She nodded, hoping the movement would make her feel less out of place. She desperately wanted to feel at ease around him. She wanted whatever invisible barriers were between them gone. "Yep."

"So what should we do now? We have at least a whole day stuck in this house together."

He was now using both hands to massage her shoulders. It felt so good, his fingers so strong and insistent, she wanted them all over her body right now. She wanted more than anything to close her eyes, drop her head to one side, give him access to her neck, beg him to slip her top off her shoulder. With the two of them alone in this big, beautiful house, it seemed like the best use of their time to just tear each other's clothes off and fall into bed.

"I don't know. You have any ideas?" she muttered. *Just kiss me.*

"Well, it's nearly Christmas and it's a little sad that there are zero decorations up in this house. How are you going to get into the holiday spirit?"

That was quite literally the last thing on her mind. This year, December 25 was simply going to be the day after the twenty-fourth and before the twenty-sixth, except it would at least be a day off. "I don't even know where we would find decorations or if they have any."

"So, we'll look."

"Doesn't that seem a little bit like snooping?"

"I doubt your friends would trust you with their enormous house unless they felt totally comfortable with you using it. Nobody wants someone they care about to spend Christmas alone with no holiday cheer."

Why was it so easy for him to convince her of things that were essentially very bad ideas? Up until he'd arrived, she'd done her best to leave behind zero trace of herself while she was here. "Okay. I suppose you have a point." She turned, flipped off the closet light, and Alex trailed her out. "I should probably get dressed."

"I don't know. I'm a big fan of the pajamas." He smiled and she thought she might melt into a puddle right there on the carpet. The bed was only paces away. He'd hardly have to do anything to have her. *Get your head out of the clouds.* She had to be sensible. That would make for a less dramatic crash back to earth whenever Alex Townsend walked out of her life.

"I think I'll go for more traditional attire today if that's okay with you."

"Whatever you think. You're in charge."

Alex hung out in the living room, watching TV for the road conditions, while Joy took her shower. The general consensus from county authorities was to stay inside and let them clear the snow. Alex didn't have a choice anyway. They wouldn't hit the 24-hour mark until that evening, and his Bugatti had too little clearance under the car body to make it through any snow at all. He'd toast the engine before he got anywhere.

His phone rang. It was Paul, his investigator. Alex hopped off the couch and rushed into the foyer, taking a peek up the stairs before he answered. "Hey. Did you find anything?" He answered in a hushed tone, quickly distancing himself from the stairwell, walking across the living room to the farthest side. If Joy came downstairs, he could end the call if needed.

"Well, I don't know. I found dozens and dozens of women with the last name Baker and the first initial J. But as far as a Joy, the only one I found is a seventy-two-year-old woman from Flagstaff, Arizona."

"Seventy-two? Definitely not the same person." He leaned against one of the mammoth wood posts that held up the vaulted ceiling, looking out the window at the stunning mountain view. All except the highest rocky peaks were blanketed in white. "I don't know that it's really necessary anyway."

"Did you strike out?"

Alex had become especially close to Paul after he discovered the true identity of Alex's former fiancée. It wasn't uncommon for them to discuss personal things. "Strike out? No. But I'm not worried about it anymore. She's a nice, kind person. We're spending some time together." Alex stopped short of disclosing the details of the storm. If Paul knew Alex was stuck in the snow, he'd suggest something ridiculous like bringing in a helicopter to rescue him, even though there was nowhere to land. Alex did not want heaven and earth moved for him. He rather enjoyed the idea that nobody could get to him right now. He had the freedom to spend time with a singular woman, someone completely unlike most people he met. Sure, she had odd habits like constantly turning off lights, but he wanted to trust her. He *could* trust for a day or two. It wasn't like he and Joy were going to get married.

"Okay. Well, let me know if you change your mind. With the internet, it's almost impossible to hide, but some people are just squeaky clean."

"Are you worried that you couldn't find her?"

"I'm only worried if you are. Worry is driving all over town because you have a five-year-old grandson who has to have an action figure for Christmas that's impossible to find."

Alex laughed quietly, realizing how stupid this all was. It was the holidays. And he only had a few days with Joy Baker, whoever she was. He should relax and have fun. That was what his brothers had told him before they went off to the Caribbean.

He loved Christmas. He should be enjoying it. December 26 he'd be headed back to Chicago. He wasn't sure how long Joy was staying, but regardless, her life was in Santa Barbara, which was a world away from his. "Definitely don't worry about my stuff. As for the action figure, go on one of those online auction sites, pay whatever outrageous price somebody wants, and be done with it. I'll foot the bill."

"Are you serious?" Paul asked. "You don't have to do that, Alex. You pay me well."

"I could always pay you better. Seriously. My treat. I just want you and your family to have a merry Christmas."

"You're the best. You know that?"

All Alex could think was that Paul was the best. He'd saved Alex's hide two years ago. "You're worth it. I'll catch up with you after Christmas, okay?"

"Deal."

Alex got off the phone just as Joy walked into the living room. The notion of a woman making his heart race made him feel like a teenager all over again, but damn, she did exactly that. She smiled softly and wandered toward him. She was wearing a fluffy white sweater with a deep V-neck and a white tank top with skinny straps underneath it. The sweater fell off her shoulder even more easily than her pajamas. She had such beautiful bone structure—her collarbone and shoulders begged to be touched. That moment in the closet was still fresh in his mind. He enjoyed giving a woman a neck rub, but he'd mostly had a hard time letting go. All he wanted to do was touch her.

"More work?" Joy asked. "Being the boss must suck."

He laughed and shook his head, advancing on her, finding himself so drawn to her it was ridiculous. There was something very freeing about the fact that he'd decided not to look into her background, to just trust her. This might be a good way for him to regain his footing when it came to women. An experiment of sorts, which was perfect since it had a logical conclusion—the day he'd leave for Chicago.

"I was just catching up with one of my employees, but no more work calls today. It's our snow day and I'd like to have some fun."

She smiled sweetly. "Honestly? I could use some fun, too. It's been a really long time since I've done anything like that."

"Perfect. Then let's go hunt for Christmas decorations."

"Project Snooping is underway."

"Don't call it snooping. We're merely attempting some necessary seasonal redecorating."

"If you're lucky, I might make Christmas cookies this afternoon."

He patted his belly. "Between scones and cookies, I'm going to need to find some way to work off all those extra calories." He hadn't planned on the naughty overtones of the statement, but he meant it.

"Maybe a snowball fight?"

He grinned at her. She'd saved him from himself. "I'm not sure you want to challenge me to that. I have a pretty killer arm. I played baseball in high school and college."

She smirked and shrugged her one naked shoulder, making everything in his body a little tighter. "I'm sure I can kick your ass in a snowball fight. I have extensive experience."

"Growing up in Santa Barbara?"

"Nope. Just lots of wintry vacations like this one."

"Oh. Right. Of course. My parents used to take us skiing all the time. That's how I fell in love with Vail. Did you used to come here often?"

"Actually, this is my first time. We used to go other places." She slipped her sweater back up onto her shoulder, taking away the view he'd been enjoying so much. "Aren't we supposed to be looking for Christmas stuff?"

For someone who hadn't been that eager to pursue this project in the first place, she'd sure changed her tune. "Yes. Where do you think we should start?"

"I think there's a storage space downstairs. No clue if there's an attic."

"I vote for the path of least resistance. Lead the way."

Off Joy went, and Alex followed, down a set of steps just off the main staircase. They took a turn, the stairwell flooded with light from an arched window, then down another five or six steps to a hall that opened up into a railed walkway overlooking a beautiful indoor pool area with a fireplace and a hot tub at one end. "Wow. This is amazing."

Joy shot him a look over her shoulder. "I know. Right? And to think this is just their vacation home. I don't think they end up coming here more than once or twice a year at most. It seems like such a waste."

Alex got what Joy was saying. There were certain excesses that came with wealth that were, well, silly. "Someone should be here enjoying this all the time."

"I totally agree. I bet that pool and hot tub haven't been used in a year."

"You haven't used it while you were here?"

"No. I've been too busy, I guess."

She stopped at the end of the walkway, then they headed down some circular stairs, ending up on the pool deck, which was covered in honed flagstone. The snow was piled high against the windows and a pair of large glass patio doors. "We're going to have to change that. We can't let the amenities go to waste. Especially that hot tub. I'm telling you right now, later today, that has our name written all over it."

"Is that your way of getting me into a bathing suit?" Joy asked.

"If it is, and I admit to it, how does that affect your willingness to do it?"

She smiled and shook her head, a breathy laugh rushing past her lips. "You're terrible. You know that, right?"

"What? You're a beautiful woman and we're stuck in this big house in a snowstorm. I'd have to be an idiot not to try."

"I'd have to be an idiot to not want you to try. At least a little."

Bingo. Things were definitely looking up. "But just so you know, I will always be gentlemanly. Always."

"Good. I like gentlemen."

"But even a gentleman wants a kiss."

She slanted her head to the side and raised her eyebrows at him. Was she considering it? He wanted to study her velvety brown eyes, but the reality was that her lips, so full and pouty, were the main attraction right now. "And a lady reserves the right to tell a gentleman that she might make him try a little harder."

"Exactly how hard?"

"If we're going to discuss hardness, I'm going to need you to buy me a drink first." She knocked into his chest with her elbow and pointed to an alcove at the back corner of the pool area. "I think the storage rooms are back there."

Alex was stuck there for a moment. Every thought he'd had before about Joy being different from other women he knew? He'd been right on the money.

He caught up to her quickly. The first room they found was full of pool equipment, but the second room contained all sorts of cardboard boxes and plastic storage tubs. "Makes you wonder why they'd store so much stuff if they only spend a few days a year here."

"It looks like they have a lot of winter gear."

Alex scanned the room. "There. Christmas." He walked over to the boxes and opened one. Inside were gold garland and boxes of ornaments. "Yes. Decorations. There's even an artificial tree."

"I don't want to do anything too over the top."

"Think of it this way. The harder we work, the more time we'll need in the hot tub."

She lifted a box while rolling her eyes, but he could see that smile she was trying to hide. "Keep trying, Alex. Just a little more."

Five

Joy plopped down the plastic tote she'd brought up from the storage area. Thoughts of dips in the hot tub with Alex and gentlemen wanting kisses danced in her head. Time had stood still after he'd said that…and she'd been sure he was going to actually do it. But he hadn't. And then she'd had to go and be coy about it. Waiting was not her strong suit.

Of course, she could have made the first move, but that just wasn't her, even when she was not a shy person. Call her old-fashioned, but she wanted him to do it. And when he hadn't, and he'd only talked a big game, she'd felt obligated to give him crap about it. But maybe she'd scared him off. That was *not* her intention.

"Should we start with putting together the tree you found?" she asked. "No telling how long that's going to take."

Alex opened the box. "I'd rather have the real thing, but this should be nice enough."

"I love the smell of a real tree. It instantly puts me in the Christmas spirit."

He pulled out the metal stand. "Where do you think we should put it? By the fireplace?"

"Sounds good." She watched as he placed the stand and the bottom section of the tree. "I can't even think of the last time I decorated for Christmas. It's been a while." It was the truth. She'd been working so much over the last several years, she hadn't had the time. Plus, living with the Marshalls had meant actual servants' quarters—cramped and not holiday-worthy. "I used to love it so much when I was a kid. Trimming the tree with my parents and my sister, listening to them fight while they untangled the lights. We would drink eggnog and listen to Christmas music. It was so great."

Alex just stood there, another section of the tree in his hands, branches sticking out every which way. It was almost like he couldn't quite compute what she'd said. "Sounds like your parents were committed to giving you a normal childhood. Our Christmas was nothing like that."

"It wasn't?" How could that possibly be true? Judging by his family's history in Chicago, surely he'd had a charmed childhood.

He shook his head and pressed his lips into a thin line as he dropped the next section of tree into place. "No. My parents had someone come in and do the decorations for us. There was a new theme every year, so we never had any favorite ornaments. My brothers and I didn't even know what to look forward to. One year my mom decided on a Miami-themed Christmas. We had aqua tinsel and pink flamingos everywhere."

"Oh, no. That sounds decidedly un-Christmas."

Alex shrugged. "I don't blame her. She was trying to please my dad by being the ultimate wife and mother. He was the one who insisted on putting on a big show. They hosted a huge party on Christmas Eve every year and their friends all came and drank too much and talked about how much money they had."

Joy couldn't even fathom it. Not a cent of his family's money had been used to build beautiful memories at the holidays. What a shame. "I'm so sorry."

"The worst part was they used to make us wear these hideous red plaid bow ties. My brothers and I just hated the whole thing. We couldn't wait until Christmas morning." Finally, he put the last section of the tree in place and began connecting the cords for the lights.

"Lots of presents under the tree, I'm sure."

"It wasn't even that. It was more that it was the one day of the year where they were nice to each other. The strain of the party was gone. My mom was distracted enough by my brothers and I that she didn't tend to drink. It was the only time we were ever really a family. There was just a whole lot of unnecessary hoopla leading up to it." He plugged in the tree and the white lights came to life. "Voila. Instant Christmas."

She smiled. It was a little thing, but having a tree up really did deliver a welcome dose of cheer. "It's so pretty. It'll look even better when we put the ornaments on it."

Joy handed Alex a box of glass ornaments in festive Santa and snowman shapes, painted in bold colors. She took a package of gold and silver metal icicles. They stood side by side, her shoulder coming up to about his armpit. The tree was small. It was hard to decorate without touching each other. Their hands kept brushing. Their elbows kept knocking.

"You're not distributing the ornaments evenly," Alex said. He scooted around her from behind, placing his hand at her waist for a moment, sending a ripple of excitement through her.

"Wow. Somebody is a little particular about the Christmas tree." She bumped her hip into him. His eyes flashed with mischief. Joy felt as though her entire body was on fire.

"I'm only particular because I haven't had the chance to do this in two years."

That seemed like an awfully specific number. "Let me guess. Girlfriend related?"

"Worse. Former fiancée."

She'd seen a mention of a broken engagement in her online snooping, but Joy assumed that was par for the course with a man like Alex, a man who had no shortage of women in his life. "Ah, so you were more deeply invested. Had to decorate for the holidays."

"Of course. She was really into it. Had my apartment all decked out. Unfortunately, it ended and my enthusiasm for doing this on my own has been lacking since then."

"I bet it was nice while it lasted." Joy had a burning need to ask him more, but she didn't want to pry. Not when they were having fun.

"It wasn't. *This* is nice," Alex said. Again, his voice was doing funny things to her, making her chest flutter. "I think the tree might tip over if we load it down with any more ornaments. We need one of those things that goes around the bottom."

"A tree skirt." Joy flipped open another box and dug around. She didn't come across what they were looking for, but she did find a suitable substitute. "This is probably meant to go on the mantle, but it'll work in a pinch." She pulled out a long swag of gold and red brocade with tassels at both ends. She held one in each hand and gave them a little twirl like a burlesque dancer. "I can do a show later if you get bored."

"Have I mentioned that I'm really bored? Things around here are chronically dull. I'm going to fall asleep unless someone entertains me."

Heat plumed in her cheeks. "You're such a flirt." The truth was that *she* was being the flirt. She desperately wanted to kiss him. She was tired of the notion of anyone trying harder or waiting longer. "Are you always like this?"

He shrugged and took one end of the swag from her. "Never. You must bring it out in me."

Yeah, right. Joy wasn't about to believe that for a second, but she did love that he wanted to create an illusion that he did things with her that he'd never done with anyone else. There was something so sexy about it, she felt light-headed.

They crouched down by the tree and wrapped the festive fabric around the base. Alex's knee was touching hers. Their shoulders brushed. They were so close she was aware of the tempo of his breaths and found her own body wanting to fall into the same rhythm. "Works like a charm."

"You're the real charm." He turned to her, his lips a heartbeat away. Everything in that library-like house became even more quiet and still.

She didn't want to put up barriers, but there was a part

of her that was naturally defensive. She just wanted one more sign that this would be okay. One more clever bit of convincing. "You should talk. You and your flirting."

"I'm just wondering if you're ever going to take the bait."

She didn't give herself another second to question whether she should do this. She'd never have a better opening than the one she had right now.

She dropped to her knees, grasped his shoulder and leaned in for a kiss. His lips were soft and warm. She reveled in that glorious instant when everything was new.

Her eyes fluttered shut and he leaned in, also on his knees. She inched closer, pressing against him—stomach, chest and lips. His fingers threaded into her hair and he gathered it at her nape, cupping the back of her head. His hand urged her to deepen the kiss, their tongues getting eagerly acquainted. She pushed her hips to meet his and felt that magical moment when he got harder.

He eased them down onto their sides. The carpet was so thick and plush, Alex all firm muscle and a capable grasp. He rolled to his back, Joy on top of him. She loved weighing him down, mostly because she knew he was so strong he wouldn't have to work at all to have wherever and however he wanted. She spread her legs wider, her knees slipping to the floor, so she was straddling his hips. She rocked into him and he groaned fiercely, slipping his warm hands up the back of her sweater, sending a bright white thrill through her. This was not only escalating quickly, it was barreling toward somewhere she'd thought it might not go. She wanted him so badly the need burned inside her. Alex might end up making her spontaneously combust.

She planted a hand in the center of his chest and

pushed back, loving the feel of his solid muscle beneath her palm. "I want to see you again," she said. She threaded her fingers beneath that beautiful cashmere sweater only to experience firsthand something far more breathtaking. The landscape of his torso was a sight to behold, especially as he arched his back, raised his arms, and let her push the sweater past his head. She spread her hands across his chest. Every inch of him was rock hard, except of course, his lips. They were soft and welcoming and she sought his kiss again, if only to get lost in how heavenly it was.

"This isn't fair," he muttered against her mouth. "You got to see me. I haven't seen a single inch of you other than your shoulder and it's been killing me."

She bit down on her lower lip. He was so damn sexy, he only made her want to be free with herself and completely let go. "Do you want to be in charge?"

"Unwrapping presents is the best part of Christmas, isn't it?"

She giggled against his neck as he pushed her until they were both sitting up, Joy's legs wrapped around his waist. His fingers curled under the hem of her tank top and she drew in a sharp breath as he raised that and the sweater slowly, lifting the fabric from her skin, leaving her exposed to him. He flung her clothes aside and placed both hands in the center of her back as he kissed the tops of her breasts, making a trail along the edge of her bra cups. He unhooked the clasp and dragged the straps down her shoulders. He ushered in a new level of intimacy as he cast aside the bra and her breasts were left naked.

Their gazes connected as he lightly pressed his palms against her nipples, rubbing up and down. Her skin went impossibly tight, the heat of blood rushing to her breasts, sending her body temperature skyward. He molded his hands around her, then let go of one side, leaning down and drawing her nipple into his warm mouth. Her eyes couldn't have stayed open if she'd wanted them to—and she did. She wanted to watch, but the feeling was too amazing, too exhilarating, so she decided the visual would have to wait. She rocked her center against his crotch, relishing the unbelievable tension between them.

"Do you have a condom?" she asked between kisses. She knew she was making a leap, but she would've launched herself off a cliff right now for him.

"I don't." He looked at her with the saddest eyes, as if she'd just shattered every dream he had in his head. It was quite possibly the sweetest thing she'd ever seen. "I'm not really the guy who walks around with condoms in his pocket."

"Good. Because I don't want to sleep with that guy." She kissed the corner of his mouth. "Lucky for you, I have some upstairs in my room." It might have been a while since she'd been with anyone, but she had moved to Santa Barbara on top of the world and feeling optimistic.

The smile that broke across his face was nearly as adorable as his broken one moments before. "What are we waiting for?"

She hopped off his lap and stood. It was hard not to notice just how much poor Alex was straining against the front of his pants. Feeling impatient and wanting to put him out of his misery, she grabbed his hand and they stole away upstairs. He followed her into her bathroom and wrapped his arms around her naked waist while she rifled through the drawers, looking for the right cosmetic bag. He was running kisses along her shoulders and along her spine, driving her wild with desire.

"Found 'em." She turned in his arms and flipped the foil packet in her fingers.

"I have never been so happy to see one of those in all my life."

Again, she doubted smooth Alex's words, but she didn't really care. He was trying and that was all that mattered. He gripped her rib cage and kissed her again, pressing her against the bathroom vanity as she tore open the wrapper.

He broke their kiss and unzipped his jeans, shoving them to the floor. Anticipation was working its way through her and now she was feeling like a woman of action more than anything else. She dropped to her knees and tugged down his gray boxer briefs. She wrapped her fingers around his steely length, stroking firmly, marveling at just how ready he was for her. Alex groaned and dug his fingers into her hair. "That feels so good, but I want to make love to you. And those jeans you're still wearing are a definite problem."

She laughed quietly and rolled on the condom, then stood and let him be in charge for a moment, watching as he dispatched her jeans and shimmied her lacy panties past her hips. Finally, there were no more clothes to worry about; there were only frantic kisses now, tongues winding around each other, his hands grasping her bottom, hers roaming the muscled landscape of his back. She couldn't wait anymore. She rose up on her tiptoes and perched on the edge of the bathroom counter, raising one leg until her ankle was on his hip. He positioned himself at her entrance and drove inside at the same moment he pulled her into the deepest kiss yet, strong and passionate. Her body struggled with how perfectly he filled her as she wrapped her other leg around his waist.

He used his ridiculous upper body strength to boost her off the counter, his craving hands cupping her bottom. His thrusts were deep. They were slow. His breaths were short and ragged, but she definitely felt like this was all about her. He was so focused on their kisses, every moan she made was met with more intensity in his touch. The tension was rattling her body, toying with her—it built, then ebbed, over and over again.

She was close—it was as if she could feel it before she came—but when she finally did, it was more than she'd been prepared for. She pitched forward and dug her fingers into his shoulders, clinging to him for dear life, her body grasping his and not willing to let go. He called out and she felt every nuance of his release, heard every subtle gasp as it left his lips.

When the pleasure subsided, he allowed her full body weight to again rest on the bathroom counter. He kissed her softly. "Let me take care of this."

Joy didn't yet have words for what had just happened, so she nodded and walked into the bedroom, climbing into the heavenly bed, sinking into the pillows and curling up under the fluffy duvet. If she persuaded Alex to make love to her here, she might die from too much bliss.

He joined her moments later, slipping under the blanket with her. His warm body quickly found hers and he wrapped his arms around her, kissed her forehead. "That's definitely the best tree-trimming party I've ever been to."

She giggled into his chest, rubbing her nose back and forth against his smooth skin. "Very funny. Technically, we still have work waiting for us downstairs. We have to put away those boxes."

"Compared to what I would normally be doing today, what's waiting for me downstairs is nothing." He tucked her hair behind her ear and left a peck on her nose. "Although all I really want right now is what's waiting for me in this bed."

Six

Alex hadn't slept with a woman in his arms in eons, but an afternoon nap? Even better. He turned his head on the pillow, buried his nose in Joy's silky hair, which was in disarray. Now he knew what that spun-sugar smell was—it was Joy. He might not like sugar in his coffee, but this sweet fragrance? He might be able to live off it, at least for a little while. For fun. For the sake of enjoying the company of a beautiful woman, even when they both had different lives, far flung from where they were now. He could enjoy their few days in Colorado together, and parting would be sad, but hopefully still happy. They could be friends. That would be nice.

Alex's stomach growled loudly. It was nearly four in the afternoon, and not only had they spent the last few hours sleeping off the exhaustion of two rounds of making love, they'd skipped lunch. He was starving.

Unfortunately, Joy was still asleep. And mumbling.

"No. Mariella. You're wrong," she muttered. Her voice was halting and breathy, like a drunk who has convinced themselves they're sober. She tossed her head from side to side.

Alex pushed up on his elbow and rubbed her arm. "Joy. It's almost four. Probably time to get up." He kissed her shoulder, but made it quick. If he got too vested in his mouth on her body, he'd never eat.

Her eyes opened halfway, then drifted shut and opened wider. "Wait. What?"

"It's almost four. You slept for more than two hours."

She sat up in bed and pulled the covers up over herself. "I did? Seriously? I never do that."

"Yeah. I think you were having a bad dream, too. You kept talking about someone named Mariella. You were saying no. Who's Mariella?"

"Who? Oh, that's my mom's cat's name."

"Why would you tell a cat that she's wrong?"

Joy shrugged. "She's very vocal. Sometimes, talking to her is the only thing that gets her to stop meowing."

"Huh. Okay." That made as much sense as anything. He guessed. "Can we eat? I can only subsist on scones for so long."

"Of course. I'll make something." She climbed out of bed and grabbed a fluffy white robe from the chair next to the bureau. "I should probably get dressed."

"Up to you. I don't mind you being not dressed."

She smiled and rolled her eyes—so adorable. "I need clothes while I'm cooking. Meet you in the kitchen in ten?" She was being distant now and he didn't want to push her further away. He was starting to understand that distant Joy might just be regular Joy. He didn't like distant Joy as much as fun, carefree Joy, but he wasn't going to worry about it. Food felt like a more pressing issue.

"Sounds like a plan." Alex grabbed his boxers from the bathroom floor and headed across the hall to the room he was staying in for a quick shower. He scrubbed his hair dry with a towel and swiped at the mirror, leaning closer. He was getting downright scruffy, but he never shaved at the gym, so he didn't have his toiletries with him, aside from deodorant. Joy would just have to live with it.

His mind stubbornly wound back to her change in mood after their nap, but he could accept that they'd managed to put themselves in a bit of an odd situation. Sleeping with someone in the first twenty-four hours was rarely accompanied by being confined to the same house. She'd been living here alone, and maybe she was a woman who enjoyed her space.

"Hey," he said to Joy when he reached the kitchen. She was busy digging through the refrigerator. "Do you think we should call someone about having the driveway plowed? Is there a caretaker?"

"No. I think they're just supposed to come as soon as they can."

"Oh. Okay." That seemed odd, but he also lived in a gated neighborhood where things like snow removal were taken care of as part of the homeowners association fees. "What's for dinner?"

"I'm trying to figure that out. Are you okay with chicken piccata? Lemon butter sauce, a little garlic, some shallot. I was thinking I'd make it with a thin spaghetti on the side, maybe some wilted spinach? That's really the only vegetable I have in the house right now other than baby carrots."

"Are you kidding? That sounds incredible. Yeah. Make that."

"Do you want to help?"

"I'm seriously no good in the kitchen. I'll just end up putting paprika in the wrong thing and then you'll hate me forever."

"First off, I could never hate you. Second, if you know what paprika is, you're getting your butt in this kitchen and helping."

Alex had no answer for that. "Okay. But you're going to have to tell me how to do everything."

He stood next to her at the stove top. She leaned closer and kissed him softly on the lips. "Something tells me you'll be a quick study."

There she was again—happy Joy. She was going to be the death of him. That was all there was to it. He'd dated plenty of sexy women, but she was simply off the charts. And perhaps it was just that she was exactly his brand of sexy. Every minute they were together, she managed to do or say something that left him wondering where she'd been all his life.

He followed her around the kitchen as she showed him the proper technique for mincing garlic, breading chicken, and sautéing. It turned out that he'd even been making pasta incorrectly all these years, not that he cooked very often. Don't use oil in the water. Any Italian would have his head for that. The room filled with heavenly smells, and he enjoyed every chance he had to watch her while his hand settled in the small of her back, or she offered him a taste of something and she'd hold on to his arm while she did it.

As good as the meal looked, it really only took about thirty minutes to prepare. They decided to forgo the stuffy dining room, which had seating for at least twenty people. Sitting next to each other at the kitchen island with a bottle of wine Alex had found in the well-stocked wine fridge was plenty romantic for him. Joy had even dimmed the lights and lit a candle.

"This is incredible. Truly." He held out his wine glass to clink with hers. "To the chef."

She smiled shyly. "Cheers. But you did just as much work as I did. There's no big mystery to cooking. Once you learn to trust your instincts, you can just go into the kitchen and have fun. That's what I do."

Trust his instincts. That was something he might be rediscovering with Joy. He still trusted his business instincts, but it was the personal side that had been lagging. She made him so comfortable; it was as if they'd known each other for months. Years, even. "Well, I'm still in awe of your talents, and the scary part is you've shown me so much in a very short amount of time. I can only imagine what mysteries Joy Baker is hiding behind that beautiful face."

"There's no big mystery to me, Alex. I love to cook. I like spending time with you. That's all you need to know."

"I seem to remember something about threatening to kick my ass in a snowball fight. It'd be good to find out what that's all about. Sounds like a lot of hot air to me."

"Snowball fight? Alex, it's dark outside. And cold."

"I know. But I have an idea."

Joy shook her head and took another sip of wine. "If it involves trudging out in the driveway in snow boots and mittens, forget it."

"Nope. It involves putting on your bathing suit and meeting me downstairs."

* * *

Joy stood in the pool area in her bikini, wondering what in the heck Alex was up to. Outside, it was pitch-black. The snow was nearly waist high. "You are certifiable."

Alex was trying to figure out the locks to the tall patio doors. "Half of the fun of a hot tub in the winter is enjoying the cold first. My brothers and I used to do this all the time when we were kids. We had a pool and hot tub in the backyard and we'd run around in the snow, then jump in. It makes the water so much nicer."

Joy was thinking that Alex's back was so much nicer. He was wearing his basketball shorts, which hung a bit low around his hips. He had no shirt on, so she could see every muscle as it rippled and twisted when he flipped through the set of keys she'd given him, trying each one. Everything about what they were doing was crazy...using the house the way they were, putting up Christmas decorations and having sex on the bathroom counter. Still, it was the most fun Joy had had in a painfully long time. The last twenty-four hours might have been the most fun she'd had with a man, ever. Alex, for all of the syllables and roman numerals in his name, was at heart, a playful guy. It was just that nothing about his upbringing, his career, or his past romantic life hinted at any of it. She had to wonder if he felt as though he'd been living half a life. It was hard to fathom given every advantage he'd had, but perhaps it was true.

"Finally." Alex turned the handle and opened one of the patio doors. Cold air rushed in with a forceful gust. The snow that had been piled up against the glass tumbled inside onto the flagstone floor.

"Oh, my God. Alex. It's freezing." Joy wrapped her

arms around her waist and turned her face away from the arctic blast. "And the snow. It's going to make a mess."

"It's frozen water. There's a drain. It's a pool area. It's meant to get wet." He approached her with a huge smile on his face. "And stop being such a wimp. Come on." He took her hand and led her to the open door.

The cold air was more and more bracing the closer she got, but it certainly made her heart race—almost as much as Alex did. "Are we really having a snowball fight?"

"Nah. That doesn't seem very fun. We're just going to run out into the snow, stand there for a minute, and run back inside. Then get in the hot tub."

"In our bathing suits. And bare feet. Right now."

"Right now." He squeezed her hand and lifted it to his lips. Such a simple gesture, but she loved it. For a nanosecond, she couldn't feel the cold.

"Okay."

Alex tore off and Joy hustled to keep up. Her bare legs shuffled into the icy snow, cold shooting up the length of her body, but this was entirely different from being in the snowbank. At least she could breathe. In fact, frozen air filled her lungs readily, but it stung in a delightful way now that she couldn't stop laughing. She was into the snow past her knees. It came to Alex's shins. She hopped from foot to foot, trying to keep warm, not letting go of Alex's hand. They were facing each other, not far apart. His cheeks were bright red, his eyes piercing. Their breaths left their lips in puffs of white.

"Have we been out here long enough yet?" she asked.

He shook his head. "Nope. I'm not dying yet."

"Wait a minute. We have to wait until you're dying? I might freeze to death before then."

"Just a few more seconds." He bobbed his head five or

six times, his hair flopping into his eyes. "Okay. Now."
Still holding her hand, he bolted for the back door.

With their entrance came several cubic feet of snow
all over the floor. Mariella Marshall would literally give
birth to a litter of kittens if she saw this. Joy wasn't about
to ruin the moment with thoughts of being found out.

Alex didn't wait. He hopped down into the hot tub. Joy
took the steps. The water was impossibly hot. Alex sub-
merged himself to his shoulders right away, but Joy had
to ease in slowly, the heat prickling her back and stomach. She held her arms above the surface of the water as
she acclimated herself, gradually sinking down.

Alex had been so right, but she wasn't quite ready to
admit it. Her blood raced through her body. Her cheeks
and lips were still ice-cold. Her body didn't know what
to do about any of it—it only knew that whatever was
going on was exciting.

Alex dipped his hand into the water and ran his fingers through his thick hair, then settled back on the stone
bench, draping his arms over the side of the hot tub.
"Well? Good?"

No longer worried about surviving the freezing temperatures, she now had the chance to admire his chest
and shoulders. Every distinct contour, the way his muscles bulged and dipped, was familiar now, but that didn't
stop her from desperately wanting to touch him. Her
hands were alive with electricity. "Better than good. Fantastic."

"Told you so." He bounced his eyebrows in that cocky
Alex way.

Joy thought she might faint. This was certainly one
of those pinch-me moments, frolicking in the snow
and hanging out in a hot tub with Alex, the impossi-

bly handsome billionaire. "You were right. I fully own up to it. Between your genius at recreational planning, your Prince Charming good looks, and the fancy car, I'm trying to figure out how you're still single."

Half a smile cracked at the corner of his lips, but he quickly adopted a more serious look. The air stood still for a moment while the water swirled around them. Their gazes connected, his icy blue eyes making her feel exposed in a way she not only was willing to admit she liked, but that she also didn't want to end. "I can't figure out how you're single, either. You're literally one of the most beautiful and fascinating women I have ever met."

Alex's words were like a dream come true. Normally a compliment like that might make her blush, or possibly roll her eyes if it wasn't delivered with sincerity. But Alex was not like a normal man. He didn't warrant an everyday reaction. "That's very sweet of you to say. Today has been so amazing." The one thought that wouldn't leave her head at this moment was that she didn't feel like less than Alex. Not anymore. She was in awe of him, but she no longer felt as though they were on uneven ground. The realization made her keenly aware of every frantic beat of her heart.

He held out his hand, his eyes heavy with desire. "Come here."

She'd never followed a request so quickly. She slipped her fingers into his grasp and he tugged her closer through the water. His other hand cupped the side of her face. That single touch had the power to make her melt. His hand was firm and strong against her skin. He leaned closer and she shut her eyes, soaking up the moment when his lips touched hers. His kiss was like heaven, just like the first time, the perfect balance of strong and soft. She tilted her head to the side if only to get closer to him. Her lips parted, then his, and their tongues found each other, winding together in a way that was now beautifully familiar. Every inch of her body was on fire now and not just because she was immersed in the hot water. She had to be closer to him, and the second his arm wrapped around her waist, she shifted herself, placing a knee on the bench and straddling his lap.

He groaned his approval as her legs settled against his hips and her elbows found his shoulders. Her fingers dug deep into his thick hair, their kiss never breaking. It only intensified. She gently nipped his lower lip and he got harder between her legs. She rocked back and forth against him, letting her body take over. His warm and masculine scent filled her nose, his damp, silky hair so soft against the tender underside of her forearms as she dug her fingers deeper into it. His hands raced up and down her sides, gripping tightly, pressing into her skin, like he couldn't get enough. And she didn't want him to go without. She reached back to the nape of her neck and untied her bikini top. He was immediately on board with her decision, undoing the tie across her back, plucking the garment from the water and tossing it onto the pool deck.

"Much better," he muttered, pulling her into another deep kiss. His hand molded around her breast, his thumb riding back and forth across her nipple.

They rocked against each other, her hips involuntarily bucking into him. She couldn't get enough and she couldn't get it fast enough, either. "I want you, Alex."

"Can I say how much I love hearing that?" The words were delivered straight to her ear, his rich voice only deepening her need for him.

"You can if you make love to me. But we have to get out. Condoms and water don't mix."

"I realize that." He flattened his palm against her belly and slid his fingers down into the front of her bikini bottoms, finding her apex. "Just relax."

Joy gasped. She dropped her chin and nestled her face into Alex's neck. Her shoulders rolled forward and his hand did his bidding, fingers moving in firm circles. The rhythm did not waver. Round and round. The tension in her hips wound tighter.

"Kiss me," he said.

She dragged her cheek across his stubble, their lips joined, tongues even hotter than the steam swirling around them. The kiss was wild. Brash. Like they were trying to outdo each other, only Alex had the advantage. Joy was under his spell. The strokes of his fingers exactly right, the pressure in the perfect spot. The energy gathering in her belly coiled, mercilessly pulling at the muscles in her thighs. Her breaths frayed. Her mind juggled too much—heat and pleasure and Alex.

The peak slammed into her. Alex broke the kiss. His other hand clutched the side of her neck. His thumb raised her chin. Joy's head dropped back then rolled to the side. A squeak left her throat as the waves kept crashing. He stilled his hand. Her body tightened, then let go. Over and over again. When the final crest faded, she collapsed against his chest. He reined her in with his strong arms. She was as vulnerable as she could be, strength wrung from her body, but she'd never felt safer.

"That was so amazing." She dotted his wet shoulder with kisses, wanting to show her appreciation.

"I loved watching you at the end." One of his hands traced up and down her spine.

"Now we have to take care of you." She was surprised she could feel anything at all between her legs right now, but Alex was even harder than he'd been minutes earlier.

"Upstairs. In your bed. All night long."

She smiled, fighting back a well of sadness inside her. Tonight had been magical, but in Joy's experience, magic didn't last. Soon enough, the snow would be gone, and her real life, the one without Alex, would resume.

Seven

The *beep beep beep* woke Alex from a deep sleep. *What the hell?* His eyelids opened and closed. What was that sound? *Oh, right.* The snowplow. Careful not to wake Joy, he peeled back the duvet, padded down the hall and looked out through the Palladian window visible from the top of the stairs. The telltale scrape of metal against the house's stone drive served as further confirmation— his time with Joy was up. Another hour or so and they would no longer be snowbound.

Which left him with a quandary. He liked Joy. A lot. Last night had been incredible. They couldn't have gotten enough of each other if they'd tried. And they'd tried. They'd even broken a condom, a feat Alex had never before accomplished. Joy hadn't seemed overly concerned. She said she was at the end of her cycle anyway. No need to worry.

That wasn't heavy on his mind, but the calendar was. He was only in town for a little more than a week. Come December 26, he'd be headed back to Chicago. Just enough time to enjoy each other a few more times. The trouble was, he didn't want to seem like he was just after her for the sex, even when there was no blowing out that candle anytime soon. They'd fallen into sync with so little effort it was uncanny. Sex with Joy was fantastic, but it wasn't the only reason he wanted to see her. Never before had Alex wished, at least for a second or two, that he had waited or taken it slower. Even when he couldn't imagine any path other than the one they had traveled together.

The other concern was its own sticking point—feelings. Eight or nine days was just enough time to get attached. Alex was fairly sure he was capable of walking away with few scars. Not none, but few. She would always have a special place in his heart. He knew that much by now. And although he knew so little about her, he did know that while she was tough at times and fiercely independent, there was a sweet side to her as deep as the ocean. No woman cooks for a man the way she did without caring. He didn't want to hurt her.

"Hey. You're up," she said from behind him. Her voice was sleepy and sexy. She was wrapped up in her robe, looking as gorgeous as he could imagine, messy hair and fresh faced.

"Yeah. Good morning." He put his arm around her waist and kissed her temple softly. They settled against each other, both leaning into the railing, watching the back-and-forth of the plow in the driveway.

"Looks like they're digging us out."

"Appears so."

She looked up at him and licked her lower lip, but her expression was difficult to decipher. The trademark Joy wariness—it was the only way to explain it. What made her like that? Was it the ex she'd talked about? Her life, at least the career and family part, all seemed perfect. If anyone was following their bliss, she was. "I'll go make coffee and then I think I'll call the bakery to see if they need me today."

If she was going back to work, that meant he should probably do the same. It was Thursday, after all. He'd turned off his phone and left it downstairs. There was no telling what fresh hell might be waiting for him when he powered it back on. *Back to reality.* "What are the chances of scones this morning?"

A delighted grin spread across her lips. She'd converted him and she would gladly take the credit. "What happened to the guy who doesn't eat breakfast?"

"He's making up for lost time. I had absolutely no idea what I was missing."

She kissed his cheek. "For you, I will make scones. Different flavor, though. I have an idea after digging through the pantry last night." She flitted down the stairs, her hair bouncing behind her. Cooking was her happy place and he envied her for that. For him, work was work. Success brought satisfaction, and there was no question he relished any time he proved his father wrong, but he wasn't drawn to his occupation the way Joy was.

He ducked down the hall into his room and grabbed a sweatshirt, then went downstairs to spend some time with Joy. When they'd been stuck in the house, it had seemed as though time had stood still. Now that the plow was almost done, it felt as though the countdown had begun, their time together had a terminus. And he would've been lying to himself if he said that he didn't want to squeeze everything from it that he could.

Alex didn't put much stock in fate. He believed that a person built their own future, their destiny. But he had to wonder if something else was at work when his car slid down that hill and he nearly ran into Joy. Was she sent to him to help him learn to trust a woman again? He hadn't felt this at ease with someone in years. He hadn't felt an instant connection like this—a bolt from the blue—in quite some time. He wasn't sure the one before this came close to matching what he already had with Joy. So one woman had hurt him…he had to stop feeling as though he was doomed to relive his own history.

He could smell Joy's scone experiment from the staircase, although he wasn't sure what it was exactly. He only knew that whatever it was, it would be good, he'd eat too many, and with snow no longer an excuse, he'd need to drag his ass to the gym today.

"Smell good?" Joy poured him a cup of coffee and handed it to him.

"Amazing. But I can't figure out what it is. Cinnamon?"

She planted a hand on her hip. "Cinnamon. You honestly think cinnamon was my experiment? Give me a little more credit than that."

"It's my inferior olfactory skills, obviously. I'm so sorry." He bounced his eyebrows and took a sip of coffee.

"You can make up for it by raving about the finished product. I think it's going to be pretty damn good." The timer rang and her eyes went wide. "We're about to find out." There was so much pure excitement in her voice, it was contagious. It was impossible to be unhappy around her. She pulled the sheet pan from the oven and plated the scones. She settled into the seat next to him at the kitchen island. "Well? Go for it."

"Aren't you going to have one?"

"I am. I just want to see the look on your face. It's the best part."

A very naughty remembrance crossed Alex's mind. "Just like the hot tub last night."

"If my scones are as good as that, you can just declare me better than Julia Child and we'll call it a day."

"I didn't think it was possible to look forward to baked goods this much." He picked up a scone and took a bite. The texture was just as perfect as the day before, but the flavor was out of this world, and honestly, quite unusual. It was warm and sweet, with a spicy edge. "Ginger?"

"Ginger and…?"

He took another bite, savoring her wizardry with butter and flour, cream and sugar. "Ginger and delicious? I have no clue."

She elbowed him in the ribs. "It's okay. I was trying to stump you. Yes, crystallized ginger, cardamom, and the secret ingredient is a tiny bit of black pepper. Gives it a little zing."

"I love it. It's absolutely brilliant. You should definitely put this in the cookbook."

She tapped her fingers on the counter and stared down at her plate. "Yeah. It's not ready for a cookbook. I need to try it out down at the bakery and see how it goes over."

"You don't trust my taste buds?"

"Oh, I do. I just think there's a chance you might be biased. I haven't slept with any of the bakery's customers."

"I would never let sex get in the way of honesty." Alex was struck by a strong and undeniable realization—he loved the effortless back-and-forth with Joy. He could get used to this.

She got up from her seat and poured herself another cup of coffee. "Do you think you could give me a ride down to the bakery? I can get a ride home from my co-worker, Natalie."

"Of course. But don't you have a car?"

She started cleaning up the kitchen. "Not right now. I've taken a cab a few times, or bummed a ride. I'm afraid to drive one of the family's cars. I'd rather drive something with a little less oomph. I'm kind of an old lady when it comes to driving."

"Yeah, I noticed there's some real firepower in the garage when I put my car in there the other night."

"Too much firepower makes me nervous."

"No worries. I'm happy to drive you into town. But first, another scone."

After breakfast, Alex collected his things, not knowing if he'd be returning to this house. Joy had said not to worry about the sheets on the bed or the towels in the bathroom. She'd take care of it, which he assumed meant the housekeeper would deal with it when she came in to clean. Joy was focused on getting down to the bakery as soon as possible. She seemed almost anxious about it, but Alex understood. He had those days at work, too. Surely, something like a cookbook had to be a daunting task. As far as he knew, she hadn't even found a publisher for it, nor did she have a literary agent. She was thinking about doing it all on her own, which he found amazing.

He and Joy went out through the garage. On the far end, in a bay with two motorcycles, sat a car-sized lump under a tarp. "This family is even more obsessed with cars than mine. Is there another one over there?" Alex pointed in that general direction.

"Just a pile of junk." Joy opened his passenger-side door and climbed in.

Alex joined her. "Why would they have junk in their garage? They should have it hauled away."

"I'll be sure to suggest that."

Alex's phone chimed with a text. "One second. I should check this." It was from his brother Jonathan, a photo of him on the beach in St. Barts with a very young-looking, buxom woman. Wish you were here. Alex shook his head.

"Everything okay?" Joy asked.

"Yeah. Fine. Just my brother's misbehaving in St. Barts. This time of year is big for picking up women, but it's not my scene."

"Not your scene now? Or never your scene?"

Alex wasn't quite sure how to answer this. "I've gone down there with them before, yes. And I did meet a lot of women. But, you know, it just isn't smart. You never know who's going to glom onto you when you have money. And people take pictures with camera phones. Just too much potential for messy situations."

Joy nodded, but her lips were pressed together in a thin line. "I see." She started to rummage in her purse.

Alex set his hand on her arm. "Really. That's not me anymore. That was a long time ago. And surely you understand the need to protect yourself when you have money."

"Of course. Makes perfect sense." She pulled back the cuff of her coat sleeve and looked at her watch. "We should get going. They really need me today."

The drive into town was a relatively quick one, although entirely too quiet for his liking. He should've thought twice before making comments about picking up women in the Caribbean. He pulled over at the far end of Vail Village, one of two main business districts. It was like a charming European village, with cobblestone walkways and quaint shops. Also, no cars, which meant he had to drop Joy off here.

"How far is the bakery?"

"About halfway down. On the left. Have you really not seen it?"

He shrugged. "I probably have and just didn't go in. But now that I know I can get the best scones in town, I'll make a habit of stopping by."

"Thanks so much for the ride and everything. It was fun," Joy said.

Alex put the car into Park. "It was more than fun for me." He turned to face her, but Joy was looking out the window.

"You're right. It was more than fun. It was great. I'll always remember it." Still, she wouldn't make eye contact, and that really amped up Alex's nervousness. How would she react to what he was about to say?

"I'd like to see you again, Joy. Take you out for a real date. Spend some more time together. I don't go back to Chicago until the 26th."

"When Christmas is said and done with your family?" She glanced at him, but only for a second.

"To put it bluntly, yes."

"I'm sorry. I didn't mean it like that."

He shook his head and finally, out of frustration, reached for her jaw and urged her to look at him. Their gazes did more than connect—they locked. This was yet another version of Joy, one he hadn't seen before. She seemed sad. "Would it be okay if I called you?"

She sighed, then nodded. It was like she was resigning herself to something. Alex didn't want her to feel obligated to see him. "Of course it would be okay. I would love it. But I also don't want you to feel like you owe me that, or like you have to say it just because we slept together. It's okay if this is goodbye. I've said it many times. It's a lot better if a guy is just up front about it."

His heart was about to beat out of his chest while he took in her words. So that's what this was. She thought he was one of those guys, the ones who say they'll call, but don't. "I'm not just saying this. I want to see you again and I'd like to call you. I don't want this to be goodbye."

He leaned in and kissed her deeply on the lips. That moment when he felt her resistance melt away was sheer heaven. He couldn't miss out on that again.

She rested her forehead against his, their noses touching. "I don't want it to be goodbye, either." She reached for the car handle. "I guess I'll just say see you later."

He grinned like a damn fool. "Yes. I'll see you later."

She closed her door and he took the chance to watch her walk away, study the particular sway that came with her determined stride. Their kiss was still on his lips, the effect of it still making waves in his body.

Even if it only happened one more time, it would be worth it.

"So? Who's the guy with the fancy car?" Natalie asked the instant Joy came through the door at the bakery.

"You saw that?" Joy had been worried about that, but she'd figured she'd be okay since Alex had to drop her off blocks away.

"I just got in a minute ago. I walked right past his car. I would've waited, but it looked like you guys were talking about something intense."

Joy didn't like calling attention to herself, nor did she like it when someone took notice. Her whole future rested on flying under the radar, earning the money she needed to earn, and getting out of the Marshalls' house. "He's just a friend. You know my car still won't start." It was her car that was the pile of junk under the tarp in the Marshalls' garage. Joy had held her breath when Alex mentioned it. If he'd decided to go look? One glance in the glove box and he would know that it was hers. Or more specifically, Joy McKinley's.

What had she gotten herself into? The whole thing had spiraled completely out of control, and she didn't know what to do about it now. Alex wanted to see her again, and she wanted to see him, too. Badly. It made her stomach wobble just to think about his touch, his proclivity for fun. The kiss in the car had practically seared itself into her memory. But he deserved better. He deserved the truth. He needed to know that the cookbook was a pipe dream, that she was working at the bakery for an actual paycheck, that she was *not* Joy Baker, the baker.

Or maybe it didn't really matter. He was leaving in less than a week and she'd never see him again after that. She hated lying, but sometimes you had to do things to survive. She only had a few more weeks in the Marshalls' house and she didn't have the money for a security deposit on an apartment. She might have to ask for an advance from the bakery or maybe ask to crash on Natalie's couch. Either way, she would keep working to turn things around so she could return to her life as Joy McKinley, distancing herself from her unfortunate history with the Marshall family and putting her career back on track.

"You know…" Natalie looped an apron over her head and gathered the ties behind her back. "My brother is a mechanic. He sometimes fixes cars on the weekend. I could send him over to your place and he could take a look at it. As long as it isn't anything major, he wouldn't charge you much money to get it running again."

That was the exact can of worms she'd been trying so hard to keep sealed tight. She couldn't go around inviting other people over to the Marshalls' house, especially not in this town where everyone knew them. "That would be amazing. Let me see if I can get it to start tonight and I'll let you know. Sometimes it's just being temperamental." Maybe she could look up some possible fixes on the internet. She'd repaired all sorts of things over the years of owning that disastrous car. And if not, she'd figure out something else. She always did. She'd push it back down the mountain if she had to.

Joy and Natalie went to work, cranking out a limited version of the daily menu since the bakery had opened late. They were in charge of pastries and cookies. A whole team of other bakers was in charge of bread, which was a separate undertaking and required getting into the bakery in the wee hours of the morning. They worked out of the larger kitchen in the back.

Joy and Natalie, with some help from Bonnie, their boss, had the smaller front kitchen as their domain. Joy loved it because they could see the customers through a glass window. Customers could also see them, and there was a narrow platform for kids to stand on, so that was part of the fun as well. They would stand with hands and faces pressed to the glass, watching in awe as Joy and Natalie did their magic. Even better was the pure satisfaction Joy got when she saw a customer bite into a cookie or Danish and roll their eyes in ecstasy or smile. Making people happy was the number one reason Joy would never find herself doing anything else.

The shorter workday whizzed by. Natalie gave Joy a ride at three, only this time, the drop-off at the house that wasn't hers was a much quicker affair since Natalie had errands to run. With no snow falling and slightly warmer temperatures, the walk up the hill wasn't quite as difficult, but in an odd way, she missed the fact that Alex wouldn't be speeding down the road, about to slide right into her. It had been the start of something special. Something short, but sweet.

As she walked the final stretch up to the Marshalls' house, she saw it differently. No, it wasn't hers and it never would be. But something good had happened there, and in a world where there just wasn't enough good, she could hold on to that. She had memories to live off of, especially if and when things got tough again.

After her usual long shower, she didn't have the energy to make a real dinner, so she had a peanut butter sandwich and headed up to bed. Alex and work had worn her out. She needed sleep. So badly that she almost didn't answer her cell phone when it rang. But what if it was Bonnie? Or Natalie? A big part of her hoped it would be Alex.

The smile on her face when she saw his name on the caller ID had to have been ridiculous—her cheeks hurt from two seconds of it. "Hello there," she answered, cozying up under the covers.

"You have no idea how nice it is to hear your voice." This was a different version of Alex. Stressed. Not playful and fun. "Seriously. I've been looking forward to this all day."

"Oh, no. Rough reentry after our snow days?"

"Yes. Work sucks, in case you're wondering. My father is impossible. My brothers are goofing off and I'm stuck picking up their slack. I don't even understand why I do it. I could walk away and I'd still be okay for money."

Joy couldn't fathom what that must be like. She'd probably still be working when she was seventy, just like her grandmother had. Still, she knew that Alex worked very hard. Every business article she'd perused had said he was known for his relentless work ethic. "I don't know. I bet you'd miss being busy."

"I'd rather be busy doing anything else. Move to Mexico and run a bait shop."

"Don't drink the water. You'll regret it." She was prepared to say anything to improve his mood. She hated hearing him like this. This was not the guy who'd suggested they go run around in the snow in their bathing suits.

He laughed quietly. "I'd probably smell like fish all the time. Not super sexy."

"I'm sure you'd find a way to pull it off."

"Maybe a surf shop would be better. In Hawaii."

"Sounds nice. Maybe I'll come visit." What a lovely thought...palm trees, blue skies, ocean breezes and Alex. He'd probably walk around barefoot in board shorts all day, ridiculously tan and even more stunning. Now that would be a life. She didn't need some big fancy house, but a dream locale would be awfully nice.

A heavy sigh came from his end of the line. "Is it weird if I say that I miss you? I know we haven't known each other for that long, but I feel like I get you. I had a hundred things I wanted to say to you today."

"You can always text me if you really have something you're dying to say." Joy was sure her smile was about seven miles wide. It surely put the one from the beginning of their conversation to shame. "But no, it's not weird. I miss you, too."

"Tell me what you miss." His rich voice and suggestive inflection was about to lead her off on an entirely different fantasy than the life in Hawaii. Or maybe she should just combine the two.

"What do you want me to say?"

"I mean exactly what I said. I'm a man. I have a horribly fragile ego. We all do. Tell me what you miss."

She had to roll her eyes at that one. Did some men need ego stroking? Absolutely. She didn't believe it about Alex for a second. He was one of the most self-assured men she'd ever met. He walked around as though he had the world at his feet, and by most measures, he did. But telling him that wasn't going to improve his day, and she had a strong suspicion that was what he needed more than anything right now.

"I miss your eyes. They're amazing." *I'd look at them forever if they didn't make me feel so exposed.*

"Okay. I like it. Go on."

She giggled, smiled, and rolled onto her side. "I miss your laugh. I miss the way that it's easy to be around you. I don't feel like I have to try very hard. It's nice."

"I don't want you to try at all. I want you to be you, having fun, cooking up a storm. I don't think you realize how cool it is to see."

Goose bumps crept over her skin. "I think eating is a lot more fun than you realized."

"True. That would be the one downside of being around someone who is a genius in the kitchen. But seriously, it's fun to be around someone who genuinely loves what they do. And you create things. You make people happy. You made me happy and I don't think I realized how unhappy I was until I met you."

"The night you nearly killed me with your car?"

He laughed heartily. "I'm never going to live that one down, am I?"

"Probably not. Sorry." In her fantasy world, the one where she lived in Hawaii with Alex, the surf shop owner, she and Alex would tell their kids that story. They would giggle and think it was so crazy, that Mommy and Daddy must be making it up. And they'd tell them again that it was true.

"But seriously, I was so focused on work that I didn't stop to appreciate much of anything."

"But you're good at what you do, and you care about it. I don't think your father's attitude would bother you if you didn't care so much. You've obviously been super successful, and that doesn't happen by accident. Maybe you just needed a break."

"A fresh perspective. You gave me that."

He was acting as though she'd given him so much, but the truth was that he'd done the same. Possibly more. "You're sweet, but you know, you did the same thing for me. We had fun together. Do you have any idea how long it's been since I've had fun, aside from at work? It's been eons."

"Then let's go have more fun. The tree lighting ceremony is going on down in town on Saturday. We can do some shopping and I'll take you to the Four Seasons.

They have the most incredible hot chocolate. Even I've been known to indulge in it."

"Decadent hot chocolate? But isn't that full of sugar and cream?"

"Precisely why it made me think of you."

It sounded so wonderful, but she needed to work at the bakery that day. "What time would we go? I should be at the bakery until three. I might be able to skip out early."

"I could pick you up straight from there. I could even drop you off in the morning if I come over tomorrow night. But I don't want to invite myself or assume."

"Assume what? That I'll go to bed with you?"

"You are really good at asking the hard questions."

She laughed under her breath. She got that from her dad. He was as hard-nosed as anyone she knew. "Well, was I wrong?"

"No. You were not wrong. I just want you to know that all that stuff about being a gentleman wasn't a line. I'm serious about it. A gentleman does not assume."

She more than adored this aspect of his personality, she needed it. She needed to be asked, she needed to feel appreciated and valued. She hadn't had that from any man she'd dated. Her ex had made her so unsure of herself that she usually didn't last more than a few dates with a guy. The minute he started to assume that he could have her anytime, the instant he showed a blip of possessiveness, she went running. Alex was giving her the space she so desperately needed, and he likely had no idea what a gift it was. It was just Alex being Alex. Who knew she'd ever feel grateful that a man had nearly run into her with his car?

"Alex, I would love to go to the tree lighting. I'd love

to have you stay over tomorrow night. I'll cook for you and everything."

"That sounds amazing. I'm really looking forward to it. Can I pick you up at the bakery tomorrow afternoon?"

"You can just wait for me where you dropped me off today." She didn't want to put him off, not when he was being so romantic, but she still had to keep her secrets safe. "We can shop for dinner then. You'll have to tell me what you like."

"You already know what I like. I like you."

Eight

The bakery was adorable. With a high-pitched roof lined with Christmas lights and inside a row of bright red bistro tables and chairs along the front window, it was welcoming and cheery. No wonder Joy liked coming here so much. Alex wasn't sure how he'd missed it the dozens of times he'd walked through quaint Vail Village, but perhaps it was that he'd been too busy trudging through life to notice. Better late than never.

He pulled the door open and nearly ran right into Joy.

"Oh. Hi." She seemed flustered, hitching her bag over her shoulder and nearly pushing him back out onto the sidewalk. She had to have had a long day.

"We have to stop running into each other like this." His joke didn't seem to make much of an impression—Joy nearly bugged her eyes at him.

"Ready? Let's go."

Alex was looking past her. A young woman was busy behind the counter. The bakery case looked nearly depleted. "Busy scone day?"

She nodded. "Yes. And I need some fresh air."

"Okay. Sure." He took her hand and they stepped outside, where there were hundreds of people milling along the wide cobblestone pedestrian shopping area. The sun was just starting to set, and although the air was cool and crisp, it was pleasant. "Beautiful night."

"It is. Sorry if I seemed out of sorts back there. I just wasn't expecting you. I thought you were going to pick me up where you dropped me off."

"That made sense yesterday, but seeing as we're going to the tree lighting, I thought I should just park and find you." Funny how he and Joy had already adopted the sort of routines couples fall into. He'd picked her up after work yesterday and they'd gone shopping for dinner, then back to her place for an unbelievable meal and an even more out-of-this-world evening in bed. He'd dropped her off this morning, but that hadn't seemed right for tonight. "Plus, this is our first real date. I wasn't going to hang out by the curb in my car. A gentleman comes to the door."

"Or the bakery, as the case may be."

"Precisely."

"Well, thank you. I appreciate that." She stopped and kissed him. "I'm sorry if I'm a little tense. This is really nice."

He smiled. It *was* really nice. Christmas was looking up. Or at least the Christmas season. Alex could feel it in his bones.

"I promise that hot chocolate is the cure for all that ails you." Their first stop was the Four Seasons, where

Alex had reserved a small table in the corner of the bar. It was warm and cozy inside, just as elegant as Alex remembered. He wanted Joy to have every fine thing she was accustomed to.

"This place is gorgeous," she said, just as the waiter brought their order. It arrived in clear glass mugs. "Is that a chocolate orb in there?"

"It is, ma'am," the waiter answered. "I pour the hot chocolate over the top and give it a gentle stir. It's quite sublime."

The look on Joy's face when she took a sip was priceless. She held her fingers to her lips; her eyes were like platters. "That is crazy good."

Alex took his own sip, which he did enjoy, although it was far richer and sweeter than anything he would normally drink. This was all about Joy. Watching her sit back in her chair, her day melting away, he knew he'd done his job and he was nothing but happy for it.

"So, I was thinking," she said, licking her spoon and making him wish they were going home soon. "You aren't leaving until the day after Christmas, right? And we've been spending so much time together. It just seems like we should spend Christmas Eve together. You can stay over and we'll make dinner. I'll even make breakfast the next morning. It'll be a nice way to say goodbye."

Goodbye. That was a word Alex was coming to hate, although he wasn't sure what to do about it. He did need to be back in Chicago for an important meeting on December 27. Circumstances were standing in their way. Plus, his time with Joy wasn't supposed to last long. It was supposed to be a way for him to test the waters. Nothing else. "That sounds really great. I would love that."

"I have a dress I think you might like, if you want to dress up."

"You want me to wear a dress?"

She laughed and swatted his arm. "No, silly. I'll wear the dress. You wear a suit."

"And how long do I have to wear it?"

"Not too long. I won't torture you." She licked her lower lip, which was like completing a circuit in Alex's body. Everything was bright and alive. "No presents, though. That's my only condition."

"What? I'm not going to spend Christmas morning with you and not buy you a gift." An idea sprang to life… maybe there was a way to extend his time with Joy at least a little bit.

"Nothing big, then. Promise?"

"Nothing too big." Alex consulted his watch. "We'd better hurry down to the tree lighting or we won't be able to see anything."

"We'll be fine. That tree is really, really tall."

Out they went, tracking back past the bakery and on to the square where the tree stood. The crowd was easily in the thousands, but the space was open enough that people weren't too horribly crammed together. Alex found them a semiquiet spot off to the side. All around them was the steady hum of people talking while holiday music played in the background. Alex stood behind Joy and wrapped his arms around her. He breathed in her hair. He kissed the top of her head.

Joy gasped and pointed skyward. "It's starting to snow."

Alex looked up. "It is. It's so pretty."

It's so perfect.

It was so perfect he'd better not get used to it. Just

then, the music ended and an emcee stepped up on a small platform. She welcomed everyone and began the countdown. The entire crowd joined in, kids and parents, couples, and groups of friends, just like it was New Year's Eve. *Five...four...three...two...one.*

The lights came on in a flash and the crowd cheered. The music started up again.

"Hey. They're playing my song."

Alex laughed. "'Joy to the World.'"

She turned in his arms, looking up at him. Her cheeks were bright pink from the cold, her eyes happy. "It's not really my song. I just made that up."

"You know what? As far as I'm concerned, I think we tell everyone it *is* your song. Nobody can possibly prove us wrong."

"I like it when you're goofy."

Alex had been called many things in life, but never that. Being with her was like seeing a side of himself he'd never even known was there. "Good. Now let's get out of here."

Alex and Joy strolled back to his car, hand in hand. He couldn't ignore the way it felt as though his feet were hardly touching the ground as they walked. Joy was amazing. Spending time with her was so enjoyable, it made everything bad seem as though it didn't matter. Sure, he'd told himself he would never fall in love again, or at least not as hard as he had in the past, but he already knew he was too far gone.

He'd never expected he would feel this way again. In fact, he'd done everything he could to prevent this from happening, but then he hit a patch of ice on a snowy road, a beautiful woman ended up in a snowbank, and the rest, as they say, was history.

They approached the parking garage valet stand and Alex handed over his claim check.

"I'll have your car for you in a just a few moments, Mr. Townsend."

Alex's arm was already wrapped around Joy's waist. He pulled her closer when the valet ran off to get the car. "Is it too much if I ask to stay over again tonight?" He kissed her cheek, then trailed his lips to her jaw. Her sweet smell and soft skin were enough to drive him crazy, but the way she bowed into him when they were close was enough to send him rocketing off into space.

"Or maybe we could go to your place? I haven't seen it yet."

As head over heels as he was, there was still this voice in the back of his head that was reluctant to truly let someone in. The last time Alex had let his heart lead the way, rather than his brain, he'd nearly ruined his entire life. But he had to get past that.

Soon.

"Tell you what? Maybe we'll spend Christmas night at my house. Is that okay? It's a longer drive to my place and your things are all at your house." All a long string of excuses. He knew that.

"Okay. Sure." Joy gave him a reassuring smile, but he could tell she wasn't entirely happy about the answer.

Just then, Alex's phone rang. The caller ID said it was his father, a call he didn't want to take, but Alex had been putting him off all day and the man was persistent. He'd just keep calling. "I'm so sorry. I should really take this. The valet will be back in a second." Alex plugged his finger into his ear and stepped away. "Dad. Hi. What's up?"

"Alex, I'm not happy."

Surprise. Surprise. Thank you for ruining my evening with the world's worst timing.

"Okay. Why don't you tell me what's going on?"

His dad launched into a diatribe about one of the Townsend mutual funds, which was currently under-performing. Alex listened but didn't say a thing. His dad always had to just get it out. Then they could really talk. Alex turned to see a man enter the parking garage. He stumbled up to the valet stand, listing to the side, unable to walk in a straight line. He was nicely dressed, in a wool coat and nice shoes, but Alex knew from experience that a good wardrobe did not make a good guy, and he was standing entirely too close to Joy now.

"Dad. I know we need to talk about this, but I'm in the middle of something important. Can I call you later? Or can we just talk about it on the 27th? It's not that far away."

"Absolutely not. You're trying to shut me out of our business, Alexander, our family business, and I won't stand for it."

Alex couldn't take his eyes off the scene unfolding at the valet stand. Where was the damn attendant? The man's lips were moving. He was looking at Joy, his eyes half-open. He said something to her. She turned away from him, then took several side steps, deliberately distancing herself. Whatever he'd said was not good. Alex's breaths became heavy. He wasn't even listening to his dad anymore. The man turned back in Alex's direction for an instant, then returned his sights to Joy, advancing on her. The hair on the back of Alex's neck stood up. *Oh, no.* Whatever came next, it was not going to happen on his watch. "Dad. I have to go."

He hung up just in time to see the man grab Joy's shoulder. Alex did the only thing he could. He sprang into action.

One minute, Joy had been having a Christmas dream date, and now this—a drunk making a pass. He'd even swiped at her shoulder. Her mind shifted into defense mode. Her body responded. She jerked away. "Don't touch me. Get your hands off me."

"Stop being such a bitch," the man slurred. "I was just trying to…"

The next thing Joy knew, Alex had the guy in a head-lock.

"Alex! Don't!" Joy jumped back.

The man struggled, but he was no match for Alex. Joy's hand clamped over her mouth, not knowing what to do. It was all happening so fast.

"Let me go!" the man shouted.

Alex must've had some sort of martial arts training, because he seamlessly released his hold and grabbed the man's upper arms. He walked him backward to the cinderblock wall of the parking garage. "You got a problem I need to know about?" Alex's voice was a growl. He'd come a little unhinged. Alex pinned the man against the wall by his shoulders, which only made Joy's stomach sink.

"Get your hands off me. I was just trying to talk to her."

Joy's pulse raced, her chest heaved. Alex had saved her. That was what good guys did. But she also knew that good guys could turn to bad guys. Like her ex. "Alex, it's okay. I'm fine. He didn't hurt me." She stepped closer.

The valet brought the car around. She heard the car door open.

"It's not okay, Joy," Alex replied, not taking his eyes off the man. "He grabbed you. I saw it with my own two eyes."

The man's head was bobbing. He'd obviously had too much to drink.

"Yeah, and he's so drunk I could probably knock him over by myself. I'm fine. Just let him go."

Alex tightened his grip on the man, his knuckles bulging. "Don't go around grabbing women. Ever, okay? I don't care how drunk you are. There's no excuse. You're lucky I didn't take you out." He finally let go, but not without an unsubtle shove.

The valet attendant approached. "Sir, is there a problem?"

"This guy has had way too much to drink. Don't give him his car. You're going to need to call him a cab." Alex pulled a bill from his wallet and handed it to the valet.

"Yes, sir. I'll take care of it." The attendant took the money, seeming confused, and opened the passenger-side door for Joy.

Joy couldn't handle any more of this scene. She was too rattled. She climbed into the car and put on her seat belt, trying to ignore the memories that kept creeping into her head. Ben had done this sort of thing many times. All another guy had to do was look at her the wrong way and Ben was in his face. If there was alcohol involved, it was always worse. At first, Joy had thought it was just protectiveness, but after a while, it became possessiveness, and if Joy wanted anything these days, it was her freedom and independence.

They drove for several minutes in near silence, winding through the mountain roads, the sky pitch-black now. Alex's grip on the steering wheel hadn't loosened at all.

His knuckles were a hard line of ripples across the tops of his hands. She glanced over and could see the fierce tension in his face, the way his jaw was tight and his brow furrowed.

"I'm sorry about that back there," she said. "You really didn't need to say anything. I would've been fine."

"Don't you dare apologize, Joy. He could've hurt you. No man should ever, ever touch a woman like that."

The tone of his voice cut right through her. Tears welled in her eyes. He was absolutely right, but she hated feeling like this. She wasn't weak. She wasn't defenseless. Her mind struggled to find the right words, coming up with nothing. All she wanted to do was apologize again, make it go away, but she had nothing to be sorry for. She only wished that man hadn't made his stupid pass, hadn't had too much to drink.

"You're right. No woman should ever have to be in that position, but that still doesn't mean I can't take care of myself."

"Would it have been better if I'd done nothing? What kind of man would I be if I sat back and watched a stranger touch a woman I care about deeply? I can't even fathom being that person. If that's what you want in a guy, then maybe I'm not the right one. Because all I know is, the instant I saw him touch you, my blood boiled over and I had to make it stop."

Joy felt like her breath couldn't find its way out of her chest. "Do you really mean that? That you care about me?"

A breathy laugh left his lips. "Yes, I care about you. What do you think today was? I want to spend time with you. You're a breath of fresh air to me. You make me laugh. You have insightful things to say. You're sweet.

And you're so damn sexy. I'd have to be a complete idiot to not care about you." He reached over and placed his hand on hers. "I'm sorry if my temper got a little out of control, but this is my weak spot, and it's a big one. I can control it most of the time, but if I'm pushed, all bets are off."

What did he mean by that? Was he saying he had a problem? Because, if he did that was a nonstarter for her. "Weak spot?"

"It's because of my mom." He ran his hand through his hair, staring intently at the road ahead. The pain on his face was evident. More tension. More angst. "Or more specifically, it's because of the way my dad treated my mom."

The air in the car began to change. Alex's anger was something quite different from what she had worried about. "Do you want to tell me about it? You don't have to if you don't want to. I mean, I understand if we haven't known each other long enough for you to tell me."

Another frustrated laugh left his lips. "Does time really matter? Does it really matter that we've only known each other for a few days?" He looked right at her, his icy blue eyes penetrating her soul with so little effort. "You and I have talked about more in the last few days than I have ever talked about with another woman."

A smile played at the corners of her lips. They had shared a lot. Or at least as much as she'd been able to divulge. "You're right. You still don't need to talk about it if you don't want to."

"But that's the thing. I want to tell you. I want to tell you everything." He pulled up to the gate, rolled down his window and entered the code. The car zipped down the driveway and up to the garage. Alex put it in Park and turned to Joy. "I'm not going to sugarcoat it. My family was totally dysfunctional when I was a kid. My dad couldn't keep it in his pants. He ignored my mom except when he needed a beautiful woman to parade around at a business dinner. When he did pay attention to her, he was verbally abusive. So she drank. To numb the pain, I guess. And as the oldest son, I tried to protect her. I wanted to. But I failed. I couldn't get either of them to stop, and eventually she paid with her life." His voice wobbled at the end, his anguish bubbling to the surface.

"I'm so sorry, Alex. You told me a little about this, but I had no idea it ended so tragically."

Alex reached out and stroked her hair. "I don't want you to feel sorry for me. Plenty of people have much sadder stories. The point of me telling you this is that I don't want you to think badly of me because I flew off the handle at the parking garage. I think you know that I'm not always like that."

"I do know that. And maybe that's why it was upsetting. Just to see you be someone I didn't think you were capable of being."

He nodded slowly, taking it all in. "I can totally understand that. And I'm sorry for that part. You know, usually I just hide the ugly stuff in my past. Ignore it. Pretend like it's not there. I've gotten pretty good at it."

How could Joy's heart feel simultaneously so heavy and yet so fundamentally happy? Alex was baring his soul to her in a way few people ever had. He cared. And she sure as hell cared right back. But there was still a barrier between them—she'd put it there and it was hers to take away.

But if she did knock down that wall, it would destroy every beautiful thing that was already between them.

And since there was an end to their romance bearing down on them, she couldn't stand the thought of sabotaging the rest of their time together. They had both needed this holiday affair. They had both needed each other, to heal, to see light. That didn't happen nearly enough in life and she wasn't about to throw that away.

She pulled Alex into a hug. "Come here." She settled her head on his shoulder and ran her hand back and forth across his back, soaking up his warmth, never wanting this to end. "You can always tell me the ugly stuff. Always. Honestly, you can't scare me. Just tell me the worst. I promise I won't run away."

Alex laughed and reared his head back. "Thank you for that. It means a lot. Truly."

She smiled, feeling so much better. They'd had such an amazing day. "Ready to go inside?"

He nodded. "With you? Always."

Nine

Joy watched Alex put on his clothes. He was half-asleep, fumbling a bit, which made him exceptionally adorable. Most of the time he was perfect while making zero effort. She loved his human moments.

"You okay? You're staring," he said, standing up from the spot where he'd been sitting on the edge of the bed.

Of course I'm staring. You're astounding.

"I'm good. Just not totally awake. Last night wore me out."

"That was a pretty rigorous tree lighting." He snickered to himself.

"Not what I meant, Mr. One More Time. Your stamina is exhausting."

He stepped closer and kissed her on the corner of her mouth. "That's not what you said last night."

"True. I guess I just have to accept that I'm going to be a step slow today."

Except there was no room in Joy's day for being a step slow. If she and Alex were going to spend Christmas together, she would need to buy him a gift. She'd thought about doing something homemade, making him a basket of his favorite pastries and maybe a jar of jam, and although it was somewhat romantic, it wouldn't last. Plus, Alex was a guy accustomed to the best of everything, and although he was sweet and she doubted he would ever, ever be unhappy about receiving some of her scones or muffins, she wanted to give him something of permanence. She would feel better about parting from him if she knew he might be walking around with something she'd given him. He could have a reminder of her, of everything they had shared—the passion, the good times, the laughter.

The only hitch was the most perpetual and pervasive problem in her life—money. She wouldn't get paid by the bakery until the end of the week, and even then, it wouldn't be enough to buy him something truly spectacular, something worth holding on to. She needed a chunk of money, real cash.

"Just about ready to go?" he asked.

"I am. I just need to get a few things. You should run downstairs and grab a cup of coffee. I just made it."

He smiled and grasped her elbow. "You're a savior." He pecked her on the nose.

As soon as he was out of sight, Joy went to the closet and grabbed a box from the top shelf, which was hidden under a pile of sweaters. This cardboard box, soft and smashed in at the corners, was filled with the most important things Joy owned. It had her grandmother's recipe cards, faded shades of pink, mint green and canary yellow, a precious bundle wrapped up in a rubber band. It also contained pictures of her family, some of which were in small frames.

She'd gotten so settled in Santa Barbara at the Marshall estate that she'd actually put the photos on the dresser in her room in the staff quarters. That was a leap she didn't make often. Once she was out of culinary school, she never stayed in one place for very long, moving from cooking job to cooking job, city to city. That was when she was on a roll, climbing the ladder of success and actually making leaps. It was a magical time that would hopefully resume at some point.

In one corner of the cardboard carton sat a small jewelry box. Not the clamshell kind from a fine jeweler, but rather the paper kind for earrings from a gift shop. Inside that was a burgundy felt pouch with her grandmother's most prized possession: a gold locket on a slender chain, a gift from the family her grandmother had spent most of her adult life cooking for.

Her grandmother had loved the family and they loved her right back. Joy's grandfather had died when Joy was just a little girl and her grandmother had taken the job, moving in with the family, as her only means of survival. Joy was the only grandchild, her mom the only child. Her grandmother's world might have been modest, but she'd filled it with love and incredible food for everyone who had been lucky enough to have been a part of it.

Joy was not about to let this necklace go forever. No way. But she had pawned it once before, to buy a ridiculously expensive textbook for culinary school, and she'd worked doubly hard to make the money to buy it back. She would do that again—she planned to ask Bonnie for extra hours at the bakery. Surely no one in a town like Vail would give one hoot about her grandmother's necklace. It was too old-fashioned, too sentimental. It wasn't flashy or showy. It was simple and unassuming, and Joy hoped that meant it could sit in the case in the pawn shop for just long enough for her to get paid and buy it back.

"Thank you for taking me to work. I realize it's not fun to get up at 6:00 a.m."

"I admire your dedication. Most people who are using a space to research a book would just show up when they feel like it."

She shrugged it off playfully, feeling nothing close to lighthearted. "I don't just talk the talk. I like to walk the walk, too."

The new day was just dawning when Alex drove her into town. Joy tried not to focus too much on the uneasy feeling in her stomach when she thought about pawning her grandmother's necklace. She tried to focus on her true goal—Alex meant something to her and she wanted him to remember her. Somewhere in the world, she wanted someone special to think of her from time to time, and maybe, for an instant, think that Joy had made their world a better place. It was the sort of thing her grandmother had done in her life, and Joy wanted the satisfaction of having accomplished at least a fraction of that.

"Here we are," Alex said as they pulled up on the side street. "Sure you don't want me to walk you in? I can get a parking spot no problem this early."

"No. It's okay. I know you have things to do."

"I do have things to do. Like going back to bed. Then shopping."

"Nothing too big. We agreed on that."

"Yes, ma'am."

"Thank you for the ride." Her lips were instantly drawn to his for a soft and gentle kiss.

His eyes were half-open when their lips parted, that look that made Joy's stomach do somersaults. Knowing he was still savoring their kiss was a wonderful feeling. "You're more than welcome. And you know, I sort of like getting up this early in the morning. It helps me imagine what it's like to be a farmer."

Joy swatted him on the arm. "Very funny. I'm guessing that nowhere in your family lineage is there a single farmer."

"You would be right about that. I think the Townsends have always been bankers."

Of course they have. "Probably even in prehistoric times when they were trading rocks and shells."

"Probably. I'm guessing your ancestors were baking scones?"

And scraping for every penny. "Not until there was baking soda and butter in the world, but at some point, yes."

Alex feigned a shiver. "I don't even want to think about a world without butter. You would be so unhappy and I don't want that."

"Me neither."

"So, tomorrow? Christmas Eve dinner? Do you need me to pick anything up? Can I do the shopping for you? I know you're busy and my enthusiasm for work is pretty slim."

Joy had forgotten about paying for groceries. Alex had picked up the tab the last time. "Actually? That would be wonderful, if you're okay with that."

"If it means I get to watch you cook, then yes. Absolutely. Text me a list and I'll get everything taken care of."

"You're the best."

"I try."

She gave him a final kiss and ventured into the cold, rushing down the cobblestone walk and ultimately into the warm safety of the bakery. The aromas that hit her nose every time she walked in the door were such a pleasant comfort, although she'd felt that way about every food-related job she'd ever had, even the bad ones. Probably because she associated the scents with her grandmother and the happiest parts of her childhood.

"Morning," Natalie said, coming in right behind Joy. "I see that the guy with the fancy car gave you a ride again. Have a good night?"

Joy looked over in time to catch a wink. Heat and embarrassment crept over her, even when it was a good seventy-five degrees in the bakery. She was past the point of pretending that Alex was just a ride. "Yes. We had a very nice time."

"Are things getting serious?" They walked to the back and put away their coats and bags in the employees' locker room, then stepped out into the hall where the stacks of clean, folded aprons sat.

Joy looped the string over her head and wrapped the tie around her waist, knotting it in the front. It gave her enough time to come up with a good answer.

If things were different between her and Alex, they might actually be getting serious. They felt serious. Whatever it was between them felt very real. But reality was so far removed from those feelings, it was ridiculous. They weren't simply residing in different states, they were on different planets, and it all boiled down to one sad truth: she had lied to him about who and what she was. There would be no coming back from that.

That meant no future for them.

"No, not serious. We're just having fun. He lives in Chicago anyway. He'll be heading home after Christmas."

Natalie drew her hair back into a high ponytail and put on a bandana to keep everything out of the way. "I wouldn't mind having fun with a guy like that. You're a lucky woman."

"I know."

And my luck is just about to run out.

Just then, Bonnie stepped out of her office.

"Hey, Bonnie. Can I talk to you for a minute?" Joy asked.

"Sure. Of course."

"I'll get the scones started," Natalie said.

"I promise I'll only be a minute," Joy countered.

Bonnie nodded in the direction of her office doorway and Joy followed her inside, taking a seat next to her desk.

"What can I do for you?" Bonnie asked, settling into her worn wooden chair.

Joy sat a little straighter. She wanted Bonnie to know how serious she was. "I know I'm new here, but I could really use some more hours, even if it's just for a few weeks."

"Strapped for cash at the holidays?"

"Something like that. I was thinking, the bread team is short one person, right?"

"I need you on pastries. You know that."

Joy nodded. "I do. But what if I started coming in early after Christmas? I could help on bread for four hours, then switch to my regular job."

Bonnie picked up a pen and tapped it on her desk. "We're talking brutal twelve-hour days."

Joy forced a smile. "I know. I figure I can do anything for a few weeks."

"If you're up for it, it's a deal. You'll really be helping me out until I can hire a new person." Bonnie got up from her seat and shook Joy's hand. "You aren't in some sort of trouble, are you?" Bonnie asked, seeming genuinely concerned.

No more than usual. "No. I just need to get some things squared away."

Bonnie sighed. "Okay. Let me know if anything changes."

Joy smiled wide, relief washing over her. "Thank you so much. Really. I appreciate it. I'd better get to work or Natalie will never let me hear the end of it."

Joy flitted into the kitchen, and she and Natalie worked together like a well-oiled machine, knocking out scones, muffins, cookies and Danish like they were nothing. As much as Joy hadn't loved her pastry courses in culinary school, she was starting to suspect her reaction had been more about her professor, who was a real wet fish and not much fun to be around. She actually loved baking. It had all the same pleasures of preparing main dishes. Maybe she really would write a baking cookbook one day. After she had a few new recipes under her belt, of course. Dreams were important, even ones of the pipe variety.

After the morning pastries were all out in the front cases, Joy and Natalie went to work on the rest of the day's tasks—cakes, pies and tarts. They had restaurant orders to fill, as well as a few special requests from customers. It was as busy and frantic a morning as they'd had since she'd started working there. When it came time for lunch, she was exhausted and wanted nothing more than to get off her feet for thirty minutes and have something to eat. But she had that errand to run.

"I need to go take care of something," Joy said, taking off her dirty apron and chucking it in the laundry. "I'll see you after lunch?"

"You need me to come with you?" Natalie asked.

Joy delivered a tentative smile. "No. It's okay. I need to do this on my own. I'll be back in a few." She rushed out of the bakery. It was a good ten-minute walk down a side street to the tiny pawn shop she'd spotted a few weeks ago.

The bell on the door rang when she walked inside. Leave it to this lovely hamlet to have a high-class pawn shop. It might have been called an emporium, but Joy knew exactly what she was dealing with. No regular store had glass cases filled with fine jewelry and musical instruments ringing the room. Joy reasoned that being in a place that wasn't the slightest bit seedy might help her get more money, which was exactly what she wanted.

"Hello, there," the man behind the counter said. He was tall and particularly thin, wearing frameless glasses and a tan pullover sweater. "What can I help you with today?"

"I have a necklace I need to pawn." Joy pulled the small pouch out of her purse, her hand trembling. She tried to focus on positive things to keep her mind off how much this necklace meant to her—she'd made her plan with Bonnie to earn the money quickly to buy it back. In the end, it would all be worth it if she made Alex happy.

He'd changed her entire mindset while she was here. A few weeks ago, she'd been as down as could be. Her Prince Charming, although he wasn't meant to be hers forever, represented a turning point, and for that, he deserved a reward.

The man pulled out a small board covered in black velvet, seeming unfazed by the way she tapped her fingers on the case. He was probably used to customers who were on edge. Joy draped the necklace across the fabric, then busied herself by browsing the other items in the store. The man was remarkably quiet while he examined the piece, leaving Joy to hum what was stuck in her head—the song that had been playing in the bakery when she left.

"I can give you two-fifty," he said, placing the necklace back on the board.

Joy took a second to think it over, but she knew this was a yes-or-no proposition. She didn't want to haggle for more money; it would only mean more to pay back in order to return it to her possession. It was far less than the necklace was worth, but the man had to have some room for profit. "Great. Thank you."

The man pulled out some paperwork, and after procuring some information from her and making a copy of her driver's license, she signed away the necklace. "You have until the 27th to buy it back for three hundred," he said.

"That's it? The last place I pawned it gave me two weeks."

The man grimaced and shook his head. "Sorry. I'm not a bank and we don't get a lot of customers. If you're in a real jam, you can come in that day and pay me ten percent for an extension."

Forget that. Like Joy had extra money to expend. "Are you open for regular hours that day?"

"Every day but Christmas."

This still was making her far too nervous. "You have my cell phone number. Can you call me if you put it out before I get back here? I don't want to take a chance that someone else might buy it."

The man sighed. "I'll make a note of it. No promises, but you seem like a nice person, so I'll do my best."

That made her feel a whole lot better. The man had a kind face. She had to believe in the goodness of strangers. "I'd really appreciate it. I'm definitely going to buy it back."

"Of course you are." His voice had a distinct edge of skepticism.

"I'm sure people say that to you all the time, but in my case, it's true. I have to have this necklace. It means too much for me to ever let it go."

"You must be in a tough spot."

Yep. I'm the queen of the tough spot.

"It's okay. I'll get out of it just fine."

Ten

Alex pulled up to Joy's place and killed the engine. Stealing a second to look in the car's visor mirror, he straightened his tie—the dark blue one. Did he look like he was walking into a business meeting? He didn't want to look like that. Not for Joy. Was his hair okay? He didn't dare mess with it too much without a comb, so he just flattened the spot in the back that never seemed to co-operate. One deep breath and he flipped up the visor. He just wanted tonight to be perfect. That was all.

He grabbed the gifts he'd bought for Joy from the pas-senger seat and scaled the steps to the front door. This would likely be his last time in this house. No matter how she reacted to the most important of the gifts tucked under his arm, tomorrow was Christmas Day and his last full day in Colorado. The meeting with his dad on December 27 could not be rescheduled and he needed

December 26 to get back in the office and prepare. Alex realized that this was a convenient out for him. If the big gift, the important one, fell flat, he could make a graceful exit and kick himself later for thinking that a woman like Joy might want more than a fling.

He rang the doorbell, remembering very well that first night when he'd stood out on this stoop and wondered if he was crazy for returning. Yes, it had been the responsible thing to do, but there had also been a great deal of curiosity woven into his thought process, whether he'd been willing to admit it to himself at the time or not. He'd wanted to know more about the beguiling Joy Baker. How much he had learned since then.

The door latch clicked and his pulse picked up, although he wasn't entirely sure why. It hadn't been that long since he'd seen her. They'd talked on the phone that morning.

The door flew open. "Oh, my God. Dinner is a disaster." Joy smiled thinly, lunged for him, kissed him on the cheek and ran off down the hall into the kitchen. "Just come in. I have no idea when we're eating."

Alex stepped into the foyer and closed the door behind him. What had just happened? He took off his coat, slung it over his arm and strode into the kitchen. Normally, Joy had everything under control. She made Martha Stewart look messy and disorganized. Today, not so much. The kitchen counter looked like a crime scene, bowls everywhere, a significant flour spill, a carton of eggs still sitting out.

"What happened?" He tossed his coat over the back of one of the chairs in the living room and casually slipped his gifts under the tree.

Joy was shaking her head and peeking through the

window in the oven door. She was wearing a long red dress with a decidedly unsexy plain black apron over the top of it. He really wanted to see the rest of the gown though—the back had a deep V, showing off a glorious stretch of her creamy skin. "I wanted to make a cheese soufflé, but I forgot to make the adjustments for the altitude, and it fell on one side. I don't know if it's going to recover. It was so dumb. I do it every day at the bakery. I did it when I baked you all those damn scones, but when it's really important, like our last big dinner together, I blow it." Her voice did something then he'd never heard—it cracked. Right in half. Strong, feisty Joy was losing it.

He approached, careful to be calm, and pulled her into his arms. "Joy, come on. Take a breath. It's going to be fine. I really don't care about dinner. I just want to be here with you."

She sucked in a sharp breath, but the exhale was a shuddering gasp. She was crying. She clung to him so hard, digging her fingers into his back. "I know. But I wanted tonight to be perfect."

He grasped her shoulders, dropping his chin and forcing her to look at him. "Tonight is perfect because you're here. I'm here. We're together. That is all that matters."

She just looked at him as a tiny tear rolled down her cheek. She was absolutely gorgeous, even with misty eyes, but it broke his heart to see her like this. She chewed on her lower lip, her head bobbing. "You're so sweet. It almost makes it worse."

He laughed and shook his head. "Worse? How could I possibly make it worse by being understanding?"

"I don't know, Alex. Maybe because I'm waiting for you to commiserate with me."

"Well, sorry. As much as I love your cooking, I really don't care that much about dinner. I care way more about everything else."

The timer buzzed and Joy snatched a pair of hot pads from the counter. She pulled the soufflé from the oven and set it down next to two plates, which already had side salads waiting on them. "If this was culinary school, I would be getting chewed out right now, big time."

"Luckily, it's not." He grabbed a piece of lettuce from the plate closest to him and popped it into his mouth. "Mmm. Good vinaigrette."

"Thank you. Hopefully the salad makes up for everything else." With a large spoon, she scooped a portion of the soufflé onto each plate. She then reached behind her and untied the apron, lifting it over her head and tossing it onto the counter behind her. "Can you get the forks?"

"Sure." Alex never should've agreed to the request. He was not capable of simple tasks right now. All he could do was drink in the vision before him—Joy in that dress. Forks were the exact last thing on his mind. "Wow."

"You haven't even tasted it yet. Let's sit in the dining room. I put out a bottle of wine, but I still need to light the candles."

"Hold on a second." He ran his fingers down the back of her bare arm as he admired her. The deep V of the gown's back was matched in the front, the neckline dipping low enough to show off the swell of her beautiful breasts. There was no way she was wearing a bra. Apparently, she was trying to kill him. With the apron gone, he could truly see how stunning she was in red, with her long chocolate-brown hair falling behind her shoulders and her eyes as warm as ever. "You are so beautiful. I mean, seriously." He wanted to say more, to be poetic, but had no clue where his command of the English language had gone. "Can I just tell you that?"

She cocked her head to the side as a smile crossed her lips, only making him want to kiss her more. "You like the dress?" She turned once and the floor-length skirt swished behind her, but when it came to a stop, he saw a flash of her leg. The dress had a very high slit. "It's not too much?"

Alex was surprised he didn't need to physically put his eyes back into his head. "Too much? No. I'm just lucky I get to look at you in it." It was official. He had zero interest in food. He'd never been less hungry. He placed his hands on either side of her neck and tilted her chin upward. "I'm just lucky I get to kiss you right now."

His lips fell on hers and there was this magical moment where the world around them fell away—no messy kitchen, no life circumstances holding them back. Only Joy's warm and giving kiss, the way her tongue sought his, was of importance now. He didn't give a damn about anything but this.

She popped up on to her tiptoes, stretched out her arms onto his shoulders and dug her delicate fingers into his hair. She deepened their kiss. He countered, and she whimpered, a sound he would never tire of hearing. He wrapped his arms tightly around her, but one hand caressed the bare skin of her back, her silky skin. He wanted to touch every inch of her more than he'd ever wanted to, which was saying a lot. He dropped one hand to her hip and gathered the skirt upward, taking a fistful of the soft fabric. His fingers reached her bare thigh and she gasped like he'd just seared her skin.

"The soufflé will get cold," she said, breathless. Gladly, there was an edge to her voice that said she didn't care, either.

"I promise I'll make it up to you." With that, he reached down and swept her into his arms, holding her tight.

She wrapped her arms around his neck and set her head against his chest. He tried not to stare down into her cleavage, reminding himself he needed to get her upstairs safely. Then he could have his reward.

He wasted no time getting up to her bedroom. He planted a knee on her bed and set her down gently.

She swished her hands across the duvet. "I love this bed. It feels so amazing."

You are amazing. Not taking his eyes off her, Alex dispatched his suit coat and tie. Why he'd ever worried about the damn color was beyond him. It clearly hadn't made a blip of a difference to Joy.

She propped up on her elbows and raised her knee, allowing the slit of her dress to fall open. He unbuttoned his shirt as fast as he could.

"I like watching you take your clothes off," she said.

He tossed the shirt aside. "I like *taking* your clothes off." He stretched out on the bed next to her, wishing he'd been smart enough to ditch his damn pants—they were entirely too confining right now—but he just wanted to touch her. That had seemed most important.

They went right back to kissing like their lives depended on it. He flattened her against the bed, she dug her fingers into his back, hitched her leg up over his hip, tracing the back of his thigh with her foot. Her other leg slipped between his and she pressed against his crotch, raising a groan from the depths of his belly and bringing it to his lips. The heat inside him was building like a wildfire on a sunny day. A windy, sunny day, at that. This was an all-new level of longing for Joy. If this was their last time together, he wanted to make it count.

He pulled one dress strap off her shoulder. Thankfully his earlier assumption had been right. No bra. He cupped her breast with his hand, her velvety skin impossibly soft against his. He lowered his head, flicking his tongue against her nipple. He loved feeling the way heat surged beneath his palm, and her skin tightened beneath his touch. She moaned softly, rubbing her leg more convincingly against his crotch as his lips closed in on the firm bud.

He lowered his hand and found the gap in the skirt, his fingers roaming higher on her thigh and lifting the voluminous fabric. When he reached her hip, he moved to her belly, and his fingers slipped beneath the silky fabric of her panties. He took his time getting to her center, teasing with a delicate touch. One well-made loop with his fingers and he knew exactly how ready she was. He didn't think he could stand the wait much longer.

She clamored for his belt buckle, unhooking it and the front of his pants. When she unzipped them and slipped her hand inside, molding her hand around his erection, he was blinded with need. All he could think about was what it was like to be inside her, to experience every inch of her. He scrambled off the bed and shucked his pants and boxers. Joy got up as well, turning her back to him and pulling her hair aside. He unzipped her dress and she pulled it forward from her shoulders. It fell to the floor in a beautiful red puddle.

Taking her hair in his hand and pulling it aside, he wrapped his other arm around her waist and pulled her snug against his body. He wanted her to feel just how turned on he was, grinding his hips against her. He kissed his way from her nape to one shoulder, then back to the other side. Joy turned in his arms, planted a hot, wet kiss on his lips before dropping to her knees. He nearly fell over from the anticipation.

She dragged her hands down his chest and stomach, then shot him a white-hot look before gripping his erection and taking him into her mouth. His eyes clamped shut, his own mouth so agape he thought he might not ever close his jaw again. It felt so impossibly good, the tenderness of her tongue, the firm hold of her lips, the attention she put into pleasing him. It would've been one thing to have this treatment from any woman, but from Joy, it was so beyond mere physical gratification. She was a rare and beautiful creature. He was lucky and he knew it.

Joy had to admit—she loved having Alex at her mercy. She paid special attention to every noise he made, every subtle twitch of the muscles in his firm thighs. She'd messed up dinner, but she was pretty sure she could get this right. Judging by the deep groans he kept unleashing, she was on the right track. Knowing they were parting tomorrow made her charge even more important. She wanted him to remember this. She knew she would. She shut out the sad feelings that threatened to take over. They had been encroaching on her thoughts all day, and she'd had enough. She would enjoy him if it was the last thing she did.

Alex caressed her shoulders, dug his fingers into her hair. "You are so damn sexy," he muttered.

She would've smiled if it wasn't going to ruin the rhythm she'd so carefully established, the one that had elicited the words in the first place. Instead, she gripped his hips a little harder and flicked her tongue from side to side, keeping as much suction as she could. The tension in his body only grew. If she didn't slow down, Alex was going to need recovery time before he could make love to her. She didn't want to wait.

He grasped her upper arms. "Come here. I need you."

Now she could smile. That was exactly what she'd been thinking. She rose to her feet and he gathered her in his arms, planting a fast and loose kiss on her lips. She opened the drawer in the bedside table and took out a condom, ripping it open and putting it on him. One more kiss and she climbed on to the bed, rolling to her back, sinking into the plush bedding and waiting for him.

He had that cocky grin on his face, the one that made her want to roll her eyes, except in this setting, it only meant she was in for a treat. He was so stunning standing before her, and even better looking when he descended on her, kissing his way up her belly and moving his attention to her breasts. He positioned himself at her entrance and drove inside.

Time stopped. Her breaths stalled. Her heart was the only thing talking as her body molded around him. It wouldn't stop saying all sorts of implausible things. *You need him. You can't let him go.*

Alex settled his weight on her, driving her crazy in the best possible way. He knew exactly what she liked, the perfect amount of pressure to send her into oblivion. How he had figured out in little more than a week what a fair number of men had *never* figured out was a mystery; she only knew that Alex had a way of getting to the heart of all matters, her body included. They moved together in the rhythm that was their own, her legs wrapped around his hips to have him as deep as he could go. Their kisses were slow and careful, and she tried once again to stop thinking of the lasts that were coming for them—the last time they would make love, the last kiss. She didn't want this to be a countdown, but it was hard not to think of it that way. And if she did, the tears would come.

The pressure of pleasure was warring in her body with the melancholy. She had to fight for the good, cling to the beauty of two people who understand each other and want to please each other. She let her thoughts go and opened her eyes, soaked up the beauty of Alex.

His breaths were tearing from his chest now, and hers were nearly the same. Tension doubled in her belly, then doubled again, and just as she felt herself teetering on the edge, she tumbled into the release and gave herself up to it. Alex's torso froze for a moment as he reached his own climax, his shoulders and hips shuddering when he relaxed and let it wash over him. He collapsed into her and she wrapped every limb she had around him as tightly as she possibly could.

A million kisses followed, or at least it felt that way—an embarrassment of riches. Dinner was a distant thought. Alex got up and used the bathroom, then Joy, and they retreated to bed, wound around each other and silent.

There wasn't much more to be said. Talking about what was coming wouldn't solve a thing. Sometimes, just giving in to the inevitability of something could be freeing.

You can't fight every last thing in life. Eventually, you'll lose.

Alex fell asleep while they were still entwined. The warm flickers from the fire lit up the side of his handsome face. Joy let her eyes roam, taking in every inch of perfection. She had to remember everything—the exact curve of his mouth, the way his lashes skimmed his cheeks when his eyes were closed, the dimple in his chin.

She was going to be so disappointed with herself in the years to come if she wasn't able to conjure up this image and make him seem real. Her memories were the only things she had left to cling to. He was about to walk out of her life. She'd known all along this was coming, and although it already hurt—although it already made a pit in her stomach and her chest blaze with a flame that might never go out—she refused to regret her time with Alex. He had given her so much. He had reminded her of the things she still loved about herself—her passion, her heart.

There had been a time in her not-so-distant past when she'd hated herself. That entire drive from Santa Barbara to Vail had been a long running dialogue about what a failure she was, how she'd created every terrible thing in her life that she hated. She'd been knee-deep in the reverberations of that self-loathing when Alex came down the hill that night. He'd lifted her out of it and shaken her into her better state, one where she didn't question her abilities, her talents, herself.

She'd thought about telling him that she was falling in love with him, but that didn't make any sense now. What good would it do? It would only make parting that much harder. It would make it painfully awkward. She wasn't about to ruin yet another good thing. She had to take the fleeting moments they had together and hold on to them in her heart forever. That was the best she could possibly do. For both of them.

She snuggled closer to him and set her head against his chest. She let his warmth seep into her, trying to ignore the worry that when he was gone, she might be left a cold and empty shell. She turned her face into his skin, inhaled his comforting smell as tears rolled down her cheeks.

He deserved to know the truth. "I'll always love you, Alex Townsend. Even after we say goodbye."

Eleven

Joy had to make up for the disaster that had been last night's dinner. They hadn't eaten until after midnight, when Alex had woken up, his stomach growling. Even then, they'd only made grilled cheese sandwiches. That flopped soufflé? Sadly, it had ended up in the trash.

She'd gone with apple cinnamon muffins—Alex had mentioned the other day how much he loved anything with cinnamon. The kitchen smelled amazing and she hoped that her perfect vision of Christmas morning would come to fruition.

She walked into the living room with a tray of coffee and breakfast. "I hope you're not disappointed, but I made muffins this morning. I can't serve you scones forever." She slid the tray onto the coffee table.

He stood and went to her, seeming exceedingly happy. "I already know I love your muffins." He gave one butt cheek a gentle squeeze and kissed her softly.

She laughed, their lips still brushing against each other before they were naturally drawn into a deeper kiss. She grasped his shoulder and bowed into him, then realized how close she was to getting pulled off track. As much as she loved sex with Alex, this morning was important for other reasons. "If we aren't careful, it'll be a repeat of our first tree lighting ceremony, right here in this room."

That day had been such an amazing turn of events. She loved reliving every moment—the flirting, the longing, the moment when they'd been unable to fight their attraction anymore and she'd finally just kissed him. It had been one of the best days of her life.

"After presents. And breakfast." He sat on the couch next to her and sipped his black coffee. If she wasn't mistaken, that was contentment on his face.

Joy handed him a muffin. "Apple cinnamon. Pretty basic, but they're still really good."

"I would say you're full of yourself, except that I know you're not." He removed the paper baking cup and took a generous bite. "Absolutely perfect."

"Thank you. That's sweet."

"Just telling you the truth." He finished off his muffin and sat back, trailing his fingers up and down Joy's back. "When do you want to open gifts?"

"I'm worried you won't like what I got you."

"Not possible. No way. You could just give me the recipe for these muffins and I'd be happy."

She knocked her fist against his knee. "I never said I was going to give you something that good." She took another sip of her coffee and got up from the couch. "Now is as good a time as any." Kneeling down, she pulled a small box out from under the tree. "You first."

The gift was wrapped in gold foil, with a red ribbon he untied. He slipped the box from the paper and lifted the lid. Inside, on a bed of cotton fluff, sat the silver money clip she'd bought him at a men's store in the village with the money from her grandmother's necklace. He picked it up and held it in the palm of his hand. She'd worried that it wouldn't make a grand enough impression, but he truly seemed to like it. "It's beautiful. What is this embossing on the top?" He ran his thumb over the irregular texture, a series of short diagonal lines.

"Do you not recognize it?" She snickered. "It's supposed to look like tire tracks. I thought it would be a fun reminder of the way we met."

He shook his head and laughed. "I'm never going to live that down, am I?"

"Just like I'll never live down diving into a snowbank." She sucked in a deep breath, but the weight of the moment lodged in her throat. That had been the beginning and they were now wedged in the end. She hated the end. She hated goodbyes. There was never a single fun thing about them, but this one was already especially painful. "I just wanted to give you something that you could remember me by. Something to carry in your pocket."

"Well, thank you. I love it. I will always keep it with me. Always." His comment was only confirmation that they really would be parting. There wasn't the slightest hint of staying another day. He was ready to say farewell. He got up and retrieved more than one box from under the tree. "I know we said we were only going to do one gift, but I cheated and got you three."

"Alex. You weren't supposed to do that. It's so mean. I only got you one."

"I know, but I just couldn't decide. I literally could've bought out the whole store when I went shopping."

"And then you would've had nothing for your money clip, so I'm glad you kept things in check." She desperately wanted to keep the tone light and fun, even when it was the opposite of what she was feeling. She just had to hold it together a little longer.

He set the packages on the coffee table, setting one apart from the others. "This one gets opened last."

"Okay." She took the first of the two remaining and tore open the paper. The instant she saw the famous red and black checks on the camel cashmere background, she knew exactly how extravagant he'd been. "A Burberry scarf? I love it. I've always wanted one of these." She'd actually fantasized about it, but never thought she'd ever actually own one. She wrapped it around her neck and bunched up her shoulders. "It's so soft."

"You were complaining about your scarf the day of the tree lighting and I thought it would look gorgeous against your dark hair. And it does."

"Well, thank you. I love it. I will keep it forever." *Forever.* She needed to avoid that word. It was only going to take its toll later. She took the second package and opened that one just as quickly. "Oh. Perfume. I never buy myself perfume." She removed the top and spritzed some on her wrists. It smelled like vanilla and sugar cookies. "Ooh. Yummy."

"This one might be stupid. I bought it because it reminded me of the way you smell when you've been baking. I just thought it would be nice." He swiped the final gift from the table. "Now this one, you're just going to have to tell me to take a hike if you don't want it. I'm not trying to make you feel hemmed in or anything."

Her brows drew together. She couldn't imagine what it could possibly be. The box was smaller than the scarf box, but the same shape—long and flat. "Now you really have me curious." She was much more careful with the paper this time, knowing this was the final part of their Christmas morning together. The tape popped free and she carefully set aside the wrapping intact. She opened the box. A folio was inside, but she still had no guess as to what this was. She opened the front flap. Inside was a plane ticket. To Fiji.

"Oh, my God. A trip."

For a moment, her heart performed the most ridiculous routine—jumping around like it wasn't attached to anything.

"Yes. Fiji. I just, I think one thing we both learned over the last few days is that we could use a vacation. A real vacation where nobody worries about work at all. And I thought that the farthest we could go away, the better. I've been to this resort and it's beautiful."

She didn't say a word. She just stared at the tickets, frozen. A tear rolled down her cheek.

"It's okay if you don't want to go. I just…" He closed his eyes and pinched the bridge of his nose.

She looked up to see him warring with himself. Was he changing his mind?

"I don't want this to end," he said.

It was the sweetest thing anyone had ever said to her. And now Joy was tangled in a web of her own making.

In her wildest dreams—or more like nightmares—she couldn't have come up with a scenario like this one. She wanted to cry and scream. She wanted to kiss Alex for being desperately romantic. She wanted to be in his arms and tell him that she loved him.

But there were about one hundred things that had to be said before that. And she was reasonably sure she'd never get that far. The tears—oh, boy, did they come, like she'd never cried in her entire life and had been waiting for this moment.

Because the truth was that the name printed on her ticket was Joy Baker. Her fake last name might as well have been Betrayal. That was what she'd done. She'd betrayed him. And for someone who'd made a zillion mistakes in her life, this one was definitely the worst.

An hour ago, Alex was sure he hadn't been this excited about Christmas morning since he was a kid. He'd certainly been nervous about how his gifts would go over with Joy. Now she was crying and hadn't said a single thing that sounded like yes.

Why had he been so stupid? How had he read it so wrong? It was too big a leap. They'd only known each other for a little more than ten days. This was not the same as asking a woman out to dinner on the fourth or fifth date. Sadly, he couldn't undo it now.

"Why are you crying?" Alex gently rested his hand on her shoulder. In some ways, touching her only made it worse. She didn't respond like she normally did. She nearly recoiled.

"I have to tell you something. I have to tell you a lot of something." She gulped for breath. She kept looking at the floor. "This isn't my name. My name is Joy McKinley. I made up Baker because I'd just spent the whole day working at the bakery and I was trying to hide my identity because nobody can know that I'm here."

Alex felt as though she had just plunged a knife into his heart. She wasn't who she said she was?

"I don't understand. Hide your identity? Is someone trying to hurt you?"

"Not exactly. I'm not really supposed to be staying in this house. It's not owned by friends of mine—it belongs to my former employer. I quit after she and I had a huge argument, and she said that if I ever gave her reason to, she would destroy my career. She and her husband are immensely powerful in the food world. If she wanted to, she could make it impossible for me to get any job as a chef, let alone pursue anything else with cooking."

"How powerful could these people be?"

"Harrison Marshall, the celebrity chef. The house belongs to him and his wife, Mariella."

"Oh, wow." Alex didn't know the ins and outs of the culinary world, but he did know who the Marshalls were. Joy's story was becoming more and more complicated. Alex was struggling to keep up. None of it made sense. "So why wouldn't you just go somewhere else? Do you not have permission at all?"

"My boss's son said I could stay here until mid-January, but nobody could know about it because his mom hates me. I had nowhere else to go. I have no money. I haven't been able to find a place I can afford. And you know I can't go home."

"You didn't have a friend you could stay with?"

"Not here. I have some in other parts of the country, but I couldn't get that far. That pile of junk under the tarp in the garage is my car. It doesn't work. That's why I need a ride everywhere."

Alex put his elbows on his knees and ran his hands through his hair. What in the hell was happening? Was fate playing some cruel trick on him? She kept launching lie after lie at him and he didn't know what he was supposed to do about any of it.

"Say something, please. I am so sorry. I never would've lied to you if I'd known what was going to happen between us. It was just one little lie after another, piled on top of the first one."

He then turned to her, his head hung low. The hurt in his heart was unfathomable. He wasn't sure he knew how to breathe anymore, or if he even wanted to. He wanted to disappear. "You couldn't bring yourself to tell me the truth before now? When you were basically backed into a corner? What about the day we went to the tree lighting? Or last night when I came over?"

"Are you serious? That would've been better? If I had ruined those beautiful, romantic moments we were sharing? For all I knew, you and I were never going to see each other again after today. You've only mentioned your departure date a dozen times, like you wanted to remind me that there was an expiration date on our affair."

His vision narrowed on her and the hurt faded, giving way to anger. "It was a fact. Nothing more than that. And it was the truth, which seems to be a big problem for you. No wonder my private investigator couldn't find anything about you. It was almost as if you didn't exist. Now I know that Joy Baker from Santa Barbara, California, doesn't actually exist. She's fake."

Joy's eyes blazed with fury. "You called your private investigator about me? Is that what you do with all women?" She got up from the couch and stared down at him. "You probably don't want to risk getting involved with anyone too messy. The perfect Alex wouldn't want to look bad."

"You want to know why I called my private investigator? Because my ex-fiancée was actually a career criminal. A con artist, trying to get at my money. Maybe you two know each other." That was a low blow, but he refused to take it back. He was too mad right now. Every happy, hopeful thought he'd dared to have over the last week had been destroyed with her version of the truth.

Joy picked up the tickets and threw them at him. "You can take your fancy Fiji trip and shove it. I wouldn't get on an airplane with you if my life depended on it. Just go by yourself and find some anonymous woman to sleep with, like you did with me. If you keep it short and sweet, you won't even have to call your PI to do a background check."

Alex picked up the money clip and tossed it in his palm. "Where'd you get the money for this? Did you steal it?" He had to know the full extent of her deception.

She started crying again, which just felt manipulative. "No. I did not steal it. I pawned the only thing I own of my grandmother's. A gold necklace that she'd gotten from one of her employers. She was a cook. Just a plain old regular cook, Alex. She worked for almost nothing, cooking for families like yours. That's why my parents didn't want me to pursue my dreams. They didn't want me to have the life I have right now, but that's just the way things are. I know I messed up. I lied to you. I fully own up to that. But you have accused me of things today that I can't live with. Because no matter what, I know now that you never trusted me. From the very beginning. That's no basis for happiness."

Alex's jaw was set firmly. He really hadn't trusted her. He'd only convinced himself that he did. Now he knew that he'd been right. "I don't think you understand what

I went through. A woman literally tried to trick me into marrying her, just so she could get my money. Do you have any idea how awful that was for me? And how this feels like more of the same?"

"I'm sure it does feel terrible. And I'm sorry. But I think you and I both know that this wasn't going to work out. You were suspicious of me all along. You just told me as much. So I think it's best if you just go. Go back to Chicago and live your life. I'm sorry I hurt you."

Alex got up from the couch, looking around the room. He didn't know what to do. He was still reeling.

"Just go, Alex. Get your things and leave."

The money clip was still in his hand. He wasn't sure he could ever look at it again. "Here. Take this back." He tried to hand it to her, but she wouldn't take it.

"No. I don't want it. I'm about to get paid. I'll get my grandmother's necklace back on my own."

"Joy. You're being ridiculous."

"I'm not. I don't want your charity. I bought you that money clip because I cared about you. You should keep it to remind yourself that somebody did. Maybe someday you'll be ready to accept that from someone." She crossed her arms and walked to the other side of the room, facing the windows, looking out at the snow.

He didn't know what to say. Was that true? Had she really cared about him? If they could rewind and undo her lies, would she have said yes to the trip? Would she have said yes to not wanting it to end? Now he would never know.

He ran upstairs and gathered his things, put on his shoes. She wanted him out and he wanted the same, if only to clear his head. He'd arrived last night with so much hope in his heart and now it was filled with nothing but black clouds and misery. He had to leave. He had to go home.

Downstairs he went. He took only one step into the living room before Joy turned to him.

"I'm going." His voice was only a trace of its normal strength. He was too hurt to muster anything with more force. "For the record, I never said I wanted things with any woman to be easy."

She closed her eyes then turned away. "Well, then, you got your wish."

Twelve

Alex left for Chicago Christmas night.

He couldn't spend another hour in Colorado. He'd normally call for the corporate jet, but there was no time for it to get to him, so he flew commercial, snagging a first-class seat on the last flight out of Denver. There was no reason to stay in Vail. There were only painful reminders of Joy there and that was the last thing he needed. The wound was plenty deep. He didn't need to claw at it. Maybe he'd just sell his place there. Or let his brothers use it. He couldn't fathom wanting to go back anytime soon.

The lights in the cabin were off as the plane began to descend. Alex stared out the window, watching the city below, pin dots of light scattered on an inky black canvas. Somewhere down there, somebody was happy. They'd had the best Christmas they'd ever had. Certainly there were children being tucked into bed, exhausted from the most incredible day they could remember. Even though he'd only had the chance to do so for a few days, he'd held out a lot of hope for this Christmas, that it would finally be the kind of day he'd always imagined—filled with love and cheer. It had certainly started out promising. He just hadn't known how badly it would crash and burn.

"Mr. Townsend. Your coat."

Alex turned to see the flight attendant handing him his jacket. She was wearing a Santa hat and jingly earrings, with long brown hair similar to Joy's. As if he needed more reminders of how much this Christmas had sucked, or of how badly his heart had been broken into two. Again. "Thank you." He took it from her and laid it across his lap, returning his sights to the city. Soon enough he'd be home.

The next day was Wednesday and Alex was up with the sun, unfortunately. Sleeping had been impossible. He just rolled around in his bed, unable to keep the thoughts of Joy out of his head. Had he been too hard on her? His gut was telling him that he hadn't. He'd been duped before, and he'd sworn to himself he would never, ever let it happen again.

He stepped on the scale after brewing a pot of coffee. He'd gained two pounds while he was away. Scone weight. He really should've been working out more while he was in Colorado. You'd think all that sex would've burned off some calories. Apparently not.

Luckily, he had a home gym in Chicago. He hopped on the treadmill and ran until he couldn't run anymore—more than an hour, listening to loud music in his earbuds, just trying to get out the anger and pain and resentment built up inside him. He sat on a weight bench when he finally gave in to exhaustion, rubbing his wet hair with a towel and sucking down water. He didn't feel any better, and all his stupid mind wanted to fixate on was what Joy was doing. At least he was fairly certain he'd sleep that night.

After a shower, he went into the office to prepare for his meeting with his father, even though no one was expecting him for another day. Striding into the offices of Townsend & Associates Investments, he knew that work was the only way to get through this. He had to put in the hours. Bury himself in numbers. He needed to blow his dad's expectations out of the water, continue to wow the world of finance. In a few months, people could gossip about him, try to guess what had gotten into him and given him such superhuman strength when it came to work.

He'd never tell a soul that it had all been fueled by a broken heart.

"Morning, Barb," he said to the receptionist.

She was on the phone, so she nodded and gave him the cursory smile. He was the boss and most people were afraid of him, so he didn't tend to get much more than that. He might need to see about changing that, too. Maybe if he spent more time with the lower-level employees, he could create an even tighter company culture. His father would be horrified by the sheer idea.

It was relatively quiet as Alex walked down the hall to his corner office. He'd given many of their employees the option of taking off the week between Christmas and New Year's. Another initiative his father did not like, but this was a slow time of year. Best to have everyone up and running at full strength after the holidays. Alex unlocked his door and got straight to work, answering emails, typing up ideas for initiatives for the new year. A little after ten, Paul poked his head into his office.

"Hey there." Paul knocked on Alex's open door.

Alex didn't believe in keeping his door closed unless absolutely necessary. It made him feel like a caged animal. He sat back in his chair. "Have a seat. How was your Christmas?"

Paul had a huge grin on his face. A mile wide, no exaggeration. "It was fantastic. I got my grandson that action figure we were talking about. I have never seen a kid so happy in my entire life. My wife loved her gifts, and she was in a great mood because both kids were there. She and our daughter made this pastry on Christmas morning that my wife hasn't made since the kids were little, a Swedish tea ring. Have you ever had one?"

Alex shook his head, while visions of scones and muffins materialized before him. "No. I haven't."

"It's delicious. Like a giant cinnamon roll. The whole house smelled amazing." Paul nodded and laughed quietly to himself. Surely he was recalling some happy moment from Christmas that he didn't feel needed to be shared. "So? How about you? What happened with that woman you wanted me to check out? Joy Baker?"

Thankfully, Alex didn't need to sugarcoat things with Paul. He could just come right out and tell him. "She lied to me about her name. It's not Baker. It's McKinley. And she's from Ohio, not California." He didn't quite know how to read the expression on Paul's face—it almost looked like remorse.

"I am so sorry. I should've dug a little deeper. So she's not a baker, either, I take it."

"No. No. That much was true. And she worked in

Santa Barbara for a while, so that was where she'd lived most recently."

"How did you find out? See her driver's license or something?"

"She told me. On Christmas morning, no less. I'd bought her tickets to Fiji. That's the thing that's so pathetic about this whole story. I really liked her. I wanted to take her away. She saw her fake name on the ticket and started to cry and she told me everything."

Paul drew in a deep breath through his nose. "Wow. That's tough. I'm so sorry. Did she say why she'd waited to tell you?"

Alex shrugged and rocked in his chair. "Well, she knew I was leaving the day after Christmas, so I guess she didn't see the point. I was coming home to Chicago. She wasn't sure where she was going next because she doesn't really have a place to live."

Paul lowered his chin and looked down his nose at Alex. "So she's homeless."

"Sort of. Not really. She was staying in the house of her former employer and she lied about her name because she didn't want me to know. She couldn't afford to go anywhere else."

"Sounds like a real mess."

"Yes. Exactly. Thank you. Her story steamrollered from there. One lie basically led to another lie, until I didn't know what was what anymore. The whole thing is a disaster and just hits way too close to home. I know you know what I mean."

"Can I speak freely?"

"Of course. You know that. I trust you. What?"

"I know you have no idea what it's like to be poor. And I'm not blaming you for that, but let me tell you, I do know. I know it very well. My family struggled when I was a teen. I had a hard time making ends meet in my twenties." Paul spoke in his characteristic calm voice, but it was even more measured than usual. "It's not fun to live your life feeling like you're up on a high wire about to fall off. You definitely reach a point where you will pretty much do anything to keep your life together. That's why it's called a survival instinct."

"So what are you saying? That I was wrong to be upset about being lied to?"

Paul shook his head. "Absolutely not. Of course not. You had every right. I'm just trying to give you some perspective, because I have a sneaking suspicion that what you were thinking in that moment when she told you the truth was that this was Sharon all over again."

"Well, it is. Isn't it?" It had felt just like Sharon when Joy had told him the truth. Although, he had to admit that he'd gone straight to feeling sad much more quickly than the first time.

"Did Sharon confess? No. I had to find out about it and you had to confront her. And what did she do when that happened?"

"Denied everything." Alex could see where Paul was going with this, but he wasn't convinced he was right. Alex had been lied to and there was no good excuse for it. He didn't care for explanations.

"Then what?"

A grumble left Alex's throat. "She stole stuff out of my apartment and tried to say that I had given it to her."

"Is that how it went down with Joy?"

"No. Not at all. She even apologized. But that still doesn't change the way I felt. That still doesn't make what she did okay."

"Of course it doesn't make it okay. And you were justified in being upset. But now that you've had time to cool down, maybe you should at least try to think this through."

Paul scooted forward to the edge of his seat. This was as close as Alex would ever get to receiving fatherly advice. "Obviously, I don't know this Joy woman. But let me just say this. That last time I talked to you, you were genuinely happy. I could hear it in your voice. And you were never like that with Sharon. Never."

"I was happy then. I just had a lot of stuff going on at work. It was a stressful time." Now he was even more confused. "I sort of thought I was happy."

"And this isn't a stressful time in your life, Alex? You're running the company now, for God's sake. The buck stops with you and you turned your phone off for twenty-four hours. You want to know what that says to me? That stress was the last thing on your mind. You met someone who was enough to take your eye off the prize. Which makes me think that she might be the real prize."

"You don't even know her."

All Alex could think was that the words he'd uttered would not have the intended effect. The truth was that he would love for Paul to meet Joy. He would love to know that he wasn't crazy, that there was a spark between the two of them that other people could see and feel. He wanted someone to tell him it was real.

"No. I don't. And there's a chance I'm totally off base."

"That doesn't help me. At all."

Paul got up out of his chair. "Look, I didn't come into your office to play psychiatrist. But I don't like what Sharon did to you. And I think you're still processing some of it. It's not fair to this other woman that you're making her pay for someone else's lies, especially when those other lies were designed to hurt you." Paul knocked his knuckle against Alex's desk. "Intent is important."

What had been behind Joy's lies? She'd been trying to protect herself. She'd been trying to survive, in a world Alex had never had to live in. "What do I do now? About Joy? I said some truly awful things to her. Terrible things." His stomach hurt just thinking about it. He'd accused her of stealing. Could he ever come back from that?

"You'll figure it out. You're a smart kid."

"I'm a few months from thirty-five, Paul. And I'm your boss."

"Hey. To me, you're still that pimply thirteen-year-old you were when I started working here. I'll always worry about you."

Alex shook his head in disbelief. How Paul could see so much was beyond him. He only knew that he did.

And now, Alex had to figure out what to do about it.

Joy had given herself one day to be sad, but now she had a sad hangover. She was also more than a little bit pissed off at herself. She had quite literally done everything she'd sworn she would never do again. Why did she keep putting herself in these situations? How did she have such a talent for creating her own unhappiness? She wasn't sure. She only knew that she couldn't allow herself to live like this anymore. She'd thrown away what she had with Alex, and he might have been the best thing that had ever happened to her. That mistake would haunt her forever. No more doing things that she couldn't stand to live with.

First thing on the day after Christmas, she called Natalie. "Hello? Joy?" Natalie sounded more than a little sleepy.

"Natalie, hey. I'm sorry if I woke you. I just figured you were up and at 'em like I am on a day off."

"Not usually, no. But I do have some stuff I need to do today."

"Okay. Well, I need to tell you some things. And I need a couch to sleep on."

Joy then launched into the entirety of the truth—where she was living, why she shouldn't be living there anymore, and that she needed help coming back down to Earth, where she belonged.

"I'll call my brother and have him come up to look at your car. I'll get him to fix it for free. You're welcome to stay on my couch for as long as you like," Natalie said.

"You're not mad I lied about the house? I asked you to drop me off at a house that I wasn't even living in. I feel horrible."

"No, I'm not mad. I don't judge people. We all have to do what we can to survive and I've been in a few jams in my life. I know you're a hard worker, a talented baker, and a good friend. You're definitely the most fun person I've ever worked with."

"We do have fun, don't we?" Joy smiled to herself. Natalie was a blessing she was so thankful to have.

"Rolling dough all day long." Natalie laughed. "Okay. Let me get some coffee and we'll get this show on the road. Text me the address."

"Will do. But you'll know it when you see it. It's the house you never would've believed I belong in." Joy hung up and got to work, collecting her things from Elana's closet, washing bedding and making the beds, cleaning the kitchen and the bathrooms, even sweeping ashes from the fireplace. She was careful to put everything exactly as it had been before. And to think she'd spent so much time worrying that Mariella Marshall would find out she was living there and would end up kicking her out. In the end, Joy was evicting herself. She never should've come here in the first place.

With every task complete, she waited to feel closer to closure, but the feeling wouldn't come. Perhaps it was because the Christmas decorations were still up. She managed to remove the first few ornaments from the tree before she started to cry. The tears streaked down her face, she gasped for air, but she kept going. Every pretty glass bauble was returned to its box, the tiny tree all packed up, and along with it, her memories of Alex.

Her tears weren't about sentimentality over the things that they'd done together—those were nothing but good and pleasant memories. The remorse was for what might have been—a chance at happiness. She'd fallen in love with him. Someday, he might've fallen in love with her. She'd had no idea he'd wanted more. She'd never expected it. And she couldn't stop asking herself why she'd never dared to think it. But now, she was starting to see the answer.

She'd doomed them from the start. She'd lied. With that first untruth, she'd made it impossible for them to ever have more—what person could ever see past that? She'd taken one look at his perfect face, his finely tailored wool coat, and his expensive car and decided they were from different worlds and that meant there was no reason to treat him with anything other than wariness and skepticism.

She'd let her circumstances harden her and turn her into something she wasn't, all because she was afraid.

When things got bad, she was allowing herself to feel just as small as Ben used to make her feel. Just as small as Mariella Marshall had made her feel. She needed to stop reacting that way when life pushed against her. Everyone had their trials. She needed to do a better job of standing up to hers. Alex would have to be the one who got away—it would always hurt. No amount of time would remove him from her head or her heart.

Late that night, she was settled at Natalie's. The couch was not as comfortable as Elana's bed, but that was fine. Joy was sleeping on this couch with full permission, with no fear of anyone discovering her whereabouts. There was a lot to be said for the peace of mind of that. But she still had unfinished business.

Things with Alex had not ended the way they should have. As upset as she'd been about the fact that he'd called his private investigator, the truth was that he was absolutely right to have done it. If he'd gotten any sort of strange vibe from her, it was completely her fault. And for that reason, she had to call him and apologize one more time. This was part of making everything right with the world.

She got his voice mail. It wasn't entirely surprising that he hadn't answered. He had every reason in the world to hate her. And she had to take some comfort in the fact that he hadn't blocked her number.

This is Alexander Townsend with Townsend & Associates Investments. Please leave a message. His voice filled her with so much regret.

"Hi, Alex. It's Joy. I'm calling to apologize. It was never my intention to lie to you. I was in a jam, and I did some things I'm not proud of. But I'm out of the Marshalls' house now and about to start working extra hours at the bakery to get my head above water." It occurred to her that he might not care about any of this, but she had to keep going. She had to get it off her chest. "I want you to know that I will always fondly look back on our time together. You're an amazing man, and any woman would be lucky to have you in her life. I hope you find happiness. I hope you live a good life." *And I love you.*

The words were threatening to burst forth from her lips, but she couldn't saddle him with that burden. This phone call was not about pulling at heartstrings. It was about making things as right as she could. "Goodbye, Alex."

She pressed the button to end the call and muted her phone, stuffing it under her pillow. She snuggled up under the blanket, closed her eyes, and willed herself to sleep. Hopefully the tears wouldn't last for long.

Joy and Natalie went into work together the next morning. Natalie took her break at eleven thirty. Joy took hers right after, just as the clock struck noon. She had to hurry. She had something important to do. Now that she was staying with Natalie, she had a brief reprieve on finding a place to live. And since her car had been fixed by Natalie's brother, Joy could use her paycheck to buy back her grandmother's necklace.

The bell on the pawn shop door rang when Joy pushed it open. It was just as dead quiet in there as it had been the first time she walked in. That seemed like a lifetime ago. When she was sure she knew how things with Alex would end. Her version would've had the same net result, but at least he would've thought well of her. He wouldn't have known the truth, but hopefully a smile would've come to his face when he remembered her.

That would've been the closest she and Alex could have come to a happy ending.

But it hadn't happened like that, and she had to continue with the baby steps toward acceptance. That was the only way to heal.

"Can I help you?" the man behind the counter asked. He wasn't really looking at her, preoccupied with polishing up an old pocket watch.

Joy pulled her paperwork out of her purse. "Yes. I'm here to buy back a necklace I pawned." She scanned the glass case but didn't see it with the other jewelry. That stuff was all more contemporary. Maybe he'd put it in another section. Joy whipped around and rushed to the other side of the store, hands on the glass, searching.

"I remember you," he said. "It's gone. A woman came in about a half hour ago to buy it."

"What? A half hour? You told me you'd call me. We talked about it."

The man shrugged. "Sorry. I guess I forgot."

Joy closed her eyes and dropped her head back. The loss shuddered through her body. How much more could she possibly lose in this world? Alex. Her pride. The necklace. What next? "Do you have the woman's information by any chance? Do you remember what she looked like or where she was going?"

"She was blonde. She mentioned something about the bakery."

"Really?"

"Yes."

Joy didn't waste another minute, hitching her bag over her shoulder and bolting out into the cold. Around the corner and down the side street she ran, as fast her impractical brown boots would carry her. When she finally stumbled through the door of the bakery, the only customer inside was an older gentleman buying a loaf of bread.

Shoot.

Joy went back out on the sidewalk and looked both ways down the street. No sign of a blonde woman. Maybe this just wasn't meant to be. She went back inside, feeling defeated, but deciding it was not the time to feel broken about anything. Her grandmother wouldn't want her to do that. She'd figure out something. She'd go back to the pawn shop tomorrow and tell the owner to call her if it turned up again. People who bought things at pawn shops often ended up taking them back.

Just then she heard a man's voice from the back hall. It made the hair on the back of her neck stand up, but not in a bad way. It was more like she was convinced that she was hearing things. It had to have been one of the bread bakers. Except that it was after noon, and they were usually gone by then. She shook it off and went in search of Natalie. The hall was now empty, just stacks of flour bags lining the walls, and the apron hooks half-empty. Natalie's laugh rang out from the front kitchen.

When Joy pushed through the aluminum swinging doors, she nearly fell over from what she saw. Alex, standing there in a baker's apron, sleeves rolled up, hair back in a bandana no less. When he turned and his eyes met hers, she thought she had died and this was the dream on the other side, the one where things work out and you get everything you always wanted. And that was before he'd said a single word.

"Hi, Joy."

"Alex. What are you doing here?"

He held up the rolling pin in his hand. "Learning how to make scones."

Natalie smiled. "He just got here a little while ago. I told him you were at lunch, so he said he'd wait."

"I tried to call you."

"You did? I didn't get any calls." Joy slapped her forehead. She'd forgotten to take her phone off mute after last night. It wasn't like she'd been expecting any important calls. She pulled her phone from her bag and sure enough, five missed calls, all from Alex. "I'm so sorry. I put my phone on mute after bed last night and totally forgot to turn it back on."

Alex stepped closer to her and Joy did the same, until they were nearly toe-to-toe. "Can we talk?" he asked.

"I can leave you two alone, if you want," Natalie offered.

"No. It's okay. I know you're busy," Joy answered. "We'll go out in the hall."

She led the way and Alex followed. She wasn't sure what to think right now. Had he listened to her message? Would he accept her apology?

He untied the apron and hung it back up on the hook, then removed the bandana from his head.

"Here. Your hair is a mess." She popped up onto her tiptoes and brushed flour from his hairline. Their lips were so close. She could smell his warm cologne. This was too much like things used to be. It was starting to hurt to look at him, like her heart was being pulled out of her chest. "I can't believe you're here."

"I had to come back. I hate the way I left things on Christmas morning."

She shook her head so fast she was surprised she didn't dislodge some brain matter. "Don't apologize for that, Alex. You were absolutely right. I'd left this gray cloud hanging over our time together and it wasn't right.

I should've said something as soon as I realized that I was romantically interested in you."

That clever smile of his crossed his lips. "The moment down by the pool?"

"The moment you didn't kiss me. That's when I should have told you that I wasn't Joy Baker, the baker."

"Which was the most adorable fake name you could've given yourself, by the way."

"It was dumb. And terribly unoriginal. I was panicked. And it wasn't fair to you." She reached for his hand. "I'll say I'm sorry every day if it means you'll give me another chance. Even if it's just one dinner."

"One kiss?"

Was that all he wanted? Even if another goodbye might kill her, she had to take this. She gripped his shoulders and leaned into him, planting her mouth on his. The second his lips parted and his tongue touched hers, she flattened him against the bakery wall. It was too good not to keep it going. It was too perfect. She could've melted right into him then and there.

Alex was the one to end it. "Wow."

She dropped down to her heels. "Sorry. I get carried away." She gazed up at his eyes knowing this was the moment when she had to lay it on the line, again. "You do that to me. Nobody else has ever done that to me. I don't know what made you come back, but I don't want you to leave. Not until we've had that dinner and we've had a chance to talk everything out."

"To start over?" His beautiful blue eyes nearly knocked the breath right out of her.

"That would be amazing." She planted one hand on his chest, watching it rise and fall with his breaths. "What made you come back?"

"Well, I needed to get a grip. That was first on my list. Second was some shopping. For jewelry." He reached into his pocket. Joy gasped when she saw what was in his hand.

"The locket." She watched as Alex draped it into her hand. "But the guy at the pawn shop said a blonde woman bought it."

Natalie poked her head out of the kitchen and waved. "Did I tell you I went to the pawn shop on my break? Not that I was eavesdropping or anything." Just like that, she ducked out of sight.

"I called the pawn shop yesterday and gave them my credit card number so I could get it back. Then I called the bakery this morning after I couldn't get through to you on the phone. Natalie answered and at that point, I figured I might as well make it a surprise, so I asked if she'd go pick it up for me."

Joy shook her head in amazement. "You did all that for me?"

"I did that for the woman I love." He smoothed back her hair with his fingers. "I'm in love with you, Joy. As crazy as that sounds, it's true. The minute I walked out of that house, I only wanted to go back in. But I also had to clear my head. I needed some perspective. Luckily it didn't take long for me to get it."

Joy grabbed his hand and squeezed it. "I love you, too. As crazy as that sounds. I do."

He nodded. "Okay. Well then, you and I have some talking to do and some decisions to make. I don't want to ask you to leave your job here, but I think you know my whole life is in Chicago. We could try long-distance for a while if you want to."

Joy looked at Alex and knew one thing—she was

done making mistakes. "I love the bakery, but I love you more."

"Yeah?" The happy lilt in his voice filled Joy's heart with contentment.

"Yeah. I think that means your scone lesson is over, mister. We need to pack up my things and head to Chicago."

Epilogue

Joy stepped on to the beach and curled her toes. She would never get over how soft the sand was in Fiji. "This is pure heaven."

Alex took her hand, his flip-flops in the other. "Agreed. Let's never leave. Ever."

They embarked on their nightly post-dinner walk. Another thing she would never get over was how beautiful the Fijian sunset was, either. "Is it just me or is it a particularly perfect night?"

"I don't think it could get much better, that's for sure."

In some ways, it felt as though the sun was putting on a command performance just for them, in ultra vivid shades of orange and gold, nothing else but the big blue ocean stretching out beneath it. She and Alex had watched the sunset every night from the deck of their private bungalow, holding hands, savoring their time together. Joy couldn't recall ever feeling so lucky, not even the day she'd landed the job with Harrison Marshall.

Colorado was a distant thought now, although it would always be in the back of her mind. She'd gone there, not realizing she was trying to escape her life, and ended up finding an entirely new one.

"It sure doesn't make me miss Chicago in January," he added.

"I don't know about that. As beautiful as it is here, I'm eager to get back home." Home—that was a concept which Joy had only toyed with over the past few years. Now she was living with Alex. His penthouse apartment in the River North neighborhood of Chicago was unbelievable—spacious, elegant, and most important, it felt like home. Of course, she'd added some of her own touches, mostly to the kitchen, but it was otherwise perfect. Every night, Joy would experiment with new recipes, they would enjoy a lovely meal together, and they would, of course, end up falling into bed. Alex had quipped about how Joy was really helping him get over his bad habit of watching too much TV. Apparently she was enough of a distraction.

Being in Chicago had also brought Alex's family into their lives. His father, Alexander Townsend II, was pretty much what Joy had expected, and he'd been kind, but she wasn't sure how much warmth she'd ever get out of the man. There wasn't a lot there, and that made her sad. Alex deserved better. Alex's brothers, Matthew and Jonathan, helped to fill that void, though. Affable and nearly as handsome as their big brother, they both clearly idolized Alex and gravitated toward him for everything from jokes to advice. Joy could see that the sibling bond fed Alex's soul, and that Alex wouldn't be leaving Chicago anytime soon.

And that meant she'd had to start looking for a job. Yes, Alex had more than enough money and hadn't asked for a cent from her, but they were a committed couple with only six weeks of togetherness under their belts. It was still early days, and Joy didn't want to be caught without a safety net if things didn't stay as wonderful as they were right now. Luckily, her career prospects were shaping up nicely.

Alex had introduced her to several friends who owned restaurants, and Joy would be going for interviews when they returned to Chicago in a few short days. He'd also touched base with a friend who worked for a big New York publisher. He was keen on her getting her foothold in the world of cookbooks if she was ready to do that as well. It was all moving so fast, but she was trying to sit back and take her good fortune as it came. She figured she'd saved up her whole life for it.

They'd made one final weekend trip before getting on the plane for Fiji, a trip for which Joy had been extremely nervous. Alex had taken her to Ohio so he could meet her parents. Of course, Joy hadn't worried about whether or not her mom and dad would like her new beau. They took to him right away. Alex was such a down-to-earth guy, he'd had no problem grabbing a beer with her dad and hanging out in the TV room watching football. He'd been very sweet with her mom, as well, complimenting her cooking and commenting that she was clearly where Joy got her beautiful, long hair and her equally long legs. Thankfully, Ben had not made his presence known, although that was likely due to Alex. Overkill or not, he'd hired two off-duty police officers to stand sentry outside her parents' house the entire time they were there. When she'd wondered aloud if it had been too much, Alex had replied that it had done the job and that was all he cared about.

It was all like a dream, but that did not mean she'd suddenly retired to the land of zero worries. She had big news for Alex, and she had no idea how he was going to react to it. Keeping secrets from him the first time had backfired and she wasn't about to do it again. The question was when the right moment would arise. Alex had been on edge all night.

"Let's get our feet wet," she said.

"Okay." Alex kneeled down and rolled up his pant legs. She'd told him one hundred times she didn't care if he wore shorts to dinner, but he'd insisted that it didn't feel right.

"Ready?" She grabbed his hand and flitted down to the water, moaning softly when her feet reached the gentle waves. "It feels so good tonight. Maybe we should go swimming." She pulled him closer and kissed him gently. "I doubt anyone would notice if we went skinny-dipping." Indeed, the resort they were staying in was so private, they could go for hours without seeing a soul.

"Maybe later. Okay?"

Joy twisted her lips and stifled a sigh. There was definitely something up with him. The man did not turn down an opportunity to be naked together. "Is everything okay? Did you not enjoy your dinner?"

"Dinner was great. It's not your food, but it was really, really good. And I'm fine. I just have a lot on my mind."

"Did your dad call you or something?"

Alex shook his head and they resumed their walk, ankle deep in the warm and tranquil water. As the sky darkened, the moon came into view, casting a moody glow. "No. I haven't dared turn on my phone. I'm here to enjoy my time with you and nothing else."

"Good. I'm glad." She felt a little better now, but only a fraction. There was still an awkward silence between them, which was not their normal dynamic. Usually, the words flowed freely. Maybe she just needed to come out with it. Tell him what was going on. Maybe that uncomfortable feeling was coming all from her. "I have something to tell you," she blurted out, surprising even herself.

Alex came to a stop. "I have something to tell you."

Oh. Was that good? Or bad? "Do you want to go first?"

"You said it first. You can go."

She sucked in a deep breath. *Here goes nothing.* "Okay—"

"Wait." He shook his head. "I'm really sorry, but the thing I have to say has literally been on the tip of my tongue all evening, and I just feel like I have to get it out or my head is going to explode."

Joy stood there, not knowing what to say. It wasn't like Alex to get flustered. "Yes. Of course."

He cleared his throat and looked at her. As beautiful as the moon was that night, his eyes put it to shame. She would've said something if the look on his face wasn't so pained and tortured. "You make me happy, Joy. Really happy. Are you happy?"

She almost laughed—wasn't the answer obvious? "Yes. Extremely."

"Okay, good." He took her other hand and then he did the most inexplicable thing—he dropped down on one knee. Which was odd enough in its own right, but they were still in the water, which meant he was now kneeling in the South Pacific. "Dammit. I didn't really plan this out very well, did I?"

Joy giggled nervously. Was this why he'd been so on edge? "It's my fault. I suggested we get our feet wet."

Alex shrugged and gazed up at her. "I'm down here, so I might as well just go with it." The most sincere smile she'd ever seen crossed his face. "I love you, Joy. And I'm happy and you're happy and I know that the world says we're supposed to be together for a few years before you go off and do something crazy like get married, but I think we should. If you want to." His vision narrowed on her. "Do you want to? Get married?"

Again, Joy wanted to laugh. Alex was so adorably out of his element right now. She also couldn't believe the timing. His question certainly segued well into her announcement. "Alex. I couldn't care less what anybody says about what we're supposed to do. We met because you nearly hit me with your car. I feel like the universe was telling us we belong together. Of course I will marry you. I love you more than anything."

Alex grinned like she'd never seen him do before, then let go of her one hand and reached into his pocket. "This is why I couldn't wear shorts. I needed bigger pockets." He opened the jewelry box and presented her with the sort of ring she never thought she'd get—a big sparkly diamond on a platinum band. Still, Alex was kneeling in the ocean and she could just imagine where this ring was going to end up if they weren't careful.

"Can I get my ring on dry land? I think it would be better."

"Yes. It's weird being in the ocean with your pants on." He clapped the ring box shut and stood, immediately planting a soft and steamy kiss on her lips. "You're sure?"

The tears she almost never shed? They were starting up. "Yes, I'm sure. One hundred percent."

Hand in hand, they walked up on shore, where he tried a second time with the ring. He took it from its velvet box and placed it on her finger. "Do you like it?"

She nodded, more fixated on him than on the ring, however beautiful it was. He was a miracle. And she was the luckiest woman in the world. "I love it."

He sighed and the perma-grin on his face grew even wider. "So what were you going to tell me?"

She still wasn't sure how to approach this. Alex had clearly been sweating the proposal. She wanted to give him his moment to bask in the sun. Still, there were no secrets between them anymore. She took his hand and flattened it against her belly. Not a word came from her lips as their gazes connected. The wonder that flickered in his eyes was everything she could've hoped for—such a pure and sweet reaction.

"You're pregnant?"

She nodded, choking back the tears, overwhelmed by the beauty of their surroundings, their perfect moment, her unbelievable man.

"But when? How?"

"I'm pretty sure we got pregnant that night the condom broke. Not that we weren't basically messing with the gods of contraception that whole time."

"True. I think we destroyed the margin for error." He laughed. "It's such amazing news."

She couldn't contain her smile. "I'm only about six weeks along. It's early. But I had to tell you as soon as I was sure."

He pulled her into his arms and kissed her forehead, then her cheek, and finally, her lips. "A baby. I'm going to be a dad. You're going to be a mom." He ran his hand through his hair. "You know what? You are going to be the best mom."

Good Lord, she was going to perish from Alex's sweetness. "And you're going to be the best dad."

He put his arm around her shoulders and they started walking back to their bungalow. Each step felt different now, like they were walking toward their happy future. "My only question is this," he said. "At what point do we teach our child how to bake scones?"

* * * * *

A BEAUMONT
CHRISTMAS
WEDDING

SARAH M. ANDERSON

To Fiona Marsden, Kelli Bruns and Jenn Hoopes – three of the nicest Twitter friends around. Thanks, ladies! You guys rock!

<u>One</u>

Matthew Beaumont looked at his email in amazement. The sharks were circling. He'd known they would be, but still, the sheer volume of messages clamoring for more information was impressive. There were emails from *TMZ, Perez Hilton* and PageSix.com, all sent in the past twenty minutes.

They all wanted the same thing. Who on earth was Jo Spears, the lucky woman who was marrying into the Beaumont family and fortune? And why had playboy Phillip Beaumont, Matthew's brother, chosen her—a woman no one had ever heard of before—when he could have had his pick of supermodels and Hollywood starlets?

Matthew rubbed his temples. The truth was actually quite boring—Jo Spears was a horse trainer who'd spent the past ten years training some of the most expensive horses in the world. There wasn't much there that would satisfy the gossip sites.

But if the press dug deeper and made the connection between Jo Spears, horse trainer, and Joanna Spears, they might dig up the news reports about a drunk-driving accident a decade ago in which Joanna was the passenger—and the driver died. They might turn up a lot of people who'd partied with Joanna.

They might turn this wedding into a circus.

His email pinged. *Vanity Fair* had gotten back to him. He scanned the email. Excellent. They would send a photographer if he invited their reporter as a guest.

Matthew knew the only way to keep this Beaumont wedding—planned for Christmas Eve—from becoming a circus was to control the message. He had to fight fire with fire and if that meant embedding the press into the wedding itself, then so be it.

Yes, it was great that Phillip was getting married. For the first time in his life, Matthew was hopeful his brother was going to be all right. But for Matthew, this wedding meant so much more than just the bonds of holy matrimony for his closest brother.

This wedding was the PR opportunity of a lifetime. Matthew had to show the world that the Beaumont family wasn't falling apart or flaming out.

God knew there'd been enough rumors to that effect after Chadwick Beaumont had sold the Beaumont Brewery and married his secretary, which had been about the same time that Phillip had very publically fallen off the wagon and wound up in rehab. And that didn't even include what his stepmothers and half siblings were doing.

It had been common knowledge that the Beaumonts, once the preeminent family of Denver, had fallen so far down that they'd never get back up.

To hell with common knowledge.

This was Matthew's chance to prove himself—not just in the eyes of the press but in his family's eyes, too. He'd show them once and for all that he wasn't the illegitimate child who was too little, too late a Beaumont. He was one of them, and this was his chance to erase the unfortunate circumstances of his birth from everyone's mind.

A perfectly orchestrated wedding and reception would show the world that instead of crumbling, the Beaumonts were stronger than ever. And it was up to Matthew, the former vice president of Public Relations for the Beaumont Brewery and the current chief marketing officer of Percheron Drafts Beer, to make that happen.

Building buzz was what Matthew did best. He was the only one in the family who had the media contacts and the PR savvy to pull this off.

Control the press, control the world—that's how a Beaumont handles it.

Hardwick Beaumont's words came back to him. When Matthew had managed yet another scandal, his father had said that to him. It'd been one of the few times Hardwick had ever complimented his forgotten third son. One of the few times Hardwick had ever made Matthew feel as if he *was* a Beaumont, not the bastard he'd once been.

Controlling the press was something that Matthew had gotten exceptionally good at. And he wasn't about to drop the ball now. This wedding would prove not only that the Beaumonts still had a place in this world but that Matthew had a place in the family.

He could save the Beaumont reputation. He could save the Beaumonts. And in doing so, he could redeem himself.

He'd hired the best wedding planner in Denver. They'd booked the chapel on the Colorado Heights University campus and had invited two hundred guests to the wedding. The reception would be at the Mile High Station, with dinner for six hundred, and a team of Percherons would pull the happy couple in either a carriage or a sleigh, weather depending. They had the menu set, the cake ordered, the favors ready and the photographer on standby. Matthew had his family—all four of his father's ex-wives and all nine of his half brothers and sisters—promising to be on their best behavior.

The only thing he didn't have under his control was the bride and her maid of honor, a woman named Whitney Maddox.

Jo had said that Whitney was a horse breeder who lived

a quiet life in California, so Matthew didn't anticipate too much trouble from her. She was coming two weeks before the wedding and staying at the farm with Jo and Phillip. That way she could do all the maid-of-honor things—dress fittings and bachelorette parties, the lot of it. All of which had been preplanned by Matthew and the wedding planner, of course. There was no room for error.

The wedding had to be perfect. What mattered was showing the world that the Beaumonts were still a family. A *successful* family.

What mattered was Matthew proving that he was a legitimate Beaumont.

He opened a clean document and began to write his press release as if his livelihood depended on it.

Because it did.

Whitney pulled up in front of the building that looked as if it was three different houses stuck together. She would not be nervous about this—not about the two weeks away from her horses, about staying in a stranger's house for said two weeks or about the press that went with being in a Beaumont Christmas wedding. Especially that.

Of course, she knew who Phillip Beaumont was—didn't everyone? He was the handsome face of Beaumont Brewery—or had been, right up until his family had sold out. And Jo Spears was a dear friend—practically the best friend Whitney had. The only friend, really. Jo knew all about Whitney's past and just didn't care. And in exchange for that unconditional friendship, the least Whitney could do was suck it up and be Jo's maid of honor.

In the high-society wedding of the year. With hundreds of guests. And photographers. And the press. And…

Jo came out to greet her.

"You haven't changed a bit!" Whitney called as she shut her door. She shivered. December in Denver was an entirely different beast from December in California. "Except you're not wearing your hat!"

"I didn't wear the hat when we watched movies in your house, did I?" Jo wore a wide smile as she gave Whitney a brief hug. "How was the drive?"

"Long," Whitney admitted. "That's why I didn't bring anyone with me. I thought about bringing the horses, but it's just too cold up here for them to be in a trailer that long, and none of my dogs do well in the car."

She'd desperately wanted to bring Fifi, her retired greyhound, or Gater, the little mutt that was pug and…something. Those two were her indoor dogs, the ones that curled up next to her on the couch or on her lap and kept her company. But Fifi did not travel well and Gater didn't like to leave Fifi.

Animals didn't care who you were. They never read the headlines. It didn't matter to them if you'd accidentally flashed the paparazzi when you were nineteen or how many times you'd been arrested for driving while intoxicated. All that mattered to animals was that you fed them and rubbed their ears.

Besides, Whitney was on vacation. A vacation with a wedding in it, but still. She was going to see the sights in Denver and get her nails done and all sorts of fun things. It didn't seem fair to bring the dogs only to leave them in a bedroom most of the time.

Jo nodded as Whitney got her bags out of the truck. "Who's watching them?"

"Donald—you remember him, right? From the next ranch over?"

"The crusty old fart who doesn't watch TV?"

Jo and Whitney shared a look. In that moment, Whitney was glad she'd come. Jo understood her as no one else did.

Everyone else in the world thought Donald was borderline insane—a holdover hippie from the 1960s who'd done too much acid back in the day. He lived off the grid, talked about animals as if they were his brothers and discussed Mother Earth as if she were coming to dinner next week.

But that meant Donald wasn't tuned in to pop culture. Which also meant he didn't know who Whitney was—who she'd been. Donald just thought Whitney was the neighbor who really should install more solar panels on her barn roof. And if she had to occasionally listen to a lecture on composting toilets, well, that was a trade-off she was willing to make.

She was going to miss her animals, but knowing Donald, he was probably sitting on the ground in the paddock, telling her horses bedtime stories.

Besides, being part of her best friend's wedding was an opportunity even she couldn't pass up. "What's this I hear about you and Phillip Beaumont?"

Jo smiled. "Come on," she said, grabbing one of Whitney's bags. "Dinner will be in about an hour. I'll get you caught up."

She led Whitney inside. The whole house was festooned—there was no other word for it—with red bows and pine boughs. A massive tree, blinking with red-and-white lights, the biggest star Whitney had ever seen perched on top, stood in a bay window. The whole place had such a rustic Christmas charm that Whitney felt herself grinning. This would be a perfect way to spend Christmas, instead of watching *It's a Wonderful Life* on the couch at home.

A small brown animal with extremely long ears clomped up to her and sniffed. "Well, hello again, Betty," Whitney said as she crouched down onto her heels. "You remember me? You spent a few months sitting on my couch last winter."

The miniature donkey sniffed Whitney's hair and brayed before rubbing her head into Whitney's hands.

"If I recall correctly," Jo said, setting down Whitney's bag, "your pups didn't particularly care for a donkey in the house."

"Not particularly," Whitney agreed. Fifi hadn't minded

as long as Betty stayed off her bed, but Gater had taken it as a personal insult that Whitney had allowed a hoofed animal into the house. As far as Gater was concerned, hoofed animals belonged in the barn.

She stood. Betty leaned against her legs so that Whitney could stroke her long ears.

"You're not going to believe this," Jo said as she moved Whitney's other bag, "but Matthew wants her to walk down the aisle. He's rigged up a basket so she can carry the flower petals and it's got a pillow attached on top so she can carry the rings. The flower girl will walk beside her and throw the petals. He says it'll be an amazing visual."

Whitney blinked. "Wait—Matthew? I thought you were marrying Phillip?"

"She is." A blindingly handsome man strode into the room—tall and blond and instantly recognizable. "Hello," he said with a grin as he walked up to Whitney. He leaned forward, his eyes fastened on hers, and stuck out a hand. "I'm Phillip Beaumont."

The Phillip Beaumont. Having formerly been someone famous, Whitney was not prone to getting starstruck. But Phillip was looking at her so intently that for a moment, she forgot her own name.

"And you must be Whitney Maddox," he went on, effortlessly filling the silence. "Jo's told me about the months she spent with you last winter. She said you raise some of the most beautiful Trakehners she's ever worked with."

"Oh. Yes!" Whitney shook her head. Phillip was a famous horseman and her Trakehner horses were a remarkably safe subject. "Joy was mine—Pride and Joy."

"The stallion who took gold in the World Equestrian Games?" Phillip smiled down at her and she realized he still had her hand. "I don't have any Trakehners. Clearly that's something I need to rectify."

She looked at Jo, feeling helpless and more than a little

guilty that Jo's intended was making her blush. But Jo just laughed.

"Too much," Jo said to Phillip as she looped her arm through his. "Whitney's not used to that much charm." She looked at Whitney. "Sorry about that. Phillip, this is Whitney. Whitney, this is Phillip."

Whitney nodded, trying to remember the correct social interaction. "It's a pleasure. Congratulations on getting married."

Phillip grinned at her, but then he thankfully focused that full-wattage smile on Jo. "Thanks."

They stared at each other for a moment, the adoration obvious. Whitney looked away.

It'd been a long time since a man had looked at her like that. And, honestly, she couldn't be sure that Drako Evans had ever looked at her quite like that. Their short-lived engagement hadn't been about love. It had been about pissing off their parents. And it had worked. The headlines had been spectacular. Maybe that was why those headlines still haunted her.

As she rubbed Betty's ears, Whitney noticed the dinner table was set for four. For the first time since she'd arrived, she smelled food cooking. Lasagna and baking bread. Her stomach rumbled.

"So," Phillip said into the silence. His piercing blue eyes turned back to her. "Matthew will be here in about forty minutes for dinner."

Which did nothing to answer the question she'd asked Jo earlier. "Matthew is...who?"

This time, Phillip's grin was a little less charming, a little sharper. "Matthew Beaumont. My best man and younger brother."

Whitney blinked. "Oh?"

"He's organizing the wedding," Phillip went on as if that were no big deal.

"He's convinced that this is the PR event of the year," Jo said. "I told him I'd be happy getting married by a judge—"

"Or running off to Vegas," Phillip added, wrapping his arm around Jo's waist and pulling her into a tight embrace.

"But he insists this big wedding is the Beaumont way. And since I'm going to be a Beaumont now…" Jo sighed. "He's taken control of this and turned it into a spectacle."

Whitney stared at Jo and Phillip, unsure what to say. The Jo she knew wouldn't let anyone steamroll her into a grandiose wedding.

"But," Jo went on, softening into a smile that could almost be described as shy, "it's going to be amazing. The chapel is beautiful and we'll have a team of Percherons pulling a carriage from there to the reception. The photographer is experienced and the dress…" She got a dreamy look in her eyes. "Well, you'll see tomorrow. We have a dress fitting at ten."

"It sounds like it's going to be perfect," Whitney said. And she meant it—a Christmas Eve ceremony? Horse-drawn carriages? Gowns? It had all the trappings of a true storybook wedding.

"It better be." Phillip chuckled.

"Let me show you to your room," Jo said, grabbing a bag.

That sounded good to Whitney. She needed a moment to sort through everything. She lived a quiet life now, one where she didn't have to navigate family relations or PR events masquerading as weddings. As long as she didn't leave her ranch, all she worried about was catching Donald when he was on a soapbox.

Jo led her through the house, pointing out which parts were original, which wasn't much, and which parts had been added later, which was most of it. She showed Whitney the part that Phillip had added, the master suite with a hot tub on the deck.

Then the hall turned again and they were in a different part, built in the 1970s. This was the guest quarters, Jo told her. Whitney had a private bath and was far enough removed from the rest of the house that she wouldn't hear anything else.

Jo opened a door and flipped on the light. Whitney had half expected vintage '70s decor, but the room was done in cozy green-and-red plaids that made it look Christmassy. A bouquet of fresh pine and holly was arranged on the mantel over a small fireplace.

Jo walked over to it and flipped a switch. Flames jumped to life in the grate. "Phillip had automatic switches installed a few years ago," she explained. On the other side of the bed was a dresser. Jo said, "Extra blankets are in there. It's going to be a lot colder here than it is at your ranch."

"Good to know." Whitney set her bag down at the foot of the bed. The only other furniture in the room was a small table with an armchair next to it. The room looked like a great place to spend the winter. She felt herself relax a little bit. "So…you and Phillip?"

"Me and Phillip," Jo agreed, sounding as though she didn't quite believe it herself. "He's—well, you've seen him in action. He has a way of just looking at a woman that's… *suggestive*."

"So I wasn't imagining that?"

Jo laughed. "Nope. That's just how he is."

This did nothing to explain how, exactly, Jo had wound up with Phillip. Of all the men in the world, Whitney would have put "playboy bachelor" pretty low on the list of possible husbands for Jo. But Whitney had no idea how to ask the question without it coming out wrong.

It could be that the Phillip in the kitchen wasn't the same as the Phillip in the headlines. Maybe things had been twisted and turned until nothing but the name was the same. More than anyone, Whitney knew how that worked.

"He has a horse," Jo explained, looking sheepish. "Sun— Kandar's Golden Sun."

Whitney goggled at her. "Wait—I've heard of that horse. Didn't he sell for seven million dollars?"

"Yup. And he was a hot mess at any price," she added with a chuckle. "Took me a week before he'd just stand still, you know?"

Whitney nodded, trying to picture a horse *that* screwed up. When Jo had come out to Whitney's ranch to deal with Sterling, the horse of hers that had developed an irrational fear of water, it'd taken her only a few hours in the paddock before the horse was rubbing his head against Jo. "A whole week?"

"Any other horse would have died of sheer exhaustion, but that's what makes Sun special. I can take you down to see him after dinner. He's an amazing stud—one to build a stable on."

"So the horse brought you together?"

Jo nodded. "I know Phillip's got a reputation—that's part of why Matthew insists we have this big wedding, to show the world that Phillip's making a commitment. But he's been sober for seven months now. We'll have a sober coach on hand at the reception." A hint of a blush crept over Jo's face. "If you'd like…"

Whitney nodded. She wasn't the only one who was having trouble voicing her concerns. "I don't think there's going to be a problem. I've been clean for almost eleven years." She swallowed. "Does Phillip know who I am?"

"Sure." Jo's eyebrow notched up in challenge. "You're Whitney Maddox, the well-known horse breeder."

"No, not that. I mean—well, you know what I mean."

"He knows," Jo said, giving Whitney the look that she'd seen Jo give Donald the hippie when he gave her a lecture on how she should switch to biodiesel. "But we understand that the past is just that—the past."

"Oh." Air rushed out of her so fast she actually sagged

in relief. "That's good. That's *great*. I just don't want to be a distraction—this is your big day."

"It won't be a problem," Jo said in a reassuring voice. "And you're right—the day will be very big!"

They laughed. It felt good to laugh with Jo again. She hadn't had to stay a whole two months with Whitney last year—Sterling hadn't been that difficult to handle—but the two of them had gotten along because they understood that the past was just that. So Jo had stayed through the slow part of the year and taught Whitney some of her training techniques. It'd been a good two months. For the first time in her adult life, Whitney hadn't felt quite so...alone.

And now she'd get that feeling again for two weeks.

"And you're happy?" That was the important question.

Jo's features softened. "I am. He's a good man who had an interesting life—to say the least. He's learned how to deal with his family with all that charm. He wasn't hitting on you—that's just how he copes with situations that make him nervous."

"Really? He must have an, um, unusual family."

Jo laughed again. "I'll just say this—they're a lot to handle, but on the whole, they're not bad people. Like Matthew. He can be a little controlling, but he really does want what's best for the family and for us." She stood. "I'll let you get freshened up. Matthew should be here in a few."

"Sounds good."

Jo shut the door on her way out, leaving Whitney alone with her thoughts. She was glad she'd come.

This was what she wanted—to feel normal. To *be* normal. To be able to walk into a room and not be concerned with what people thought they knew about her. Instead, to have people, like Phillip, take her at face value and make her feel welcome.

And he had a brother who was coming to dinner.

What did Matthew Beaumont look like? More to the

point, what did he act like? Brothers could like a lot of the same things, right?

What if Matthew Beaumont looked at her the way his brother did, without caring about who she'd been in the past? What if he talked to her about horses instead of headlines? What if—? What if he wasn't involved with anyone?

Whitney didn't hook up. That part of her life was dead and buried. But…a little Christmas romance between the maid of honor and the best man wouldn't be such a bad thing, would it? It could be fun.

She hurried to the bathroom, daring to hope that this Matthew Beaumont was single. He was coming to dinner tonight and it sounded as if he would be involved with a lot of the planned activities. She was here for two weeks. Perhaps the built-in time limit was a good thing. That way, if things didn't go well, she had an out—she could go home.

Although…it had been eleven years since she'd attempted anything involving the opposite sex. Making a pass at the best man might not be the smartest thing she could do.

She washed her face. A potential flirtation with Matthew Beaumont called for eyeliner, at the very least. Whitney made up her face and decided to put on a fresh top. She dug out the black silk before putting it aside. Jo was in jeans and flannel, after all. This was not a fancy dinner. Whitney decided to go with the red V-neck cashmere sweater—soft but not ostentatious. The kind of top that maybe a single, handsome man would accidentally brush with his fingers. Perfect.

Would Matthew be blond, like Phillip? Would he have the same smile, the same blue eyes? She was brushing out her short hair when, from deep inside the house, a bell chimed.

She slicked on a little lip gloss and headed out. She tried to retrace her steps, but she got confused. The house had a bunch of hallways that went in different directions. She tried one set of stairs but found a door that was locked at the bottom. That wasn't right—Jo hadn't led her through a door.

She backtracked, trying not to panic. Hopefully, everyone wasn't downstairs waiting on her.

She found another stairwell, but it didn't seem any more familiar than the first one had. It ended in a darkened room. Whitney decided to go back rather than stumble around in the dark. God, she shouldn't have spent so much time getting ready. She should have gone back down with Jo. Or gotten written directions. Getting lost was embarrassing.

She found her room again, which had to count for something. She went the opposite direction and was relieved when she passed the master suite. Finally. She picked up the pace. Maybe she wasn't too late.

She could hear voices now—Jo's and Phillip's and another voice, deep and strong. Matthew.

She hurried down the steps, then remembered she was trying to make a good impression. It wouldn't do to come rushing in like a tardy teenager. She needed to slow down to make a proper entrance.

She slammed on the brakes in the middle of a step near the bottom and stumbled. Hard. She tripped down the last two steps and all but fell into the living room. She was going down, damn it! She braced for the impact.

It didn't come. Instead of hitting the floor or running into a piece of furniture, she fell into a pair of strong arms and against a firm, warm chest.

"Oof," the voice that went with that chest said.

Whitney looked up into a pair of eyes that were a deep blue. He smiled down at her and this time, she didn't feel as if she were going to forget her own name. She felt as if she'd never forget this moment.

"I've got you."

Not blond, she realized. Auburn hair. A deep red that seemed just right on him. And he did have her. His arms were around her waist and he was lifting her up. She felt secure. The feeling was *wonderful*.

Then, without warning, everything changed. His warm smile froze as his eyes went hard. The strong arms became iron bars around her and the next thing she knew, she was being pushed not up but away.

Matthew Beaumont set her back on her feet and stepped clear of her. With a glare that could only be described as ferocious, he turned to Phillip and Jo.

"What," he said in the meanest voice Whitney had heard in a long time, "is Whitney Wildz doing here?"

Two

Matthew waited for an answer. It'd better be a damn good one, too. What possible explanation could there be for former teen star Whitney Wildz to be in Phillip's house?

"Matthew," Jo said in an icy tone, "I'd like you to meet my maid of honor, Whitney Maddox."

"Try to stop being an ass," Phillip said under his breath.

"Whitney," Jo went on, as if Phillip hadn't spoke, "this is Matthew Beaumont, Phillip's brother and best man."

"Maddox?" He turned back to the woman who looked as though she'd been stepped on by a Percheron. At least they could all agree her first name was Whitney. Maybe there was a mistake? But no. There was no missing that white streak in her hair or those huge pale eyes set against her alabaster skin. "You're Whitney Wildz. I'd recognize you anywhere."

Her eyes closed and her head jerked to the side as if he'd slapped her.

Someone grabbed him. "Try *harder*," Phillip growled in his ear. Then, louder, Phillip said, "Dinner's ready. Whitney, is iced tea all right?"

Whitney Wildz—Matthew had no doubt that was who she was—opened her eyes. A wave of pain washed over him when she looked up at him. Then she drew herself up.

"Thank you," she said in that breathy way of hers. Then she stepped around him.

Memories came back to him. He'd watched her show, *Growing Up Wildz*, all the time with his younger siblings Frances and Byron. Because Matthew was a good brother—the best—he'd watched it with them. He'd even scored VIP tickets to the *Growing Up Wildz* concert tour when it came through Denver and taken the twins, since their father couldn't be bothered to remember that it was their fifteenth birthday. Matthew was a good brother just taking care of his siblings. That was what he told everyone else.

But that wasn't, strictly, the truth.

He'd watched it for Whitney.

And now Whitney was here.

This was *bad*. This was quite possibly the worst thing that could have happened to this wedding—to him. It would have been easier if Phillip were screwing her. That sort of thing was easy to hush up—God knew Matthew had enough practice covering for his father's indiscretions.

But to have Whitney Wildz herself standing up at the altar, in front of the press and the photographers—not to mention the guests?

He tried to remember the last time she'd been in the news. She'd stumbled her way up on stage and then tripped into the podium, knocking it off the dais and into a table. The debate hadn't been about *if* she'd been on something, just *what*—drugs? Alcohol? Both?

And then tonight she'd basically fallen down the stairs and into his arms. He hadn't minded catching a beautiful woman at the time. The force of her fall had pressed her body against his and what had happened to him was some sort of primal response that had taken control of his body before he'd realized it.

Mine, was the only coherent thought he'd managed to produce as he'd kept her on her feet. Hell, yeah, he'd responded. He was a man, after all.

But then he'd recognized her.

What was she on? And what would happen if she stumbled her way down the aisle?

This was a disaster of epic PR proportions. This woman was going to mess up all of his plans. And if he couldn't pull off this wedding, would he ever be able to truly call himself a Beaumont?

Phillip jerked him toward the table. "For the love of everything holy," he hissed in Matthew's ear, "be a gentleman."

Matthew shook him off. He had a few things he'd like to say to his brother and his future sister-in-law. "Why didn't you tell me?" he half whispered back at Phillip. "Do you know what this *means* for the wedding?"

On the other side of the room, Jo was at the fridge, getting the iced tea. Whitney stood next to her, head down and arms tucked around her slender waist.

For a second, he felt bad. Horrible, actually. The woman who stood thirty feet away from where he and Phillip were didn't look much like Whitney Wildz. Yes, she had Whitney's delicate bone structure and sweetheart face and yes, she had the jet-black hair with the telltale white streak in it. But her hair was cut into a neat pixie—no teased perm with blue and pink streaks. Her jeans and sweater fit her well and were quite tasteful—nothing like the ripped jeans and punk-rock T-shirts she'd always worn on the show. And she certainly wasn't acting strung out.

If it hadn't been for her face—and those pale green eyes, like polished jade, and that hair—he might not have recognized her.

But he did. Everything about him did.

"It means," Phillip whispered back, "that Jo's friend is here for the wedding. Whitney Maddox—she's a respected horse breeder. You will knock this crap off now or I'll—"

"You'll *what*? You haven't been able to beat me up since we were eight and you know it." Matthew tensed. He had a scant half inch on Phillip but he'd long ago learned to make the most of it.

Phillip grinned at him. It was not a kind thing on his face. "I'll turn Jo loose on you and trust me, buddy, that's a fate worse than death. Now knock it off and act like a decent human being."

There was something wrong about this. For so long, Matthew had been the one who scolded Phillip to straighten up and fly right. Phillip had been the one who didn't know how to act in polite company, who'd always found the most embarrassing thing to say and then said it. And it'd been Matthew who'd followed behind, cleaning up the messes, dealing with the headlines and soothing the ruffled feathers. That was what he did.

Briefly, Matthew wanted to be proud of his brother. He'd finally grown up.

But as wonderful as that was, it didn't change the fact that Whitney Wildz was not only going to be sitting down for dinner with them tonight, but she was also going to be in the Beaumont wedding.

He would have to rethink his entire strategy.

"Dinner," Jo called out. She sounded unnaturally perky about it. There was something odd about Jo being perky. It did nothing to help his mood.

"I really wish you had some beer in the house," he muttered to Phillip.

"Tough. Welcome to sobriety." Phillip led the way back to the table.

Matthew followed, trying to come up with a new game plan. He had a couple of options that he could see right off the bat. He could go with denial, just as Phillip and Jo seemed to be doing. This was Whitney Maddox. He had no knowledge of Whitney Wildz.

But that wasn't a good plan and he knew it. He'd recognized her, after all. Someone else was bound to do the same and the moment that someone did, it'd be all over. Yes, the list of celebrities who were attending this wedding was long but someone as scandalous as Whitney Wildz would create a stir no matter what she did.

He could go on the offensive. Send out a press release announcing that Whitney Wildz was the maid of honor. Hit the criticism head-on. If he did it early enough, he might defuse the situation—make it a nonissue by the big day. It could work.

Or it could blow up in his face. This wedding was about showing the world that the Beaumonts were above scandal—that they were stronger than ever. How was that going to happen now? Everything Whitney Wildz did was a scandal.

He took his seat. Whitney sat to his left, Phillip to his right. Jo's ridiculous little donkey sat on the floor in between him and Whitney. Good. Fine. At least he didn't have to look at Whitney, he reasoned. Just at Jo.

Who was not exactly thrilled with him. Phillip was right—Matthew was in no mood to have Jo turned loose on him. So he forced his best fake smile—the one he used when he was defusing some ticking time bomb created by one of his siblings. It always worked when he was talking to reporters.

He glanced at Phillip and then at Jo. Damn. The smile wasn't working on them.

He could *feel* Whitney sitting next to him. He didn't like that. He didn't want to be aware of her like that. He wasn't some teenager anymore, crushing in secret. He was a grown man with real problems.

Her.

But Phillip was staring daggers at him, and Jo looked as though she was going to stab him with the butter knife. So Matthew dug deep. He could be a gentleman. He could put on the Beaumont face no matter what. Being able to talk to a woman was part of the Beaumont legacy—a legacy he'd worked too hard to make his own. He wasn't about to let an unexpected blast from his past undermine everything he'd worked for. This wedding was about proving his legitimacy and that was that.

Phillip glared at him. Right. The wedding was about Phillip and Jo, too. And now their maid of honor.

God, what a mess.

"So, Whitney," Matthew began. She flinched when he said her name. He kept his voice pleasant and level. "What are you doing these days?"

Jo notched an eyebrow at him as she served the lasagna. *Hey,* he wanted to tell her. *I'm trying.*

Whitney smiled, but it didn't reach her eyes. "I raise horses." She took a piece of bread and passed the basket to him. She made sure not to touch him when she did it.

"Ah." That wasn't exactly a lot to go on, but it did explain how she and Jo knew each other, he guessed.

When Whitney didn't offer any other information, he asked, "What kind of horses?"

"Trakehners."

Matthew waited, but she didn't elaborate.

"One of her horses won gold in the World Equestrian Games," Phillip said. He followed up this observation with a swift kick to Matthew's shin.

Ow. Matthew grunted in pain but he managed not to curse out loud. "That's interesting."

"It's amazing," Phillip said. "Not even Dad could breed or buy a horse that took home gold." He leaned forward, turned on the Beaumont smile and aimed it squarely at Whitney.

Something flared in Matthew. He didn't like it when Phillip smiled at her like that.

"Trust me," Phillip continued, "he tried. Not winning

gold was one of his few failures as a horseman. That and not winning a Triple Crown."

Whitney cut Matthew a look out of the corner of her eye that hit him funny. Then she turned her attention to Phillip. "No one's perfect, right?"

"Not even Hardwick Beaumont," he agreed with a twinkle in his eye. "It turns out there are just some things money can't buy."

Whitney grinned. Suddenly, Matthew wanted to punch his brother—hard. This was normal enough—this was how Phillip talked to women. But seeing Whitney warm to him?

Phillip glanced at Matthew. *Be a gentleman*, he seemed to be saying. "Whitney's Trakehners are beautiful, highly trained animals. She's quite well-known in horse circles."

Whitney Wildz was well-known in horse circles? Matthew didn't remember any mention of that from the last article he'd read about her. Only that she'd made a spectacle of herself.

"How long have you been raising horses?"

"I bought my ranch eleven years ago." She focused her attention on her food. "After I left Hollywood."

So she really was Whitney Wildz. But…eleven years? That didn't seem right. It couldn't have been more than two years since the last headline.

"Where is your ranch?"

If Matthew had known who she really was, he would have done more digging. Be Prepared wasn't just a good Boy Scout motto—it was vital to succeeding in public relations.

One thing was abundantly clear. Matthew was not prepared for Whitney, whatever her last name was.

"Not too far from Bakersfield. It's very…quiet there."

Then she gazed up at him again. The look in her eyes stunned him—desperate for approval. He knew that look—he saw it in the mirror every morning.

Why would she want his approval? She was Whitney

Wildz, for crying out loud. She'd always done what she wanted, when she wanted—consequences be damned.

Except...nothing about her said she was out of control—except for the way she'd fallen into his arms.

His first instinct had been to hold her—to protect her. To claim her as his. What if...?

No.

There was no "what if" about this. His first duty was to his family—to making sure this wedding went off without a hitch. To making sure everyone knew that the Beaumonts were still in a position of power. To making sure he proved himself worthy of his father's legacy.

At the very least, he could be a gentleman about it.

"That's beautiful country," he said. Compliments were an important part of setting a woman at ease. If he were smart, he would have remembered that in the first place. "Your ranch must be lovely."

A touch of color brightened her cheeks. His stomach tensed. *She* was beautiful, he realized. Not the punk-rock hot she'd been back when he'd watched her show, but something delicate and ethereal.

Mine.

The word kept popping up in his head, completely unbidden. Which was ridiculous because the only thing Whitney was to him was a roadblock.

Phillip kicked him again. *Stop staring*, he mouthed at Matthew.

Matthew shook his head. He hadn't realized he was staring.

"Matthew, maybe we should discuss some of the wedding plans?" Jo said it nicely enough but there was no mistaking that question for an order.

"Of course," he agreed. The wedding. He needed to stay on track here. "We have an appointment with the seamstress tomorrow at ten. Jo, it's your final fitting. Whitney, we ordered your dress according to the measurements you sent in, but we've blocked out some additional time in case it requires additional fittings."

"That sounds fine," she said in a voice that almost sounded casual.

"Saturday night is the bachelorette party. I have a list of places that would be an appropriate location for you to choose from."

"I see," she said. She brushed her hand through her hair. He fought the urge to do the same.

What was wrong with him? Seriously—*what* was wrong with him? He went from attracted to her to furious at everyone in the room and now he wanted to, what—stroke her hair? Claim her? Jesus, these were exactly the sort of impulses he'd always figured had ruled Phillip. The ones that had ruled their father. See a beautiful woman, act on the urge to sweep her off her feet. To hell with anything else.

Matthew needed to regain control of the situation—of himself—and fast.

"We'll need to get the shoes and jewelry squared away. We need to get you in to the stylist before then to decide how to deal with your hair, so we'll do that after the dress fitting." He waited, but she didn't say anything.

So he went on. "The rehearsal dinner is Tuesday night. Then the wedding is Christmas Eve, of course." A week and a half—that didn't leave him much time to deal with the disruption of Whitney Wildz. "The ladies will get manicures that morning before they get their hair done. Then we'll start with the photographs."

Whitney cleared her throat—but she still didn't meet his gaze. "Who else is in the wedding party?"

He wanted her to look at him—he wanted to get lost in her eyes. "Our older brother Chadwick will be walking with his wife, Serena. Frances and Byron will be walking together—they're twins, five years younger than I am." For a second,

Matthew had almost said *we*—as in he and Phillip. Because he and Phillip were only six months apart.

But he didn't want to bring his father's infidelity into this conversation, because that meant Whitney would know that he was the second choice, the child his father had never really loved. Or even acknowledged, for that matter. So he said *I*.

"That just leaves the two of us," he added, suddenly very interested in his plate. How was he going to keep this primal urge to haul her off under control if they were paired up for the wedding?

He could not let her distract him from his goals, no matter how much he wanted to. He had to pull this off—to prove that he was a legitimate Beaumont. Ravishing the maid of honor did not fall anywhere on his to-do list.

"Ah." He looked up when he heard her chair scrape against the floor. She stood and, without looking at him, said, "I'm a little tired from the drive. If you'll excuse me." Jo started to stand, but Whitney waved her off. "I think I can find my way."

Then she was gone, walking in a way that he could only describe as graceful. She didn't stumble and she didn't fall. She walked in a straight line for the stairs.

Several moments passed after she disappeared up the stairs. No one seemed willing to break the tense silence. Finally, Matthew couldn't take it anymore.

"What the *hell*? Why is Whitney Wildz your maid of honor and why didn't either of you see fit to tell me in advance? Jesus, if I'd known, I would have done things differently. Do you have any idea what the press will do when they find out?"

It was easier to focus on how this was going to screw up the wedding than on how his desire was on the verge of driving him mad.

"Gosh, I don't know. You think they'll make a big deal out of stuff that happened years ago and make Whitney feel like crap?" Phillip shot back. "You're right. That would really suck."

"Hey—this is not my fault. You guys sprung this on me."

"I believe," Jo said in a voice so icy it brought the temperature of the room down several degrees, "I told you I was asking Whitney Maddox to be my maid of honor. Whitney Wildz is a fictional character in a show that was canceled almost thirteen years ago. If you can't tell the difference between a real woman and a fictional teenager, then that's *your* problem, not hers."

"It *is* my problem," he got out through gritted teeth. "You can't tell me that's all in the past. What about the headlines?"

Phillip rolled his eyes. "Because everything the press prints is one hundred percent accurate, huh? I thought you, of all people, would know how the headlines can be manipulated."

"She's a normal person," Jo said. Instead of icy, though, she was almost pleading. "I retrained one of her horses and we got to spend time together last winter. She's a little bit of a klutz when she gets nervous but that's it. She's going to be fine."

"If *you* can treat her like a normal person," Phillip added. "Man—I thought you were this expert at reading people and telling them what they wanted to hear. What happened? Hit your head this morning or something?"

Matthew sat there, feeling stupid. Hell, he wasn't just feeling stupid—he *was* stupid. His first instinct had been to protect her. He should have stuck with it. He could do that without giving in to his desire to claim her, right?

Right. He was in control of his emotions. He could keep up a wall between the rest of the world and himself. He was good at it.

Then he made the mistake of glancing at that silly donkey, who gave him a baleful look of reproach. Great. Even the donkey was mad at him.

"I should apologize to her."

Phillip snorted. "You think?"

Damn it, he felt like a jerk. It didn't come naturally to him. Chadwick was the one who could be a royal pain simply because he wasn't clued in to the fact that most people had actual feelings. Phillip used to be an ass all the time because he was constantly drunk and horny. Matthew was the one who smoothed ruffled feathers and calmed everyone down.

Phillip was right. Matthew hadn't been reading the woman next to him. He'd been too busy thinking about old headlines and new lust to realize that she might want his approval.

"Which room is she in?"

Jo and Phillip shared a look before Phillip said, "Yours."

Three

Whitney found her room on the first try and shut the door behind her.

Well. So much for her little fantasy about a Christmas romance. She doubted that Matthew would have been less happy to see her if she'd thrown up on his shoes.

She flopped down on her bed and decided that she would not cry. Even though it was really tempting, she wouldn't. She'd learned long ago this was how it went, after all. People would treat her just fine until they recognized her and then? All bets were off. Once she'd been outed as Whitney Wildz, she might as well give up on normal. There was no going back.

She'd thought for a moment there she might get to do something ordinary—have a little Christmas romance between the maid of honor and the best man. But every time she got it in her foolish little head that she could be whoever she wanted to be…well, this was what would happen.

The thing was, she didn't even blame Matthew. Since he recognized her so quickly, that could only mean that he'd read some of the more recent headlines. Like the last time she'd tried to redeem Whitney Wildz by lending her notoriety to the Bakersfield Animal Shelter's annual fund-raising gala dinner. She'd been the keynote speaker—or would have been if she hadn't gotten the fancy Stuart Weitzman shoes she'd bought just for the occasion tangled up in the microphone cords on her way up to the podium.

The headlines had been unforgiving.

Whitney shivered. Boy, this was going to be a long, *cold* two weeks.

As she was getting up to turn her fireplace back on, she heard it—a firm knock.

Her brain diverted all energy from her legs to the question of who was on the other side of that door—Jo or a Beaumont?—and she tripped into the door with an audible *whump*.

Oh, for the love of everything holy. Just once—once!—she'd like to be able to walk and chew gum at the same time. She could sing and play the guitar simultaneously. She could do complicated dressage moves on the back of a one-ton animal. Why couldn't she put one foot in front of the other?

She forced herself to take a deep breath just as a male voice on the other side of the door said, "Is everything all right in there, Miss…uh…Ms. Maddox?"

Matthew. Great. How could this get worse? Let her count the ways. Had he come to ask her to drop out of the wedding? Or just threaten her to be on her best behavior?

She decided she would not cower. Jo had asked her to be in the wedding. If Jo asked her to drop out, she would. Otherwise, she was in. She collected her thoughts and opened the door a crack. "Yes, fine. Thanks."

Then she made the mistake of looking at him. God, it wasn't fair. It just *wasn't*.

Matthew Beaumont was, physically, the perfect man to have a Christmas romance with. He had to be about six foot one, broad chested, and that chin? Those eyes? Even his deep red hair made him look distinctive. Striking.

Gorgeous.

Too darned bad he was an ass.

"Can I help you?" she asked, determined to be polite if it killed her. She would not throw a diva fit and prove him right. Even if there would be a certain amount of satisfaction in slamming the door in his face.

He gave her a grin that walked the fine line between awkward and cute. He might be even better-looking than his brother, but he appeared to possess none of the charm. "Look, Ms. Maddox—"

"Whitney."

"Oh. Okay. Whitney. We got off on the wrong foot and—"

She winced.

He paused. "*I* got off on the wrong foot. And I want to apologize to you." His voice was strong, exuding confidence. It made everything about him that much sexier.

She blinked at him. "What?"

"I jumped to conclusions when I realized who you were and I apologize for that." He waited for her to say something but she had nothing.

Was he serious? He looked serious. He wasn't biting back laughter or— She glanced down at his hands. They were tucked into the pockets of his gray wool trousers. No, he wasn't about to snap an awful photo of her to post online, either.

He pulled his hands from his pockets and held them at waist level, open palms up, as if he knew what she was thinking. "It's just that this wedding is incredibly important for rebuilding the public image of the Beaumont family and it's my job to make sure everyone stays on message."

"The…public image?" She leaned against the door, staring up at him. Maybe he wasn't a real man—far too handsome to be one. And he was certainly talking like a space alien. "I thought this was about Jo and Phillip getting married."

"That, too," he hurried to agree. This time, his smile was a little more charming, like something a politician might pull out when he needed to win an argument. "I just— Look. I just want to make sure that we don't make headlines for the wrong reason."

Embarrassment flamed down the back of her neck. She looked away. He was trying to be nice by saying *we* but they both knew that he meant *her*.

"I know you don't believe this, but I have absolutely no desire to make headlines. At all. Ever. If no one else recognized me for the rest of my life, that'd be super."

There was a moment of silence that was in danger of becoming painful. "Whitney..."

The way he said her name—soft and tender and almost reverent—dragged her eyes up to his. The look in his eyes hit her like a bolt out of, well, the blue. He had the most amazing eyes...

For that sparkling moment, it almost felt as if...as if he was going to say something that could be construed as romantic. Something that didn't make her feel as though the weight of this entire event were being carried on her shoulders.

She wanted to hear something that made her feel like Whitney Maddox—that being Whitney Maddox was a good thing. A great thing. And she wanted to hear that something come out of Matthew's mouth, in that voice that could melt away the chilly winter air. Desire seemed to fill the space between them.

She leaned toward him. She couldn't help it. At the same time, his mouth opened as one of his hands moved. Then, just as soon as the motion had started, it stopped. His mouth closed and he appeared to shake himself. "I'll meet you at the dress fitting tomorrow. To make sure everything's—"

"On message?"

He notched up an eyebrow. She couldn't tell if she'd offended him or amused him. Or both. "Perfect," he corrected. "I just want it to be perfect."

"Right." There would be no sweet words. If there was one thing she wasn't, it was perfect. "Will it just be you?"

He gave her a look that was surprisingly wounded. She couldn't help but grin at him, which earned her a smile that looked more...real, somehow. As though what had just passed between them was almost...flirting.

"No. The wedding planner will be joining us—and the seamstress and her assistants, of course."

"Of course." She leaned against the door. Were they flirting? Or was he charming her because that was what all Beaumonts did?

God, he was *so* handsome. He exuded raw power. She had no doubt that whatever he said went.

A man like him would be hard to resist.

"Tomorrow, then," she said.

"I look forward to it." He gave her a tight smile before he turned away. Just as she was shutting the door, he turned back. "Whitney," he said again in that same deep, confident and—she hoped—sincere voice. "It truly is a pleasure to meet you."

Then he was gone.

She shut the door.

Heavens. It was going to be a *very* interesting two weeks.

"So," Whitney began as they passed streetlights decorated like candy canes. The drive had, thus far, been quiet. "Who's on the guest list again?"

"The Beaumonts," Jo said with a sigh. "Hardwick Beaumont's four ex-wives—"

"Four?"

Jo nodded as she tapped on the steering wheel. "All nine of Phillip's siblings and half siblings will be there, although only the four he actually grew up with are in the wedding—Chadwick, Matthew, Frances and Byron."

Whitney whistled. "That's a *lot* of kids." Part of why she'd loved doing the show was that, for the first time, she'd felt as though she'd had a family, one with brothers and sisters and parents who cared about her. Even if it were all just pretend, it was still better than being the only child Jade Maddox focused on with a laserlike intensity.

But ten kids? *Dang.*

"And that doesn't count the illegitimate ones," Jo said in a conspiratorial tone. "Phillip says they know of three, but there could be more. The youngest is…nineteen, I think."

As much as she hated gossip… "Seriously? Did that man not know about condoms?"

"Didn't care," Jo said. "Between you and me, Hardwick Beaumont was an old-fashioned misogynist. Women were solely there for his entertainment. Anything else that happened was their problem, not his."

"Sounds like a real jerk."

"I understand he was a hell of a businessman, but…yeah. On the whole, his kids aren't that bad. Chadwick's a tough nut to crack, but his wife, Serena, balances him out really well. Phillip's… Well, Phillip's Phillip." She grinned one of those private grins that made Whitney blush. "Matthew can come on a bit strong but really, he's a good guy. He's just wound a bit tight. Very concerned with the family's image. It's like…he wants everything to be perfect."

"I noticed." Whitney knew she was talking about the coming-on-strong part, but her brain immediately veered back to when she'd stumbled into his arms. His strong arms.

And then there was the conversation they'd had—the private one. The one that could have been flirting. And the way he'd said her name…

"We're really sorry about last night," Jo repeated for about the fifteenth time.

"No worries," Whitney hurried to say. "He apologized."

"Matthew is…very good at what he does. He just needs to lighten up a little bit. Have some fun."

She wondered at that. Would fun be a part of this? The dinner had said no. But the conversation after? She had no idea. If only she weren't so woefully out of practice at flirting.

"I can still drop out," she said. "If that'll make it simpler."

Jo laughed—not an awkward sound, but one that was

truly humorous. "You're kidding, right? Did I mention the ex-wives? You know who else is going to be here?"

"No…"

"The crown prince of Belgravitas."

"You're kidding, right?" God, she hoped Jo was kidding. She didn't want to make a fool of herself in front of honest-to-God royalty.

"Nope. His wife, the princess Susanna, used to date Phillip."

"Get *out*."

"I'm serious. Drake—the rapper—will be there, as well. He and Phillip are friends. Jay Z and Beyoncé had a scheduling conflict, but—"

"Seriously?" It wasn't as though she didn't know that Phillip Beaumont was a famous guy—all those commercials, all those stories about parties he hosted at music festivals—but this was crazy.

"If you drop out," Jo went on, "who on earth am I going to get to replace you? Out of the two hundred people who'll be at the wedding and the six hundred who'll be at the reception, you know how many I invited? My parents, my grandma Lina, my uncle Larry and aunt Penny, and my parents' neighbors. Eleven people. That's it. That's all I have. And you."

Whitney didn't know what to say. She didn't want to do this, not after last night. But Jo was one of her few friends. Someone who didn't care about Whitney Wildz or *Growing Up Wildz* or even that horrible Christmas album she'd put out, *Whitney Wildz Sings Christmas, Yo.*

She didn't want to disappoint her friend.

"Honestly," Jo said, "there's going to be so many egos on display that I doubt people will even realize who you are. Don't take that the wrong way."

"I won't," Whitney said with a smile. She could do this. She could pull off normal for a few weeks. She couldn't compete with that guest list. She was just the maid of honor. Who would notice her, anyway? Besides Matthew, that was...

"And you're right. It won't be like that last fund-raiser."

"Exactly," Jo said, sounding encouraging. "You were the headliner there—of course people were watching you. Matthew only acted like he did because he's a perfectionist. I truly believe you'll be fine." She pulled into a parking lot. "It'll be fine."

"All right," Whitney agreed. She didn't quite believe the sentiment but she couldn't disappoint Jo. "It will be fine."

"Good."

They got out. Whitney stared at the facade of the Bridal Collection. This was it. Once she was in the dress, there was no backing out.

Oh, who was she kidding? There was no backing out anyway. Jo was right. They were the kind of people who didn't have huge social circles or celebrities on speed dial. They were horse people. She and Jo got along only because they both loved animals and they both had changed their ways.

"You're really having a wedding with Grammy winners and crown princes?"

"Yup," Jo said, shaking her head. "Honestly, though, it's not the over-the-top wedding that matters. It's the marriage. Besides," she added as they went inside, "David Guetta is going to be doing the music for the reception. How cool is that?"

"Pretty cool," Whitney agreed. She didn't recognize the name, but then, why would she? She wasn't famous anymore.

Maybe Jo was right. No one would care about her. She'd managed to stay out of the headlines for almost three years, after all—that was a lifetime in today's 24/7 news cycle. In that time, there'd been other former teen stars who'd grabbed much bigger headlines for much more scandalous reasons.

They walked into the boutique to find Matthew pacing between rows of frothy white dresses and decorations that were probably supposed to be Christmas trees but really looked more as though someone had dipped pipe cleaners in glitter. The whole place was so bright it made her eyes hurt.

Matthew—wearing dark gray trousers and a button-up shirt with a red tie under his deep green sweater—was so out of place that she couldn't *not* look at him. She wouldn't have thought it possible, but he looked even better today than he had the other night. As she appreciated all the goodness that was Matthew Beaumont, he looked up from his phone.

Their eyes met, and her breath caught in her throat. The warmth in his eyes, the curve to his lips, the arch in his eyebrow—heat flooded Whitney's cheeks. Was he happy to see her? Or was she misreading the signals?

Then he glanced at Jo. "Ladies," he said in that confident tone of his. It should have seemed wholly out of place in the midst of this many wedding gowns, but on him? "I was just about to call. Jo, they're waiting for you."

"Where's the wedding planner?" Whitney asked. If the planner wasn't here, then she and Jo weren't late. Late was being the last one in.

"Getting Jo's dress ready."

Dang. Whitney tried to give her friend a smile that was more confident than she actually felt. Jo threaded her way back through racks of dresses and disappeared into a room.

Then Whitney and Matthew were alone. Were they still almost flirting? Or were they back to where they'd been at dinner? If only she hadn't fallen into him. If only he hadn't recognized her. If only…

"Is there someone else who can help me try my dress on?"

"Jo's dress requires several people to get her into it," he said. Then he bowed and pointed the way. "Your things are in here."

"Thanks." She held her head high as she walked past him.

"You're welcome." His voice trickled over her skin like a cool stream of water on a too-hot day.

She stepped into a dressing room—thankfully, one with a door. Once she had that door shut, she sagged against it. That voice, that face were even better today than they'd been last night. Last night, he'd been trying to cover his surprise and anger. Today? Today he just looked happy to see her.

She looked at the room she'd essentially locked herself in. It was big enough for a small love seat and a padded ottoman. A raised dais stood in front of a three-way mirror.

And there, next to the mirrors, hung a dress. It was a beautiful dove-gray silk gown—floor length, of course. Sleeveless, with sheer gathered silk forming one strap on the left side. The hemline was flared so that it would flow when she walked down the aisle, no doubt.

It was stunning. Even back when she'd walked the red carpet, she'd never worn a dress as sophisticated as this. When she was still working on *Growing Up Wildz*, she'd had to dress modestly—no strapless, no deep necklines. And when she'd broken free of all the restrictions that had hemmed her in for years, well, "classic" hadn't been on her to-do list. She'd gone for shock value. Short skirts. Shorter skirts. Black. Torn shirts that flashed her chest. Offensive slogans. Safety pins holding things together. Anything she could come up with to show that she wasn't a squeaky-clean kid anymore.

And it'd worked. Maybe too well.

She ran her hands over the silk. It was cool, smooth. If a dress could feel beautiful, this did. A flicker of excitement started to build. Once, before it'd been a chore, she'd liked to play dress-up. Maybe this would be fun. She hoped.

Several pairs of shoes dyed to match were lined up next to the dress—some with four-inch heels. Whitney swallowed hard. There'd be no way she could walk down the aisle in those beauties and not fall flat on her face.

Might as well get this over with. She stripped off her parka and sweater, then the boots and jeans. She caught a glimpse of herself in the three-way mirror—hard not to with those angles. Ugh. The socks had to go. And…

Her bra had straps. The dress did not.

She shucked the socks and, before she could think better about it, the bra. Then she hurried into the dress, trying not to pull on the zipper as the silk slipped over her head with a shushing sound.

The fabric puddled at her feet as she tried to get the zipper pulled up, but her arms wouldn't bend in that direction. "I need help," she called out, praying that an employee or a seamstress or anyone besides Matthew Beaumont was out there.

"Is it safe to come in?" Matthew asked from the other side of the door.

Oh, no. Whitney made another grab at the zipper, but nothing happened except her elbow popped. *Ow.* She checked her appearance. Her breasts were covered. It was just the zipper….

"Yes."

The door opened and Matthew walked in. To his credit, he didn't enter as if he owned the place. He came in with his eyes cast down before he took a cautious glance around. When he spotted her mostly covered, the strangest smile tried to crack his face. "Ah, there you are."

"Here I am," she agreed, wondering where else on earth he thought she could have gotten off to in the ten minutes she'd been in here. "I can't get the zipper up all the way."

She really didn't know what to expect at this point. The majority of her interactions with Matthew ranged from outright rude to surly. But then, just when she was about to write him off as a jerk and nothing more, he'd do something that set her head spinning again.

Like right now. He walked up to her and held out his hand, as if he were asking her to dance.

Even in the cramped dressing room, he was impossibly

handsome. But he'd already muddled her thoughts—mean one moment, sincere the next. She didn't want to let anything physical between them confuse her even further.

When she didn't put her hand in his, he said, "Just to step up on the dais," as if he could read her thoughts.

She took his hand. It was warm and strong, just as his arms had been. He guided her up the small step and then to the middle. "Ah, shoes," he said. Then he let her go.

"No—just the zipper," she told him, but he was already back by the shoes, looking at them.

Lord. She knew what was about to happen. She was all of five-four on a good day. He would pick the four-inch heels in an attempt to get her closer to Jo's height. And then she'd either have to swallow her pride and tell him she couldn't walk in them or risk tripping down the aisle on the big day.

"These should work," he said, picking up the pair of peep-toed shoes with the stacked heel only two inches high. "Try these on."

"If you could just zip me up first. *Please.*" The last thing she wanted to do was wobble in those shoes and lose the grip she had on the front of her dress.

He carried the shoes over to her and set them on the ground. Then he stood.

This time, when his gaze traveled over her, it didn't feel as if he were dismissing her, as he had the first time. Far from it. Instead, this time it was almost as if he was appreciating what he saw.

Maybe.

She felt him grab the edges of the dress and pull them together. Something about this felt…intimate. Almost too intimate. It blew way past possible flirting. She closed her eyes. Then, slowly, the zipper clicked up tooth by tooth.

Heat radiated down her back, warming her from the inside out. She breathed in, then out, feeling the silk move over her bare flesh. Matthew was so close she could smell his cologne—something light, with notes of sandalwood. Heat built low in her back—warm, luxurious heat that made her want to slowly turn in his arms and stop caring whether or not the dress zipped at all.

She could do it. She could hit on the best man and find out what had been behind that little conversation they'd had in private last night. And this time, she wouldn't trip.

Except…except for his first reaction to her—if she hit on him, he might assume she was out to ruin his perfect wedding or something. So she did nothing. Matthew zipped the dress all the way up. Then she felt his hands smoothing down the pleats in the back, then adjusting the sheer shoulder strap.

She stopped breathing as his hands skimmed over her.

This had to be nothing. This was only a control freak obsessively making sure every detail, every single pleat, was perfect. His touch had nothing to do with *her*.

She felt him step around her until he was standing by her side. "Aren't you going to look?" he asked, his voice warm and, if she didn't know any better, inviting.

She could feel him waiting right next to her, the heat from his body contrasting with the cool temperature of the room. So she opened her eyes. What else could she do?

The sight that greeted her caused her to gasp. An elegant, sophisticated woman stood next to a handsome, powerful man. She knew that was her reflection in the mirror, but it didn't look like her.

"Almost perfect," Matthew all but sighed in satisfaction.

Almost. What a horrible word.

"It's amazing." She fought the urge to twirl. Someone as buttoned-up as Matthew probably wouldn't appreciate a good twirl.

The man in the reflection grinned at her—a real grin, one that crinkled the edges of his eyes. "It's too long on you. Let's try the shoes." Then, to her amazement, he knelt down and held out a shoe for her, as if this were some backward version of *Cinderella*.

Whitney lifted up her skirt and gingerly stepped into the shoe. It felt solid and stable—not like the last pair of fancy shoes she'd tried to walk in.

She stepped into the other shoe, trying not to think about how Matthew was essentially face-to-knee or how she was in significant danger of snagging these pretty shoes on the edge of the dais and going down in a blaze of glory.

When she had both shoes firmly on, Matthew sat back. "How do those feel?"

"Not bad," she admitted. She took a preliminary step back. "Pretty good, actually."

"Can you walk in them? Or do you need a ballerina flat?"

She gaped at him. Of all the things he might have asked her, that wasn't even on the list. Then it hit her. "Jo told you I was a klutz, right?"

He grinned again. It did some amazing things to his face, which, in turn, did some amazing things to the way a lazy sort of heat coiled around the base of her spine and began to pulse.

"She might have mentioned it."

Whitney shouldn't have been embarrassed, and if she was, it shouldn't have bothered her anymore. Embarrassment was second nature for her now, as ordinary as breathing oxygen.

But it did. "Because you thought I was drunk."

His Adam's apple bobbed, but he didn't come back with the silky smile he'd pulled out on her last night, the one that made her feel as if she was being managed.

"In the interest of transparency, I also considered the option that you might have been stoned."

Four

Whitney blinked down at him, her delicate features pulled tight. Then, without another word, she turned back to the mirror.

What happened? Matthew stood, letting his gaze travel over her. She was, for lack of a better word, stunning. "The color suits you," he said, hoping a compliment would help.

It didn't. She rolled her eyes.

Transparency had always worked before. He'd thought that his little admission would come out as an ironic joke, something they could both chuckle over while he covertly admired the figure she cut in that dress.

What was it about this woman that had him sticking his foot in his mouth at every available turn?

It was just because she wasn't what he'd been expecting, that was all. He'd been up late last night, digging into the not-sordid-at-all history of Whitney Maddox, trying to get his feet out of his mouth and back under his legs. She *was* a respected horse breeder. Her horses *were* beautiful animals and that one *had* won a gold medal. But there weren't any pictures of Whitney Maddox anywhere—not on her ranch's website, not on any social media. Whitney Maddox was like a ghost—there but not there.

Except the woman before him was very much here. His hands still tingled from zipping her into that dress, from the glimpse of her panties right where the zipper had ended. How he itched to unzip it, to expose the bare skin he'd seen but not touched—slip those panties off her hips.

He needed to focus on what was important here, and that was making sure that this woman—no matter what name she went by—did not pull this wedding off message. That she did not pull *him* off message. That was what he had to think about. Not the way the dress skimmed over her curves or the way her dark hair made her stand out.

Before he knew what he was doing, he said, "You look beautiful in that dress."

This time, she didn't roll her eyes. She gave him the kind of look that made it clear she didn't believe him.

"You can see that, right? You're stunning."

She stared at him for a moment longer. "You're confusing me," she said.

She had a sweet smell to her, something with warm vanilla notes overlaying a deeper spice. Good enough to eat, he thought, suddenly fascinated with the curve of her neck. He could press his lips against her skin and watch her reaction in the mirror. Would she blush? Pull away? Or lean into his touch?

She looked away. "I could change my hair."

"What?"

"I could try to dye it all blond, although," she said with a rueful smile, "it didn't turn out so well the last time I tried it. The white streak won't take dye, for some reason. God knows I've tried to color it over, but it doesn't work. It's blond or nothing."

"Why on God's green earth would you want to dye your hair?"

He couldn't see her as a blonde. It would be wrong on so many levels. It'd take everything that was fine and delicate about her and make it washed-out, like a painting left out in the rain.

"If I'm blonde, no one will recognize me. No one would ever guess that Whitney Wildz is standing up there. That way, if I trip in the shoes or drop my bouquet, people will just think I'm a klutz and not assume I'm stoned. Like they always do."

Shame sucker punched him in the gut. "Don't change your hair." He reached out and brushed the edge of her bangs away from her face.

She didn't lean away from him, but she didn't lean into him, either. He didn't know if that was a good thing or not.

"But…" She swallowed and tried to look tough. She didn't make it. "I look like me. People will *recognize* me. I thought you didn't want that to happen."

"You say that as if looking like yourself is a bad thing."

In the mirror's reflection, her gaze cut to him. "Isn't it?"

He took a step closer to her, close enough that he could slide his fingers from the fringe of her hair down her neck, down her arm. He couldn't help it, which was something outside of his experience entirely. He'd *always* been able to help himself. He'd never allowed himself to get swept up in something as temporary, as fleeting, as emotional attraction. He'd witnessed firsthand what acting on attraction could do, how it could ruin marriages, leave bastard babies behind— leave children forgotten.

With the specter of his father hovering around him, Matthew managed to find some of the restraint that normally came so easy to him. He didn't slide his hand down her bare arm or pull her into his chest. Instead, he held himself to arranging the shoulder of the dress. She watched him in the mirror, her eyes wide. "You are *beautiful*," he said. It came out like something Phillip would say—low and seductive. It didn't sound like Matthew talking at all.

She sucked in a deep breath, which, from his angle, did

enticing things to her chest. He wanted to sweep her into his arms. He wanted to tell her he'd had a crush on her back in the day. He wanted to get her out of that dress and into his bed.

He did none of those things.

Focus, damn it.

He took a step back and tried his hardest to look at her objectively. The heels helped, but the hem of the dress still puddled around her. She'd need it hemmed, but they had to settle on the shoes first.

"Let's see how you walk in those." There. That was something that wasn't a come-on and wasn't a condemnation. Footwear was a safe choice at this point.

She stood for a moment, as if she was trying to decide what his motivations were. So he held out his arm for her. He could do that. She'd walk back down the aisle on his arm after the ceremony. Best they get used to it now.

After a brief pause, she slipped her hand around his elbow and, after gathering her skirts in one hand, stepped off the dais. They moved toward the door, where he opened it for her.

She walked ahead of him, the dress billowing around her legs just as he'd wanted it to. The salon had a bouquet of artificial flowers on a nearby table. He handed them to her. "Slow steps, big smile."

"Right," she said, an odd grin pulling up at the corners of her mouth. "No skipping. Got it."

She walked down the aisle, then turned and came back toward him with a big fake smile on her face. Then, just as she almost reached him, the toe of her shoe caught in the too-long hem of the dress and she stumbled. The bouquet went flying.

He caught her. He had to, right? It wasn't about pulling her into his arms. This was a matter of personal safety.

He had her by her upper arms. "Sorry," she muttered as he pulled her back onto her feet.

"Don't worry about it."

She gave him a hard look, her body rigid under his hands. "I had to worry about it yesterday. You're sure I'm not on anything today?"

Okay, yes, he deserved that. That didn't make it any less sucky to have it thrown back in his face.

Without letting go of her, he leaned down and inhaled deeply. "No trace of alcohol on your breath," he said, staring at her lips.

She gasped.

Then he removed one of his hands from her arm and used it to tilt her head back until she had no choice but to look him in the eyes.

Years of dealing with Phillip while he was drunk had taught Matthew what the signs were. "You're not on anything."

"You...can tell?"

He should let her go. She had her balance back. She didn't need him to hold her up and she certainly didn't need him to keep a hand under her chin.

But he didn't. Instead, he let his fingers glide over her smooth skin. "When you become a Beaumont, you develop certain skills to help you survive."

She blinked at him. "When you *become* a Beaumont? What does that mean? Aren't you a Beaumont?"

Matthew froze. Had he really said that? Out loud? He *never* drew attention to his place in the family, *never* said anything that would cast doubt on his legitimacy. Hell, his whole life had been about proving to the whole world that he was a Beaumont through and through.

What was it about this woman that made him stick his foot into his mouth?

Whitney stared at him. "You're confusing me again,"

she repeated, her voice a whisper that managed to move his heart rate up several notches. Her lips parted as she ever so slightly leaned into his hand.

"You're the one who's confusing me," he whispered back as he stroked his fingertips against her skin. For a woman who was neither here nor there, she was warm and solid and so, *so* soft under his hands.

"Then I guess we're even?" She looked up at him with those pale green eyes. He was going to kiss her. Long. Hard. He was going to taste her sweetness, feel her body as it pressed against his and—

"Whitney? Matthew?"

Jo's voice cut through the insanity he'd been on the brink of committing. He let go of Whitney, only to grab her immediately when she took a step back and stepped on her hem again.

"I've got you," he told her.

"Repeatedly," she said. He couldn't tell if she was amused or not.

Then Jo came around the corner, seamstresses and salon employees trailing her. She pulled up short when she saw the two of them and said, "I need to go," as the wedding planner started unfastening the back of her dress.

"What?" Matthew said.

"Why?" Whitney said at the same time.

"A mare I'm training out on the farm is having a meltdown and Richard is afraid she's going to hurt herself." She looked over her shoulder at the small army of women who were attempting to get her out of her dress. "Can you go any faster?"

There were murmurs of protest from the seamstresses as the wedding planner said, "We can't risk tearing the dress, Ms. Spears."

Jo sighed heavily.

Whitney and Matthew took advantage of the distraction

to separate. "I'll come with you," Whitney said. "I can help. You taught me what to do."

"No, you won't," he said.

It must have come out a little harsher than he meant it to, because every woman in the room—all six of them—stopped and looked at him. "I mean," he added, softening his tone, "we have too much to do. We have to get your dress hemmed, we have an appointment with the stylist this afternoon— everyone is set except you. We *must* keep your schedule."

There was a moment of silence, broken only by the sound of Jo's dress rustling as the seamstresses worked to free her from the elaborate confines.

Whitney wasn't looking at him. She was looking at Jo. She'd do whatever Jo said, he realized. Not what he said. He wasn't used to having his orders questioned. Everyone else in the family had long ago realized that Matthew was always right.

"Matthew is right," Jo said. "Besides, having a new person show up will only freak out Rapunzel. I need to do this alone."

"Oh," Whitney said as if Jo had just condemned her to swing from the gallows. "All right."

"Your dress is amazing," Jo said, clearly trying to smooth over the ruffled feathers.

"Yours, too," Whitney replied. Jo's compliment must have helped, because Whitney already sounded better.

That was another thing Matthew wasn't expecting from Whitney Wildz. A willingness to work? A complete lack of interest in throwing a diva fit when things didn't go her way?

She confused him, all right. He'd never met a woman who turned his head around as fast and as often as Whitney did. Not even the celebrities and socialites he'd known made him dizzy the way she did. Sure, such women made plays for him—he was a Beaumont and a good-looking man. But none of them distracted him from his goal. None of them got him off message.

He tried telling himself it was just because he'd liked her so many years ago. This was merely the lingering effects of a crush run amok. His teenage self was screwing with his adult self. That was all. It didn't matter that Whitney today was a vision in that dress—far more beautiful than anything he'd ever imagined back in the day. He had a job to do—a wedding to pull off, a family image to rescue, his rightful place to secure. His adult self was in charge here.

No matter what the Beaumonts put their minds to, they would always come out on top. That'd been the way Hardwick Beaumont had run his business and his family. He'd amassed a huge personal fortune and a legacy that had permanently reshaped Denver—and, one could argue, America. He expected perfection and got it—or else.

Even though Chadwick had sold the Beaumont Brewery, even though Phillip had crashed and burned in public, Matthew was still standing tall. He'd weathered those storms and he would pull this wedding off.

"There," one of the seamstresses said. "Mind the edge..."

Jo clutched at the front of the dress. "Matthew, if you don't mind."

Right. He turned his back to her so she could step out of the $15,000 dress they'd chosen because it made Jo, the tomboy cowgirl, look like a movie-star goddess, complete with the fishtail bodice and ten-foot-long train. The Beaumonts were about glamour and power. Every single detail of this wedding had to reflect that. Then no one would ever question his place in the family again.

Not even the maid of honor.

He looked down at Whitney out of the corner of his eye. She was right. With her fine bone structure, jet-black hair with the white stripe and those large eyes, he could dress her in a burlap sack and she'd still be instantly recognizable. The dress only made her features stand out that much more.

So why hadn't he agreed that a drastic change to her hair was a good idea?

It'd be like painting pouty ruby-red lips on the *Mona Lisa*. It'd just be wrong.

Still, he felt as if he'd done very little but insult her in the past twenty-four hours, and no matter what his personal feelings about Whitney were, constantly berating a member of the wedding party was not the way to ensure things stayed on message.

"I'll take you to lunch," he offered. "We'll make a day of it."

She gave him the side eye. "You normally spend your day styling women for weddings?"

"No," he said with a grin. "Far from it. I'm just making sure everything is—"

"Perfect."

"Exactly."

She tilted her head to one side and touched her cheek with a single fingertip. "Aren't you going to miss work?"

"This is my job." Again, he got the side eye, so he added, "I do the PR for Percheron Drafts, the beer company Chadwick started after he sold the Beaumont Brewery." He'd convinced Chadwick that the wedding needed to be a showcase event first. It hadn't been that hard. His older brother had learned to trust his instincts in the business world, and Matthew's instincts told him that marrying former playboy bachelor Phillip Beaumont off in a high-profile high-society wedding would pay for itself in good publicity.

Convincing Phillip and Jo that their wedding was going to be over-the-top in every possible regard, however, had been another matter entirely.

"I see," she said in a way that made it pretty clear she

didn't. Then she cleared her throat. "Won't your girlfriend be upset if you take me out to lunch?"

That was what she said. What she meant, though, was something entirely different. To his ears, it sure sounded as though she'd asked if he had really been about to kiss her earlier and whether he might try it again.

He leaned toward her, close enough he caught the scent of vanilla again. "I'm not involved with anyone," he said. What he meant?

Yeah, he might try kissing her again. Preferably someplace where seamstresses wouldn't bust in on them.

He watched the blush warm her skin. Again, his fingers itched to unzip that dress—to touch her. But… "You?"

His web searches last night hadn't turned up anything that suggested she was in a relationship.

She looked down at the floor. "I find it's best if I keep to myself. Less trouble that way."

"Then lunch won't be a problem."

"Are you sure? Or will you need to search my bag for illegal contraband?"

Ouch. Her dig stung all the more because he'd earned it. Really, there was only one way to save face here—throw himself on his sword. If he were lucky, she'd have mercy on him. "I'm sure. I'm done being an ass about things."

She jolted, her mouth curving into a smile that, no matter how hard she tried, she couldn't repress. "Can I have that in writing?"

"I could even get it notarized, if that's what it'd take for you to forgive me."

She looked at him then, her eyes full of wonder. "You already apologized last night. You don't have to do it again."

"Yes, I do. I keep confusing you. It's ungentlemanly."

Her eyebrows jumped up as her mouth opened but behind them, someone cleared her throat. "Mr. Beaumont? We're ready to start on Ms. Maddox's dress."

Whitney's mouth snapped shut as that blush crept over her cheeks. Matthew looked around. Jo and her dress were nowhere to be seen. He and Whitney had been standing by themselves in the middle of the salon for God knows how long, chatting. Flirting.

Right. They had work to do here.

But he was looking forward to lunch.

Five

"I'm sorry, sir, but the only seats we have are the window seats," the hostess said.

Matthew turned to look at Whitney. He hadn't expected Table 6 to be this crowded. He'd thought he was taking her to a quiet restaurant where they could talk. Where he could look at her over a table with only the bare minimum interruption.

But the place was hopping with Christmas shoppers taking a break. Shopping bags crowded the aisle, and there were more than a few people wearing elf hats and reindeer antlers. The hum of conversation was so loud he almost couldn't hear Bing Crosby crooning Christmas carols on the sound system.

"We can go someplace else," he offered to Whitney.

She pulled down her sunglasses and shot him a look, as if he'd dared her to throw a diva fit. "This is fine."

Matthew glanced around the restaurant again. He really didn't want to sit at a bar-high counter next to her. On the other hand, then he could maybe brush against her arm, her thigh.

They took the only two spots left in the whole place. A shaft of sunlight warmed their faces. Whitney took off her sunglasses and her knit hat and turned her face to the light.

She exhaled, a look of serene joy radiating from her. She was so beautiful, so unassuming, that she simply took his breath away.

Then it stopped. She shook back to herself and gave him an embarrassed look. "Sorry," she said, patting her hair back into place. "It's a lot colder here than it is in California. I miss the sun."

"Don't apologize." Her cheeks colored under his gaze. "Let's order. Then tell me about California." She notched a delicate eyebrow at him in challenge. "And I mean more than the basics. I want to know about *you*."

The corners of her mouth curved up as she nodded. But the waitress came, so they turned their attention to the daily specials. She ordered the soup and salad. He picked the steak sandwich. The process seemed relatively painless.

But Matthew noticed the way the waitress's eyes had widened as Whitney had asked about the soup du jour. *Oh, no*, he thought. The woman had recognized her.

Maybe it wouldn't be a problem. The restaurant was busy, after all. The staff had better things to do than wonder why Whitney Wildz had suddenly appeared at the counter, right?

He turned his attention back to Whitney. Which was not easy to do, crammed into the two seats in this window. But he managed to pull it off. "Now," he said, fixing her with what he really hoped wasn't a wolfish gaze, "tell me about you."

She shrugged.

The waitress came back with some waters and their coffee. "Anything else?" she asked with an ultraperky smile.

"No," Matthew said forcefully. "Thank you."

The woman's eyes cut back to Whitney again and she grinned in disbelief as she walked away. Oh, hell.

But Whitney hadn't noticed. She'd unwrapped her straw and was now wrapping the paper around her fingers, over and over.

Matthew got caught up in watching her long fingers bend the wrapper again and again and forgot about the waitress.

"You're confusing me," she said, staring hard at her scrap of paper. "Again."

"How?" She gave him the side eye. "No, seriously—please tell me. It's not my job here to confuse you."

She seemed to deflate, just a little. But it didn't last. "You're looking at me like that."

He forced his attention to his own straw. Hopefully, that would give her the space she needed. "Like how?"

The silence stretched between them like a string pulling tight. He was afraid he might snap. And he never snapped. He was unsnappable, for God's sake.

But then his mind flashed back to the bare skin of her back, how the zipper had ended just at the waistband of her panties. All he'd seen was a pretty edge of lace. Now he couldn't get his mind off it.

"I can't decide if you think I'm the biggest pain in the neck of your life or if you're— If you—" She exhaled, the words coming out in a rush. "If you like me. And when you look at me like that, it just…makes it worse."

"I can't help it," he admitted. It was easier to say that without looking at her. Maybe this counter seating wasn't all bad.

Her hands stilled. "Why not?" There was something else in her voice. That something seemed to match the look she'd given him last night, the one that craved his approval.

He couldn't tell her why not. Not without telling her… what? That he'd nursed a boyhood crush on her long after he'd left boyhood behind? That he'd followed her in the news? That this very afternoon, she'd been the most beautiful woman he'd ever seen?

"Tell me about you," he said, praying that she'd go along with the subject change. "Tell me about your life."

He felt her gaze on him. Now it was his turn to blush. "If I do, will you tell me about you?"

He nodded.

"Okay," she agreed. He expected her to begin twisting her paper again, but she didn't. She dug out her phone. "This is Pride and Joy," she said, showing him a horse and rider holding a gold medal.

The picture was her phone's wallpaper. Her pride and joy, indeed. "That was the Games, right?"

"Right." Her tone brightened considerably at his memory. "I'd been getting close to that level but…I wanted him to win, you know? Having bred a horse that could win at that level made me feel legitimate. Real. I wasn't some crazy actress, not anymore. I was a real horse breeder."

She spoke calmly—no hysterics, no bravado. Just someone determined to prove her worth.

Yeah, he knew that feeling, too. Better than he wanted to.

"There are people in this world who don't know about that show," she said, staring at her phone. "People who only know me as Whitney Maddox, the breeder of Pride and Joy. You have no idea how *huge* that is."

"I'm starting to get one." He lifted the phone from her hand and studied the horse. He'd seen a similar shot to this one online. But she wasn't in either one.

She slid her fingertip over the screen and another horse came up. Even he could tell this was a younger one, gangly and awkward looking. "This is Joy's daughter, Ode to Joy. I own her mother, Prettier Than a Picture—Pretty for short. She was a world-champion dressage horse, but her owner got indicted and she was sold at auction. I was able to get her relatively cheap. She's turned out some amazing foals." The love in her voice was unmistakable. Pretty might have been a good business decision, but it was clear that the horse meant much more to Whitney than just a piece of property. "Ode's already been purchased," she went on. "I could keep studding Joy to Pretty for the rest of my life and find buyers."

"Sounds like job security."

"In another year, I'll deliver Ode," she went on. "She's only one right now." She flicked at her screen and another photo came up. "That's Fifi," she told him. "My rescued greyhound."

The sleek dog was sprawled out on a massive cushion on the floor, giving the camera a don't-bother-me look. "A greyhound?"

"I was fostering her and just decided to keep her," Whitney replied. "She'd run and run when she was younger and then suddenly her life stopped. I thought—and I know this sounds silly because she's just a dog—but I thought she understood me in a way that most other living creatures don't."

"Ah." He didn't know what else to say to that. He'd never felt much kinship with animals, not the way Phillip did with his horses. His father had never really loved the horses he'd bought, after all. They'd been only investments for him—investments that might pay off in money or prestige. "You foster dogs?"

She nodded enthusiastically. "The no-kill shelter in Bakersfield never has enough room." Her face darkened briefly. "At first they wouldn't let me take any animals but..." Her slim shoulders moved up and down. Then the cloud over her face was gone. "There's always another animal that needs a place to stay."

He stared at her. It could have been a naked play for pity—poor little celebrity, too notorious to be entrusted with animals no one else wanted. But that was not how it came out. "How many animals have you fostered?"

She shrugged again. "I've lost count." She flicked the screen again and a strange-looking animal appeared.

He held the phone up so he could get a better look, but the squished black-and-white face stayed the same. "What is *that*?"

"That," she replied with a giggle that drew his gaze to her face, "is Gater. He's a pug-terrier-something."

Hands down, that was the ugliest mutt Matthew had ever seen. "How long have you had him?"

"Just over two years. He thinks he rules the house. Oh, you should have seen him when Jo and Betty stayed with me. He was furious!" She laughed again, a sweet, carefree sound that did more to warm him than the sun ever could.

"What happened?"

"He bit Betty on the ankle, and she kicked him halfway across the living room. No broken bones or skin," she hurried to add. "Just a pissed-off dog and donkey. Gater thinks he's the boss, and Fifi doesn't care as long as Gater stays off her cushion."

Whitney leaned over and ran her fingers over the screen again. A photo of some cats popped up, but that was not what held Matthew's attention. Instead, it was the way she was almost leaning her head against his shoulder, almost pressing her body against his arm.

"That's Frankie and Valley, my barn cats."

"Frankie and Valley? Like Frankie Valli, the singer?"

"Yup." Without leaning away, she turned her face up toward his. Inches separated them. "Frankie was a…stray." Her words trailed off as she stared at Matthew's face, his lips. Her eyes sparkled as the blush spread over her cheeks like the sunrise after a long, cold night.

He could lean forward and kiss her. It'd be easy. For years, he'd thought about kissing Whitney Wildz. He'd been young and hormonal and trying so, *so* hard to be the Beaumont that his father wanted him to be. Fantasies about Whitney Wildz were a simple, no-mess way to escape the constant effort to be the son Hardwick Beaumont wanted.

Except he didn't want to kiss that fantasy girl anymore. He wanted to kiss the flesh-and-blood woman sitting next to him. She shouldn't attract him as she did. He should see nothing but a headache to be managed when he looked at her. But he didn't, damn it. He didn't.

Matthew couldn't help himself. He lifted the hand that

wasn't holding her phone and let the tips of his fingers trail down the side of her cheek.

Her breath caught, but she didn't turn away—didn't look away. Her skin was soft and warmed by the sun. He spread his fingers out until the whole of his palm cradled her cheek.

"I didn't realize you were such a fan of Frankie Valli," she said in a breathy voice. Her pupils widened as she took another deep breath. As if she was waiting for him to make his move.

"I'm not." The problem was, Matthew didn't have a move to make. Phillip might have once moved in on a pretty woman without a care in the world about who saw them or how it'd look in the media.

But Matthew cared. He had to. It was how he'd made a place for himself in this family. And he couldn't risk all of that just because he wanted to kiss Whitney Maddox.

So, as much as it hurt, he dropped his hand away from her face and looked back at the screen. Yes. There were cats on the screen. Named after an aging former pop idol.

He could still feel Whitney's skin under his touch, still see her bare back...

Something outside the window caught his eye. He looked up to see two women in their mid-twenties standing on the sidewalk in front of the restaurant. One had her phone pointed in their general direction. When they saw that he'd noticed them, they hurried along, giggling behind their hands.

Dread filled him. Okay, yes, Whitney was recognizable—but she wasn't the only woman in the world with an unusual hair color, for crying out loud. This had to be...a coincidence.

He turned his attention back to the phone, but pictures of cats and dogs and horses barely held his attention. He wanted their food to come so they could eat and get the hell out of here. He wanted to get Whitney to a place where even if people did recognize her, they had the decency not to make a huge deal out of it.

She flicked to the last photo, which was surprisingly *not* of an animal. Instead, it was of a cowgirl wearing a straw hat and tight jeans, one foot kicked up on a fence slat. The sun was angled so that the woman in the picture was bathed in a golden glow—alone. Perfect.

Whitney tried to grab the phone from him, but he held on to it, lifting it just out of her reach. "Is this…you?"

"May I have that back, please?" She sounded tense.

"It *is* you." He studied the photo a little more. "Who took it?"

"Jo did, when she was out last winter." She leaned into him, reaching for the phone. "Please."

He did as the lady asked. "So that's the real Whitney Maddox, then."

She froze, her fingertip hovering over the button that would turn the screen off. She looked down at the picture, a sense of vulnerability on her face. "Yes," she said in a quiet voice. "That's the real me." The screen went black.

He cleared his throat. "I think I like the real you."

Even then she didn't look at him, but he saw the smile that curved up her lips. "So," she said in a bright voice, "your turn."

Hell. What was he supposed to say? He looked away— and right at the same two women he'd seen earlier. Except now there were four of them. "Uh…"

"Oh, don't play coy with me," she said as she slipped her phone back into her jacket pocket. Then she nudged him with her shoulder. "The real you. Go."

This time, when the women outside caught him looking, they didn't hurry off and they sure didn't stop pointing their cameras. One was on her phone.

It was then that he noticed the noise. The restaurant had gone from humming to a hushed whisper. The carols over the sound system were loud and clear. He looked over his shoulder and was stunned to find that a good part of the restaurant was staring at them with wide eyes. Cell phones were out. People were snapping pictures, recording videos.

Oh, hell. This was about to become a PR nightmare. Worse—if people figured out who he was? And put two and two together? Nightmare didn't begin to cut what this was about to become.

"We need to leave."

The women outside were headed inside.

"Are you trying to get…out…?" Whitney saw the women, then glanced around. "Oh." Shame flooded her cheeks. She grabbed her sunglasses out of her bag and shoved them back onto her face. "Yes."

Sadly, the glasses did little to hide who she was. In fact, they gave her an even more glamorous air, totally befitting a big-name star.

Matthew fished a fifty out of his wallet and threw it on the counter, even though they weren't going to eat anything they'd ordered.

As they stood, the small group of women approached. "It's really you," one of the woman said. "It's really Whitney Wildz!"

The quiet bubble that had been building over the restaurant burst and suddenly people were out of their seats, crowding around him and Whitney and shoving camera phones in their faces.

"Is this your boyfriend?" someone demanded.

"Are you pregnant?" someone else shouted.

"Are you ever going to clean up your act?" That insult was shouted by a man.

Matthew was unexpectedly forced into the role of bouncer. He used his long arms to push people out of Whitney's way as they tried to walk the twelve feet to the door. It took several minutes before they were outside, but the crowd moved with them.

He had his arm around her shoulders, trying to shield her as he rushed for his car. With his long legs, he could have left half of these idiots behind, but Whitney was much shorter than he was. He was forced to go slow.

Someone grabbed Whitney's arm, shouting, "Why did you break Drako's heart?"

Matthew shoved and shoved hard. They were at his car, but people were pushing so much that he had trouble getting the passenger door open. "Get back," he snarled as he hip-checked a man trying to grab a lot more than Whitney's arm. "Back off."

He got the door open and basically shoved her inside, away from what had rapidly become a mob. He slammed the door shut, catching someone's finger. There was howling. He was feeling cruel enough that he was tempted to leave the finger in there, but that would be the worst sort of headline—Beaumont Heir Breaks Beer Drinker's Hand. So he opened the door just enough to pull the offending digit out and then slammed it shut again.

Whitney sat in the passenger seat, already buckled up. She stared straight ahead. She'd gotten her hat back on, but it was too late for that. The parts of her face that were visible were tight and blank.

Matthew stormed around to the driver's side. No one grabbed him, but several people were recording him. Great. Just freaking great.

He got in, fired up the engine on his Corvette Stingray and roared off. He was furious with the waitress—she'd probably called her girlfriends to tell them that Whitney Wildz was at her table. He was furious with the rest of the idiots, who'd descended into a mob in mere minutes.

And he was furious with himself. He was the Beaumont who always, always handled the press and the public. Image was everything and he'd just blown his image to hell and back. If those people hadn't recognized him from the get-go, it wouldn't take much online searching before they figured it out.

This was exactly what he hadn't wanted to happen—Whitney Wildz would turn this wedding and his message into a circus of epic proportions. Yeah, he'd been a jerk to her about it last night, but he'd also been right.

Even if she was a cowgirl who fostered puppies and adopted greyhounds, even if she was a respected horse breeder, even if she was *nothing* he'd expected in the best possible ways, it didn't change the perception. The perception was that Whitney Wildz was going to ruin this wedding.

And he wouldn't be able to control it. Any of it. Not the wedding, not the message—and not himself.

He was screwed.

Six

They drove in silence. Matthew took corners as if he were punishing them. Or her. She wasn't sure.

She wished she had the capacity to be surprised by what had happened at the restaurant, but she didn't. Not anymore. That exact scene had played out time and time again, and she couldn't even feel bad about it anymore.

Instead, all she felt was resigned. She'd known this was going to happen, after all. And if she was disappointed by how Matthew had reacted, well, that was merely the by-product of him confusing her.

She'd allowed herself to feel hopeful because, at least some of the time, Matthew liked her.

The real her.

She thought.

She had no idea where they were, where they were going, or if they were going there in a straight line. He might be taking the long way just in case any of those fans had managed to follow them.

"Are you all right?" he growled out as he pointed his sleek car toward what she thought was downtown Denver.

She wouldn't flinch at his angry tone. She'd learned a long time ago that a reaction—any reaction—would be twisted around. Best to be a placid statue. Although that hadn't always worked so well, either.

"I'm fine."

"Are you sure? That one guy—he *grabbed* you."

"Yes." Had that been the same man whose hand had gotten crushed in the door?

Even though she had her gaze locked forward, out of the corner of her eye she could see him turn and give her a look of disbelief. "And that doesn't piss you off?"

This time, she did wince. "No."

"Why the hell not? It pissed me off. People can't grab you like that."

Whitney exhaled carefully through her nose. This was the sort of thing that someone who had never been on the receiving end of the paparazzi might say. Normal people had personal space, personal boundaries that the rest of humanity agreed not to cross. You don't grab my butt, I won't have you arrested.

Those rules hadn't applied to her since the days after her show had been canceled. The day she'd bolted away from her mother's overprotective control.

"It's fine," she insisted again. "It's normal. I'm used to it."

"It's bullshit," he snapped. "And I won't stand by while a bunch of idiots take liberties with you. You're not some plaything for them to grope or insult."

She did turn to look at him then. He had a white-knuckle grip on the steering wheel as he glared at the traffic he was speeding around. He was serious.

She couldn't remember the last time someone hadn't just stood by and watched the media circus take her down.

Like the time she'd flashed the cameras. She hadn't had on any panties because the dress made no allowances for anything, the designer had said. Yeah, she'd been high at the time, but had anyone said, "Gee, Whitney, you might want to close your legs"? Had anyone tried to shield her from the cameras, as Matthew had just done, until she could get her skirt pulled down?

No. Not a single person had said anything. They'd just kept snapping pictures. And that next morning? One of the worst in her life.

He took another corner with squealing tires into a parking spot in front of a tall building. "We're here."

"Are you on my side?" she asked.

He slammed the car into Park, causing her to jerk forward. "What kind of question is that?"

"I mean…" Was he the kind of guy who would have told her she was flashing the cameras? Or the kind who would have gotten out of the way of the shot? "No one's ever tried to defend me from the crowds before."

Now it was his turn to look at her as if she were nuts. "No one?"

This wasn't coming out well. "Look, like you said—in the interest of transparency, I need to know if you're on my side or not. I'm not trying to mess up your message. I mean, you saw how it was." Suddenly, she was pleading. She didn't just want him on her side, watching her back—she *needed* him there. "All I did was take off my hat."

He gave her the strangest look. She didn't have a hope in heck of trying to guess what was going on behind his deep blue eyes.

"That's just the way it is," she told him, her voice dropping to a whisper. Every time she let her guard down—every time she thought she might be able to do something normal people did, like go out to lunch with a man who confused her in the best possible ways—this was always what would happen. "I—I wish it wasn't."

He didn't respond.

She couldn't look at him anymore. Really, she didn't expect anything else of him. He'd made his position clear. His duty was to his family and this wedding. She could respect that. She was nothing but a distraction.

A distraction he'd almost kissed in a crowded restaurant. So when he reached over and cupped her face in his hand, lifting it until she had no choice but to look at him, she was completely taken off guard. "I refuse to accept that this is 'just the way it is.' I *refuse* to." His voice—strong and confident and so close—did things to her that she barely recognized. "And you should, too."

Once, she'd tried to fight back, to reclaim her name and her life. She'd tried to lend her celebrity status to animal shelters. It'd gotten her nothing but years of horrible headlines paired with worse pictures. She hadn't done anything public since the last incident, over two years ago.

She looked into his eyes. If only he were on her side… "What I do doesn't matter and we both know it."

He gave her another one of those looks that walked the fine line between anger and disgust. "So what are you going to do about it?"

She glared at him. She couldn't get mad at those people—but him? She could release a little rage on him. After all, he'd been barely better than those people last night. "I'm not going to sit around and fume and mope about how I'm nothing but a *commodity* to people. I'm not going to sit around and feel bad that once upon a time I was young and stupid and crazy. And I'm not going to let anyone else sit around and feel bad for me. I'm not an object of your pity *or* derision. Because that's not who I am anymore."

If he was insulted by her mini tirade, he didn't show it. He didn't even let go of her. Instead, one corner of his mouth curled up into an amused grin.

"Derision, huh?" He was close now, leaning in.

"Yes."

That'd been last night. Right after she'd first fallen into his arms. After she'd dared to hope she might have a little Christmas romance. The memory made her even madder.

"So if you're going to ask me to drop out, just get on with it so I can tell you I already told Jo I would and she begged me not to because *you* invited a bunch of strangers to her wedding and she wants one friend standing next to her. Now, are you on my side or not?"

Because if he wasn't, he needed to stop touching her. She was tired of not knowing where she stood with him.

He blinked. "I won't let anyone treat you like that."

"Because it's bad for your message?"

His fingers pulled against her skin, lifting her face up. Closer to him. "Because you are *not* a commodity to me."

The air seemed to freeze in her lungs, making breathing impossible. He was going to kiss her. God, she wanted him to. Just as she'd wanted him to kiss her in the restaurant.

And see what had happened? She could still feel that man's hand on her butt.

As much as she wanted to kiss Matthew—to be kissed for the real her, not the fake one—she couldn't.

"I'm going to ruin the wedding." It was a simple statement of an unavoidable fact.

It worked. A shadow clouded his face, and he dropped his hand and looked away. "We're going to be late."

"Right." She didn't want to do this anymore, didn't want to be the reason the wedding went off script. She wanted to go back to her ranch—back where dogs and cats and horses and even Donald, the crazy old coot, didn't have any expectations about Whitney Wildz.

Matthew opened her door and held out his hand for her. She'd promised Jo. Until Jo told her she could quit, she couldn't. She wouldn't. That was that.

So she sucked it up, put her hand in Matthew's and stood.

He didn't let go of her, didn't step back. Instead, he held on tighter. "Are you sure you're okay?"

She put on a smile for him. She wouldn't be okay until she was safely back home, acres of land between her and the nearest human. Then she'd put her head down and get back to work. In a while—a few weeks, a few months—this wedding would be superseded by another celebrity or royal doing something "newsworthy." This would pass. She knew that now. She hadn't always known it, though.

"I'm fine," she lied. Then, because she couldn't lie and look at him, she stared up at the white building. "Where are we?" Because the sign said Hotel Monaco.

"The Veda spa is inside the hotel."

He still didn't let her go. He tucked her hand into the crook of his elbow, as if they'd walked out of 1908 or something. When she shot him a look, he said, "Practice."

Ah, yes. That whole walking-down-the-aisle thing.

So she put on her biggest, happiest smile and held an imaginary bouquet in front of her. She'd been an actress once, after all. She could fake it until she made it.

He chuckled in appreciation. "That's the spirit," he said, which made her feel immensely better. He handed his keys to a valet and they strode through the hotel lobby as if they owned the place.

"Mr. Beaumont! How wonderful to see you again." The receptionist at the front desk greeted them with a warm smile. Her gaze flicked over Whitney. "How can I help you today?"

"We're here for the spa, Janice," he said. "Thank you." As he guided Whitney down a hallway, she gave him a look. "What?"

Jealousy spiked through her. "You check into a hotel in your hometown in the middle of the day often? So often they know you by name?"

He pulled up right outside the salon door. "The Beaumonts have been using the hotel for a variety of purposes for years. The staff is exceedingly discreet. Chadwick used it for board meetings, but our father was...fond of using it for other purposes." Then he blushed. The pink color seemed out of place on his cheeks.

Ah—the father who sired countless numbers of children. She bit her tongue and said, "Yes?"

"Nothing," he said with more force than she expected. "The Beaumonts have a long business relationship with the hotel, that's all. I personally do not check into the rooms."

He opened the door to the spa. Another receptionist stood to greet them. "Mr. Beaumont," she said with a deferential bow of the head. "And this is—" she checked a tablet "—Ms. Maddox, correct?"

"Yes," Whitney said, feeling her shoulders straighten a bit more. If she could get through this as Ms. Maddox, that'd be great.

"This way. Rachel is ready for you."

They went back to a private room. Whitney hadn't been in a private salon room in a long time. "This is nice," she said as Matthew held the door open for her.

"And it better stay that way. Rachel," he said to the stylist with every color of red in her hair, "can you give me a moment? I have something I need to attend to."

"Of course, Mr. Beaumont." Rachel turned to face her. "Ms. Maddox, it's a delight to meet you."

Whitney tried not to giggle. A delight? Really? Still, this was a good test of her small-talk skills. At the wedding, she would be meeting a lot of people, after all. "A pleasure," she agreed.

She sat in the chair, and Rachel fluffed her hair several times. "Obviously, the bride will have her hair up," Rachel said. "Ms. Frances Beaumont has requested Veronica Lake waves, which will look amazing. Ms. Serena Beaumont will have a classic twist. You…" Her voice trailed off as she fingered Whitney's home-cut pixie.

"Don't have a lot to work with," Whitney said. "I know. I was thinking. Maybe we should take it blond."

Rachel gasped in horror. "What? Why?"

"She's not taking it blond," Matthew announced from the door as he strode in. He didn't look at Whitney—he was too busy scowling at his phone. But the order was explicit.

"Of course not," Rachel hurriedly agreed. "That would be the worst possible thing." She continued fluffing. "We could add in volume and extensions. Blond is out but colored strands are very hot right now."

Whitney cringed. Extensions? Volume? Colored streaks?

Why not just put her in a torn T-shirt emblazoned with the *Growing Up Wildz* logo and parade her down the street?

"Absolutely not," Matthew snapped. "We're going for a glamorous, classic look here."

If the stylist was offended by his attitude, she didn't show it. "Well," she said, working her fingers through Whitney's hair, "I can clean up the cut and then we can look at clips? Something bejeweled that matches the dresses?"

"Perfect," Matthew agreed.

"People will recognize me," Whitney reminded him, just because she felt as if she should have some say in her appearance. She glanced at the stylist, who had the decency to not stare. "Just like they did at the restaurant. If you won't let her dye it, at least get me a wig."

"No." But that was all he said as he continued to scowl at his phone.

"Why the heck *not*?"

He looked up at her, his eyes full of nothing but challenge. "Because you are beautiful the way you are. Don't let anyone take that away from you." Then his phone buzzed and he said, "Excuse me," and was gone.

Whitney sat there, stunned, as Rachel cleaned up her pixie cut.

Beautiful?

Was that how he thought of her?

Seven

This was going south on him. Fast. Matthew struggled to keep his cool. He'd learned a long time ago that losing his temper didn't solve anything. But he was getting close to losing it right now.

When the photo of him and Whitney, taken from the sidewalk while they sat inside the restaurant, had popped up on Instagram with the caption OMG WHITNEY WILDZ IN DENVER!?! he'd excused himself from the stylist's room so that he could be mad without upsetting Whitney. She'd had enough of that already.

He'd already reported the photo, but he knew this was just the beginning. And after years of cleaning up the messes his siblings and stepmothers had left behind, he also knew there was no way to stop it.

He was going to make an effort, though. Containment was half the battle. The other half? Distraction.

If he could bury the lead on Whitney under some other scandal...

He scanned the gossip sites, hoping that someone somewhere had done something so spectacularly stupid that no one would care about a former teen star having lunch.

Nothing. Of all the weeks for the rest of the world to be on its best behavior.

In the days of old—when he'd found himself faced with a crowd of paparazzi outside his apartment, demanding a re-action about his second stepmother's accusation that she'd caught Hardwick Beaumont in bed with his mistress in this very hotel—Matthew had relied on distraction.

He'd called Phillip, told him to make a scene and waited for the press to scamper off. It'd worked, too. Bailing Phillip out was worth it when Hardwick had called Matthew into his office and told him he'd done a nice job handling the situation.

"You're not mad at Phillip? Or…me?" Matthew had asked, so nervous he'd been on the verge of barfing. The only other times Hardwick had called Matthew into his office had been to demand to know why he couldn't be more like Chadwick.

Hardwick had gotten up and come around his desk to put his hands on Matthew's shoulders. Hardwick had been older then, less than five years from dying in the middle of a board meeting.

"Son," Hardwick had said with a look that could have been described only as fatherly on his face. It'd looked so unnatural on him. "When you control the press, you rule the world—that's how a Beaumont handles it."

Son. Matthew could count on both hands the number of times that Hardwick had used that term of affection. Mat-thew had finally, *finally* done something the old man had no-ticed. For the first time in his life, he'd felt like a Beaumont.

"You just keep looking out for the family," Hardwick had said. "Remember—control the press, rule the world."

Matthew had gotten very good at controlling the press—the traditional press. It was the one thing that *made* him a Beaumont.

But social media was a different beast, a many-headed hydra. You cut off one Instagram photo, another five popped up.

He couldn't rely on Phillip to cause a scene anymore, now that the man was clean and sober. Chadwick was out, as well—he didn't deal with the press beyond the controlled environment of interviews that Matthew prescreened for him.

Matthew stared at his phone. He could call his sister Frances, but she'd want to know why and how and details before she did anything. And once she found out that her former childhood idol Whitney Wildz was involved...

That left him one choice. He dialed his younger brother Byron.

"What'd I do now?" Byron said. He yawned, as if Matthew had woken him up at two in the afternoon.

"Nothing. Yet." There was silence on the other end of the line. "You *are* in Denver, right?"

"Got in this morning." Byron yawned again. "Hope you appreciate this. It's a damn long flight from Madrid."

"I need a favor."

"You mean beyond flying halfway around the world to watch Phillip marry some horse trainer?" Byron laughed.

Matthew gritted his teeth. Byron sounded just like Dad. "Yes. I need you to be newsworthy today."

"What'd Phillip do this time? I thought he was getting married."

"It's not Phillip."

Byron whistled. "What'd you get into?"

Matthew thought back to the photo he'd already reported. Whitney—sitting right next to him. Those people hadn't known who he was, but it wouldn't take long for someone to figure out that Whitney Wildz was "with" a Beaumont. "I just need a distraction. Can you help me out or not?"

This was wrong. All wrong. He was trying to prove that the Beaumont family was back on track, above scandal. He was trying to prove that he had complete control over the situation. And what was he doing?

Asking his brother to make a mess only days before the wedding...to protect Whitney.

What was he thinking?

He was thinking about the way her face had closed down the moment she realized people were staring, the way she sat in his car as if he were driving her to the gallows instead of a posh salon.

He was thinking about the way she kept offering to change her hair—to drop out—so that he could stay on message.

He was thinking how close he'd come to kissing her at that lunch counter.

"How big a distraction?"

"Don't kill anyone."

"Damn," Byron said with a good-natured chuckle. "You'll bail me out?"

"Yeah."

There was a pause that made Matthew worry. "Hey—did you invite Harper to the wedding?"

"Leon Harper, the banker who forced Chadwick to sell the Brewery?"

"Yeah," was the uninformative response. But then Byron added, "Did you invite him?"

"No, I didn't invite the man who hated Dad so much he took it out on all of us. Why?"

"I'll only help you out if you invite the whole Harper family."

"He has a *family*?" Matthew had had the displeasure of meeting Harper only a few times, at board meetings or other official Brewery functions. The man was a shark—no, that was unfair to sharks everywhere. The man was an eel, slippery and slimy and uglier than sin.

Plus, there was that whole thing about hating the Beaumonts enough to force the sale of the family business

"Are you serious? Why on God's green earth would you want Harper there?"

"Do you want me to make headlines for you or not?" Byron snapped.

"They can't come to the wedding—there's no room in the chapel. But I'll invite them to the reception." There would be plenty of room for a few extra people at the Mile High Station. And in a crowd of six hundred guests—many of whom were extremely famous—the odds of Harper running into a Beaumont, much less picking a fight with one, were slim. Matthew could risk it.

"Done. Don't worry, big brother—I've got a bone or two to pick now that I'm Stateside." Byron chuckled. "Can't believe you want me to stir up trouble. You, of all people."

"I have my reasons. Just try not to get a black eye," Matthew told him. "It'll look bad in the photos."

"Yeah? This reason got a name?"

The back of Matthew's neck burned. "Sure. And does the reason you ran off to Europe for a year have a name?"

"I was working," Byron snapped.

"That's what I'm doing here. Don't kill anyone."

"And no black eyes. Got it." Byron hung up.

Matthew sagged in relief. Byron had been in Europe for over a year. He claimed he'd been working in restaurants, but really—who could tell? All that Matthew knew was that Byron had caused one hell of a scene at a restaurant before winding up in Europe. There he'd kept his head down long enough to stay the heck out of the headlines. That'd been good enough for Matthew. One less mess he had to clean up.

This would work. He'd send out a short, boring press release announcing that Whitney Maddox, former star of *Growing Up Wildz* and close friend of the bride, was in Denver for the Beaumont wedding. The Beaumonts were pleased she would be in the wedding party. He'd leave it at that.

Then tonight Byron would go off the rails. Matthew was reasonably sure that his little brother wouldn't actually kill anyone, but he'd put the odds of a black eye at two to one. Either way, he was confident that Byron would do something that washed Whitney right out of the press's mind. Who cared about a former child star when the prodigal Beaumont had returned to raise hell at his brother's wedding?

"Mr. Beaumont?" Rachel, the stylist, opened the door and popped her head out. "We're ready for the big reveal."

"How'd she turn out?" Now that he had his distraction lined up, he could turn his attention back to Whitney. *All* of his attention.

Rachel winked at him. "I think you'll be pleased with the results."

Matthew walked into the private room. Whitney's back was to him. Her hair wasn't noticeably shorter, but it was shaped and sleek and soft-looking. A large rhinestone clip was fastened on one side, right over her white streak. He walked around to the front. Her eyes were closed. She hadn't seen yet.

God, she was beautiful. *Stunning.* The makeup artist had played up her porcelain complexion by going easy on the blush and heavy on the red lips. Instead of the smoky eye that Frances and Serena were going to wear, the artist had gone with a cat's-eye look.

"Whoa," he heard himself say. How could people look at this woman and only see Whitney Wildz?

Because the woman sitting in the chair in front of him was so much *more* than Whitney Wildz had ever been.

Whitney's nose wrinkled at him, but there was no missing the sweet little smile that curved up the corners of her mouth.

He was *going* to kiss her. Just as soon as they didn't have hairstylists and makeup artists hanging around, he was going to muss up that hair and smudge that lipstick and he wasn't going to feel bad about it at all.

"Ready, Ms. Maddox?" Rachel said. She spun Whitney's chair around and said, "Ta-da!"

Whitney blinked at her reflection, her pale eyes wide with shock.

Rachel's smile tensed. "Of course, it'll look better with the dress. And if you don't like it…"

"No, it's perfect," Matthew interrupted. "Exactly how I want her to look. Great job."

Whitney swallowed. "Perfect?" It came out as a whisper. He noticed her chest was rising and falling with increasing speed.

He knew what was happening. His sister Frances had always done the same thing when she'd been busted for sneaking around with the hired help. The shallow, fast breathing meant only one thing.

Whitney was about to freak out.

"If you could give us a moment," he said to the stylist.

"Is everything—?" Rachel asked, throwing a worried look back at Whitney as Matthew hurried the woman out of the room.

"It's perfect," Matthew reassured her as he shut the door in her face. Then he turned back to Whitney.

She'd come up out of the chair and was leaning into the mirror now. His mind put her back in her dress. "You're going to look amazing."

She started, as if she'd forgotten he was still there. Meeting his gaze in the mirror's reflection, she gave him a nervous grin. "I don't look like…*her* too much?"

Like Whitney Wildz.

He couldn't see anything of that ghost of the past in the woman before him—anything beyond a distinctive hair color. She *wasn't* Whitney Wildz—not to him. She was someone else—someone better.

Someone he liked.

Someone he'd defend, no matter what the cost.

He couldn't help it. He closed the distance between them and brushed the careful edge of her hairstyle away from her cheek. Then he tilted her head back to face him.

"You look like *you*," he assured her.

Her gaze searched his. The desperation was undisguised this time. He wanted to make her feel better, to let her know that he'd take care of her. He wouldn't throw her to the wolves or leave her hanging.

His lips brushed hers. Just a simple, reassuring kiss. A friendly kiss.

Yeah, right.

Except…she didn't close her eyes. He knew this because he didn't, either. She watched him kiss her. She didn't throw her arms around his neck and she didn't kiss him back. She just…watched.

So he stopped.

She was even paler now, practically a ghost with red lips as she stared at him with those huge eyes of hers.

Damn it. For once he'd let his emotions do the thinking for him and he'd screwed up.

"Whitney…"

"Knock-knock!" Rachel said in a perky voice as the door opened. "What did we decide?"

He ran the back of his hand over his mouth and then looked at Whitney. "I think she's perfect."

Eight

Matthew had been right. The staff at the hotel and spa were exceedingly discreet. There were no cameras or phones pointed at her when she walked out of the hotel. No one yelled her name as the valet pulled up with Matthew's car. Not a single person tried to grab her while the doorman opened her door and waited for her to get seated.

But Matthew had kissed her. Somehow, that made everything worse. And better.

She didn't know which. All she knew was that when he'd touched her—when he'd looked at her—and said she looked like herself, she'd wanted to kiss him and not kiss him and demand to know which "you" she looked like.

Which Whitney he thought he was kissing.

God, her brain was a muddled mess. She knew what to expect from the crowd at the restaurant. She did not know what to expect from Matthew Beaumont.

Except that he was probably going to keep confusing her.

Which he did almost immediately.

"I have the situation under control," he told her as they drove off for what she hoped was Jo and Phillip's farm. She couldn't take any more of this gadding about town. "I've done a press release announcing your involvement in the wedding."

"You're *announcing* I'm here? I thought that's what you wanted to avoid." She was feeling better now. Ridiculous, yes. But the sight of her in that mirror, looking like…well, like a Hollywood movie star, but a classic one, had short-circuited her brain. And then he'd kissed her.

"Trust me—after what happened at the restaurant, everyone knows you're here. There's no putting that genie back in the bottle."

"This does not make me feel better." She ran her hand over her hair. It felt much smoother than normal. She didn't feel normal right now.

"As I was saying," Matthew went on with a tense voice, "I've sent out a short, hopefully boring press release announcing that we're happy you're here. Then tonight my younger brother Byron will do something excessive and highly Beaumont-like."

"Wait, what?"

He didn't look at her—traffic was picking up—but his grin was hard to miss. "Byron's going to bury the lead. That's you."

"I—I don't understand. I thought you wanted the Beaumonts to stay *out* of the headlines." She was sure that he'd said something to that effect yesterday.

"I do. Byron was going to be newsworthy anyway. He flew off to Europe over a year ago and even I don't know why. This is just…building on that buzz."

She gave him a look. Was he serious?

He was.

"And it's the kind of situation I'm used to dealing with," he went on. "I can control this kind of press. I'm not going to let people manhandle you." He said it in such a serious tone that she was momentarily stunned.

"Why?"

"Why what?"

She swallowed, hoping she wouldn't trip over her words.

At least she was safely buckled in a car. The chances of her tripping over her feet were almost zero. "Why are you doing this for me?"

"Because it's the right thing to do."

She wanted to believe that. Desperately. But... "You're going to throw a Beaumont under the bus for me? You don't even know me."

"That's not true. And it's not throwing Byron under the bus if he willingly agrees. The situation is under control," he said again, as if it was a mantra.

She wasn't sure she believed that, no matter how many times he said it. "You don't even *know* me," she repeated. "Yesterday you wouldn't have just thrown me under the bus to stay on message—you would have backed the bus over me a few times for good measure."

"I know you breed award-winning horses, rescue dogs, name your cats after aging pop singers and will do anything for your friends, even if it puts you in the line of fire." He glanced over at her. "I know you prefer jeans and boots but that you can wear a dress as well as any woman I've ever seen. I know that once you were a rock star but now you're not."

Her cheeks warmed at the compliments, but then she realized what he'd said. Rock star? She'd played a rock star on television. Most people considered her an actress first—if they considered her a musician at all.

Unless... There was something going on here, something that she had to figure out right now. "You recognized me. Right away."

He didn't respond immediately, but she saw him grip the steering wheel even tighter. "Everyone recognizes you. You saw what happened at lunch today."

"Women recognize me," she clarified. "Who watched the show when they were kids."

"I'm sure they do." Did he sound tense? He did.

She was getting closer to that *something*. "Did you watch my show?"

"Frances did." He sounded as if he was talking through gritted teeth. "My younger sister."

"Did you watch it with her?"

The moment stretched long enough that he really didn't have to answer. He used to watch the show. He used to watch *her*. "Did you see me in concert? Is that why you called me a rock star?"

In response, he honked the horn and jerked the car across two lanes. "Stupid drivers," he muttered.

Normally, she wouldn't want to know. She didn't want people's version of her past to project onto her present. But she needed to know—was this the reason why he'd run so hot and cold with her?

"Matthew."

"Yes, okay? I used to watch your show with Frances and Byron. Frances, especially, was a huge fan. We never missed an episode. It was the only time when I could *make* time for them, make sure they didn't feel forgotten by the family. Our father had already moved on to another wife, another set of new children and another mistress. He never had time for them, for any of us. And I didn't want my brother and sister to grow up like I had. So I watched the show with them. Every single one of them. And then your concert tour came through Denver the week before their fifteenth birthday, so I got them front-row tickets and took them. Our father had forgotten it was their birthday, but I didn't."

She sat there, flabbergasted. Jo had said Hardwick Beaumont was a bastard of a man, but to not even remember your own kids' birthdays?

"And…and you were amazing, all right? I'd always wondered if you really did the singing and guitar on the show or if it was dubbed. But it was all you up on that stage. You put on a hell of a show." His voice trailed off, as if he was lost in the memory, impressed with her musical talents all over again. "I'd always…" He sighed heavily.

"What? You'd always *what*?"

"I'd always had a crush on you." His voice was quiet, as if he couldn't believe he was saying the words out loud. "Seeing you in person—seeing how talented you really were—only made it worse. But then the show got canceled and you went off the rails and I felt…stupid. Like I'd fallen for a lie. I'd let myself be tricked because you were so pretty and talented. I was in college by then—it really wasn't cool to crush on a teen star. And the headlines—every time you made headlines, I felt tricked all over again."

Okay, so how was she supposed to reply to *that*? *Gosh, I'm sorry I destroyed a part of your childhood? That I never had a childhood?*

She'd had people tell her they loved her before—had it shouted at her on sidewalks. Love letters that came through her agent—he forwarded them to her with the quarterly royalty checks. And she'd had more than a few people tell her how disappointed they were that she wasn't a proper role model, that she wasn't really a squeaky-clean rock star.

That she wasn't what they wanted her to be.

"You weren't— Last night…you weren't mad at me?"

He chuckled. It was not a happy sound. "No. I was mad at myself."

Why hadn't she seen it earlier? He'd had a crush on her. He might have even fancied himself in love with her.

No, not with her. With Whitney Wildz.

"But *you* kissed *me*."

True, it hadn't been a let's-get-naked kind of kiss, but that didn't change the basic facts. He'd told her she was beautiful at several important points throughout the day, gone out of his way to reassure her, listened to her talk about her pets and…kissed her anyway.

He scrubbed a hand through his hair, then took an exit off

the highway. It was several minutes before he spoke. "I did." He said it as though he still didn't believe it. "My apologies."

"You're apologizing? For the kiss? Was it that bad?"

Yeah, he'd sort of taken her by surprise—she'd been in a state of shock about her face—but that wasn't going to be *it*, was it? One strike and she was out of luck?

"You didn't kiss me back."

"Because I didn't know who you thought you were kissing." Point of fact, despite all the illuminating personal details he'd just revealed, she *still* didn't know who he'd thought he was kissing.

"You," he said simply. "I was kissing you."

She opened her mouth to ask, *Who?*

This was not the time for ambiguous personal pronouns. This was the time for clarity, by God. Because if he still thought he was kissing a rock star or an actress, she couldn't kiss him back. She just couldn't.

But if he was kissing a klutz who rescued puppies…

She didn't get the chance to ask for that vital clarification, because suddenly they were at the guard gate for Beaumont Farms. "Mr. Beaumont, Ms. Maddox," the guard said, waving them through.

Matthew took the road back to the house at what felt like a reckless speed. They whipped around corners so fast she had to hold on to the door handle. Then they were screeching to a halt in front of Phillip and Jo's house. The place was dark.

Whitney's head was spinning from more than just his driving. She couldn't look at him, so she stared at the empty-looking house. "Who am I? Who am I to you?"

Out of the corner of her eye, she saw his hands flex around the steering wheel. After today she wouldn't be surprised if he'd permanently bent it out of shape, what with all the white-knuckle gripping he'd been doing.

He didn't answer the question. Instead, he said, "Can I walk you inside?"

"All right."

They got out of the car. Matthew opened the door to the house for her and then stood to the side so she could enter first. She had to stop—it was dark and she didn't know where the light switches were located.

"Here." Matthew's voice was close to her ear as he reached around her. She stepped back—back into the wall.

He flipped the light on but he didn't move away from her. Instead, he stood there, staring down at her with something that looked a heck of a lot like hunger.

What did people do in this situation?

To hell with what other people did. What did *she* want to do?

She still wanted the same thing she'd wanted when she'd shown up here—a little Christmas fling to dip her toes back into the water of dating and relationships. She still wanted to feel sexy and pretty and, yes, graceful.

But the way that Matthew was looking down at her...there was something else there, something more than just a casual attraction that might lead to some really nice casual sex.

It scared her.

"I don't think they're home," he said, his voice husky.

"That's a shame," she replied. He'd made her feel pretty today, but right now? That hunger in his eyes?

She felt sexy. Desirable.

He wanted her.

She wanted to be wanted.

Just a Christmas fling. The maid of honor and the best man. Something that'd be short and sweet and so, *so* satisfying.

He hesitated. "Is it?"

"No." She turned until her back was against the wall.

His other arm came up beside her, trapping her in between them. "I'll stop. If you want me to."

She touched one of his cheeks. His eyelashes fluttered. But he hadn't answered her question.

He seemed to realize it. "I don't know what you are to me," he told her, the words coming out almost harsh. He leaned down and touched his forehead to hers. "But I know *who* you are."

This time, she knew the kiss wouldn't be the soft, gentle thing he'd pressed against her lips before. This time, it would be a kiss that consumed her.

She wanted to be consumed.

But he hadn't clarified anything, damn it. She put her hands on his chest and pushed just hard enough to stop him. Not hard enough to push him away. "Tell me, Matthew. Tell me who you're going to kiss."

Now both of his hands were cradling her face—pulling her up to him. "Whitney," he whispered. The length of his body pressed her back against the wall, strong and hard and everything she wanted it to be. "Whitney Maddox."

She didn't wait for him to kiss her. She kissed him first. She dug her fingers into the front of his sweater and hauled him down so she could take possession of his mouth, so she could offer up her own for him.

He groaned into her as she nipped at his lower lip. Then he took control of the kiss. His tongue swept into hers as his hands trailed down her cheeks, onto her neck and down her shoulders. Then he picked her up. The sudden change in altitude caused her to gasp.

"You need to be taller," he told her as he kissed along her cheek to her neck, her ear. His hands were flat against her bottom, boosting her to make up for the eight-inch height difference between them. Then he squeezed.

She had no choice. Her legs went around his waist, pulling him into her. She could feel his erection straining against his pants, pressing against her. She trembled, suddenly filled with a longing she couldn't ignore for a single second more.

Then his hips moved, rocking into hers. The pressure was intense—*he* was intense. Even though she had on jeans, she could feel the pads of his fingertips through the denim, squeezing her, pulling her apart.

His body rocked against hers, hitting the spot that sent the pressure spiraling up. She wanted to touch him, wanted to feel all the muscles that were holding her up as if she weighed nothing at all, but suddenly she had to hold on to him for dear life as he ground against her.

Her head fell back and bounced off the wall, but she didn't care—and she cared a whole lot less when Matthew started nipping at her neck, her collarbone. His hips flexed, driving him against her center again and again.

"Oh," she gasped. "Oh, Matthew."

"Do you like it," he growled against her chest.

"Yes."

"Louder." He thrust harder.

"Yes—*Oh!*" She gasped again—he was— She was going to—

He rocked against her again, in time with his teeth finding the spot between her shoulder and neck. He bit down and rubbed and—and—

"Oh yes, oh yes, *oh yes!*" she cried out as he pinned her back against the wall and held her up as she climaxed.

"Kiss me back," he told her, his forehead resting against hers. He was still cupping her bottom in his hands, but instead of the possessive squeezing, he was now massaging her. The sensation was just right. *He* was just right. "Always kiss me back."

So she kissed him, even as the climax ebbed and her body sagged in his arms. She kissed him with everything she had, everything she wanted.

Because she wanted everything. Especially a man who put her first.

"Tell me what you want," he said. Already his hips were

moving again, the pressure between her legs building. "I want this to be perfect for you. Tell me everything you want."

She cupped his cheeks in her hands. "Perfect?"

He gave her a look that started out as embarrassed but quickly became wicked. "Do you doubt me?"

After that orgasm? For heaven's sake, they were still fully clothed! What was he capable of when they were naked?

She grinned at him, feeling wicked in her own right. "Prove it."

Nine

"Oh, I'll prove it," Matthew told her. He hefted her up again. Then they were moving. He carried her through the house. He knew where they were going—his old room. If he didn't get all these clothes off them and bury himself in her body soon, he might just explode.

She wasn't helping. True, she didn't weigh very much and, since he was carrying her, she didn't trip or stumble into him. But the way she busied herself by scraping her teeth over his earlobe? He was going to lose it. Him, who was always in control of the situation. Of himself.

She'd stripped that control away from him the moment she'd walked into his life.

"This is my old room," he told her when they got to her door. He managed to get the door open. Then he kicked it shut.

Then he laid her out on the bed. Normally, he took his time with women. He was able to keep a part of himself back—keep a certain distance from what he was doing, what they were trying to do to him. Oh, they enjoyed it—he did, as well—but that level of emotional detachment was important somehow. He didn't know why. It just was.

Besides, being detached made it easier to make sure the women he was with were getting what they wanted from him.

But seeing Whitney on his old bed? Her hair was mussed now, her red lipstick smudged. She was no longer the perfect beauty he'd tentatively—yes, detachedly—kissed in the salon.

She was, however, his. His for right now. And he couldn't hold back.

He stripped off his coat while she tried to wriggle out of her jeans. Then, just as he had his sweater over his head, she kicked him in the stomach.

"Oof," he got out through clenched teeth. He stepped out of range and jerked the sweater the rest of the way off.

"Sorry! Oh, my gosh, I'm so sorry." Whitney lay on her back. She had one leg halfway out of her jeans, the other stuck around the ankle. "I didn't— I wasn't trying to— Oh, *damn*."

He caught the jeans, now practically inside out, and yanked them off her. Then he climbed onto the bed. Her blush was anything but pale or demure. An embarrassing red scorched her cheeks.

"I'm sorry," she whispered, looking as if she might start crying.

He straddled her bare legs as he pinned her wrists by her head. "None of that," he scolded her. "Nervous?"

She dropped her gaze and gave him a noncommittal shrug.

"Look at me," he told her. "Do you still want to do this?"

She didn't look. "I'm such a klutz. I'm sorry I kicked you."

"*Look* at me, Whitney," he ordered. When she didn't, he slid her wrists over her head so he could hold them with one hand and then he took her by the jaw and turned her face to his.

There was so much going on under the surface. She was trying to hide it by not looking at him, but he wasn't having any of it. "Apology accepted. Now forget it happened."

"But—"

He cut her off with a kiss, his hand sliding down her neck. "One of the things I like about you is that you get clumsy when you're nervous. It's cute."

Defiance flashed over her face. Good. "I don't want to be cute."

"What do you want?"

She sucked in a tiny breath—and was silent.

Oh, no, you don't, he thought. He snaked his hand down her front and then up under her sweater until he found her breast.

God, what a breast. Full and heavy and warm—and so responsive. Even through her bra, her nipple went to a stiff point as he teased her. "Is that what you want?"

She didn't answer. Not in words. But her breathing was faster now, and she'd tucked her lower lip into her mouth.

What control he had regained when she'd kicked him started to fray like a rope. He rolled her nipple between his finger and thumb. Her back arched into him, so he did it again, harder. "Is that what you want?"

She nodded.

"Say it," he told her. "Say it or I will tie you to this bed and *make* you say it."

The moment the words left his mouth, he wondered where they'd come from. He didn't just randomly tie people up. He wasn't into that kinky stuff. And when he'd dreamed of making it with Whitney Wildz, well, hell, back then, he hadn't even known people did that sort of thing.

But she didn't reply. Her eyes got huge and she was practically panting, but she didn't utter a word.

Then she licked her lips. And he lost his head.

Challenge accepted.

He let go of her breast and pulled her up, then peeled her sweater off her. The bra followed. She said nothing as he tore her clothes off, but when he kissed the side of her breast, when he let his tongue trace over her now-bare shoulder, she shuddered into him.

He couldn't stop whatever this was he'd started. He'd made her cry out in the entry hall. He'd make her do it again. He wrenched his tie off, then looped it around her wrists. Not tight—he didn't want to hurt her. But knowing her, she'd hit him in the nose with her elbow and nothing ruined some really hot sex like a bloody nose.

The tie secure around her wrists, he loosely knotted it to the headboard. Then he got off the bed.

Whitney Maddox was nude except for a thin pair of pale pink panties that looked so good against her skin. Her breasts were amazing—he wanted to bury his face in them and lick them until she cried his name over and over.

And she was tied to his bed.

Because she'd let him do that. Because she'd *wanted* him to do that.

He'd never been so excited in his life.

He stripped fast, pausing only long enough to get the condom out of his wallet. He rolled it on and then went to her. "I want to see all of you," he said, pulling her panties down. She started to lift her legs so he could get them off her ankles, but he held her feet down. "I'm in charge here, Whitney."

He trailed a finger down between her breasts, watching her shiver at his touch. Finally, *finally*, she spoke.

"I expect perfection."

"And that's what you'll get."

He climbed between her legs and stroked her body. She moaned, her head thrashing from side to side as he touched her.

He couldn't wait much longer. "You okay?" he asked. He wanted to be sure. They could play this little game about making her say it, but he also didn't want to hurt her. "If it's not okay, you tell me."

"This is okay. This is…" She tried to shift her hips closer to his dick. "Am I…am I sexy?"

"Oh, babe," he said. But he couldn't answer her, not in words. So he fit his body to hers and thrust in.

"Matthew!" she gasped in the same breathless way she'd cried his name in the hall.

"Yeah, louder," he ground out as he drove in harder.

"Matthew!" she cried again. Her legs tried to come off the bed, and she almost kneed him in the ribs.

"Oh, no, you don't," he told her as he grabbed her legs and tucked them up under his arms. Then he leaned down into her.

She was completely open to him, and he took advantage of that in every way he knew how—and a few he didn't even know he knew.

"Is this what you want?" he demanded over and over.

"Yes." Always, she said yes.

"Say it louder," he ordered her, riding her harder.

"Yes! Oh, Matthew—*yes*!"

There was nothing else but the moment between when he slid out of her body and drove back in. No thoughts of family or message or public image. Nothing but the woman beneath him, crying out his name again and again.

Suddenly her body tensed up around his. "Kiss me," she demanded. "Kiss me!"

"Kiss me back," he told her before he lowered his lips to hers.

Everything about her went tight as she kissed him. Then she fell back, panting heavily.

Matthew surrendered himself to her body. He couldn't fight it anymore.

Then he collapsed onto her chest. Her legs slid down his, holding him close. He knew he needed to get up—he didn't want to lose the condom—but there was something about holding her after what he'd done to her…

Jesus—had he really tied her up? Made her cry out his name? That was…something his father would have done.

"Can you untie me now?" she asked, sounding breathless and happy.

Focus, he told himself. So he sat back and undid the tie from the headboard. He'd really liked that tie, too, but he doubted it'd ever be the same.

He started to get out of bed to get cleaned up and dressed, but she sat up and tackle-hugged him so hard it almost hurt. But not quite. After he got over his momentary shock, he wrapped his arms around her.

"Thank you," she whispered. "It was…"

"Perfect?" He hoped so, for her sake.

At that, she leaned back and gave him the most suggestive smile he'd ever seen. He could take her again. He had another condom. He could loop his demolished tie back through the headboard and…

"I'm not sure. We might have to do it again later. Just to have a point of comparison, you understand." Then a shadow of doubt crossed her face. "If you wanted to," she hurried to add.

He pulled her back into his arms. "I'd like that. I'd like that a lot. You were amazing. Except for the kicking part."

She giggled, her chin tucked in the crook of his neck. He grabbed one of her wrists and kissed where he'd had it bound.

Then, from the floor, his phone chimed Phillip's text message chime.

And the weight of what he was supposed to be doing came crushing back down on him.

Why was he lolling away the afternoon in bed with Whitney? This was not the time to be tying people up, for crying out loud. He had a wedding to pull off—a family image to save.

An image that was going to be a whole hell of a lot harder to save when Byron got done with it.

Matthew had to keep the wheels from falling off. He had

to take care of the family. He had to prove he was one of them. A Beaumont.

Then Whitney kissed his jaw. "Do you need to go?"

"Yeah."

He didn't want to. He wanted to stay here, wrapped up with her. He wanted to say to hell with the wedding, the message—he didn't care. He'd done the best he could.

He cared about Whitney. He shouldn't—her old image was going to keep making headaches for him and it'd been only twenty-four hours since he'd met her.

But that didn't change things.

And yet it changed everything.

The phone chimed again. And again. Different chimes. It sounded as though Byron had pulled his stunt.

"I've got to go bail out Byron," he told her. "But I'll see you soon." He got off the bed, trashed the condom and got dressed as fast as he could. By now his phone sounded like a bell choir.

"When?" She sat on the bed, her knees tucked up under her chin. Except for the part where she was completely nude—or maybe because of it—there was an air of vulnerability about her.

"Lunch, tomorrow. You've got to choose where you want to have the bachelorette party. I'll take you to all the places I've scouted out." He picked up his phone. Jeez, that was a lot of messages in less than five minutes. "What a mess," he muttered at his phone. "I'll get you at eleven—that'll give you time with Jo and it'll give me time to fix this."

He leaned down and gave her a quick, hard kiss. Then he was out the door.

He knew he shouldn't be surprised that Phillip was standing in the living room—this was his house, after all—but the last thing Matthew needed right now was to be confronted by his brother.

Phillip looked at him with a raised eyebrow. But instead

of asking about Whitney, he said, "Byron got picked up. He said to tell you he's sorry, but the black eye was unavoidable."

Matthew's shoulders sagged. His little brother had done exactly what he wanted him to—but damned if it didn't feel as though Matthew was suddenly right back at the bottom of the very big mountain he was doomed to be constantly climbing—Mount Beaumont. "What'd he do?"

"He went to a restaurant, ordered dinner, asked to see the chef and proceeded to get into a fistfight with the man."

Matthew rubbed the bridge of his nose. "And?"

"The media is reporting he ordered the salmon."

"Ha-ha. Very funny. I'll get him."

He was halfway to the door when Phillip said, "Everything okay with Whitney?"

"Fine," he shot back as he picked up the pace. He had to get out of here, fast.

But Phillip was faster. He caught up to Matthew at the door. "Better than yesterday?"

"Yes. Now, if you'll excuse me…"

Phillip grinned. "Never thought you had it in you, man. You always went for such…boring women."

"I don't know what you're talking about."

Denial—whether it was to the press or his family—came easily to Matthew. He had years of practice, after all.

"Right, right." He gave Matthew the smile that Matthew had long ago learned to hate—the one that said *I'm better than you are*. "Just a tip, though—from one Beaumont to another—always wipe the lipstick off *before* you leave the bedroom."

Matthew froze. Then he scrubbed the back of his hand across his mouth. It came away bright red.

Whitney's lipstick.

"Uh…this isn't what it looks like."

"Really? Because it looks like you spent the afternoon sleeping with the maid of honor." Matthew's fists curled, but

Phillip threw up his hands in self-defense. "Whatever, man. I'm not about to throw stones at your glass house. Say," he went on in a too-casual voice, "this wouldn't have anything to do with Byron telling me he'd done what you asked him to, would it? Except for the black eye, of course."

Matthew moved before he realized what he was doing. He grabbed Phillip by the front of his shirt. "Do. Not. Give. Her. Crap."

"Dude!" Phillip said, trying to peel Matthew's hands away from his shirt. "Down, boy—down!"

"Promise me, Phillip. After all the messes I cleaned up for you—all the times I saved your ass—*promise me* that you won't torture that woman. Or Byron won't be the only one with a black eye at this wedding."

"Easy, man—I'm not going to do anything."

Matthew let go of his brother. "Sorry."

"No, you're not. Go." Phillip pushed him toward the door. "Bail Byron out so we can all line up for your perfect family wedding. That's what you want, isn't it?"

As Matthew drove off, his mind was a jumble of wedding stuff and family stuff and Whitney. Zipping Whitney into the bridesmaid dress. Stripping her out of her clothes. Admiring her perfectly done hair. Messing her hair up.

He had to pull this wedding off. He had to stay on message. He had to prove he belonged up there with the other Beaumonts, standing by Phillip's side.

That was what Matthew wanted.

Wasn't it?

Ten

She checked her watch. Three to eleven. She'd gotten up at her regular time and gone out with Jo to look at the young mare she was working with. Jo hadn't pressed her about Matthew, except to say, "You and Matthew…" there'd been a rather long pause, but Whitney hadn't jumped into the breach "…do all right yesterday?" Jo had finally finished.

"Yeah. I think you were right about him—he seems like a good guy who's wound a bit too tight."

Which *had* to be the explanation as to why he'd tied her to the bed with a necktie.

Which did nothing to explain why she'd let him do it and explained even less why she'd enjoyed it.

And now? Now she was going to spend the afternoon with him again. Which was great—because it'd been so long since she'd had sex with another person and Matthew wasn't just up to the task—he was easily the best lover she'd ever had.

But it was also nerve-racking. After all, he'd tied her to the bed and made her climax several times. How was she supposed to look him in the eye after that? Yes, she'd slept around a lot when she'd been an out-of-control teenager trying to prove she was an adult. Yes, she'd had some crazy sex. The gossips never let her forget that.

But she'd never had that kind of sex clean and sober. She'd never had any kind of sex sober. She'd never looked a lover in the eye without some sort of chemical aid to cover up her anxiety at what she'd done, what she might still do.

And now, as she adjusted her hat and sunglasses, she was going to have to do just that. She had no idea what to do next. At least she had Betty—the small donkey's ears were soft, and rubbing them helped Whitney keep some sort of hold on her anxiety. It would be fine, she kept telling herself as she petted Betty. *It* will *be fine.*

At exactly eleven, Matthew walked through the door at Phillip and Jo's house, cupped her face in his hands and made her forget everything except the way she'd felt beneath his hands, his body. Beautiful. Sexy.

Alive.

"Hi," he breathed as he rested his forehead against hers.

Maybe this wouldn't be complicated. It hadn't seemed complicated when he'd pinned her to the wall yesterday. Maybe it would be…easy. She grinned, slipping her arms around his waist. "Hi." Then she looked at him. "You're wearing a tie?"

Color touched his cheeks, but he didn't look embarrassed. If anything, he looked the way he had yesterday—hungry for more. Hungry for her.

"I usually wear ties." Heat flushed down her back and pooled low. But instead of pulling that tie off, he added, "Are you ready?"

She nodded, unable to push back against the anxiety. This time, at least, it didn't have anything to do with him. "We have to go, right?"

He leaned back and adjusted her hat, making sure her hair was fully tucked under it. "We'll just look at the places. And after yesterday, I cut a couple of the other options off the list, so it's only four places. We'll park, go in, look at the menu and come back out. Okay?"

"What about lunch?" Because the going-in part hadn't been the problem yesterday.

"I decided we'll have lunch at my apartment."

She looked at him in surprise. "You decided, huh?"

Thus far, she hadn't actually managed to successfully make it through a meal with him. If they were alone at his place, would they eat or…?

He ran his thumb over her lower lip. "I did." Then Betty butted against his legs, demanding that he pet her, too. "You getting ready to walk down the aisle, girl?" he asked as he checked his phone. "We need to get going."

Despite the kiss that followed this statement—how was she going to make it to lunch without ripping his clothes off?—by the time they got into the car and were heading off the farm, she was back to feeling uneasy. She didn't normally fall into bed with a man she'd known for a day. Not since she'd started over.

Matthew had said he knew she was Whitney Maddox… but had he, really? He'd admitted having a huge crush on her back in the day.

"You're nervous," he announced when they were back on the highway, heading toward Denver.

She couldn't deny it. At least she'd made it into the car without stepping on him or anything. But she couldn't bring herself to admit that she was nervous about him. So she went with the other thing that was bothering her. "How's your brother—Byron?"

Matthew exhaled heavily. "He's fine. I got him bailed out. Our lawyers are working to get the charges dropped. But his black eye won't be gone by the wedding, so I had to add him to the makeup artist's list."

"Oh." He sounded extremely put out by this situation, but she was pretty sure he'd told his brother to do something dramatic. To bury her lead. She couldn't help but feel that, at the heart of it, this was her fault.

"The media took the bait, though. You didn't even make the website for the *Denver Post*. Who could pass up the chance to dig up dirt on the Beaumont Prodigal Son Returned? That's the headline the *Post* went with this morning. It's already been picked up by *Gawker* and *TMZ*."

She felt even worse. That wasn't the message Matthew wanted. She was sure that this was exactly what he'd wanted to avoid.

"You're quiet again," he said. He reached over and rubbed her thigh. "This isn't your fault."

The touch was reassuring. "But you're off message. Byron getting arrested isn't rehabilitating the Beaumont family image."

"I know." He exhaled heavily again. "But I can fix this. It's what I do. There's no such thing as bad PR."

Okay, that was another question that she didn't have an answer to. "Why? Why is *that* what you do?"

Matthew pulled his hand back and started drumming his fingers against the steering wheel. "How much do you know about the Beaumonts?"

"Um…well, you guys were a family beer company until recently. And Jo told me your father had a bunch of different children with four different wives and he had a lot of mistresses. And he forgot about your sister and brother's birthday."

"Did Jo say anything else?"

"Just that you'd threatened all the ex-wives to be on their best behavior."

"I did, you know." He chuckled again, but there was at least a little humor in it this time. "I told them if they caused a scene, I'd make an example out of them. No one's hands are clean in this family. I've buried too many scandals." He shot her an all-knowing grin. "They won't risk pissing me off. They know what I could do to them."

She let that series of ominous statements sink in. Suddenly, she felt as if she was facing the man who'd caught her the first night—the man who'd bury her if he got the chance.

But that wasn't the man who'd made love to her last night—was it? Had he offered his brother up as bait to protect her…or because that was still an easier mess to clean up than the one she'd make?

"Are your hands clean?"

"What?"

"You said no one's hands in your family are clean. Does that include you?"

His jaw tensed, and he looked at her again. He didn't say it, but she could tell what he was thinking. Not anymore. Not since he tied her to the bed.

Just then his phone chimed. He glanced down at the screen before announcing, "We need to keep to the schedule."

Right. They weren't going to talk about him right now.

He obviously knew a great deal about her past, but what did she know about him? He was a Beaumont, but he was behind the scenes, keeping everyone on message and burying leads.

"We're here," he announced after a few more minutes of driving. She nodded and braced herself for the worst.

The restaurant seemed overdone—white walls, white chairs, white carpet and what was probably supposed to be avant-garde art done in shades of black on the wall. A white tree with white ornaments stood near the front. It was the most depressing Christmas tree Whitney had ever seen. If a restaurant was capable of trying too hard, this one was. Whitney knew that Jo would be miserable in a place like this.

"Seriously?" she whispered to Matthew after reading the menu. Most of it was in French. She had no idea what kind of food they served here, only that it would be snooty.

"One of the best restaurants in the state," he assured her.

Then they went to a smaller restaurant with only six tables

that had a menu full of locally grown microgreens and other items that Whitney wasn't entirely sure qualified as food. Honest to God, one of the items touted a kind of tree bark.

"How well do you even know Jo?" she asked Matthew as they sped away from the hipster spot. "I mean, really. She's a cowgirl, for crying out loud. She likes burgers and fries."

"It's a nice restaurant," he defended. "I've taken dates there."

"Oh? And you're still seeing those women, are you?"

Matthew shot her a comically mean look.

She giggled at him. This was nice. Comfortable. Plus, she hadn't had to take her hat or sunglasses off, so no one had even looked twice at her. "Gosh, maybe it was your pretentious taste in dining, huh?"

"Careful," he said, trying to sound serious. The grin, however, completely undermined him. "Or I'll get my revenge on you later."

All that glorious heat wrapped around the base of her spine, radiating outward. What was he offering? And more to the point—would she take him up on it this time?

Still, she didn't want to come off as naive. "Promises, promises. Do either of the remaining places serve real food?"

"One." His phone chimed again. "Hang on." He answered it. "Yes? Yes, we're on our way. Yes. That's correct. Thanks."

"*We're* on our way?"

That got her another grin, but this one was less humorous, hungrier. "You'll see."

After a few more minutes, they arrived at their destination. It wasn't so much a restaurant but a pub. Actually, that was its name—the Pub. Instead of the prissiness of the first two places, this was all warm wood and polished brass. "A bar?"

"A pub," he corrected her. "I know Jo doesn't drink, so I was trying to avoid places that had a bar feel to them. But if I left it up to Frances, she'd have you all down at a male strip club, shoving twenties into G-strings."

Realization smacked her upside the head. This wasn't about her or even Jo—this whole search for a place to have a bachelorette party was about managing his sister's image. "You were trying to put us in places that would look good in the society page."

His mouth opened, but then he shut it with a sheepish look. "You're right."

The hostess came forward. "Mr. Beaumont, one moment and I'll get your order."

"Wait, what?"

He turned to her and grinned. "I promised you lunch." He handed her a menu. "Here you go."

"But…you already ordered."

"For the bachelorette party," he said, tipping the menu toward her.

She looked it over. There were a few oddities—microgreens, again!—but although the burgers were touted as being locally raised and organic, they were still burgers. With fries.

"In the back," Matthew explained while they were waiting, "they have a more private room." He leaned down so that his mouth was right by her ear. "It's perfect, don't you think?"

Heat flushed her neck. She certainly hadn't expected Denver at Christmas to be this…warming. "You knew I was going to pick this place, didn't you?"

"Actually, I reserved rooms in all four restaurants. There'll be people looking to stalk the wedding party no matter what. And since we've been seen going over the menu at three of the places, they won't know where to start. This will throw them off the trail."

She gaped at him. *That* was what covering your bases looked like. She'd never been able to plan like that. Which was why she was never ready for the press.

"Really? I can't decide if that's the most paranoid thing I've ever heard or the most brilliant."

He grinned, brushing his fingers over her cheek. "You can't be too careful."

He was going to kiss her. In public. She, more than anyone, knew what a bad idea that was. But she was powerless to stop him, to pull away. Something about this man destroyed her common sense.

The hostess saved Whitney from herself. "Your order, Mr. Beaumont."

"Thank you. And we have the private room for Friday night?"

"Yes, Mr. Beaumont."

Matthew grabbed the bagged food. "Come on. My place isn't too far away."

Matthew pulled into the underground parking lot at the Acoma apartments. He'd guessed right about the Pub, which was a good feeling. And after Whitney's observations about burgers and fries, he felt even better about ordering her that for lunch.

But best of all was the feeling of taking Whitney to his apartment. He didn't bring women home very often. He'd had a couple of dates that turned out to be looking for a story to tell—and sell. Keeping his address private was an excellent way to make sure that he wouldn't get up in the morning and find paparazzi parked outside the building, ready to catch his date leaving his place in the same outfit she'd had on the night before.

He wasn't worried about that happening with Whitney. First off, he had no plans of keeping her here all night long—although that realization left him feeling strangely disappointed. But second?

As far as he could tell, no one had made him as the man sitting next to Whitney Wildz the other day. Frankly, he couldn't believe it—it wasn't as if he were an unknown quantity. He talked to the press and his face was more than recognizable as a Beaumont.

Still, it was a bit of grace he was willing to use as he led Whitney to the elevator that went up to the penthouse apartment.

Inside, he pressed her back against the wall and kissed her hungrily. Lunch could wait, right?

Then she moaned into his mouth, and his body responded. He'd wanted to do this since he'd walked into Phillip's house this morning—show her that he could be spontaneous, that he could give her more than just one afternoon. He wanted to show her that there was more to him than the Beaumont name.

Even as the thought crossed his mind, the unfamiliarity of it struck him as...wrong. Hadn't it *always* been about the Beaumont name?

"Oh, Matthew," she whispered against his skin.

Yeah, lunch could wait.

Then the doors opened. "Come on," he said, pulling her out of the elevator and into his penthouse.

He wanted to go directly to the bedroom—but Whitney pulled up short. "Wow. This is...perfect."

"Thanks." He let go of her long enough to set the lunch bag down on a counter. But before he could wrap his arms around her again, she'd walked farther in—not toward the floor-to-ceiling windows but toward the far side of the sitting room.

The one with his pictures.

As Whitney stared at the Wall of Accomplishments, as he thought of it, something Phillip had said last night came back to him. *You always went for such boring women.*

They hadn't been boring. They'd been *safe.* On paper, at least, they'd been perfect. Businesswomen who had no interest in marrying into the Beaumont fortune because they had their own money. Quiet women who had no interest in scoring an invite to the latest Beaumont Brewery blowout because they didn't drink beer.

Women who wouldn't make a splash in the society pages.

Whitney? She was already making waves in his life—waves he couldn't control. And he was enjoying it. Craving more. Craving *her.*

"This…" Whitney said, leaning up on her tiptoes to look at the large framed photo that was at the center of the Wall of Accomplishments. "This is a wedding photo."

Eleven

"Yes. That's my parents' wedding."

The tension in his voice was unmistakable.

"But you're in the picture. That's you, right? And the boy you're standing next to—that's Phillip? Is the other one Chadwick?" The confusion pushed back at the desire that was licking through her veins. She couldn't make sense out of what she was looking at.

"That's correct." He sounded as if he were confirming a news story.

"But…you're, like, five or something? You're a kid!"

A tight silence followed this statement. She might have crossed some line, but she didn't care. She was busy staring at the photo.

A man—Hardwick Beaumont—was in a very nice tuxedo. He stood next to a woman in an exceptionally poofy white dress that practically dripped crystals and pearls. She had giant teased red hair that wasn't contained at all by the headband that came to a V-point in the middle of her forehead. The look spoke volumes about the high style of the early '80s.

In front of them stood three boys, all in matching tuxedos. Hardwick had his hand on Chadwick's shoulder. Next to Chadwick stood a smaller boy with blond hair. He wore a wicked grin, like a sprite out to stir up trouble. And standing in front of the woman was Matthew. She had her hand on his shoulder as she beamed at the camera, but Matthew looked as though someone were jabbing him with a hatpin.

When he did speak, he asked, "You didn't know that I wasn't born a Beaumont?"

She turned to stare at him. "What? No—what does that mean?"

He nodded, nearly the same look on his face now that little-kid Matthew had worn for that picture. "Phillip is only six months older than I am."

"Really?"

He came to stand next to her, one arm around her waist. She leaned into him, enjoying this comfortable touch. Enjoying that he wasn't holding himself apart from her.

"It was a huge scandal at the time—even by Beaumont standards. My mother was his mistress while he was still married to Eliza—that's Phillip and Chadwick's mother." He paused, as if he were steeling himself to the truth. "Eliza didn't divorce him for another four years. I was born Matthew Billings."

"Wait—you didn't grow up with your dad?"

"Not until I was almost five. Eliza found out about me and divorced Hardwick. He kept custody of Chadwick and Phillip, married my mom and moved us into the Beaumont mansion."

She stared at him, then back at the small boy in the photo. *Matthew Billings.* "But you and Phillip seem so close. You're planning his wedding. I just thought…"

"That we'd grown up together? No." He laughed, a joyless noise. "I remember her telling me how I'd have my daddy and he'd love me, and I'd have some brothers who'd play with me, so I shouldn't be sad that we were leaving everything behind. She told me it was going to be perfect. Just…perfect."

The way he said it made it pretty clear that it wasn't. Was this why everything had to be *just so*? He'd spent his life chasing a dream of perfection?

"What happened?"

He snorted. "What do you think? Chadwick hated me—deeply and completely. Sometimes Phillip was nice to me because he was lonely, too." He pointed at the wedding photo. "Sometimes he and Chadwick would gang up on me because I wasn't a real Beaumont. Plus, my mom got pregnant with Frances and Byron almost immediately and once they were born…well, they were Beaumonts without question." He sighed.

His dad had forgotten about him. That was basically what Jo had said Hardwick Beaumont did—all those wives, mistresses and so many children that they didn't even know how many there were. What a legacy. "So how did you wind up as the one who takes care of everyone else?"

He moved, stepping back and wrapping both arms around her. "I had to prove I belonged—that I was a legitimate Beaumont, not a Billings." He lowered his head so that his lips rested against the base of her neck.

She would not let him distract her with something as simple, as perfect, as a kiss. Not when the key to understanding *why* was right in front of her.

"How did you do that?"

His arms were strong and warm around her as they pulled her back into his chest. All of his muscles pressed against her. and for a moment she wondered if he was going to push her against the wall and make her cry out his name again, just to avoid answering the question.

But then he said, "I copied Chadwick. I got all As, just like Chadwick did. I went to the same college, got the same MBA. I got a job at the Brewery, just like Chadwick. He was the perfect Beaumont—still is, in a lot of ways. I thought—It sounds stupid now, but I thought if I could just *be* the perfect Beaumont, my mom would stop crying in her closet and we'd be a happy family."

"Did it work?" Although she already knew the answer to that one.

"Not really." His arms tightened around her, and he splayed his fingers over her ribs in an intimate touch. She leaned into him, as if she could tell him that she was here for him. That he didn't have to be perfect for her.

"When Frances and Byron were four, my parents got divorced. Mom tried to get custody of us, but without Beaumont money, she had nothing and Hardwick's lawyers were ruthless. I was ten."

"Do you still see her?"

"Of course. She's my mother, after all. She works in a library now. It doesn't pay all of her bills, but she enjoys it. I take care of everything else." He sighed against her skin, his hands skimming over her waist. "She apologized once. Said she was sorry she'd ruined my life by marrying my father."

"Do you feel the same way?"

He made a big show of looking around his stunning apartment. "I don't really think this qualifies as 'ruined,' do you?"

"It looks perfect," she agreed. But then, so did the wedding photo. One big happy family.

"Yeah, well, if there's one thing being a Beaumont has taught me, it's that looks are everything. Like when a jealous husband caught Dad with his wife. There was a scene—well, that's putting it mildly. I was in college and walked out of my apartment one morning and into this throng of reporters and photographers and they were demanding a good reaction quote from me—they wanted something juicy, you know?"

"I know." God, it was like reliving her own personal hell all over again. She could see the paparazzi jostling for position, shouting horrible things.

"I didn't know anything about what had happened, so I just started…making stuff up." He sounded as if he still didn't believe he'd done that. "The photos had been doctored. People would do anything for attention, including lay a trap for the richest man in Denver—and we would be suing for libel. The family would support Hardwick because he was right. And the press—they took the bait. Swallowed it hook, line and sinker. I saved his image." His voice trailed off. "He was proud of me. He told me, 'That's how a Beaumont handles it.' Told me to keep taking care of the family and it'd be just fine."

"Was it?"

"Of course not. His third wife left him—but he bought her off. He always bought them off and kept custody of the kids because it was good for his image as a devoted family man who just had really lousy luck when it came to women. But I'd handled myself so well that when a position in the Brewery public relations department opened up, I got the job."

He'd gone to work for his brother after that unhappy childhood. She wasn't sure she could be that big of a person. "Do your brothers still hate you?"

He laughed. "Hell, no. I'm too valuable to them. I've gotten Phillip out of more trouble than he even remembers and Chadwick counts me as one of his most trusted advisors. I'm…" He swallowed. "I'm one of them now. A legitimate Beaumont—the brother of honor at the wedding, even. Not a bastard that married into the family five years too late." He nuzzled at the base of her neck. "I just… I wish I'd known it would all work out when I was a kid, you know?"

She knew. She still wished she knew it would all work out. Somehow. "You know what I was doing when I was five?"

"What?"

"Auditions. My mother was dragging me to tryouts for commercials," she whispered into the silence. "I didn't care about acting. I just wanted to ride horses and color, but she wanted me to be famous. *She* wanted to be famous."

She'd never understood what Jade Maddox got out of it,

putting Whitney in front of all those people so she could pretend she was someone else. Hadn't just being herself been enough for her mother?

But the answer had been no. Always no. "My first real part was on *Larry the Llama*—remember that show? I was Lulu."

Behind her, Matthew stilled. Then, suddenly, he was laughing. The joy spilled out of him and surrounded her, making her smile with him. "You were on the llama show? That show was terrible!"

"Oh, I know it. Llamas are *weird*. Apparently everyone agreed because it was canceled about six months later. I'd hoped that was the end of my mother's ambitions. But it wasn't. I *dreamed* about having brothers or sisters. I didn't even meet my dad until I became famous, and then he just asked for money. Jade's the one who pushed me to audition for *Growing Up Wildz*, who pushed them to make the character's name Whitney."

His eyebrows jumped. "It wasn't supposed to be Whitney?"

"Wendy." She gave him a little grin. "It was supposed to be Wendy Wildz."

"Wow. That's just…" he chuckled. "That's just wrong. Sorry."

"It is. And I went along with it. I thought it'd be cool to have the same name as the character. I had no idea then it'd be the biggest mistake of my life—that I'd never be able to get away from Whitney Wildz."

He spun her around and gazed into her eyes. "That's not who you are to me. You know that, right?"

She did know. She was pretty sure, anyway. "Yes."

But then his mouth crooked back into a smile. "But… Lulu?"

"Hey, it was a great show about a talking llama!" she shot

back, unable to fight back the giggle. "Are you criticizing quality children's programming written by adults on drugs?"

"What was it ol' Larry used to say? 'It's Llama Time!' And then he'd spit?" He tried to tickle her.

She grabbed his hands. "Are you mocking llamas? They're majestic animals!"

He tested her grip, but she didn't let go. Suddenly, he wasn't laughing anymore and she wasn't, either.

She found herself staring at his tie. It was light purple today, with lime-green paisley amoebas swimming around on it. Somehow, it looked good with the bright blue shirt he was wearing. Maybe that was because he was wearing it.

He leaned down, letting his lips brush over her forehead, her cheek. "What are you going to do?" he asked, his voice husky. "Tie me up? For making fun of a llama?"

Could she *do* that? It'd been one thing to let him bind her wrists in a silk necktie yesterday. He'd been in control then—because she'd wanted him to be. She'd wanted him to make the decisions. She'd wanted to be consumed.

But today was different. She didn't want to be consumed. She wanted to do the consuming.

She pushed him back and grabbed his tie, then hauled his face down to hers. "I won't stand for you disparaging llamas."

"We could sit." He nodded toward a huge dining-room table, complete with twelve very available chairs surrounding it. The chairs had high backs and latticed slats. But he didn't pull his tie away from her hand, didn't try to touch her. "If you want to."

"Oh, I want to, mister. No one gets away with trash-talking *Larry the Llama*." She jerked on his tie and led him toward the closest chair.

"Larry was ridiculous," Matthew said as she pushed him down.

"You're going to regret saying that." She yanked his tie

off. It still had the knot in it, but she didn't want to stop to undo it. She didn't want to stop and think about what she was doing.

"Will I?" He held his hands behind his back.

"Oh, you will." She had no idea how to tie a man up in the best of times. So she looped the tie around his wrists and tried to tie it to the slat that was at the correct height. "There. That'll teach you."

"Will it?" Matthew replied. "Llamas look like they borrowed their necks from gira—"

She kissed him, hard. He shifted, as if he wanted to touch her, but she'd tied him to a chair.

She could do whatever she wanted, and he couldn't stop her.

Sexy. Beautiful. Desirable. That was what she wanted.

She stepped away from him and began to strip. Not like yesterday, when she'd been trying to get out of her clothes so fast she'd kicked him. No, this time—at a safe distance— she began to remove her clothing slowly.

First she peeled her sweater over her head, then she started undoing the buttons on her denim shirt—slowly. One at a time.

Matthew didn't say anything, not even to disparage llamas.

Instead, Matthew's gaze was fastened to Whitney's fingertips as one button after another gave.

A look of disappointment blotted out the desire when he saw the plain white tank top underneath.

"It's cold here," she told him. "You're supposed to dress in layers when it's cold."

"Did the llamas tell you that? They lie. You should be naked. Right now."

She was halfway through removing her tank top when he said that. She went ahead and pulled it the rest of the way off, but said, "Just for that, I'm not going to get naked."

His eyes widened in shock. "What?"

She stuck her hands on her hips, which had the handy effect of thrusting her breasts forward. "And you can't touch me, because you're tied up." Just saying it out loud gave her a little thrill of power.

For too damn long, she'd felt powerless. The only way she'd been able to control her own life was to become a hermit, basically—just her and the animals and crazy Donald up the valley. People took what they wanted from her—including deciding who she was—and they never gave her any say in the matter.

Not Matthew. He'd let her do whatever she wanted—be whoever she wanted.

She could be herself—klutzy and concerned about her animals—and he still looked at her with that hunger in his eyes.

She kicked off her boots and undid her jeans. Miracle of miracles, she managed to slide them off without tipping over and falling onto the floor.

Matthew's eyes lit up with want. With *need*. She could see him breathing faster now, leaning forward as if he could touch her. Heat flooded her body—almost enough to make up for the near-nudity. She felt sexy. Except for the socks.

Well, she'd already told him she wasn't going to get naked. Although she was having a little trouble remembering why, exactly.

Plus, he was sitting there fully clothed. And she didn't know where any condoms were. "Condoms?" They were required. She'd been accused of being falsely pregnant far too many times to actually risk a real pregnancy. The last thing she needed in her life were more headlines asking, Wildz Baby Daddy?

"Wallet." The tension in his voice set her pulse racing. "Left side."

"You just want me to touch you, don't you?"

He grinned. "That is the general idea. Since you won't let me touch you."

"I stand for llama solidarity," she replied as she walked toward him. "And until you can see reason…"

"Oh, I can't. No reason at all. Llamas are nature's mistake."

"Then you'll just have to stay tied up." She straddled him, but she didn't rest her weight on his obvious erection. Instead, she slid her hands over his waist and down around to his backside until she felt his wallet. She fished it out, dropped it onto the table and then ran her hands over him again. "I didn't really get to feel all of this last time," she told him.

"You were a little tied up."

She ran her hands over his shoulders, down his pecs, feeling the muscles that were barely contained by the button-down shirt and cashmere sweater. Then she leaned back so she could slide her hands down and feel what was behind those tweed slacks.

Matthew sucked in a breath so hot she felt it scorch her cheek as she touched the length of his erection. He leaned forward and tried to kiss her, but she pulled away, keeping just out of his reach. "Llama hater," she hissed at him.

"You're killing me," he ground out as he tried to thrust against her hand.

"Ah-ah-ah," she scolded. This was…*amazing.* She knew that, if he wanted to, he could probably get out of the tie and wrap her in his arms and take what she was teasing him with. And she'd let him because, all silliness aside, she wanted him *so* much.

But he wasn't. He wouldn't, because she was in control. She had all the power here.

Tension coiled around the base of her spine, tightening her muscles beyond a level that was comfortable. She let her body fall against his, let the contact between them grow.

"Woman," Matthew groaned.

She tsked him as she slid off. "You act like you've never been tied up before."

"I haven't." His gaze was fastened to her body again. She felt bold enough to strike a pose, which drew another low groan from him.

"You…haven't?"

"No. Never tied anyone up before, either." He managed to drag his gaze up to her face. "Have you?"

"No." She looked at him, trying to keep her cool. He hadn't done this before? But he'd seemed so sure of himself last night. It wasn't as though she expected a man as hot and skilled as he was to be virginal, but there was something about being the first woman he'd wrapped his necktie around—something about her being the first woman he'd let tie him to a chair—that changed things.

No. No! This was just a little fling! Just her dipping her sexual toes back in the sexy waters! This was not about developing new, deeper feelings for Matthew Beaumont!

She snagged the condom off the table. "I demand an apology on behalf of Larry the Llama and llamas everywhere." Then—just because she could—she dropped the condom and bent over to pick it up.

He sucked in another breath at the sight she was giving him. "I beg of your forgiveness, Ms. Maddox." She shifted. *"Please,"* he added, sounding desperate. "Please forgive me. I'll never impugn the honor of llamas again."

Ms. Maddox.

She needed him. Now.

She slid her panties off but kept the bra on. She undid his trousers and got them down far enough that she could roll the condom on. Then, unable to wait any longer, she let her body fall onto his.

She grabbed his face and held it so she could look into his eyes. "Matthew…"

But he was driving up into her and she was grinding down onto him and there wasn't time for more words. They had so very little time to begin with.

"Want to…kiss you," Matthew got out, each word punctuated with another thrust.

His clothing was rubbing against her, warming her bare skin. Warming everything. "Kiss me back?" she asked, knowing what the answer would be.

"Always," he replied as she lowered her lips to his. "Always."

Always. Not just right now but always.

She came apart when their lips met, and he came with her.

She lay on top of him, feeling the climax ebb from her body. It was then that she wished she hadn't tied him up, because she wanted him to hold her.

"I had no idea that llamas got you so worked up," he told her as his lips trailed over her bare shoulder. "I'll make a mental note of it."

She leaned back and grinned at him. "Was that okay? I didn't hurt you or anything—? Oh! I should untie you!"

"Uh—wait—" he said, but she was already at the back of the chair.

The tie lay in a heap on the ground. Not around his wrists. Not tied to the chair. She blinked at the puddle of bright fabric. Confusion swamped her. "When— Wait—if you weren't tied up, why didn't you touch me?"

He stood and adjusted his pants before turning around. He was, for all intents and purposes, the same as he'd been before, minus one necktie. And she was standing here in her socks and a bra. She couldn't even tie a man up.

"Why didn't you touch me?" she asked again.

He came to her then, wrapping his arms around her and holding her tight to him. "Because," he said, his lips pressing against her forehead, "you tied me up. It was kind of like…making a promise, that you were in charge. I keep my promises."

"Oh," she breathed. People didn't often keep promises, not to her. Her mother hadn't protected her, hadn't managed

her money. Her former fiancé hadn't kept a single promise to her.

She had crazy Donald, who didn't know who she was, and…Jo, who'd promised that she wouldn't tell anyone about the months she'd spent with Whitney, wouldn't tell a living soul where Whitney lived.

And now Matthew was promising to follow her wishes.

She didn't know what to make of this.

From somewhere far away, his phone chimed. "Our lunch is probably ice-cold," he said without letting her go or answering his phone.

At the mention of the word *cold*, she shivered. She was mostly naked, after all. "We haven't had a successful meal yet."

The phone chimed again. It seemed louder—more insistent. "I need to deal with some things. But if you want to hang out for a bit, I can take you home and we can try to have dinner out at the farm?"

"I'd like that."

"Yeah," he agreed, brushing his lips over hers as his phone chimed again and again. "So would I."

Twelve

It was a hell of a mess. And what made it worse was that it was self-inflicted. He'd made this bed. Now he had to lie in it.

Matthew tried to focus on defusing the situation—which wasn't easy, given that Whitney was exploring his apartment. Normally, he didn't mind showing off his place. It was opulent by any normal standard—truly befitting a Beaumont.

But now? What would she see when she looked at his custom decorating scheme? Would she see the very best that money could buy or…would she see something else?

None of the other women he'd brought back here had ever focused on his parents' wedding picture. They might have made a passing comment about how cute he was as a kid, but the other women always wanted to know what it was like being Phillip's brother or meeting this actor or that singer. They wanted to know how awesome it was to be one of the famous Beaumont men.

Not Whitney. She already knew what fame felt like. And she'd walked away from it. She didn't need it. She didn't need other people's approval.

What must she think of him, that he *did* need it? That he had to have the trappings of wealth and power—that he had to prove he was not just *a* Beaumont but the best one?

Focus. He had a job to do—a job that paid for the apartment and the cars and, yes, the ties. Matthew didn't know why Byron had gone after that chef. His gut told him there was a history there, but he didn't know what it was and Byron wasn't talking.

So Matthew did what he always did. He massaged the truth.

He lied.

The other guy had swung first. All Byron had done was complain about an underdone salmon steak, and the chef took it personally. Byron was merely defending himself. So what if that wasn't what the police report said? As long as Matthew kept repeating his version of events—and questioning the motives of anyone who disagreed with him—sooner or later, his reality would replace the true events.

"What's in here?" Whitney called out. Normally, he didn't like people in general and women in particular to explore his space on their own. He kept his apartment spotless, so it wasn't that. He liked to explain how he'd decided on the decorating scheme, why the Italian marble was really the only choice, how a television that large was really worth it. He liked to manage the message of his apartment.

He liked to manage the people in his apartment.

However, Whitney was being so damned adorable he couldn't help but smile.

"Where?" he shouted back.

"Here— Oh! That's a *really* big TV!"

He chuckled. "You're in the theater room!"

"Wow…" Her voice trailed off.

He knew that in another five minutes they'd have almost the exact same conversation all over again.

Matthew realized he was humming as he gave his official Beaumont response to the "unfortunate" situation again and again. Byron was merely noting his displeasure with an undercooked dish. The Beaumonts were glad the cops were called so they could get this mess straightened out. They would have their day in court.

Then a new email popped up—this one wasn't from a journalist but from Harper, his father's nemesis.

"Thank you for inviting us to the reception of Phillip Beaumont and bride at the last second, but sadly, no one in the Harper family has the least interest in celebrating such an occasion."

The old goat hadn't even bothered to sign the kiss-off. Nice.

Normally, it would have bothered Matthew. Maybe it did, a little. But then Whitney called out, "You have your own gym? Really?"

And just like that, Matthew didn't care about Harper.

"Really!" he called back. He sent off a short reply stating how very much Harper would be missed—Hardwick Beaumont had always counted him as a friend. Which was another bold-faced lie—the two men had hated each other from the moment Hardwick had seduced Harper's first wife less than a month after Harper had married her. But Harper wasn't the only one who could write a kiss-off.

Speaking of kissing…Matthew checked the weather, closed his computer and went looking for Whitney. She was standing in his bathroom, of all places, staring at the wide-open shower and the in-set tub. "It's just you, right? Even the bathroom is monster huge!"

"Just me. You need to make a decision."

Her eyes grew wide. "About what?"

He brushed his fingers through her hair. It'd gotten mussed up when she'd stripped for him. He liked it better that way. "The weather might turn later tonight. If you want to go back to the farm, we'll need to leave soon."

One corner of her mouth curved up. "*If*? What's the other option?"

"You are more than welcome to stay here with me." He looked around his bathroom. "I have plenty of room. And then I could show you how the shower works. And the bath." He'd like to see that—her body wet as he soaped her up.

She gave him a look that was part innocence, part sheer seduction. A look that said she might like to be soaped up— but the thought scared her, as well. "I don't have any of my things…"

He nodded in agreement. Besides, he tried to reason with himself, just because there hadn't been paparazzi waiting for them when they got to the building didn't mean that there wouldn't be people out there in the morning. And the last thing he needed right now was someone to see him and the former Whitney Wildz doing the walk of shame.

"Besides," she went on, looking surprisingly stern, "it's Christmas—almost, anyway—and you don't even have a tree. Why don't you have a tree? I mean, this place is amazing—but no tree? Not a single decoration? Really?"

He brushed his fingertips over her cheeks again. He didn't normally celebrate Christmas here. "I spend Christmas night with my mom. If they're in town, Frances and Byron come by. She always has stockings filled with cheesy gifts like yo-yos and mixes for party dips. She has a small tree and a roasted turkey breast and boxed mashed potatoes—not high cuisine by any stretch." He wouldn't dare admit that to anyone else.

Christmas night was the one night of the year when he didn't feel like Matthew Beaumont. Back in Mom's small apartment, cluttered with photos of him and her and Frances and Byron—but never Hardwick Beaumont—Matthew felt almost as if he were still Matthew Billings.

It was a glimpse into the past—one that he occasionally let himself get nostalgic about, but it never lasted very long. Then, after he gave his mother the present he'd picked out for her—something that she could use but a nicer version than she could afford herself—he'd kiss her goodbye and come back to this world. His world. The world where he would never admit to being Matthew Billings. Not even for an afternoon.

Except he'd just admitted it to Whitney. And instead of the clawing defensiveness he usually felt whenever anyone brought up the Billings name, he felt…lighter.

Whitney gave him a scolding look. "It sounds lovely. I watch *It's a Wonderful Life* and share a ham with Gater and Fifi. I usually bring carrots to the horses, that sort of thing." She sighed, leaning into his arms. "I miss having someone to celebrate with. That's why I came to this wedding. I mean, I came for Jo, but…"

"Tell you what—we'll head back to the farm now, because it looks all Christmassy, and then—" his mouth was moving before he realized what he was saying "—then after the wedding, maybe we can spend part of Christmas together before you go home?"

"I'd like that." Her cheeks flushed with warmth. "But I don't have a present for you."

He couldn't resist. "You are the only present I want. Maybe even tied up with a bow…." He gathered her into his arms and pressed her back against the tiled wall with a rather heated kiss.

Several minutes passed before she was able to ask, "Are you done with your work?"

"For now, yes." Later he'd have to log back in and launch another round of damage control. But he could take a few hours to focus on Whitney. "Let me take you home."

She giggled. "I don't think I have much of a choice in that, do I? My truck's still out on the farm." A look of concern crossed her face. "Can you drive your car in the snow?"

"I'm a Beaumont," he said, his words echoing off the tiled walls of the bathroom. "I have more than one vehicle."

After a comfortable drive out to the farm in his Jeep, Whitney asked him if he'd stay for dinner. Jo had already set a place for him at the table and Phillip said, "Hang out, dude."

So, after a quick check of his messages to make sure that

nothing else had blown up, Matthew sat down to dinner—
homemade fried chicken and mashed potatoes. Finally, over
easy conversation about horses and celebrities, he and Whitney managed to successfully eat a meal together.

Then Jo said, "We're going to watch *Elf*, if you want to
join us."

"I auditioned for that movie," Whitney said, leaning into
him. "But I was, um, under the influence at the time and
blew it pretty badly, so Zooey Deschanel got the part. It's
still a really funny movie. I watch it every year."

Matthew looked at Phillip, who was pointedly not smiling at the way Matthew had wrapped his arm around Whitney's waist. "Sure," Matthew heard himself say. "It sounds
like fun."

As the women popped popcorn and made hot chocolate,
of all things, Phillip pulled him aside under the pretense of
discussing the sound for the movie. "Who are you," he said
under his breath, "and what have you done with my brother
Matthew?"

"Shove it," Matthew whispered back. He didn't want to
have this conversation. Not even with Phillip.

His brother did no such shoving. "Correct me if I'm
wrong," he went on, "but weren't you on the verge of personally throwing her out of the wedding a few nights ago?"

"Shove. It."

"And yesterday—well, she's an attractive woman. I can't
fault you for sleeping with her. But today?" Phillip shook
his head, clearly enjoying himself. "Man, I don't think I've
ever seen you be so…lovey-dovey."

Matthew sighed. He wanted to deck Phillip so badly, but
the wedding was in a matter of days. "Lovey-dovey?"

"Affectionate. I can't remember the last time I've seen
you touch a woman, outside of handshakes and photo ops.
And you *never* just sit around and watch a movie. You're
always working."

"I'll have to log back on in a few hours. I'm still working."

Phillip looked at him out of the corner of his eye. "You can't keep your hands off her."

Matthew shrugged, hoping he looked noncommittal. He touched women. He took lovers. He was a Beaumont—having affairs was his birthright.

Boring women, he remembered Phillip calling them yesterday. Women he took to stuffy restaurants and to their own place to bed them so no one would see that he'd had a guest overnight.

It wasn't that he wasn't affectionate. It was that he was careful. He had to be.

He wished Jo and Whitney would hurry the hell up with that popcorn. "I like her."

"Which her? The fallen star or the horse breeder?"

"The horse breeder. I like her."

Phillip clapped him on the shoulder. "Good answer, man. Good answer. The movie is ready, ladies," he added as Jo and Whitney made their way over to them.

Matthew hurried to take the full mugs of cocoa—complete with marshmallows—from Whitney. Then Jo produced blankets. She and Phillip curled up on one couch with the donkey sitting at their feet as they munched popcorn and laughed at the movie.

Which left him and Whitney with the other couch. He didn't give a rat's ass for the popcorn. He set his cocoa down where he could reach it, then patted the couch next to him. Whitney curled up against his side and pulled the blankets over them.

"Do you watch a lot of movies?" he asked in a quiet voice, his mouth against her ear.

"I do. I get up really early when it's warm—farmer's hours—and I'm pretty tired at night. Sometimes I read—I like romances." He could see the blush over her face when she said that, as if he'd begrudge her a happy ending. "It took a while before I could watch things like this and not think a bunch of what-ifs, you know?"

He wrapped his arms around her waist and lifted her onto his lap. Maybe Phillip was right. Maybe he wasn't normally affectionate with the women who came into his life. But he *had* to touch Whitney.

They watched the movie. Whitney and Jo had clearly watched it together before. They laughed and quoted the lines at each other and had little inside jokes. Matthew's phone buzzed a few times during the show, but he ignored it.

Phillip was right about one thing—when was the last time he'd taken a night off and just hung out? It'd been a while. Matthew tried to think—had he planned on taking a couple of days off after the wedding? No, not really. The wedding was the unofficial launch of Percheron Drafts, Chadwick's new craft beer. Matthew had a 30 percent stake in the company. They were building up to a big launch just in time for the Big Game in February. The push was going to be hard.

He'd made plans to have dinner with his mother. That was all the time he'd originally allotted for the holiday. But now? He could take a few days off. He didn't know when Whitney was heading back to California, but if she wanted to stick around, he would make time for her.

By the time the movie ended, he and Whitney were lying down, spooning under their blankets. He hadn't had any popcorn, and the cocoa was cold, but he didn't care. With her backside pressed against him, he was having a hard time thinking. Other things were also getting hard.

But there was a closeness that he hadn't anticipated. He liked just holding her.

"I should go," he said in her ear.

She sighed. "I wish you didn't have to."

Phillip and Jo managed to get untangled from their covers first. "Uh, Matthew?"

"Yeah?" He managed to push himself up into a sitting position without dumping Whitney on the floor.

"Icy."

"You see what?"

"No, icy—as in ice. On your car. And the driveways."

"Damn, really?" He waited long enough for Whitney to sit up. Then he walked to a window. Phillip was right. A glaze of ice coated everything. "The weather said snow. Not ice. Damn. I should have…"

"You're stuck out here, man." Phillip gave him a playful punch in the shoulder. "I know it'll be a real hardship, but you can't drive home on ice."

Matthew looked at Whitney. She'd come to stand next to him. "Ice…wow," she said in the same tone she'd used when she'd been exploring his apartment. "We don't get ice out in California. Not like this!" She slipped her hand into his and squeezed.

He could stay the night. One night wrapped up in Whitney and then he could fall asleep with her in his arms. Wake up with her there, too. He didn't do that often. Okay, he didn't ever do that.

Only one problem. "I didn't bring anything."

"We have guest supplies," Jo called out.

Phillip stood up straight and looked Matthew over. "Yeah, we probably still wear the same size."

"Stay," Whitney said in a voice that was meant only for him. "Stay with me. Just for the night. Call it…an early Christmas present."

It really wasn't an argument. He couldn't drive home on ice and honestly? He didn't want to. Suddenly he understood why Phillip had always preferred the farmhouse. It was warm and lived-in. If Matthew went back to his apartment—monster huge, as Whitney had noted, and completely devoid of holiday cheer—and Whitney wasn't there with him, the place would feel…empty.

Lonely.

It'd never bothered him before. But tonight he knew it would.

"I'll need to log on," he told everyone. "We still have a wedding to deal with."

"Of course," Jo said. She was smiling, but not at him. At Whitney. "You do what you need to do."

Matthew spent an hour answering the messages he'd ignored. Whitney had gone up to read so she wouldn't distract him from his work. He knew he was rushing, but the thought of her in his room again—well, that was enough to make a man hurry the hell up.

When he opened his door, the fire was blazing in the hearth, and Whitney was in bed. She looked...perfect. He couldn't even see Whitney Wildz when he looked at her anymore. She was just Whitney.

The woman he wanted. "I was waiting for you," she told him.

"I'll make it worth the wait." Then she lifted up the covers and he saw that she was nude.

Thank God for ice.

Thirteen

The day of the bachelorette party came fast. Whitney got to stay on the farm for a couple of days, which should have made her happy. She was able to work with Jo and some of the many horses on the farm—Appaloosas, Percherons and Sun, the Akhal-Teke. Phillip treated her like a close friend and the staff on the farm was the definition of discreet and polite at all times. They made cookies and watched holiday shows. Even the farm manager, an old hand named Richard, took to calling her Whit.

By all rights, it should have been everything she wanted. Quiet. Peaceful. Just her and a few friends and a bunch of horses. No cameras, no gossips, no anything having to do with Whitney Wildz. Except...

She missed Matthew.

And that wasn't like her. She didn't miss people. She didn't get close enough to people to miss them when they went.

Well, that wasn't true. She'd missed the easy friendship with Jo when Jo had hitched her trailer back up to her truck and driven on to the next job.

But now, after only two days without him, she missed Matthew. And she shouldn't. She just shouldn't. So he'd made love to her that night, rolling her onto her stomach to do things to her that *still* made her shiver with desire when she thought about them. And so she'd woken up in his arms the next morning and they'd made love so sweetly that she still couldn't believe she hadn't dreamed the whole thing.

How long had it been since she'd woken up with a man in bed? A long time. Even longer since the man in question had made love to her. Told her how beautiful she was, how good she was. How glad he was that he'd stayed with her.

It was a problem. A huge one. This was still a temporary thing, a Christmas fling that would end with the toss of the bridal bouquet. If she were lucky, she'd get Christmas morning with him. And that'd be it. If she missed Matthew now, after just a couple of good days, how bad off would she be when she went home? When she wouldn't have to wait another day to see him?

How much would she miss him when she wasn't going to see him again?

It'd hurt to watch him get into his car and slowly drive away. He'd offered to let her come with him, but she'd refused. She was here for Jo and, anyway, Matthew had things he needed to do. Weddings to manage, PR debacles to control. Just another reminder of how far apart their lives really were.

To her credit, Jo hadn't said much about the sudden relationship. Just, "Are you having a good time with Matthew?"

"I am," Whitney had said truthfully. Although *fun* seemed as if it wasn't strong enough of a word. Fun was a lovely day at an amusement park. Being with Matthew? It was amazing. That was all there was to it. He was *amazing*.

"Good." That was all Jo said about it.

Now, however, Whitney and Jo were driving in to the Pub to meet the other women in the wedding party. Matthew would be out with Phillip and all their brothers—bowling, of all things. Although Whitney wasn't sure if that was one of those fake activities Matthew had planned to keep the paparazzi guessing.

Whitney kept her hat on as the hostess showed them back to the private room. There were already several other women there, as well as a small buffet laid out with salads, burgers and fries. *Matthew*, Whitney thought with a smile as she took off her hat and sunglasses. Maybe he did know Jo better than she thought.

"Hi, all," Jo said. "Let me introduce—"

"*Oh, my God*, it's really you! You're Whitney Wildz!" A young woman with bright red hair came rushing up to Whitney. In the brief second before she grabbed Whitney by the shoulders, Whitney could see the unmistakable resemblance to both Matthew and Phillip—but especially Matthew. The red hair helped.

"You really *are* here! And you know Jo! *How* do you know Jo? I'm Frances Beaumont, by the way."

"Hi," Whitney tried out. She'd known this was going to happen—and today was certainly a more controlled situation than normal. She had Jo and there were only a few women in the room. But she'd never really mastered the proper response to rabid fans.

"Yes, as I was saying," Jo said in a firm voice as she pried Frances's hands off Whitney's shoulders, "this is Whitney Maddox. She's a horse breeder. I know her because we've worked horses together." She tried to steer Frances away from Whitney, but it didn't work.

"You're really *here*. Oh, my God, I know you probably have this happen all the time, but I was your *biggest* fan. I loved your show *so* much and one time Matthew took me to see you in concert." Before Whitney could dodge out of the way, Frances threw her arms around her and pulled Whitney into a massive hug. "I'm *so* glad to meet you. You have no idea."

"Um…" was all Whitney could get out as her lungs were crushed. Frances was surprisingly strong for her size. "I'm getting one."

"Frances," Jo said, the warning in her voice unmistakable. "Could you at least let Whitney get her coat off before you embarrass yourself and go all fangirl?"

"Right, right! Sorry!" Frances finally let go. "I'm just so excited!" She pulled out her cell phone. "Can I get a picture? Please?"

"Um…" Whitney looked around, but she found no help. Jo looked pissed and the other women were waiting for her to make a decision. She was on her own here. What would Matthew do? He'd manage the message.

"If you promise not to post it on social media until after the wedding." She smiled at how in control that sounded.

"Of course! I don't have to post it at all—this is just for me. You have *no* idea how awesome this is." She slung her arm around Whitney's shoulders and held the camera up overhead before snapping the selfie. "That is so awesome," she repeated as she approved the picture. "Can I send it to Byron and Matthew? We always used to watch your show together."

"I've already met him. Matthew, that is." Suddenly, she was blushing in an entirely different way. And there was no hiding from it, since everyone in the room was staring at her.

Another woman stood up. "You'll have to excuse Frannie," this woman said with a warm smile. She looked nothing like a Beaumont, but beyond that, she was holding a small baby that couldn't be more than a month old. "She's easily excitable. I'm Serena Beaumont, Chadwick's wife. It's delightful to meet you." She shifted the baby onto her shoulder and held out a hand.

"Whitney." She didn't have a lot of experience dealing with babies, but it had to be safer than another hug attack from Frances. "How old is your baby?"

"Six weeks." Serena smiled. She turned so that Jo and Whitney could see the tiny baby's face. "This is Catherine Beaumont."

"She's adorable." She was actually kind of wrinkly and still asleep, but Whitney had no other points of reference, so the baby was adorable by default.

"Her being pregnant made getting the bridesmaids' dresses a mess," Frances said with a dramatic roll of her eyes. "Such a pain."

"Said the woman who is not now, nor has ever been, pregnant," Serena said. But instead of backbiting, the whole conversation was one of gentle teasing. The women were clearly comfortable with each other.

Whitney was introduced to the rest of the women in attendance. There was Lucy Beaumont, a young woman with white-blond hair who did not seem exactly thrilled to be at the party. She left shortly after the introductions, claiming she had a migraine.

Whitney also met Toni Beaumont, who seemed almost as nervous as Whitney felt. "Toni's going to be singing a song at the wedding," Jo explained. "She's got a beautiful voice."

Toni blushed, looking even more awkward. She was considerably younger than the other Beaumonts Whitney had met. Whitney had to wonder if she was one of Hardwick Beaumont's last children? If so, did that make her...maybe twenty? She didn't get the chance to find out. Toni, too, bailed on the proceedings pretty quickly.

Then it was just Jo, Frances, Serena and Whitney—and a baby who was sleeping through the whole thing. "They seem...nice," Whitney ventured.

"Lucy doesn't really like us," Frances explained over the lip of her beer. She was the only one drinking. "Which happens in this family. Every time Dad married a new wife, the new one would bad-mouth the others. That's why Toni isn't comfortable around us, either. Her mom told her we were all out to get her."

"And," Serena added, giving Frances a sharp look, "if I understand correctly, you *were* out to get her when you were a kid."

Frances laughed. "Maybe," she said with a twinkle in her eye. "There might have been some incidents. But that was more between Lucy and Toni. I was too old to play with *babies* by that point. Besides, do you know how much crap Phillip used to give me? I swear, he'd put me on the meanest horse he could find just to watch me get bucked off and cry. But I showed him," she told Whitney. "I learned how to stay on and I don't cry."

Serena rolled her eyes and looked at Whitney. "It's a strange family."

Whitney nodded and smiled as if it were all good fun, but she remembered Matthew telling her how his older brothers used to blame him for, well, *everything*.

"Okay, yeah," Frances protested. "So we're all a little nuts. I mean, I'm never going to get married, not after having *that* many evil stepmothers. Never going to happen. But that's the legacy we were born into as Beaumonts—all except Matthew. He's the only one who was ever nice to all of us. That's why Lucy and Toni were here today—he asked them to come. Said it was important to the family, so they came. The only person who doesn't listen to him is Eliza, Chadwick and Phillip's mom. Everyone else does what he says. And seriously? That man not only wouldn't let me take you guys to the hottest club, but he wouldn't even let me hire a stripper." She scoffed while rolling her eyes, a practiced gesture of frustration. "He can be such a control freak. He probably even picked out your shoes or something."

There was a pause, and then both Frances and Serena turned to look at Whitney.

Heat flooded Whitney's cheeks. Matthew had, in fact, picked out her shoes. And her hairstyle. And her lipstick. Right before he'd mussed them all up. She wasn't about to argue the control-freak part. But then, he'd also let her tie him up. He'd kept up the illusion even though her knot hadn't held. Just so she could be in control.

"So," Frances said in a too-bright tone. "You *have* met Matthew."

"Yes." The one word seemed safer. She wasn't used to kissing and telling. Heck, she was still getting used to the kissing thing. She was absolutely not going to tell anyone about it.

"And?" Frances looked as if she were a lioness about to pounce on a wounded wildebeest.

Whitney hated being the wildebeest. "We're just working to make sure that the wedding goes smoothly. No distractions." She thought it best not to mention the shoes. Or the ties.

Serena nodded in appreciation, but Frances made a face of exasperation. "Seriously? He's had a huge crush on you for, like, forever! I bet he can barely keep his hands off you. And frankly, that man could stand to get distracted."

"Frannie!" Jo and Serena said at the same time. The baby startled and began to mew in tiny-baby cries.

"Sorry," Serena said, draping a blanket over her shoulder so she could nurse, Whitney guessed.

"Well, it's true! He's been driving us all nuts with this wedding, insisting it has to be perfect. Honestly," Frances said, turning her attention back to Whitney, "I'm not sure he ever just does something for fun. It'd be good for him, you know?"

Whitney was so warm she was on the verge of sweating. She thought of the way he'd ignored his phone while they cuddled on the couch, watching a Christmas movie. Was that fun?

"He had a crush on Whitney Wildz," she explained, hoping her face wasn't achieving a near-fatal level of blush. "That's not who I am."

They'd cleared that up before the clothes had started to come off. He knew that she was Whitney Maddox. He liked her for being her, not because she'd once played someone famous. End of discussion.

Except…Matthew was, in fact, having trouble keeping his hands off her. Off *her*, right? Not Whitney Wildz?

She didn't want the doubt that crept in with Frances's knowing smile. But there it was anyway. She couldn't be 100 percent sure that Matthew wasn't sleeping with Whitney Wildz, could she? Just because he'd called her Ms. Maddox a few times—was that really all the proof she needed?

"Sure," Frances said with a dismissive wave of her hand. "Of course."

"You're being obnoxious," Serena said. Then she added to Whitney, "Frances is good at that."

"I'm just being honest. Matthew's way too focused on making sure we all do what he thinks we should. This is a rare opportunity for him to do something for himself. Lord knows the man needs more fun in his life. You two should go out." She paused, a smile that looked way too familiar on her face. "If you haven't already."

This was it. After all these years, all those headlines and horrible pictures and vicious, untrue rumors, Whitney was finally going to die of actual embarrassment. She'd have thought she couldn't feel it this much anymore—that she was immune to it—but no. All it took was one affair with a Beaumont and an "honest" conversation with his little sister and *boom*. It was all over.

Jo sighed. "Are you done?"

"Maybe," Frances replied, looking quite pleased with herself.

"Because you know what Matthew's going to do to you when he finds out you're treating my best friend like this, don't you?"

At that, a look of concern managed to blot out Frances's satisfied smile. "Well…hey, I've been on my best behavior ever since you guys decided to get married. No headlines, no trouble. I leave that to Byron."

And Byron had gotten into trouble only because Matthew had asked him to. For her. There was a moment of silence, during which Whitney considered getting her coat and going. Except she couldn't leave without Jo. Damn it.

Then the silence was broken. "But what about—?" Serena said, joining the fray.

"Or the one time when you—" added Jo.

"Hey!" Frances yelped, her cheeks turning almost as red as her hair. "That's not fair!"

"We're just being honest," Serena said with a grin that bordered on mean.

Jo nodded in agreement, giving Whitney an encouraging grin. "What did Phillip tell me about that one guy? What did he call you? His Little Red—"

Frances's phone chimed. "Sorry, can't listen to you make fun of me. Must answer this very important text!" She read her message. "Byron says he can't believe that's really Whitney Wildz." She began to type a reply.

"What are you going to tell him?" Whitney asked.

"What do you think?" Frances winked at her. "That your name is Whitney Maddox."

"Is that...Whitney Wildz?" Byron held his phone up to his good eye. "Seriously?"

"What?" Matthew grabbed the phone away from his brother. "Jesus." It was, in fact, Whitney, standing next to Frances, smiling for the camera. She looked good. A little worried but that was probably because Frances had a death grip on her shoulders.

He was going to kill both of them. Why would Whitney let anyone take her picture? And hadn't he warned Frances not to do anything stupid? And didn't taking a picture of Whitney and plastering it all over the internet count as stupid?

The phone chimed as another message popped up.

Tell Matthew that she made me promise to only send it to you. No social media.

Matthew exhaled in relief. That was a smart compromise. He could only hope Frances would hold up her end of that promise. He handed the phone back over, hoping he appeared nonchalant. "That was a character she played," he said in his most diplomatic tone. "Her name is Whitney Maddox." He shot a look at Phillip, who was enjoying a cigar on Matthew's private deck.

Phillip gave him his best innocent face, then mimed locking his lips and throwing away the key.

The guys had managed to arrive at Matthew's place without notice. It was just the five of them. Byron didn't get along with their other half brothers David and Johnny at all and Mark was off at college. Matthew had decided to keep the guest list to the wedding party. Just the four Beaumont men who could tolerate each other. Most of the time.

Plus the sober coach, Dale. When Phillip was out on the farm, he was fine, but he'd been sober for only seven months now and with the pressure of the wedding, no one wanted a relapse. Hands down, that would be the worst thing to happen to the wedding. There would be no recovering from that blow to the Beaumont image and there would be no burying that lead. It would be game over.

Matthew and Phillip had made sure that Dale would be available for any event that took place away from the farm. Currently, Dale was sitting next to Phillip, talking horses. This was what the Beaumont men had come to—soda and cigars on a Saturday night. So this was what getting old was like.

"Who?" Chadwick asked, taking the phone.

"Whitney Wildz." Byron was studying the picture. "She was this squeaky-clean girl who starred in a rock-and-roll update of *The Partridge Family* called *Growing Up Wildz*. Man," he went on, "she looks *amazing*. Do you know if she's—?"

"She's not available," Matthew said before he could stop himself. But Byron was a Beaumont. There was no way Matthew wanted his little brother to get it into his head that Whitney was fair game.

All three of his brothers gave him a surprised look. Well, Chadwick and Byron gave him a look. Phillip was trying too hard not to laugh, the rat bastard. "I mean, if anyone tried to hit on her, it'd be a media firestorm. Hands off."

"Wait," Chadwick said, studying the picture again. "Isn't this the woman who's always stoned or flashing the camera?"

"She's not like that," Matthew snapped.

"What Matthew means to say," Phillip added, "is that in real life, Whitney raises prize-winning horses and lives a fairly quiet life. She's definitely *not* a fame monster."

"*This* is the woman who's the maid of honor?" Chadwick's voice was getting louder as he glared at the phone. "How is this Whitney Wild person not going to make this wedding into a spectacle? You know this is the soft opening for Percheron Drafts, Matthew. We can't afford to have anything compromise the reception."

"Hey—easy, now, Chad." Chadwick flinched at Phillip's nickname for him. Which Phillip used only when he was trying to piss off the oldest Beaumont. Yeah, this little bachelor party was going downhill, fast. "It's going to be fine. She's a friend of Jo's and she's not going to make a spectacle of anything. She's perfectly fine. Matthew was worried, too, but he's seen that she's just a regular woman. Right?" He turned to Matthew. "Back me up here."

"Phillip's correct. Whitney will be able to fulfill her role in the wedding with class and style." *And*, he added mentally, *with a little luck, some grace*. He hoped he'd put her in the right shoes. "She won't be a distraction. She'll help demonstrate that the Beaumonts are back on top."

Funny how a few days ago he'd been right where Chadwick was—convinced that a former star would take advantage of the limelight that went with a Beaumont Christmas wedding and burn them all. Now all Matthew was worried about was Whitney getting down the aisle without tripping.

He glanced up to see Byron staring at him. "What?"

It was Chadwick who spoke first. "We can't afford any *more* distractions," he said, half punching Byron on the arm. "I'm serious."

"Fine, fine. I prefer to eat my own cooking anyway." Byron walked off to lean against the railing on the balcony. Then he looked back at Matthew.

Matthew knew what that meant. Byron wanted to talk. So he joined his little brother. Then he waited. It was only when Phillip distracted Chadwick by asking about his baby daughter that Matthew said, "Yes?"

"Did you ask Harper?" Byron kept his voice low. Yeah, there was no need to let Chadwick in on this conversation. If Chadwick knew that they'd asked his nemesis to the wedding... Well, Matthew hated bailing people out.

"I did. He refused. The Harpers will not be joining us at the reception."

"Not even...?" Byron swallowed, staring out at the mountains cloaked in darkness. "Not even his family? His daughter?"

Suddenly, Matthew understood. "No. Is she the reason you've got a black eye?"

Byron didn't answer. Instead, he said, "Is Whitney Wildz *your* reason?"

"Her name," Matthew said with more force than he probably needed, "is Whitney Maddox. Don't you forget it."

Byron gave him the look—the same look all the brothers shared. The Beaumont smile. "Exactly how 'not available' is she, anyway?"

Deep down, Matthew had to admire how well his little brother was handling himself. In less than a minute, he'd completely redirected the conversation away from Harper's daughter and back to Matthew and Whitney. "Completely not available."

"Well," Phillip announced behind them, "this has been

lovely and dull, but I've got a bride-to-be waiting for me who's a lot more entertaining than you lot."

"And I've got to get home to Serena and Catherine," Chadwick added.

"I swear," Byron said, "I leave for one lousy year and I don't even know you guys anymore. Chadwick, not working? Phillip, sober and monogamous? And you?" He shot Matthew a sidelong glance. "Hooking up with Whitney Wild—"

"Maddox," Matthew corrected.

Byron gave him another Beaumont smile and Matthew realized what he'd just done—tacitly agreed that he was, in fact, hooking up with Whitney. "Right. You hooking up with anyone. Next thing you know, Frances will announce she's joining a nunnery or something."

"We can only hope," Chadwick grumbled before he turned to Phillip and Dale. "You okay to get home?"

Dale spoke. "You're going straight home to the farm?"

"Yeah," Phillip replied, slapping the man on the shoulder. "Jo's waiting on me. Thanks for—"

Matthew cut him off. "I'll see that he gets home."

"What—" Phillip demanded. He sounded pissed.

Matthew didn't look at him. He focused on Dale and Chadwick. "There's been a lot of pressure with this wedding. We can't be too careful."

"—the hell," Phillip finished, giving him a mean look.

Matthew refused to flinch even as he wondered what he was doing. At no point during the wedding planning had Phillip been teetering on the brink of dependency. Why was Matthew implying that he suddenly needed a babysitter?

Because. He wanted to see Whitney.

"Good plan," Chadwick said. "Dale, is that okay with you?"

"Yeah. See you tomorrow at the rehearsal dinner." Dale took off.

When it was just the four brothers, there was a moment of

awkward silence. Then the awkwardness veered into painful. What was Matthew doing? He could see the question on each man's face. Byron's black eye. Casting doubts on Phillip's sobriety. That wasn't who Matthew was. He was the one who did the opposite—who tried to make the family sound better, look better than it really was. He put the family name first. Not his selfish desire to see a woman who was nothing but a PR headache waiting to happen.

Phillip glared at him. Yeah, Matthew had earned that. "Can we go? Or do you need to take a potshot at Chadwick, too?"

Chadwick paused. He'd already headed for the door. "Problem?"

"No. Nothing I can't handle," Matthew hurried to say before Byron and Phillip could tattle on him.

He could handle this. His attraction to Whitney? A minor inconvenience. A totally amazing, mind-blowing inconvenience, but a minor one. He could keep it together. He had to. That was what he did.

Chadwick nodded. That he was taking Matthew at his word was something that should have made Matthew happy. He'd earned that measure of trust the hard way. It was a victory.

But that didn't change the fact that he was, at this exact moment, undermining that trust, as well.

Yeah, he could handle this.

He hoped like hell.

Fourteen

The drive out to the farm was fast and tense.

"After this wedding," Phillip finally said as he fumed in the passenger seat, "you and I are going to have words."

"Fine." Matthew had earned it, he knew.

"I don't get you," Phillip went on, clearly deciding to get those words out of the way now. Matthew thought that it'd be better if they could just fight and get it over with. "If you wanted to come out to the farm and see her, you could have just come. Why'd you have to make it sound like I had my finger on the trigger of a bottle? Because I don't."

"Because."

"What the hell kind of answer is that?"

Matthew could feel Phillip staring at him. He ignored him. Yeah, he'd bent the truth. That was what he did. Besides, he'd covered up for Phillip so many times they'd both lost count.

"You don't have to hide her. Not from us. And certainly not from me. I already know what's going on."

The statement rankled him. The fact that it was the truth? That only made it worse. "I'm not hiding."

"Like hell you're not. What else would you call that little show you put on back there? Why else does Byron have a black eye? You can dress it up as you're protecting her because that's what you do but damn, man. There's nothing wrong with you liking the woman and wanting to spend time with her. You think I'd hold that against you?"

"You would have. In the past."

"Oh, for crying out loud." Phillip actually threw his hands up. "There's your problem right there. You're so damn concerned with what happened last year, five years ago—thirty-five years ago—that you're missing out on the *now*. Things change. People change. I'd have thought that hanging out with Whitney would have shown you that."

Matthew didn't have a comeback to that. He didn't have one to any of it.

Phillip moved in for the kill. Matthew wasn't entirely used to the new, improved, changed Phillip being this right and certainly not right about Matthew. "Even Chadwick would understand if you've got to do something for *you*. You don't have to manage the family's image every single minute of your life. Figure out who you are if you're not a Beaumont."

Matthew let out a bark of laughter. "That's rich, coming from you."

If he wasn't a Beaumont? Not happening. He'd fought too hard to earn his place at the Beaumont table. He wasn't going to toss all that hard work to "figure out" who he was. He already knew.

He was Matthew Beaumont. End of discussion.

"Whatever, man. But the next time you want to cover your tracks, don't use me as a human shield. I don't play these games anymore."

"Fine."

"Good."

The rest of the drive was silent.

Matthew was mad. He was mad at Phillip—but he wasn't sure why. Because the man had spoken what felt uncomfortably like the truth? And Byron—he'd gotten that damn black eye. Because Matthew had asked him to do something dramatic.

And he was—he was mad at Whitney. That was what this little verbal skirmish was about, wasn't it? Whitney Maddox. Why did she have to be so—so—so *not* Whitney Wildz? Why couldn't she be the kind of self-absorbed celebrity he knew how to manage—that he knew how to keep himself distant from? Why did she have to be someone soft and gentle and—yeah, he was gonna say it—innocent? She shouldn't be so innocent. She should be jaded and hard and bitter. That way he wouldn't be able to love her.

They pulled up at the farmhouse. Matthew didn't want to deal with Phillip anymore. Didn't want to deal with any of it. He was not hiding her, damn it.

He strode into the house as if he owned the thing, which he didn't. Not really. But it was Beaumont Farms and he was a Beaumont, so to hell with it.

He found Jo and Whitney on the sofas, watching what looked like *Rudolph the Red-Nosed Reindeer*, the one he'd watched back when he was a kid. Whitney was already in her pajamas. Jo's ridiculous donkey, Betty, was curled up next to Whitney. She was petting Betty's ears as if it were a normal everyday thing.

Why didn't he feel normal anymore? Why had he let her get close enough to change him?

"Hi," she said in surprise when she looked up. "Is everything—?"

"I need to talk to you." He didn't wait for a response. Hell, he couldn't even wait for her to get up. He scooted Betty out of the way and pulled Whitney to her feet.

"Are you—*whoa*!"

Matthew swept her legs up and, without bothering to look back at where Phillip was no doubt staring daggers at him— hell, to where the donkey was probably staring daggers at him—he carried Whitney up the stairs.

She threw her arms around his neck as he took the steps two at a time. "Are you okay?"

"Fine. Just fine." Even as he said it, he knew it wasn't true. He wasn't fine and she was the reason.

But she was the only way he knew how to make things fine again.

"Bachelor party went okay?" she asked as he kicked open the door to her room.

"Yeah. Fine." He threw her down on the bed and wrenched off his tie.

Her eyes went wide. "Matthew?"

"I—I missed you, okay? I missed you." Why did saying it feel like such a failure? He didn't miss people. He didn't miss women. He didn't let himself care enough to miss them.

But in two damn days, he'd missed her. And it made him feel weak. He wrapped the tie around his knuckles and pulled, letting the bite of silk against his skin pull him back. Pull him away from her.

She clambered up to her knees, which brought her face almost level with his. "I missed you, too."

"You did?"

She nodded. Then she touched his face. "I...I missed waking up with you."

At her touch—soft and gentle and innocent, damn it all—something in him snapped. "I don't want to talk."

She was the reason he was the mess he was. He had to—he didn't know. He had to put her in her place. He *had* to keep himself distanced from her, for his own sanity. And he couldn't do that while she was touching him so sweetly, while she was telling him she missed him.

One eyebrow notched up. Too late, he remembered announcing that the whole reason he was sweeping her off her feet was to talk to her.

But she didn't say anything. Instead, she pushed herself up onto her feet and stripped her pajama top off. Then, still standing on the bed—not tipping over, not accidentally kicking him—she shimmied out of her bottoms, which was fine because it was damnably hard to think the lustful thoughts he was thinking about someone who was wearing pink pants covered with dogs in bow ties. Then she sank back down to her knees in front of him.

No talking. No touching. He would keep a part of himself from her, just as he did with everyone else. No one would know what she meant to him. Not even him.

Then he had her on her back, but that was still too much. He couldn't look into her eyes, pale and wide and waiting for him. He couldn't see what he meant to her. He couldn't risk letting her see what she meant to him. So he rolled her onto her belly and, after getting the condom, buried himself in her.

She didn't say a word, not even when her back arched and her body tightened down on his and she grabbed the headboard as the climax rolled her body. She was silent as he grabbed her hips and drove in deep and hard until he had nothing left to give her.

They fell onto the bed together, panting and slick with sweat. He'd done what he needed to—what a Beaumont would. This was his birthright, wasn't it? White-hot affairs that didn't involve feelings. His father had specialized in them. He'd never cared about anyone.

Matthew needed to get up. He needed to walk away from Whitney. He needed to stay a Beaumont.

Then she rolled, looped her arms over his neck and held him. No words. Just her touch. Just her not letting him go.

How weak was he? He couldn't even pull himself away from her. He let her hold him. Damn it all, he held her back.

It was some time before she spoke. "After the wedding… after Christmas morning…"

He winced. "Yes?" But it was surprisingly hard to sound as if he didn't care when his face was buried in the crook of her neck.

"I mean," she hurried on, her arms tightening around his neck, "that'll be... We'll be..."

It. That'll be it. *We'll be* done. That was what she was trying to say. Then—and only then—did he manage to push himself up. But he couldn't push himself away from her. "My life is here in Denver, and you..." He swallowed, wishing he were stronger. That he could be stronger for her. "You need the sun."

She smiled—he could see her trying—but at the same time, her eyes began to shine and the corners of her mouth pulled down. She was trying not to cry. "Right."

He couldn't watch her, not like this. So he buried his face back against her neck.

"Right," he agreed. *Fine*, he thought, knowing it wasn't. At least that would be clean. At least there wouldn't be a scene that he'd have to contain. He should have been relieved.

"Anytime you want to ride the Trakehners," she managed to get out, "you just let me know."

Then—just because she made him so weak—he kissed her. Because no matter how hard he tried, he couldn't hold himself back. Not around her.

Fifteen

They spent the next morning looking over the carriage that would pull Phillip and Jo from the chapel to the reception. The whole thing was bedecked with ribbons and bows of red-and-green velvet, which stood out against the deep gray paint of the carriage. Whitney wasn't sure she'd ever really grasped what the word *bedecked* meant, but after seeing the Beaumont carriage, she understood completely. "It's a beautiful rig."

"You like it?" Matthew said. He'd been quiet all morning, but he'd held her hand as they walked around the farm together. In fact, he had hardly stopped touching her since they'd woken up. His foot had been rubbing against her calf during their breakfast; his hands had been around her waist or on her shoulders whenever possible.

Whitney had been worried after last night. Okay, more than worried. She'd originally thought that he was mad at her because of the picture with Frances, but there'd been something else going on.

After the intense sex—and the part where he'd agreed that this relationship was short-term—she had decided that it wasn't her place to figure out what that "something else" was. If he wanted to tell her, he would. She would make no other claims to him.

She would try not to, anyway.

"I do." She looked at the carriage, well and truly bedecked. "It's going to look amazing. And with Jo's dress? *Wow*."

He trailed his hand down her arm. She leaned into his touch. "Do you have a carriage like this?"

She grinned at him. He really didn't know a whole lot about horses, but he was trying. For her. "Trakehners aren't team horses, so no."

He brushed his gloved fingertips over her cheek. She could feel the heat of his touch despite the fabric. "Want to go for a ride?"

She pulled up short. "What?"

"I'll have Richard hook up the team. Someone can drive us around."

"But…it's for the wedding."

"I know. You're here *now*." Then he was off, hunting up a hired hand to take them on a carriage ride around Beaumont Farms.

Now. Now was all they had. Matthew gallantly handed her up into the carriage and tucked the red-and-green-plaid blankets around her, then wrapped his arm around her shoulder and pulled her into him. Then they were off, riding over the snow-covered hills of the farm. It was…magical.

She tried not to overthink what was happening between them—or, more to the point, what wasn't going to happen in a few days. What was the point of dwelling on how she was going to go back to her solitary existence, with only her animals and crazy Don to break up the monotony?

This was what she wanted—a brief, hot Christmas-vacation romance with a gorgeous, talented man. A man who would make her feel as if Whitney Maddox was a woman who didn't have to hide anymore, who could take lovers and have relationships. This was getting her out of the safety of her rut.

This time with Matthew was a gift, plain and simple. She couldn't have dreamed up a better man, a better time. He was, for lack of a better word, *perfect*.

That had to be why she clung to him extra hard as they rode over the ice-kissed hills, the trees shimmering under the winter sun. This was, hands down, the most romantic thing she'd ever done—even though she knew the score. She had him now. She didn't want to miss any of that.

So when it was time to go to the rehearsal, she went early with Matthew. They were supposed to eat lunch, but they wound up at his palatial apartment, tangled up in the sheets of his massive bed, and missed lunch entirely. Which was fine. She could eat when she was alone. And the dinner after the rehearsal would be five-star, Matthew promised.

They made it to the chapel for the rehearsal almost an hour ahead of everyone else—of course they did. The place was stunning. The pews were decorated with red-and-gray bows that matched the ones on the carriage perfectly atop pine garlands, making the whole place smell like a Christmas tree. The light ceilings had dark buttresses and the walls were lined with stained-glass windows.

"We're going to have spotlights outside the windows so the lights shine at dark," Matthew explained. "The rest of the ceremony will be candlelit."

"Wow," Whitney breathed as she studied the chapel. "How many people will be here for the wedding?"

"Two hundred," he said. "But it's still an intimate space. I've been working with the videographers to make sure they don't overtake the space. We don't want anything to distract from the happy couple."

She took a deep breath as she held an imaginary bouquet in front of her. "I should practice, then," she said as she took measured steps down the aisle. "Should have brought my shoes."

Matthew skirted around her and hurried to the altar. Then he waited for her. Her cheeks flushed warm as an image of her doing this not in a dove-gray gown but a long white one forced its way across her mind.

Now, she thought, trying not to get ahead of herself. *Stay in the now.*

That got harder to do when she made it up to the altar, where Matthew was waiting. He took her hands in his and, looking down into her eyes, he smiled. Just a simple curve of the lips. It wasn't rakish; it wasn't predatory—heavens, it wasn't even overtly sexual.

"Ms. Maddox," he said in a voice that was as close to reverent as she'd ever heard him use.

"Mr. Beaumont," she replied because it seemed like the thing to do. Because she couldn't come up with anything else, not when his gaze was deepening in its intensity.

It was almost as if, standing here with Matthew, in this holy place…

No. She would not hope, no matter how intense his gaze was, no matter how much his smile, his touch affected her. She would not hope, because it was pointless. She had three more days before she left for California. Tonight, Christmas Eve and maybe Christmas morning. That was it. No point in thinking about something a little more permanent with him.

He leaned forward. "Whitney…"

Say something, she thought. *Something to give me hope.*

"Hello? Matthew?"

To his credit, he didn't drop Whitney's hands. He did lean back and tuck her fingers into the crook of his arm. "Here," he called down the aisle as the wedding planner came through the doors. Then, to Whitney, he said, "Shall we practice a few times before everyone gets here?"

"Yes, let's." Which were not words of hope.

That was fine. She didn't want any.

Really.

* * *

Against his will, Matthew sent Whitney home with Jo and took Phillip back to his place. Even though they were going to shoot photos before the ceremony, Jo had decided that she wanted to at least get ready without Phillip in the house.

Phillip wasn't exactly talking to Matthew, which was fine. Matthew had things to do anyway. The press was lining up, and Matthew had to make sure he was available for them before they wandered off and started sniffing around.

This was his job, his place in this world. He had to present the very best side of the Beaumonts, contain any scandals before they did real damage and...

His mind drifted back to the carriage ride across the farm with Whitney—to the way she'd looked standing hand in hand with him at the altar.

For such a short time, it hadn't mattered. Not the wedding, not the public image—not even the soft launch of Percheron Drafts. His showroom-ready apartment, his fancy cars—none of that mattered.

What had mattered was holding a beautiful woman tight and knowing that she was there for him. Not for the family name, the fortune, the things.

Just him.

And now that time was over and he was back to managing the message. The good news was that Byron's little brawl had done exactly what Matthew had intended it to—no one was asking about Whitney Wildz.

He checked the social media sites again. Whitney had insisted on keeping her hat on during the rehearsal and the following dinner and had only talked with the embedded press representatives when absolutely required. He knew he should be thankful that she was keeping her profile as low as possible, but he hated that she felt as if she had to hide.

All was as calm as could be expected. As far as he could tell, no one in attendance had connected the quiet maid of

honor with Whitney Wildz. Plus, the sudden influx of famous people eating in restaurants and partying at clubs was
good press, reinforcing how valuable the Beaumont name
was without Matthew being directly responsible for their
actions.

It wouldn't last, he knew. He sent out the final instructions
to the photographer and videographer, which was semipoint-
less. Whitney was in the wedding party, after all. And he
hadn't let her change her hair. They'd have to take pictures
of her. But reminding the people on his payroll what he expected made him feel better anyway.

They just had to get through the wedding. Whitney had
to make it up the aisle and back down without incident.

Just as she'd done today. She'd been downright cute, mim-
ing the action in a sweater and jeans and that hat, of course.
But tomorrow?

Tomorrow she'd be in a gown, polished and proper and
befitting a Beaumont wedding. Tomorrow she'd look perfect.

He could take a few days after the wedding, couldn't he?
Even just two days off. This thing had swallowed his life for
the past few months. He'd earned some time. Once he got
Phillip and Jo safely off on their honeymoon and his siblings
and stepmothers back to their respective corners, once he
had Christmas dinner with his mom, he could…

He could go see Whitney. See her in the sun. Ride her
horses and meet her weird-looking dogs and her pop-singer
cats.

This didn't change things, he told himself as he began to
rearrange his schedule. This was not the beginning of something else, something *more*. Far from it. They'd agreed that
after the wedding, they were…done.

Except the word felt wrong. Matthew had never had a
problem walking away from his lady friends before. When
it was over, it was over. There were no regrets, no look-

ing back and absolutely no taking time off to spend a long weekend together.

It was close to midnight when he found himself sending her a text. What are you doing? But even as he hit Send, he knew he was being foolish. She was probably in bed. He was probably waking her up. But he couldn't help himself. It'd been a long day, longer without her. He just wanted… Well, he just wanted her.

A minute later, his phone pinged and there was a blurry photo of Whitney with a tiny donkey in her lap. He could just see the silly dogs in bow ties on her pajama pants. Jo had leaned over to grin into the frame, but there was no missing Whitney's big smile. Watching Love Actually and eating popcorn, came the reply.

Good. Great. She was keeping a low profile and having fun at the same time.

Then his phone pinged again.

Miss you.

He could take a couple of days. Maybe a week. Chadwick would understand. As long as they made it through the wedding with no big scandals—as long as all the Beaumonts stayed out of the news while he was gone—he could spend the time with Whitney.

Miss you, too, he wrote back. Because he did.

He was pretty sure he'd never missed anyone else in his life.

The day of the wedding flew by in a blur. Manicures, pedicures, hairstylists, makeup artists—they all attacked Whitney and the rest of the wedding party with the efficiency of a long-planned military campaign. Whitney couldn't tell if that was because Matthew had everything on a second-by-second schedule or if this was just what happened when you had the best of the best working for you.

She finally met Byron Beaumont, as he was next in the makeup artist's chair after they finished painting Whitney's lips scarlet-red. She winced as she looked at the bruise around his face that was settling into purples and blues like a sunset with an attitude.

"Ms. Maddox," he said with an almost formal bow. But he didn't touch her and he certainly didn't hug her, not as Frances had. Heck, he didn't even call her Whitney Wildz. "It's an honor."

"I'm sorry about your eye," she heard herself say, as if she were personally responsible for the bruising. Byron looked a great deal like Matthew. Maybe a few inches shorter, and his eyes were lighter, almost gray. Byron's hair was almost the same deep auburn color as Matthew's, but his hair was longer with a wave to it.

Byron grinned at her then—almost the exact same grin that Matthew had and that Phillip had. "Anything in the service of a lady," he replied as he settled into the chair, as if he had his makeup done all the time.

By four that afternoon, the ladies were nibbling on fruit slices with the greatest of care to sustain them through the rest of the evening. "We don't want anyone to pass out," the wedding planner said as she stuck straws into water bottles and passed them around.

Then they were at the chapel, posing for an endless series of photos. She stood next to Jo, then next to Frances, then between Frances and Serena. They took shots with Jo's parents, her grandmother, her aunt and uncle. Since Toni Beaumont was singing a song during the wedding, they had to have every permutation of who stood where with her, too.

Then the doors to the chapel opened, and Whitney heard Matthew say, "We're here." The men strode down the aisle as if they owned the joint. At first she couldn't see them

clearly. The chapel wasn't well lit and the sunlight streaming in behind them was almost blinding. But then, suddenly,
Matthew was leading the Beaumont men down the aisle.

She gasped at them. At him. His tuxedo was exquisitely
cut. He could have been walking a red carpet, for all the
confidence and sensuality he exuded.

"We're keeping to the schedule, right, people?" he demanded. Then their gazes met and the rest of the world—
the stylists and wedding planner chatting, the photographer
bossing people around—all of it fell away.

"Perfect," he said.

"You, too," she murmured. Beside her, Frances snickered.
Oh, right—they weren't alone. Half the Beaumont family
was watching them. She dropped her gaze to her bouquet,
which was suddenly very interesting.

Matthew turned his attention to the larger crowd. "Phillip's ready for the reveal."

"Everyone out," the photographer announced. "I want to
get the bride and groom seeing each other for the first time.
Joey," he said to Jo. He'd been calling her that for half an
hour now. Whitney was pretty sure it wouldn't be much longer before Jo cracked and beat the man senseless with his
own camera. "You go back around and walk down the aisle."

Jo glanced at Whitney and rolled her eyes, which made
them both giggle. Whitney gathered up Jo's train, and they
hurried down the aisle as fast as they could in these dresses.
It was only when they had themselves tucked away that Frances gave the all clear.

Whitney and Frances peeked as Jo made her way up the
aisle to where Phillip was waiting for his bride. "I don't
know if I've ever seen him that happy," Frances whispered
as Phillip blinked tears of joy out of his eyes. "I hope it lasts."

"I think it will," Whitney decided.

"I just..." Frances sighed. "I just wish we could all stop

living in our father's shadow, you know? I wish I could believe in love. Even if it's just for them."

"Your time will come," Whitney whispered as she looked at Frances. "If you want it to."

"I don't. I'm never getting married," Frances announced. Then, standing up straighter, she added, "But if you want to marry Matthew, can I be your bridesmaid?"

Whitney opened her mouth and then closed it because as much as she wanted to tell Frances her head was in the clouds and that after tonight Whitney and Matthew were going their separate ways, she couldn't dismiss the image of him standing with her at the very same altar where Jo and Phillip now stood. For that brief moment—when she'd wanted him to say something that would give her hope that they weren't done after this. When she'd thought he was going to do just that. And then they'd been interrupted.

Finally, she got her mouth to work. "I'm not going to marry Matthew."

"Pity," Frances sniffed. "I saw how he looked at you. Trust me, Matthew doesn't look at other people like that."

So everyone had seen that look. Whitney sighed. But before she could respond, a deep voice behind them said, "Like what?"

The women spun around at Matthew's voice. Whitney teetered in her shoes, but Matthew caught her before she could tip forward. Then his arms were around her waist, and he was almost holding her. But not quite. They managed to keep a glimmer of space between them.

"Hi," Whitney breathed. She wanted to tell him how much she'd missed him. She wanted to ask if they could spend this last night together, after the reception, so that their Christmas morning could start off right. She wanted to tell him that he was the most handsome man she'd ever seen.

She didn't get the chance.

"Like that," Frances said with obvious glee.

"Frannie." Matthew's voice was as clear a warning as Whitney had heard since that very first night, when he'd realized who she'd once been. The space between him and Whitney widened ever so slightly. "Go make sure Byron stays out of trouble, please."

Frances rolled her eyes. "Fine. I'm going, I'm going. But he's not the one I'm worried about right now." Then, with a rustle of silk, she was gone.

And they were alone in the vestibule. "You look amazing," she managed to get out.

"So do you," he said as his arms tightened around her.

"I'd kiss you, but…"

"Lipstick," he agreed. "We're going to have to go out for more photos soon."

A quick moment. That was all they had. But she wanted more. She at least wanted tonight. One more night in his arms. Then, somehow, she'd find a way to let him go. "Matthew…" she said.

At the same time, he said, "Whitney…"

They paused, then laughed. But before she could ask for what she wanted, the photographer called out, "The best man and maid of honor? Where are you, people?"

"Tonight," Matthew said as he looped his arm through hers. "We'll talk at the reception, all right?"

All she could do was nod as they walked down the aisle together, toward the happy couple and the bossy photographer.

Whitney didn't trip.

Sixteen

Everything went according to plan. After they finished the photos in the chapel—including a series of shots with Betty in her flower-girl-slash-ring-bearer harness—the whole party went to a nearby park and took shots with snow-covered trees and ground as the backdrop. They also did the shots of Jo and Phillip getting into and out of the carriage.

Then, just because everything was going so smoothly, Matthew asked the photographer to take pictures of each of the couples with the carriage, just so he and Whitney could have a photo of the two of them with the Percheron team. So they'd have something to remember this week by.

Serena and Chadwick didn't mind, but Frances and Byron clearly thought he was nuts and Matthew didn't miss the look Phillip gave him.

He wasn't hiding how he felt about Whitney, okay? He *wasn't*. That wasn't why he had the photographer take extra shots of all the couples by themselves. He reasoned that Chadwick and Serena had had a small ceremony—absolutely no pomp and circumstance had been allowed. True, Serena had been about seven months pregnant and, yes, Chadwick had already had a big wedding for his first marriage. Serena's parents had walked her down the aisle while Phillip,

Matthew and Frances stood as witnesses. Cell phone photos didn't count. So Matthew was really doing this for Chadwick and Serena, so they'd have beautiful photos of them at their very best. And if Matthew and Whitney got some memories out of it, so much the better.

And because he was not hiding how he felt about her, he had his arms on her while the photographer snapped away. An arm around her waist when they leaned underneath the evergreen tree, its branches heavy with glistening snow. Handing her up into the carriage. Tucking her against his waist.

For their part, his family was…okay with it. Byron had slapped him on the back and said, "Some women are worth the bruises, huh?" Matthew had ignored his baby brother.

Chadwick's big comment was, "The situation is under control, correct?"

To which Matthew had replied, "Correct." Because it was.

For the moment, anyway.

"You doing okay?" Matthew whispered to Phillip as they stood at the front of the chapel. He could see that Phillip had started to fidget.

"Why is everything going so slow?" Phillip whispered back as Frances did the "step, pause, step, pause" walk down the aisle to Pachelbel's *Canon in D*. "I want Jo."

"Suck it up and smile. Remember, the cameras are rolling."

Matthew looked out over the full house in the chapel. Phillip's mother had a place of honor in the front, although she had chosen not to sit with Jo's family. Which didn't surprise Matthew a bit. Eliza Beaumont was not a huge fan of anything that had to do with the Beaumont family, a list that started with Matthew and went on for miles.

But Phillip had wanted his mother at his wedding and Matthew had the means to make it happen, so the woman was sitting in the front row, looking as relaxed as a prisoner before a firing squad and pointedly ignoring everyone.

Serena was headed down the aisle now, although she was moving at a slightly faster clip than Frances had been. "Beautiful," Chadwick whispered from the other side of Matthew. "I have to say, I'm impressed you pulled this off."

"Don't jinx it, man," Matthew hissed through his smile.

Then Serena was standing next to Frances and everyone waited.

Matthew could see Whitney, standing just inside the doors. *Come on, babe,* he thought. *One foot in front of the other. You can do it. It'll be fine.*

Then the music swelled and she took the first step. Paused. Second step. Paused. Each foot hit the ground squarely. She didn't wobble and she didn't trip on her hem. She *glided* down the aisle as if she'd been born with a bouquet in her hand and a smile on her face. The whole time, she kept her gaze fastened on him. As though she was walking not just to him but *for* him.

God, she was *so* beautiful. Simply perfect. But then, the woman in her doggy pajamas had been perfect, too. Even when she was klutzy and nervous and totally, completely Whitney, she was absolutely perfect.

How was he going to let her go?

She reached the altar and took her place. He could see how pleased she was with herself, and frankly, he was pretty damn happy, too.

Then there was a moment that should have been silent as the music changed to the wedding march and Jo made her big entrance.

Except it wasn't silent. A murmur ran through the crowd—the highest of Denver's high society, musicians and actors and people who were famous merely for being famous.

Then he heard it. "...Whitney Wildz?" Which was followed by "...that hair!" More murmurs followed. Then a click. The click of a cell phone snapping a picture.

He looked at Whitney. She was still smiling, but it wasn't

the same natural, luminous thing it'd been earlier. Her face was frozen in something that was a mockery of joy.

It'll be okay, he wanted to tell her. He wanted to believe it.

Then the music swelled up, drowning out the whispers and the clicks. Everyone stood and turned to the entrance. Betty tottered down the aisle as the daughter of one of the brewery's employees tossed rose petals onto the ground. Betty should have held everyone's attention.

But she didn't. Not even a mini donkey wearing a basket and a crown of flowers over her floppy ears could distract from Whitney Wildz. People were holding their devices high to get the best shot of her.

Jo came down the aisle on the arms of her parents. Matthew took advantage of this to get the wedding rings untied from the small pillow on Betty's back, and then the farm manager, Richard—looking hilariously uncomfortable in a suit—led the small animal off before she started munching on the floral arrangements.

When he stood back up, Matthew caught Whitney's eye as Jo took her place at the altar. He gave her an encouraging nod, hoping that she'd get the message. *Ignore them. Don't let them win.*

When the music stopped this time, the murmuring was even louder. The preacher took his place before the happy couple. Jo handed Whitney her bouquet.

The murmuring was getting louder. People weren't even trying to whisper now. Matthew wanted to shout at the crowd, *This is a wedding, for God's sake! Have some decency!* But he'd long since learned that you didn't feed the fire like that. Ignoring the excited whispers was the only way to make it through this.

"Matthew," Chadwick said in the quietest of whispers, and Matthew knew what his older brother was thinking. This was having the situation under control? *This* was handling it?

The preacher began to talk about vows and love, but he had to stop and pitch his voice up in volume to be heard.

Matthew kept his attention on the happy couple—and on Whitney. She was blinking too fast, but her smile was locked. Her face looked as if it were going to crack in half. She didn't look at him, but she didn't need to. He could read her well enough.

This was just like the restaurant all over again. She'd done nothing—not even tripped, much less fallen, and yet she was setting off a media firestorm. He had the sinking feeling that if he got out his phone and checked social media, Whitney would already be trending.

Then, out of the corner of his eye, he saw it. Movement, in the aisle. As best he could without turning and staring, he looked.

Oh, hell. People were getting up and exiting the pews—coming into the aisles. Phones and cameras were raised. They were jostling—yes, jostling—for a better shot. Of Whitney. Of someone they thought was Whitney Wildz.

"If I may," the preacher said in a tone better suited for a fire-and-brimstone Sunday sermon than a Christmas Eve wedding. "If I may have *silence*, please."

That was when Whitney turned her stricken face to his. He saw the tears gathering, saw how fast she was breathing. "I'm sorry," she said, although he couldn't hear her over the crowd. He read her lips, though. That was enough.

"No," he said, but she didn't hear him. She was already turning to hand Jo's bouquet to Serena and then she was running down the aisle, arms stiffly at her side.

Gone.

Oh, hell.

"Ms. Maddox?"

Whitney realized that she was outside.

The horse-drawn carriage was parked in front of the chapel, waiting for the happy couple. The happy couple whose wedding she'd just ruined. She vaguely recognized the driver as one of the farmhands, but he wasn't wearing jeans and flannel. "Is everything okay?"

"Um…" No. Nothing was okay. And worse? She didn't know when it would start being okay again. The chapel was on a college campus. She had to walk…that way to get to a main road?

Snow began to fall on her bare shoulders. She hadn't even managed to snag her cape, but who cared. She wasn't going back in there. She was going…

Home. That was where she was headed. Back to her solitary ranch where she could live out her solitary life. That was where she belonged. Where she wouldn't embarrass herself, which was bad enough. She was used to that.

She'd ruined Jo's wedding. Her best friend—hell, her only friend—and Whitney had ruined the wedding. She hadn't fallen, hadn't even dropped her bouquet.

She'd just been herself.

Why had she ever thought she could do that?

She wrapped her arms around her waist to try and keep warm as she walked away from the carriage and the driver. She didn't really have a plan at this point, but she knew she couldn't take off in the wedding carriage. The very carriage she'd ridden in yesterday, snuggled in Matthew's arms. She'd already messed up the wedding. She drew the line at stealing the carriage.

"Ms. Maddox?" the driver called behind her, but she ignored him. She needed to get back to the farm so she could get her things and go—and there was no way the horse and carriage could get her there.

She'd walk to the main road and catch a taxi. Taxis could get her to the farm and from there, she could leave. There. That was a plan.

The snow was coming down thick and fast, each flake

biting into her bare shoulders with what felt like teeth. It felt as if it were trying to punish her, which was fine. She deserved it.

She'd tried. She'd tried *so* hard. She'd offered to step aside. She'd tried to convince Matthew to let her change her hair. And she damn well had on panties today. Industrial-strength Spanx in opaque black, just to be extra sure.

But it wasn't enough. It would never be enough. She would *always* be Whitney Wildz. And every time she got it into her foolish little head that she wasn't—that she could be whoever she wanted to be—well, this was what would happen. If she didn't hurt herself, she'd hurt the people she cared for. People like Jo.

People like Matthew.

God, she couldn't even think of him without pain. She'd *told* him she was going to ruin the wedding, but the man had decided that through the sheer force of his will alone, she wouldn't. He'd been bound and determined—literally—to have the perfect Beaumont wedding. He was a man who was used to getting what he wanted. He'd given her a chance to show him—to show everyone—that she was Whitney Maddox. For a beautiful moment—a too-short moment—she'd thought they had succeeded.

But that'd been just an illusion and they were both the poorer for indulging in it. He had to hate her now. She was living proof that he couldn't control everything. He'd never be able to look at her and see anything but imperfection.

She slipped but managed not to fall. The sidewalks were getting slicker by the second and these shoes weren't suited for anything other than plush carpeting. She could hear the sounds of traffic getting closer, and she trudged on. Good. The farther she could get from the wedding, the better.

Her stomach turned again. She hoped Jo and Phillip were still *able* to get married. What if the whole thing had devolved into a brawl or something? What if the preacher decided Whitney's running was a sign from God that Jo and Phillip shouldn't be married? It was on her head. All of it.

She'd just come upon the main street when she heard "Whitney?" from behind her.

Matthew. No, God, please—not him. She couldn't look at him and see his failure and know it was hers.

She waved her hands, hoping there was a taxi somewhere. Anywhere. And if there wasn't, she'd keep walking until she found one.

"Whitney, wait! Babe," she heard him shout. Damn it, he was getting closer.

She tried to hurry, but her foot slipped. Stupid heels on the stupid snow. The whole universe was out to get her. She thought she would keep her balance but she hit another slick spot and started to fall. Of course. Maybe someone would get a picture of it. It'd make a great headline.

Instead of falling, though, she was in his arms. The warmth of his body pushed back against the biting cold as he held her tight. It was everything she wanted and nothing she deserved. "Let me go," she said, shoving against him.

"Babe," he said, pointedly not releasing her from his grip. If anything, he held on tighter. "You're going to freeze. You don't even have your cape."

"What does it matter, Matthew? I ruined the wedding. You saw how it was. You and I both knew it was going to happen and…and we let it." The tears she'd been trying not to cry since the first whisper had hit her ears threatened to move up again. "Why did I let it happen?"

He came around to her front and forced her to look at him. He was not gentle about it. "Because you're Whitney Maddox, damn it. And I don't care about Whitney Wildz. You're enough for me."

"But I'm not and we both know it. I'm not even enough for me. I can never be the perfect woman you need. I can never be perfect." The tears stung at her eyes almost as much as the snow stung against her skin. And that, more than any-thing else, hurt the most.

"You *are*," he said with more force. "And you didn't ruin the wedding. Those people—they did. This is on them. Not you."

She shook her head, but before she could deny it—because Matthew had never been more wrong in his life—shouts of "Whitney? Whitney!" began to filter through the snow.

A taxi pulled up next to them and the cabbie shouted, "You need a cab, lady?"

Matthew got a fierce look on his face. "Let me handle them," he said as he stripped off his tuxedo jacket and wrapped it around her shoulders. "Follow my lead. I can fix this."

She wanted to believe it. She wanted him to protect her, to save her from herself.

But she couldn't. She couldn't let him throw away every-thing he'd worked for because of her. She wasn't worth it.

"Don't you see? I can't be another mess you have to clean up. I just can't." She ducked under his arm and managed to get the taxi door open on the second try. "It has to be this way," she told him.

Before the press could swarm, she got in the taxi and slammed the door. Matthew stood there, looking as if she'd stabbed him somewhere important. It hurt to look, so she focused on the cabbie.

"Where to, lady?" he asked.

"Can you take me to the Beaumont Farms? Outside the city?"

The cabbie stared at her dress, then at Matthew and the press, complete with flashing cameras and shouting. "You can pay?"

"Yes."

The fare would be huge, but what did it matter?

This evening had already cost her everything else.

Seventeen

Matthew was going to punch something. Someone. Several someones.

Hard.

Whitney's taxi sped off, its wheels spinning for traction on the newly slick streets. Then the press—the press *he* had invited to the wedding—was upon him like hungry dogs fighting over the last table scrap.

"Matthew, tell us about Whitney!"

"Matthew! Did you see Whitney Wildz drinking before the wedding? Can you confirm that Whitney Wildz was drunk?"

"Was she on drugs?"

"Is there something going on, Matthew? Are you involved with Whitney Wildz?"

"Did Whitney have a baby bump, Matthew? Who's the father?"

"Is Byron the father? Is that why he has a black eye? Did you two fight over her?"

The snow picked up speed, driving into his face. It felt good, the pain. It distracted him from the gut-wrenching agony of Whitney's face right before she ran down the aisle. Right before she got into the taxi.

"Ladies and gentlemen," he said in his meanest sneer. There were no such people before him. Just dogs with cameras.

No one blinked. The sarcasm was lost on them entirely. They just crowded closer, microphones in his face, cameras rolling. For a moment, he felt as if he were back in college and, at any second, someone was going to ask him what he thought about those photos of his father with his pants around his ankles.

Panic clawed at him. No one had ever asked if he wanted to manage the Beaumont public image. It was just something he'd fallen into and, because he was good at it, he'd stuck with it. Because it earned him a place in the family. Because defending his father, his brothers, his stepmothers—that was what made him a Beaumont.

Figure out who you are if you're not a Beaumont.

Phillip's comment came back to Matthew, insidious little words that Matthew had thought were Phillip's attempt at chipping away at Matthew's hard-won privilege.

But if being a Beaumont meant he had to throw Whitney to the dogs…could he do that? Did he want to?

No. That was not what he wanted. It'd never been, he realized. Hadn't he asked Byron to generate some press? Hadn't that been putting Whitney first?

Who am I? Her voice whispered in his ear. *Who am I to you?*

She'd said those words to him in the front seat of his car, right before he'd tied her to the bed.

She was Whitney Maddox. And she was Whitney Wildz. She was both at the same time.

Just as he was Matthew Beaumont and Matthew Billings. He'd never stopped being Matthew Billings. That lost little boy had always been standing right behind Matthew, threatening to make him a nobody again.

Because if he wasn't a Beaumont, who was he? He'd always thought the answer was a nobody. But now?

Who was *he* to *her*?

Who was he?

He was Matthew Beaumont. And being a Beaumont was saying to hell with what people thought of you—to hell with even what your family thought of you. It was not giving a rat's ass what the media said.

Being a Beaumont was about doing what you wanted, whenever you wanted to do it. Wasn't that what was behind all of those scandals he'd swept under the rug for all these years? No one else in his family ever stopped to think. They just *did*. Whatever—whoever—they wanted.

He looked at the cameras still rolling, the reporters all jostling for position to hear what juicy gossip he was going to come up with. The headlines tomorrow would be vicious—but for the first time in his life, he didn't care.

"Ladies and gentlemen," he began again, "I have no comment."

Dead silence. Matthew smirked. He'd truly managed to stun the lot of them into silence.

Then he turned and hailed a cab. Mercifully, one pulled right up to the curb.

"Where to, buddy?" the cabbie asked as Matthew shut the door on the gaping faces of the press.

Who was he? What did he want?

Whitney.

He had to get her. "The Beaumont Farms, south of the city."

The cab driver whistled. "That's gonna cost you."

"Doesn't matter." Then, with a smile, he added, "I'm a Beaumont."

Eighteen

"Ms. Maddox?" The guard stepped out of the gate when Whitney climbed out of the taxi. "Is everything all right?"

She really wished people would stop asking that question. Wasn't the answer obvious? "I…I need to pay him and I don't have any money. On me. I have some cash in the house…" She shivered. The cabbie had turned the heat on full blast for her, but it hadn't helped. Matthew's jacket wasn't enough to fend off the elements. The snow was coming down thick and fast and the cabbie was none too happy about the prospect of making it home in this weather.

The guard stared at her with obvious concern. Then he ushered her into the guard house. "I'll pay the driver and then get a truck and take you to the house. Don't move."

He said it as if he was afraid she might go somewhere, but she didn't want to. There was heat in this little building. Plus, she was almost back to the farmhouse. This nice guard would take her the rest of the way. She'd get out of this dress and back into her own clothes. She didn't have much. She could be packed within twenty minutes. And then…

If she left immediately, she could be home by tomorrow afternoon. Back to the warmth and the sun and her animals and crazy Donald, none of whom would ever care that she'd ruined the Beaumont Christmas wedding. Yes. Back to the safety of solitude.

The guard came back with a truck and helped her into the passenger seat. He didn't tell her how much it had cost to get the cabbie to drive away. She'd pay it back, of course. She'd use the money from the royalty checks for *Whitney Wildz Sings Christmas, Yo*. Fitting.

"I'm going home," she told him when he pulled up in front of the house and got out to unlock the front door for her. "Tonight."

"Ms. Maddox, the snow is going to continue for some time," he said, the worry in his voice obvious. "I don't think—"

"I can drive on snow," she lied. She couldn't stay here. That much she knew.

"But—"

Whitney didn't listen. She said, "Thank you very much," and shut the door in the man's face. Which was a diva thing to do, but it couldn't be helped.

She didn't get lost on her way back to what had been her room and Matthew's room. Their room. Well, it wasn't that anymore.

She changed and started throwing things into her bags. She'd have time when she got home to shake out the wrinkles. She didn't have that time now.

The dress…it lay in a heap on the floor, as if she'd wounded it in the line of duty. She'd felt beautiful in the dress. Matthew had thought so. She'd felt…

She'd felt like the woman she was supposed to be when she'd worn it. Glamorous and confident and sexy and worthy. And not scandalous. Not even a little.

She picked it up, shook it out and laid it on the bed. Then she did the same with his tuxedo jacket. In her mind's eye, she saw the two of them this afternoon, having their pictures taken in a park, in a carriage bedecked in Christmas bows.

They hadn't even gotten to walk down the aisle together. She'd ruined that, too.

Her bags were heavy and, because she hadn't packed carefully, extra bulky. Getting them both out of the door and down the hall was bad enough. She was navigating the stairs one at a time when she heard the front door slam open.

"Whitney?"

Matthew. *Oh, no.* That was all that registered before she lost her grip on one of her bags. It tangled with her feet and suddenly she was falling down the last few stairs.

And right into his arms. He caught her just as he had before—just as he was always doing.

Then, before she could tell him she was sorry or that she was leaving and she'd pay back the cab fare, he was kissing her. His hair was wet and his shirt was wet and he was lifting her up to him, sliding his hands around her waist and holding her.

And he was kissing her. She was so stunned by this that she couldn't do anything but stare at him.

He pulled away, but he didn't let her go. Hell, he didn't even set her on her feet. He just held her as though his life depended on it.

She needed to get out of his arms so she could go back to being invisible Whitney Maddox. But she couldn't. Was it wrong to want just a few more minutes of being someone special? Was it wrong to want that hope, even if she was going to get knocked down for daring to hope almost immediately?

Matthew spoke. "*Always* kiss me back," he said, as if this were just another wild Tuesday night and not the ruination of everything. Then her bags—which had come crashing down after her—seemed to register with him. "Where are you going?"

"Home," she told him. She would not cry. Crying solved

nothing. And really, this was everything she'd expected. "I don't belong here. I never did."

"That's not true."

Oh, so they were just going to deny reality? Fine. She could do that. "Why are *you* here? Why aren't you at the wedding?" Then, because she couldn't help herself—because she might never get another chance to have him in her arms—she placed her palm on his cheek.

He leaned into her touch. "I had this revelation," he said as he touched his forehead to hers. "It turns out that I'm not a very good Beaumont."

"What?" she gasped. She'd heard him say how hard it was to earn his place at the table—at the altar. Why would he say that about himself? "But you're an amazing man—you take care of people and you took your sister and brother to my concert and the whole wedding was *amazing*, right until I ruined it!"

His grin was sad and happy and tired, all at the same time. Her feet touched the ground, but he didn't let her go.

"A Beaumont," he said with quiet conviction, "wouldn't care what anyone else thought. They wouldn't care how it played in the media. A Beaumont would do whatever he wanted, whenever he wanted, consequences be damned. That's what makes a Beaumont. And I've never done that. Not once." He paused, lifting her up even closer. "Not until I met you."

Hope. It was small and felt foreign in her mind—so foreign that she almost didn't recognize it for what it was. "Me?"

"You. For the first time in my life, I did something because I wanted to, regardless of how it'd play in the press." He touched her hair, where the bejeweled clip still held her stubborn white streak in place. "I fell in love with you."

Her heart stopped. Everything stopped. Had he just said… that he'd fallen in love with her? "I—" But she didn't have anything else.

Then, to her horror, she heard herself ask, "Who am I to you?"

He gave her a little grin, as if he'd known she was going to ask the question but had hoped she wouldn't. "You're a kind, thoughtful, intelligent woman who can get clumsy when you're nervous. You'd do anything for your friends, even if it puts you in the line of fire."

"But—"

He lifted her face so she had to look at him. "And," he went on, "you're beautiful and sexy and I can't hold myself back when I'm around you. I can't let you go just because of how it'll look in a headline."

"But the press—tomorrow—" She shuddered. The headlines would be cruel. Possibly the worst in her life, and that was saying something. The Beaumont public image would be in tatters, thanks to her. "Your family… I ruined *everything*," she whispered. Why couldn't he see that?

His grin this time was much less sweet, much more the look of a man who could bend the press to his will. "You merely generated some PR, that's all. And there's no such thing as bad PR."

"That's not— What?"

"Don't let the guessing games that complete strangers play hold you back, Whitney. Don't let a manufactured scandal keep us apart."

"But—but—but your life is here. And I need the sun. You said so yourself."

"The Beaumonts are here," he corrected her. "And we've already established that I'm not a very good Beaumont."

The thing that was hope began to grow inside of her until it was pulsing through her veins, spreading farther with each heartbeat. "What are you saying?"

"Who am I?" His voice was low and serious. It sent a chill up her spine that had nothing to do with his wet shirt. "If I'm not a Beaumont, who am I to you?"

"You're Matthew." He swallowed, his Adam's apple bobbing nervously. "It never mattered to me what your name is—Billings, Beaumont—I don't care. I came here thinking it'd be nice to meet a man who could look at me without thinking about Whitney Wildz or all the headlines. A man who could make me feel sexy and wanted, who could give me the confidence to maybe start dating. Who could show me it was even possible."

He cupped her face in his hands, his thumbs stroking her cheeks. "And?"

"And…that man was you. Eventually," she added with an embarrassed smile, remembering the first time she'd fallen into his arms. "But now the wedding's over. And I—" Her voice caught. "I can't be another mess you have to manage, Matthew. And I can't ever be perfect. You know I can't."

"I know." For the briefest of seconds, it felt like a book being slammed shut. "But," he added, "I don't want perfection. Because I'll never get it. I can try and try to be the perfect Beaumont until I lie down and die and I'll never make it. That's what you've shown me."

A little choked sob escaped her lips. No matter what she did, she'd never be perfect, either. Not even to him. "Great. Glad to help."

"Be *not* perfect with me, Whitney. Let me be a part of your life. Let me catch you when you fall—and hold me up when I stumble."

"But…the press—the headlines—"

"They don't matter. All that matters is what you and I know. And this is what I know. I have never *let* myself fall in love before, because I've been afraid that loving someone else will take something away from me. Make me less of a man, less of a Beaumont. And you make me more than that. More than my name. You make me whole."

The impact of his words hit her hard. Suddenly, those tears that she hadn't allowed herself to cry because the

disappointment and shame were always to be expected—
suddenly, those tears were spilling down her cheeks. "I didn't
expect to find you. I didn't expect to fall in love with you.
I don't—I don't know how to do this. I don't want to mess
this up. More than I already have."

"You won't," he said, brushing his lips over hers. "And if
you try, I'll tie you to the bed." She giggled, and he laughed
with her. "We will make this work because I'm not going
to let you go. You will always be my Whitney. Although,"
he added with a wicked grin, "I was thinking—you might
want to try out a new last name. Maybe something that starts
with a *B*."

"What are you saying?"

"Marry me. Let me be there for you, *with* you."

"Yes. Oh, God—*Matthew*." She threw her arms around
his neck. The tears were coming faster now, but she couldn't
hold them back. It was messy and not perfect but then, so was
life. "You see me as I really am. That's all I ever wanted."

"I *love* you as you really are." He swept her feet out from
underneath her and began to climb the stairs back to his
room. Their room. "Love me back?"

"Always," she told him. "Always."

* * * * *

COLD CONSPIRACY

CINDI MYERS

To the ladies of GJWW.

Chapter One

"Come on, Donna. We need to head back to the house or I'll be late for work." Rayford County Sheriff's Deputy Jamie Douglas turned to look back at her nineteen-year-old sister, Donna, who was plodding up the forest trail in snowshoes. Short and plump, her brown curls like a halo peeking out from beneath her pink knit cap, cheeks rosy from the cold, Donna reminded Jamie of the Hummel figurines their grandmother had collected. On a Monday morning in mid-January, the two sisters had the forest to themselves, and Jamie had been happy to take advantage of a break in the weather to get outside and enjoy some exercise. But now that she needed to get home, Donna was in no rush, stopping to study a clump of snow on a tree branch alongside the trail, or laughing at the antics of Cheyenne, one of their three dogs. The twenty-pound terrier-Pomeranian mix was the smallest and easiest to handle of the canines, so Donna had charge of him. Jamie had a firm hold on the leashes for the other two—a Siberian husky named Targa, and a blond Lab mix, Cookie. "Donna!" Jamie called again, insistent.

Donna looked up, her knit cap slipping over one eye. "I'm coming!" she called, breaking into a clumsy jog.

"Don't run. You'll fall and hurt yourself." Jamie started

back toward her sister, but had taken only a few steps when Donna tripped and went sprawling.

"Oh!" It was Jamie's turn to run—not an easy feat in snowshoes, though she managed to reach Donna's side quickly. "Are you okay?"

Donna looked up, tears streaming down her plump cheeks. "I'm all wet," she sniffed.

"Come on, let's get you up." Jamie took her sister's arm. "It's not far to the car." Though Down syndrome had delayed her development, Donna was only a few inches shorter than Jamie and outweighed her by twenty pounds. Getting her to her feet while both women were wearing snowshoes made for a clumsy undertaking. Add in three romping dogs, and by the time Donna was upright, both sisters were tired and damp.

Once she was assured Donna would stay on her feet, Jamie took charge of Cheyenne, adjusting her grip on all three leashes. But just then, something crashed through the undergrowth to their left. Barking and lunging, Targa tore from her grasp, quickly followed by Cookie and Cheyenne. All three dogs took off across the snow, on the trail of the mule deer buck who was bounding through the forest.

"A deer!" Donna clapped her hands. "Did you see him run?"

"Targa! Cookie! Come here!" Jamie called after the dogs, even as the clamor of their barking receded into the woods. Silently cursing her bad luck, she slipped off her pack and dropped it at Donna's feet. "Stay here," she ordered. "I'm going after the dogs."

Running in snowshoes was probably like dancing in clown shoes, Jamie thought as she navigated through the thick undergrowth. She could still hear the dogs—that was good. "Targa, come!" she shouted. She needed to find the dogs soon. Otherwise, she'd be showing up late for the mandatory meeting Sheriff Travis Walker had called, and she hated to think what he would have to say. As the department's newest deputy, she couldn't count on him cutting her much slack.

The dogs' tracks were easy to follow through the snow, which was churned up by their running paws. Here and there she spotted the imprints of the deer, too. She replayed the sight of the big animal crashing out of the woods toward them. What had made the buck run that way—before the dogs had even seen it? Was a mountain lion stalking the animal?

Fighting back a shiver of fear, she scanned the forest surrounding her. She saw nothing, but she couldn't shake a feeling of uneasiness—as if she really was being watched.

She crashed through the underbrush and emerged in a small clearing. The dogs were on the other side, all wagging tails and happy grins as they gathered around a man on snowshoes, who scowled at the three of them. Jamie's heart sank when she recognized the uniform of a wildlife officer—what some people called a game warden. He looked up at her approach. "Are these your dogs?" he asked.

"Yes, Nate. They're my dogs." She crossed the clearing to him and gathered up the leashes. Worse even than having her dogs caught in the act of breaking the law by a wildlife officer was being caught by Nate Hall. The big blond outdoorsman managed to look like a conquering Viking, even in his khaki uniform, though Jamie could remember when he had been a gawky boy. The two of them had been pretty successfully avoiding each other since he had moved back to Eagle Mountain four months ago, after an absence of seven years. "My sister fell and I was helping her up when they got away from me," Jamie said.

"Jamie, you ought to know better," Nate said. "The deer

and elk are already stressed this winter, with the deep snow. Allowing dogs to chase them stresses them further and could even result in their death."

What made him think he had the right to lecture her? "I didn't *allow* the dogs to chase the deer," she said. "It was an accident." She glared down at the three dogs, who now sat at her feet, tongues lolling, the pictures of innocence.

"Hello!" They both turned to see Donna tromping toward them. She towed Jamie's pack behind her, dragging it through the snow by its strap.

"Donna, you were supposed to wait for me," Jamie said.

"I wanted to see what you were doing." Donna stopped, dropped the pack and turned to Nate. "Hello. I'm Donna. I'm Jamie's sister."

"Hello, Donna," Nate said. His gaze swept over Donna, assessing her. "Your sister said you fell. Are you okay?"

"Just wet." Donna looked down at the damp knees of her snow pants.

"We really need to be going." Jamie picked up her pack with one hand, while holding all three leashes in the other. "I have to get to work."

"Let me take the dogs." Not waiting for her reply, Nate stepped forward and took the leashes. She started to argue, then thought better of it. If the dogs got away from him, maybe he wouldn't be so quick to blame her.

"Nice day for snowshoeing," he said as he fell into step beside Jamie, Donna close behind.

She didn't really want to make small talk with him. The last real conversation they had had—seven years ago— had not been a pleasant one. Though she didn't remember much of anything either of them had said, she remembered the pain behind their words. The hurt had faded, leaving an unsettled feeling in its place.

The dogs trotted along like obedience school protégés.

When Targa tried to pull on the leash, Nate reined her in with a firm "No!" and she meekly obeyed—something she never did for Jamie. Apparently, muscles and a deep, velvety voice worked to impress female canines, too.

"It's a beautiful day," Donna said. "It's supposed to be Jamie's day off, but now she has to go to work."

"Something come up?" he asked. His gray eyes met hers, clearly telegraphing the question he didn't want to voice in front of Donna—*Any more murders?* Over the past three weeks, a serial killer had taken the lives of five local women. Dubbed the Ice Cold Killer, because of the calling cards he left behind with the words *Ice Cold* printed on them, the serial murderer had eluded all attempts by local law enforcement to track him down. Heavy snow and avalanches that closed the only road out of town for weeks at a time had further hampered the investigation.

"Nothing new," Jamie said. "The sheriff has called a meeting to go over everything we know so far."

Nate nodded and faced forward again. "When I moved back to town I was surprised to find out you were a sheriff's deputy," he said. "I never knew you were interested in law enforcement."

"There's a lot you never knew about me." She hadn't meant the words to come out so sharply and hurried to smooth them over. Otherwise, Nate might think she was still carrying a torch for him. "I stopped by the department one day to get an application to become a 911 dispatcher," she said. "I found out they were recruiting officers. They especially wanted women and would pay for my training, as long as I agreed to stay with the department three years. The starting salary was a lot more than I could make as a dispatcher, and I thought the work sounded interesting." She shrugged. "And it is."

"A little too interesting, sometimes, I imagine," Nate said.

"Well, yeah. Lately, at least." She had been one of the first on the scene when the killer's third victim, Fiona Winslow, had been found. Before then, she had never seen the body of someone who had died violently. Then she had responded to the call about a body in a car in the high school parking lot and found the killer's most recent victim, teacher Anita Allbritton. The deaths had shocked her, but they had also made her more determined than ever to do what she could to stop this killer.

"The sheriff is getting married soon," Donna said.

"Yes, he is." Nate looked back at her. "I'm going to be in the wedding."

"You are?" Donna sounded awed, as if Nate had announced that he was going to fly to the moon.

"I'm one of the groomsmen," Nate said.

"I didn't know you knew Travis that well," Jamie said.

"We ended up rooming together in college for a while," Nate said. "He's really the one who talked me into coming back to Eagle Mountain, when an opening came up in my department."

So Nate had returned to his hometown because of Travis—not because of anyone else he had left behind.

They reached the trailhead, where Jamie's SUV was parked. Nate helped her get the dogs into the vehicle. "Where is your car?" Donna asked, looking around the empty parking area.

"I hiked over from the base of Mount Wilson," Nate said. "I'm checking on the condition of the local deer and elk herds. The department is thinking of setting up some feeding stations, to help with survival rates this winter. All this snow is making it tough for even the elk to dig down and get enough food."

"I could help feed deer!" Donna's face lit up.

"I appreciate the offer," Nate said. "But they're too wild

to come to people. We put out pelleted food and hay in areas where the animals congregate, and monitor them with remote cameras."

Nate had intended to study wildlife biology in college, Jamie remembered. He was in his element out here in the snowy woods. That his job involved carrying a gun and arresting poachers would only make the work more interesting to him. He had always had a strong sense of wrong and right. Some people might even call him idealistic.

She didn't have much room for idealism in her life these days—she had to focus on being practical. "We have to go," she said, tossing her pack in after the dogs and shutting the hatch. "Buckle up, Donna."

She started around the side of the car to the driver's seat, but Nate blocked her way. "I'm glad I ran into you this afternoon," he said. "We didn't have much chance to visit at the scavenger hunt at the Walker Ranch."

She shook her head. Fiona Winslow had died that day—no one had been in a visiting mood. "I'm sure we'll run into each other from time to time," she said. Eagle Mountain was a small town in a remote area—she saw a lot of the same people over and over again, whether she wanted to or not. "But don't get any ideas about picking up where we left off." She shoved past him and opened the car door.

After she made sure Donna was buckled in, she backed the SUV out of the lot. Donna waved to Nate, who returned the wave, though the look on his face wasn't an especially friendly one.

Donna sat back in her seat. "He was cuuuute!" she said.

"Don't you remember Nate?" Jamie asked. "He used to come over to the house sometimes, when he and I were in middle school and high school."

"I remember boys," Donna said. "He's a man. You should go out with him."

"I'm not going out with anybody," Jamie said. She wasn't going to deny that Nate was good-looking. He had been handsome in high school, but time and working out, or maybe the demands of his job, had filled out and hardened his physique. Though the bulky parka and pack he had on today didn't reveal much, the jeans and sweater he had worn to the party at the ranch had showed off his broad shoulders and narrow waist in a way that had garnered second and third looks from most of the women present.

"Why don't you have a boyfriend?" Donna asked. It wasn't a new question. Donna seemed determined to pair up her sister with any number of men in town.

"I'm too busy to have a boyfriend," Jamie said. "I work and I take care of you, and I don't need anyone else."

"But I want you to have a boyfriend," Donna said.

"Sorry to disappoint you."

"I have a boyfriend!" Donna grinned and hugged herself.

"Oh?" This was the first Jamie had heard that Donna was interested in anyone in particular. "Who is your boyfriend?"

"Henry. He works in produce."

Donna worked part-time bagging groceries at Eagle Mountain Grocery. Jamie made a note to stop by the store and check out Henry. Was he another special-needs young adult like Donna, or the local teen heartthrob—or even an adult who might have unknowingly attracted her? It was an easy mistake for people to think of Donna as a perpetual child, but she was a young woman, and it was up to Jamie to see to it that no one took advantage of her.

She slowed to pass a blue Chevy parked half off the road. The car hadn't been there when they had come this way earlier. If she had more time, she would stop and check it out, but a glance at the clock on the dash showed she was cutting it close if she was going to drop Donna off at Mrs. Simmons's house and change into her sheriff's department uniform before the meeting.

"What is wrong with that car?" Donna looked back over her shoulder. "We should stop and see."

"I'll let the sheriff's office know about it," Jamie said. "They'll send someone out to check."

"I really think we should stop." Donna's expressive face was twisted with genuine concern. "Someone might be hurt."

"I didn't see anyone with the car," Jamie said.

"You didn't stop and look!" Donna leaned toward her, pleading. "We need to go back. Please? What if the car broke and someone is there, all cold and freezing?"

Her sister's compassion touched Jamie. The world would be a better place if there were more people like Donna in it. She slowed and pulled to the shoulder, preparing to make a U-turn. "All right. We'll go back." Maybe the sheriff would accept stopping to check on a disabled vehicle as an excuse for her tardiness.

She drove past the car, then turned back and pulled in behind it, angling her vehicle slightly, just as if she had been in a department cruiser instead of her personal vehicle. "Stay in the car," she said to Donna, who was reaching for the buckle on her seat belt.

Donna's hand stilled. "Okay," she said.

Cautiously, Jamie approached the vehicle. Though she didn't usually walk around armed, since the appearance of the Ice Cold Killer, she wore a gun in a holster on her belt at all times. Its presence eased some of her nervousness now. The late-model blue Chevrolet Malibu sat parked crookedly, nose toward the snowbank on the side of the road, the snow around it churned by footsteps, as if a bunch of people had hastily parked it and piled out.

She leaned forward, craning to see into the back seat, but nothing appeared out of order there. But something wasn't right. The hair rose up on the back of her neck and she put a hand on the gun, ready to draw it if necessary.

But she didn't need a gun to defend herself from the person in the car. The woman lay on her back across the front seat, eyes staring at nothing, the blood already dried from the wound on her throat.

Chapter Two

Nate reached his truck parked at the base of Mount Wilson just as his radio crackled. Though a recently installed repeater facilitated radio transmission in this remote area, the pop and crackle of heavy static often made the messages difficult to understand. He could make out something about needing an officer to assist the sheriff's department. He keyed the mic and replied. "This is Officer Hall. What was that location again?"

"Forest Service Road 1410. That's one-four-one-zero."

"Copy that. I'm on my way." The trailhead on 1410 was where he had left Jamie and her sister. Had they found something? Or had something happened to them?

He pressed down harder on the gas pedal, snow flying up around the truck as he raced down the narrow path left by the snowplow. The Ice Cold Killer's next to last victim, Lauren Grenado, had been found on a Forest Service road not that far from here. Maybe Nate shouldn't have left Jamie and her sister alone. He could have asked them to give him a ride back to his truck, as an excuse to stay with them. But Jamie had said she was running late for work, so she probably would have turned him down.

Who was he kidding? She definitely would have turned him down. She clearly didn't want anything to do with him, apparently still holding a grudge over their breakup all those years ago.

And yeah, maybe he hadn't handled that so well—but he'd been nineteen and headed off to college out of state. He had thought he was doing the right thing by ending their relationship when it was impossible for them to be together. He had told himself that eventually she would see the sense in splitting up. Maybe she would even thank him one day. But she wasn't thanking him for anything—the knowledge that he could have hurt her that deeply chafed at him like a stone in his boot.

He spotted her SUV up ahead, parked behind a blue sedan. Jamie, hands in the pockets of her parka, paced alongside the road. He didn't see Donna—she was probably in the car.

He pulled in behind Jamie's SUV and turned on his flashers. Jamie whirled to face him. "What are you doing here?" she demanded.

"I got a call to assist the sheriff's department." He joined her and nodded toward the car. "What have you got?"

"Another dead woman." Her voice was flat, as was her expression. But he caught the note of despair at the end of the sentence and recognized the pain shining out from her hazel eyes. He had a sharp impulse to pull her close and comfort her—but he knew right away that would be a very bad idea. She wasn't his friend and former lover Jamie right now. She was Deputy Douglas, a fellow officer who needed him to do his job.

"I've got emergency flashers in my car," he said. He glanced toward her SUV. Donna sat in the front seat, hunched over and rocking back and forth. "Is your sister okay?"

"She's upset. Crying. Better to leave her alone for a bit."

"Do you know who the woman is?"

She shook her head. "No. But I think it's the Ice Cold Killer. I didn't open the door or anything, but she looks like his other victims—throat cut, wrists and ankles wrapped with tape."

He walked back to his truck, retrieved the emergency beacons and set them ten yards behind his bumper and ten yards ahead of the car. As he passed, he glanced into the front seat and caught a glimpse of the dead woman, staring up at him. Suppressing a shudder, he returned to Jamie, as a Rayford County Sheriff's cruiser approached. The driver parked on the opposite side of the road, and tall and lanky Deputy Dwight Prentice got out. "Travis is on his way," he said, when they had exchanged greetings.

"I was headed back to town to get ready for our meeting when I saw the car," Jamie said. "It wasn't here when I drove by earlier, on my way to the Pickaxe snowshoe trail."

"The meeting has been pushed back to four o'clock." Dwight walked over to the car and peered inside. "Do you know who she is?"

"I don't recognize her, and I never opened the car door," Jamie said. "I figured I should wait for the crime scene team."

"Did you call in the license plate?" Dwight asked.

Jamie flushed. "No. I… I didn't think of it."

"I'll do it," Nate said.

Radio transmission was clearer here and after a few minutes he was back with Jamie and Dwight, with a name. "The car is registered to Michaela Underwood of Ames, Iowa."

The sound of an approaching vehicle distracted them. No one said anything as Sheriff Travis Walker pulled in behind Dwight's cruiser. Tall and trim, looking like a law enforcement recruiting poster, the young sheriff showed the strain of the hunt for this serial killer in the shadows beneath his eyes and the grim set of his mouth. He pulled on gloves as he crossed to them, and listened to Jamie's story. "What time did you drive by here on your way to the trail?" he asked.

"I left my house at five after nine, so it would have been about nine thirty," she said.

"Your call came in at eleven fifty-two," Travis said. "How long was that after you found her?"

"I had to drive until I found a signal, but it wasn't that long," Jamie said. "We stopped here at eleven forty-five. I know because I kept checking the time, worried I was going to be late for work."

Travis glanced toward her car. "Who is that with you?"

"My sister, Donna. She never got out of the car." One of the dogs—the big husky—stuck its head out of the partially opened driver's-side window. "I have my dogs with me, too," Jamie added.

"All right. Let's see what we've got."

The others stood back as Travis opened the driver's-side door. He leaned into the vehicle and emerged a few moments later with a small card, like a business card, and held it up for them to see. The bold black letters were easy to read at this short distance: ICE COLD. "Butch is on his way," Travis said. Butch Collins, a retired doctor, served as Rayford County's medical examiner. "Once he's done, Dwight and I will process the scene. I've got a wrecker on standby to take the car to our garage."

"It must be getting crowded in there," Nate said—which earned him a deeper frown from the sheriff.

"Nate, can you stay and handle traffic, in case we get any lookie-loos?" Travis asked.

"Sure."

"What do you want me to do?" Jamie asked.

"Take your sister home. I'll see you at the station this afternoon. You can file your statement then."

"All right."

Nate couldn't tell if she was relieved to be dismissed—or upset about being excluded. He followed her back to her SUV and walked around to the passenger side. The dogs began barking but quieted at a reprimand from Jamie. Donna eased the door open a crack at Nate's approach. "Hello," Nate said. He had a vague memory of Donna as a sweet, awkward little girl. She wasn't so little anymore.

"Hello." She glanced toward the blue sedan, where Dwight and Travis still stood. "Did you see the woman?"

"She's not anyone we know," Nate said. "A tourist, probably." More than a few visitors had been stranded in Eagle Mountain when Dixon Pass, the only route into town, closed due to repeated avalanches triggered by the heavy snowfall.

"Why did she have to die?" Donna asked.

Because there are bad people in the world, he thought. But that didn't seem the right answer to give this girl, who wanted reassurance. "I don't know," he said. "But your sister and I, and Sheriff Walker and all his deputies, are going to do everything we can to find the person who hurt her."

Donna's eyes met his—sweet, sad eyes. "I like you," she said.

"I like you, too," he answered, touched.

"All right, Donna. Quit flirting with Nate so he can get back to work." Jamie turned the key in the ignition and started the SUV.

"You okay, Jamie?" he asked.

The look she gave him could have lit a campfire. "Why wouldn't I be okay?" she asked. "I'm a deputy. I know how to handle myself."

"I wasn't implying you didn't." He took a step back.

"But this kind of thing shakes up everybody. If you asked the sheriff, he'd probably tell you he's upset." At least, Nate had known Travis long enough to recognize the signs that this case was tearing him up inside.

"I'm fine," Jamie said, not looking at him. "And I need to go."

Look me in the eye and let me see that you're really okay, he thought. But he only took another step back and watched as she drove away. Then he walked into the road, to flag down the ambulance he could see in the distance.

JAMIE SHIFTED IN the driver's seat of the SUV, as uncomfortable as if her clothes were too tight. Nate had looked at her as if he expected her to dissolve into tears at any minute. He ought to know she wasn't like that. She was tough—and a lot tougher now than she was when they had been a couple. She had had to develop a thick skin to deal with everything life had thrown at her.

She was a sheriff's deputy, and she had seen dead people before. She wasn't going to fall apart at the sight of a body. Though she had forgotten to call in the license plate of the car, which she should have done, even if she wasn't on duty. And she should have stayed and helped process the crime scene.

If she had been a man, would the sheriff have asked her to stay? No, she decided, her gender didn't have anything to do with this. Travis Walker was as fair a man as she had ever known. But she had had Donna with her. She had to look after her sister, and the sheriff knew that. They had discussed her situation before he hired her. With their parents dead and no other relatives living nearby, Jamie was responsible for Donna, and might be for the rest of her life. While Donna might one day want to live on her own, with some assistance, most programs that would allow that were only available in larger cities—not small towns like Eagle Mountain. As long as Donna wanted to stay in their childhood home, Jamie would do whatever she could to make that happen.

She was happy to take care of her sister, but it meant making certain adjustments. She wasn't free to go out whenever she liked. She couldn't be spontaneous, because she had to make sure Donna was safe and looked after. She didn't think many men her age would be open to that kind of life.

Which was fine. She didn't need a man to make her complete.

She didn't need Nate Hall. When his plans changed and he decided to go away for college, he had shed her as easily as if he had been getting rid of last year's winter coat or a pair of shoes he'd outgrown.

He had told her he loved her, but when you loved someone, you didn't treat them like you were doing them a favor when you said goodbye.

"I'm hungry. We missed lunch."

Jamie guessed Donna wasn't too traumatized, if she was thinking about food. "I'll make you a sandwich before I drop you off at Mrs. Simmons's," she said. "I think there's still some tuna in the refrigerator. Would you like that?"

"I don't want to go to Mrs. Simmons's house," Donna said. "I want to stay home."

"I have to work this afternoon," Jamie said. "And I may be late. You can't stay in the house by yourself."

"Why not?" Donna asked. "I know how to dial 911 if something bad happens."

Jamie tightened her hands on the steering wheel until her knuckles ached. "It's not safe for you to stay by yourself," she said. Even if Donna's mental capacity had matched her physical age, Jamie wouldn't have wanted to leave her alone. Not with a killer preying on women in Eagle Mountain.

"I'm old enough to stay home by myself," Donna said.

"Mrs. Simmons's feelings will be hurt if you don't stay with her," Jamie said. For sure, their older neighbor would miss the money Jamie paid her to watch over Donna while Jamie worked.

"You could explain it to her." But Donna sounded doubtful. She was very sensitive to other people's feelings—perhaps because her own had been wounded so often by unthinking remarks.

"If you don't go see her, you'll miss your shows," Jamie said. Every afternoon, Mrs. Simmons and Donna watched old sitcoms and dramas on a classic TV station. Since Jamie didn't subscribe to the expensive cable package required for such programming, Mrs. Simmons was Donna's only source for her beloved shows.

Donna sighed—a long, dramatic sigh that would have done any teen girl proud. "I guess I had better go, then."

"Thank you." Jamie leaned over and squeezed her sister's arm. "I really appreciate you being so nice about it."

"What time will you be home?" Donna asked.

"I don't know. I have this meeting, but if the sheriff wants me to work after that, I will." She sat up straighter, her next words as much a pep talk for herself as for her sister. "The work I do is important. I'm helping to keep people safe." Though she and her fellow deputies hadn't been able to keep Michaela Underwood and the Ice Cold Killer's other victims safe. The knowledge hurt, and it goaded her to do more. To do better.

"Will you see Nate at the meeting?" Donna asked.

Jamie frowned. "Nate is a wildlife officer—he doesn't work for the sheriff's department."

"He's nice," Donna said. "And cute."

"You think every man you see is cute," Jamie teased.

"I don't think Mr. McAdams is cute." Donna made a face. Mr. McAdams was the meat market manager at Eagle Mountain Grocery. Jamie had to admit he bore a startling resemblance to the photo of last year's Grand Champion steer that graced the door to the meat freezer at the grocery.

"Is Henry cute?" Jamie asked.

Donna grinned. "Oh, yeah. Henry is cuuuute!" She dissolved into giggles, and Jamie couldn't help giggling, too. She could never feel gloomy for long when she was with Donna. Her sister had a real gift for bringing joy into the lives of everyone she knew.

They reached home and the dogs piled out of the SUV and raced into the house, then out into the backyard, through the dog door Jamie's father had installed years before. Three laps around the yard, noses to the ground, then they were back inside, lined up in formation in front of the treat cabinet. "Treat!" Donna proclaimed and took out the bag that held the beloved bacon snacks. She carefully doled out one to each dog, pronouncing "Good dog!" as each treat was devoured.

The next hour passed in a blur of lunch, changing clothes and hustling Donna two houses down to Mrs. Simmons, who met them at the door, a worried expression on her face. "There's some cookies for you on the table," Mrs. Simmons said to Donna. "You go get them while I talk to Jamie."

When Donna had left them, Mrs. Simmons said, keeping her voice low. "I heard they found another woman's body."

"Yes." There was no sense denying it. Half the town listened to the emergency scanner, the way some people listened to music on the radio. "I don't know anything to tell you," she added quickly, before Mrs. Simmons could press her for more information.

"I never thought I'd see the day when I didn't feel safe around here," Mrs. Simmons said.

Jamie wanted to reassure the woman that she would be fine—that there was nothing to worry about. But with six women dead and the department no closer to finding the killer, the words would be empty and meaningless. "I have to go," she said. "I'm not sure how late I'll be. If it will be later than nine, I'll call you."

"Don't worry about us," Mrs. Simmons said. "Donna is welcome to spend the night if she needs to. She's good company."

Ten minutes later, Jamie parked her SUV in the lot behind the sheriff's department. She stowed her purse in her locker and made her way down the hall to the conference room. Dwight and Travis's brother, Deputy Gage Walker, were already there, along with Ryder Stewart from Colorado State Patrol, and US Marshal Cody Rankin, his arm in a sling.

"How's the arm?" Jamie asked as she took a seat at the table across from Cody.

"The arm's fine. The shoulder hurts where they took the bullet out, but I'll live." He had been shot by an ex-con who had been pursuing him and the woman who was catering Travis's upcoming wedding. "I'm not officially on duty," Cody added. "But Travis asked me to sit in and contribute what I could."

The sheriff entered and everyone moved to seats around the table. Though newspaper reports almost always included at least one reference to the sheriff's "boyish good looks," today he looked much older, like a combat veteran who has seen too many battles. He walked to the bulletin board in the center of the wall facing the conference table and pinned up an eight-by-ten glossy photo of a smiling, dark-haired woman. The image joined five others of similarly smiling, pretty females. The victims of the Ice Cold Killer.

"Her name is Michaela Underwood," Travis said. "Twenty-two years old, she moved to Eagle Mountain to live near her parents. She recently started a new job at the bank." He turned to face them. "These killings have got to stop," he said. "And they have to stop now."

Chapter Three

The meeting at the sheriff's department had already begun when Nate arrived. He slipped into the empty seat next to Jamie. She glanced at him, her expression unreadable, then turned her attention back to the sheriff, who was speaking.

"We're putting every resource we've got behind this case," Travis said. "We're going to look at every bit of evidence again. We're going to reinterview everyone even remotely connected with the women who died, everyone in the areas where they were killed—anyone who might have possibly seen or heard anything."

"What about suspects?" Nate asked. He indicated a board on the far left side of the room, where photos of several men were pinned.

"Where we can, we'll talk to them again." Travis said. "We've ruled them out as the murderers, but they may know something." He rested his pointer on photos of a pair of young men at the top of the chart. "Alex Woodruff and Tim Dawson drew our attention because they were at the Walking W Ranch the day the third victim, Fiona Winslow, was killed. They didn't have an alibi for the previous two murders, of Kelly Farrow and Christy O'Brien. Once the road reopened, they disappeared. I'm still trying to confirm that they returned to Fort Collins, where they're supposedly attending Colorado State University."

He shifted the pointer to a photo of a handsome, dark-haired man. "Ken Rutledge came to our attention because he lived next door to Kelly Farrow and had dated her business partner, Darcy Marsh. When he attacked Darcy several times and eventually kidnapped her, we thought we had found our killer. But since his arrest, there have been three more murders."

Quickly, Travis summarized the case against the remaining suspects—three high school students who had been seen the night Christy O'Brien was murdered, and a veterinarian who resented Kelly Farrow and Darcy Marsh setting up a competing veterinary practice. "They all have solid alibis for most of the murders, so we had to rule them out," he concluded.

He moved back to the head of the conference table. "We're putting together profiles of all the victims, to see if we can find any common ground, and we're constructing a detailed timeline. If you're not out on a call, then I want you studying the evidence, looking for clues and trying to anticipate this killer's next move."

They all murmured agreement.

"Some of this we've already done," Travis said. "But we're going to do it again. The person who did this left clues that tell us who he is. It's up to us to find them. Colorado Bureau of Investigation has agreed to send an investigator to work with us when the road opens again, but we don't know when that will be. Until then, we're on our own. I want to start by considering some questions."

He picked up a marker and wrote on a whiteboard to the left of the women's pictures, speaking as he wrote. "Why is this killer—or killers—here?"

"Because he lives here," Gage said.

"Because he was visiting here and got caught by the snow," Dwight added.

"Because he came here to kill someone specific and found out he liked it," Jamie said. She flushed as the others turned to look at her. "It would be one way to confuse authorities about one specific murder," she said. "By committing a bunch of unrelated ones."

Travis nodded and added this to their list of reasons.

"Are we talking about one man working alone, or two men working together?" Ryder asked.

"That was my next question." Travis wrote it on the whiteboard.

"I think it has to be two," Gage said. "The timing of some of the killings—Christy O'Brien, Fiona Winslow and Anita Allbritton, in particular—required everything to be carried out very quickly. The woman had to be subdued, bound, killed and put into her vehicle. One man would have a hard time doing that."

"Maybe he's a really big guy," Cody said. "Really powerful—powerful enough to overwhelm and subdue the women."

"I agree with Gage that I think we're probably looking at two men," Travis said. "But that should make it easier to catch them. And if we find one, that will probably lead us to the second one." He turned to write on the board again. "What do we know for certain about these murders?"

"The victims are all women," Dwight said. "Young women—all of them under forty, most under thirty."

"They're all killed out of doors," Nate said. "Away from other people."

"Except for Fiona," Jamie said. "There were a lot of people around when she was killed."

"They were all left in vehicles, except Fiona," Ryder said. "And they were alone in their vehicles."

"The killer uses the weather to his advantage," Gage

said. "The snow makes travel difficult and covers up his tracks."

"I think he likes to taunt law enforcement," Ryder said. "He leaves those cards, knowing we'll find them."

"He wants us to know he's committing the murders, but is that really taunting?" Dwight asked.

"He killed Fiona at the Walker Ranch," Gage said. "When the place was crawling with cops." He shifted to look at Jamie and Nate. "I wouldn't be surprised if he knew the two of you were nearby when he killed Michaela this morning."

Jamie gasped. "That deer!"

Nate touched her arm. "What deer?"

"When my sister and I were on the trail this morning, a buck burst out of the underbrush suddenly, as if something had startled it," she said. "That's what my dogs were chasing. I wondered at the time if a mountain lion was after it. And when I was trying to catch the dogs I felt…unsettled." Her eyes met his, tinged with fear. "As if someone was watching me."

"That could be a good thing, if he thinks he's taunting us," Travis said. "We might be able to draw him out into the open."

"So far he's been very good at evading us," Gage said.

"He has, but from now on, we're going to be better." Travis pointed to Nate. "Did you see anyone else when you were in the area near the murder this morning?"

"I talked to an ice fisherman—checked his fishing license. A local guy." He searched his memory. "Abel Crutchfield."

"Gage, find him and interview him," Travis said.

Gage nodded.

"Anyone else?" Travis asked.

Nate shook his head. "Nobody else—except Jamie—Deputy Douglas—and her sister."

"Jamie, did you see anyone while you and your sister were out there?"

"No one," she admitted. "We didn't even pass any cars once we turned off the main highway."

"You start with the women," Travis told her. "See if you can find any commonalities—or any one woman who had a reason someone might want to kill her. Enough that he would kill others to cover up the crime."

"Yes, sir."

Travis gave the others their assignments—Nate was going to work with Gage on re-canvassing people who might have been in the vicinity of the two murders that occurred on forest service land.

The meeting ended and they filed out of the conference room, unsmiling and mostly silent. Nate stayed close to Jamie. "Is Donna upset about all this?" he asked.

"A little." She shook her head. "Not too much. She does a good job of living in the moment, and I try to keep things low-key—not bring the job home or act upset around her."

"These killings have everyone on edge," he said.

"It's frustrating, having him do this right under our noses. I realize it might be more than one person, but it's awkward to keep saying 'killer or killers.'"

"I get that," Nate said. "We all say 'he,' even though we suspect more than one person is involved."

"This is a small community," Jamie said. "We ought to be able to spot someone like this."

"He knows how to blend in," Nate said. "Or to hide."

She rolled her shoulders, as if shrugging off some burden. "I was surprised to see you here this afternoon," she said.

"The sheriff asked me to sit in. I've been one of the

first on the scene for three of the murders. I spend a lot of time in the backcountry, where several of the women were found. He's trying to pull in every resource that might help. And I want to help. There's not a law enforcement officer in the county who doesn't want to catch this guy."

"Of course. Well, I'd better get to work. I'm going to start reviewing all the information we have about the victims." She started to turn away, but Nate touched her arm, stopping her.

"Now that I'm back in Eagle Mountain, I'd really like us to be friends again," he said.

The look she leveled at him held a decided chill. "I don't have a lot of time for hanging out and reminiscing about the old days," she said.

She shrugged out of his grasp and started down the hall but was stopped by Adelaide Kinkaid. The seventy-something office manager alternately nagged and nurtured the sheriff and his deputies, and kept her finger on the pulse of the town. She peered over the tops of her purple bifocals at Jamie. "Where's the sheriff?" she asked. "There's someone here to see him."

"I think he's still in the conference room, talking to Gage," Jamie said.

"I'll get him." Adelaide started to move past Jamie, then said, "You go on up front and stay with the couple who are waiting. I'm thinking this might benefit from a woman's touch."

Nate followed Jamie into the small front lobby of the sheriff's department. A man and a woman in their early thirties huddled together near the door, arms around each other, the man's head bent close to the woman's. They both looked up when Jamie and Nate arrived, the woman's face a mask of sorrow, her eyes puffy and red from crying.

"I'm Deputy Douglas." Jamie introduced herself. "The sheriff will be here shortly. Can I help you in the meantime?"

"We're Drew and Sarah Michener." The man offered his hand. "We came to find out everything we could about… about Michaela Underwood's death." He looked down at his wife, who had bowed her head and was dabbing at her eyes with a crumpled tissue. "We just heard the news, from her parents."

"Michaela is…was…my sister," the woman—Sarah— said. "We heard she was killed in the woods near here this morning. I want to know if that man—Al—killed her."

"Who is Al?" Jamie asked.

"The man she was supposed to meet this morning, to go snowshoeing," Sarah said. "If you found her by herself, and he wasn't there, he must have been the one to kill her."

"I'm Sheriff Walker." Travis joined them in the lobby. "I understand you wanted to talk to me."

"This is Drew and Sarah Michener." Jamie made the introductions. "Michaela Underwood's sister and brother-in-law."

Travis shook hands with the Micheners. "We'd better talk about this in my office," he said. Jamie started to turn away, but Travis stopped her. "Deputy Douglas, you come, too."

Nate moved aside to let them pass, Travis leading the way to his office, Jamie bringing up the rear.

Gage joined him in the lobby. "What's up?" he asked, watching the couple disappear into Travis's office.

"Michaela's sister and her husband think they know who killed her," Nate said. "Or at least, she was supposed to meet a man—someone named Al—to go snowshoeing this morning."

"And you didn't see any sign of him out there with her, did you?" Gage asked.

"No." He continued to study the closed door, wishing he could hear what was going on in there. "Even if he didn't kill Michaela, the sheriff is going to want to find him and talk to him."

Gage put his hand on Nate's shoulder. "Right now, the sheriff wants me to talk to this ice fisherman, Abel Crutchfield. You up for coming with me?"

"Sure." He'd planned to finish his report on the condition of elk and deer herds in the area, but that could wait. A murder investigation took precedence over everything.

JAMIE FOLLOWED THE Micheners into Travis's office, closing the door after her. She stood by the door, while the Micheners occupied the two chairs in front of Travis's desk. Even if Jamie could have found more seating, there wasn't room for it in the small room.

Travis settled behind the desk, a neat, uncluttered space with only a laptop and a stack of files visible. "I'm very sorry for your loss," he said. "Losing a loved one is always hard, but losing them to murder is especially tough. We're doing everything we can to find who did this, but if you have anything you think can help us, we certainly want to know."

Sarah looked at her husband, who cleared his throat. "Can you tell us more about what you already know?" he asked. "We got the call this morning from Sarah's father—Michaela lived with them, so I assume that's how you knew to contact them. But they're understandably upset and didn't have a lot of details."

"We found Michaela's body in her vehicle on the side of Forest Service Road 1410," Travis said. "The medical examiner thinks she was killed earlier this morning. Do you know why she would have been in that area?"

"She had a date to go snowshoeing with a man," Sarah

said. "Someone named Al. I don't know his last name."
She leaned forward, clenched hands pressed to her chest.
"I told her not to go out with someone she didn't know—
especially not to someplace where there weren't a lot of
other people around. Especially not with this...this mad-
man going around killing women. But she wouldn't listen to me." Her face crumpled. "If only she had listened."

Drew rubbed his wife's back as she struggled to pull
herself together. "Michaela was young," he said. "Only
twenty-two. And she trusted people. She still thought she
was invincible."

"How did she meet this man?" Travis asked.

Sarah sniffed, straightening her shoulders. "She met
him at the bank. She just started the job on the first of the
month. She's a teller. I guess they flirted, and the next day
he came back and asked her out. She said...she said he was
really nice and cute, and that she thought the idea of going
snowshoeing was fun, and would be a good way to get to
know each other without a lot of pressure."

"When was this—when they met?" Travis asked.

"I think it was Thursday when he first came into the
bank." Sarah nodded. "Yes, Thursday. Because Friday she
and I met for lunch and she told me about him—then she
called me later that day to tell me he'd come back in and
they'd made a date for Monday. She had the day off, and
I guess he did, too."

"Did she say where he worked?" Travis asked. "Or what
kind of work he did?"

"No." Sarah sighed. "I asked her that, too. She said
she didn't know and it didn't matter, because that was the
kind of thing they could get to know about each other on
Monday. She told me I was too uptight and I worried too
much. But I was right to worry! He must have been the
one who killed her."

"What time were they supposed to meet?" Travis asked. "Or did he arrange to pick her up at your parents' house?"

"She said they were meeting at eight thirty at the trailhead for the snowshoe trails," Sarah said. "She told me she was being smart, driving herself, because if the date didn't go well, it would be easy for her to leave."

Travis looked to Jamie. "You said you got to the trailhead about nine thirty?"

"Yes," Jamie said. "There wasn't anyone else there. And no other cars in the parking area. We didn't pass any cars on the way in, either."

"Her parents said she left their house at eight," Drew volunteered.

"She didn't tell them she was meeting a man," Sarah said. "Just that she was going snowshoeing with friends."

Travis nodded. "Tell me everything your sister said to you about this man—even if you don't think it's important. Did she describe what he looked like? Did she say where he lived, or if he gave her his phone number?"

"She just said he was cute. And funny. I guess he made some joke about how nobody could rob the bank with the road closed, because they wouldn't be able to go very far and she thought that was funny."

"What was he doing at the bank that day?" Travis asked. "Was he making a deposit or cashing a check?"

"I don't know. Sorry. I don't know if she had his number, though I think she said she gave him hers." She shook her head. "I've been thinking and thinking about this ever since we got the call from my dad, and there really isn't anything else. She got kind of defensive when I started quizzing her about the guy, and I didn't want to make her mad, so I changed the subject. I made her promise to call me when she got back to the house and let me know how things went, but I wasn't worried when I didn't hear from her by lunch. I just figured they were having a good time and decided to go eat together. But all that time, she was already dead." She covered her hand with her mouth and took a long, hiccupping breath.

Travis took a box of tissues from a drawer of his desk and slid it over to her. "Thank you for coming to talk to us," he said. "We'll follow up with the bank, see if anyone there remembers this man. If we're lucky, he'll be on the security footage. And we may want to talk to you and to your parents again."

"Of course," Drew said. He stood and helped his wife to her feet, also. "Please keep us posted on how things are going."

"We will." Travis came around the desk to escort the Micheners to the lobby. Jamie stepped aside, then followed them into the hall. She was still standing there, reviewing everything the Micheners had said, when Travis returned.

"I've got Dwight checking Michaela's phone records for a call or text that might be from Al," he said. "Meanwhile, I want you to come to the bank with me. I'll call Tom Babcock and ask him to meet us there. We need to get those security tapes and see what this guy looks like. Maybe we'll recognize him."

"Do you really think he's the Ice Cold Killer?" Jamie quickened her steps to keep up with the sheriff's long strides.

"He's the best lead we've had so far," Travis said. "I'm not going to let him get away."

Chapter Four

Abel Crutchfield lived in a mobile home on the west side of town that backed up to the river. His truck sat beneath a steel carport next to the trailer home, which was painted a cheerful turquoise and white. A trio of garden gnomes poked out of the snow around the bottom of the front steps, and a Christmas wreath with a drooping red ribbon still adorned the door.

Abel answered Gage's knock and his eyes widened at the sight of the two officers on his doorstep. "Is something wrong?" he asked.

"We'd like to ask you a few questions." Gage handed him a business card.

Abel read it, then looked past Gage to Nate. "You're the game warden I talked to this morning, aren't you?"

"Yes." Nate gave him a reassuring smile. "This isn't about that. We're hoping you can help us with something else."

"You'd better come in." Abel pushed open the screened door. "No sense standing out in the cold."

The front room of the trailer was neat but packed with furniture—a sofa and two recliners, a large entertainment unit with a television and a stereo system, and two tall bookshelves filled with paperback books and ceramic figurines of dogs, bears, more gnomes, angels and others

Nate couldn't make out. Abel threaded his way through the clutter and sat in one of the recliners and motioned to the sofa. "It's my wife's afternoon for her knitting club," he said. "So I'm here by myself. What can I help you with?"

"Did you see anyone else while you were fishing this morning?" Gage asked.

"Nope. I had the lake to myself."

"What about on the way to and from the lake?" Nate asked. "Did you see anyone on the road, or in the parking area?"

"What's this about?" Abel asked. "Not that it makes any difference in my answers, but I'd like to know."

"Another young woman was killed in that area this morning," Gage said.

Abel sat back, clearly shocked. "You don't think I killed her, do you?" he asked. "I was just out there fishing. I go fishing every Monday. Usually I bring home something for supper."

"We're not accusing you," Gage said. "But we're hoping you might have seen or heard something that could help us find the killer. Where were you between eight and ten this morning?"

"I was at the lake. I always try to get there by eight, and I leave about eleven to come home for lunch." He turned to Nate. "You saw me there. It must have been about nine or so when we talked."

Nate nodded. "That's about right. And you didn't see anyone else while you were at the lake?"

"Not a soul. I passed a couple of cars on the highway on my way out there, but once I turned onto the Forest Service Road, I didn't see any other cars, and none in the parking lot. I saw a woman out walking, but that was all."

Gage tensed. "A woman out walking? Where? What did she look like?"

"She was on the forest road, about a mile before the turnoff to the lake. She was tall and thin, with long blond hair—a lot of it."

"What was she doing?" Gage asked.

"Just walking along, talking on the phone. She didn't even look up when I passed."

"What else can you tell me about her?" Gage asked. "Did you recognize her?"

"She was wearing jeans and hiking boots and a black parka. I didn't get that good a look at her. She had her head bent, with that phone pressed to her ear and her hair falling all in her face."

"Had you ever seen her out there before?" Nate asked.

"No. I usually don't see anybody—not in the winter, anyway," Abel said. "I don't think there are any houses out that way."

"Didn't you think it was odd she was walking out there by herself?" Gage asked.

Abel shrugged. "People like to walk. It's none of my business. She didn't look like she was in trouble or anything. Just walking along, talking on the phone."

"What time was this that you saw her?" Gage asked.

"Well, it was before eight. Maybe seven fifty."

"Which direction was she walking?" Nate asked.

"North. Same direction I was headed."

They talked to him a few more minutes, but he couldn't tell them anything further. They said goodbye and returned to Gage's cruiser. Neither man spoke until they were headed back to the sheriff's department.

"The woman he saw wasn't Michaela," Gage said. "She has short, dark hair. And what was a woman doing out there by herself at that time of morning, anyway?"

"Something else really strange about that whole story," Nate said.

"I know what you're thinking," Gage said. "What was she doing on the phone?"

"Right. Jamie had to drive a ways to call in when she found Michaela. There's no phone signal out that way. None at all."

BANK PRESIDENT TOM BABCOCK met Travis and Jamie at the Mountain States Bank, a worried expression on his face. "I hope we can help you," he said as he led them past the teller windows to the back of the building. "It's unnerving to think a murderer is one of our customers."

"If he is a customer, it will make it easier for us to find him," Travis said.

"You said on the phone you wanted to see footage from our security cameras," Babcock said. "I've asked our IT specialist, Susan Whitmore, to meet with us. She knows her way around the system much better than I do." He opened the door to a small office filled with computer equipment. "While we wait for her, can you tell me a little more about this? You said our teller, Michaela Underwood, was murdered? And this man she met at the bank might be her killer?"

"We don't know that he killed her," Travis said. "But he was supposed to meet her this morning. It may be he knows something about what happened. Were you here on Thursday?"

"Yes. Michaela worked eight to five that day. She took lunch from eleven thirty to twelve thirty, and was the only teller on duty from twelve thirty to three."

"Do you remember her talking to a young man?" Travis asked. "Flirting with him?"

"I can't say that I noticed anything like that." He frowned. "Michaela was always very friendly. Customers liked her.

We're going to really miss her. I can't imagine anyone wanting to hurt her…"

His voice trailed away as a chime sounded. "That will be Susan now." He leaned out of the open door. "We're back here, Susan," he called.

Susan Whitmore was a trim woman with very short platinum hair and piercing blue eyes. "Tom filled me in on the phone," she said after introductions were made. "Just tell me what you need, Sheriff, and I'll do my best to help."

"Michaela Underwood made a date to go snowshoeing this morning with a man she told her sister she met here at the bank Thursday," Travis explained. "He returned Friday and asked her out. We need to find this guy and talk to him. All we have is a first name—Al. If we can spot him talking to her on your security footage, we're hoping that will help us locate him."

"If you find him, we can look at the time stamp on the image and I can link him to a particular transaction," Tom said. "That should give you a name if he was cashing a check or making a deposit, or a payment on an account with us."

"Do you have a particular time you want to look at?" Susan asked. "Or the whole day?"

"Let's start with twelve thirty to three," Travis said. "When Michaela was the only teller working."

"All right." Susan inputted information into a computer and pulled up a black-and-white image showing four screens—ATM, front door, back door and a wider shot that took in most of the lobby. She clicked on the lobby view and enlarged it. "We'll start here, since this gives us a good view of Michaela. I'll scroll forward and stop on any male customers."

Jamie and Travis leaned in as Susan began to forward the film. Michaela waited on an older couple, a young woman with a child and two middle-aged women. Then a single man approached the counter. "Stop," Travis ordered.

Susan stilled the film. Jamie studied the image of a slender man, maybe six feet tall or just under. He wore a dark knit hat pulled down on his head, the collar of his dark coat turned up.

"Can you zoom in?" Travis asked.

Susan enlarged the image until it began to blur. Travis furrowed his brow. "Is there another camera, focused on the teller, which would give us a view of his face?" he asked.

"No," Susan said.

Travis sighed and stepped back. "The way he's standing, we can't tell anything about his face. We can't even tell whether his hair is light or dark."

"Do you think that's deliberate?" Jamie asked.

"Maybe," Travis said. "If he is the killer, he wouldn't want to be seen on video. The hat and coat do a good job of obscuring his face. He's wearing jeans and hiking boots."

"Maybe the brand of the boots will tell us something," Jamie said.

"We'll try," Travis said. He nodded to Susan. "Advance the tape again. Let's see what he does."

They had a clear view of Michaela, smiling and at one point even laughing, as the man stood in front of her. Then he left. But instead of turning to face the camera, he took a few steps back, still talking to Michaela. When he was almost out of reach of the camera, he whirled, head down, and hurried out of the frame.

"I'm willing to bet he knew about the security camera and didn't want to be seen," Travis said. "Let's see the footage for Friday."

But the footage from Friday yielded no sign of the man. They spent almost an hour running through everything and saw no images of him. "Maybe she met him outside the bank," Jamie said. "On her lunch break or something."

"Maybe," Travis said. "It would be easy enough for him to wait for her in the parking lot or on the sidewalk and stop her before she went into the bank." He turned to Tom. "Did anything about him look familiar to you—like someone who had come into the bank before?"

Tom shook his head. "I'm sorry, no."

"What about the name Al? Does that make you think of anyone in particular?"

"I know an Allen and an Alvin, but both of them are in their fifties or sixties. And that wasn't them we saw on the video just now."

"I'm going to need all your security footage from the past week, including what we looked at today. It's possible this guy came in earlier, checking things out."

"Of course. Susan will get it for you."

"Can you tell us what kind of transaction he was making here Thursday?" Travis asked. "The time stamp on the security footage showed he walked up to the teller window at two sixteen."

Tom walked to a computer farther down the counter and began typing. A few moments later, he groaned. "Looks like it was a cash transaction."

"Such as?" Jamie asked.

"Breaking a large bill or cashing in rolled coins," Tom said.

"Here are the security discs for the time period you wanted." Susan handed Travis an envelope. Travis wrote out a receipt for her, then he and Jamie left.

"I got chills when Tom said it was a cash transaction," Jamie said when they were in Travis's cruiser. "Al had to know we couldn't trace that."

"Or maybe he was using the transaction as an excuse

to hit on the cute teller," Travis said. He rubbed his hands along the steering wheel. "Not that I really believe that. I think we're on to something."

"This might be the killer." A shiver ran through Jamie as she said the words.

"Maybe." He shifted the cruiser into gear and began backing out of the parking spot. "In any case, this feels like the closest we've gotten."

NATE AND GAGE returned to the sheriff's department and waylaid Travis and Jamie as soon as they returned. "We got something from Abel Crutchfield that might be useful," Gage said as they followed Travis into his office. Jamie hung back, then followed, too, squeezing in to stand next to Nate. The soft, herbal scent of her hair made his heart race with a sudden memory of the two of them making out in the old Ford pickup he had driven at the time. Hastily, he shoved the memory away and focused on the conversation between the sheriff and his brother.

"Abel says he saw a woman—tall, thin, blonde—walking along Forest Service Road 1410 this morning," Gage said. "She was alone, no car around. He said he didn't get a real good look at her, because she had her head bent, talking on her phone."

"Except there isn't a phone signal out there," Nate said. "For any carrier."

"That does seem suspicious," Travis said.

Beside Nate, Jamie shifted. "Maybe it isn't really suspicious," she said.

She flushed when all three men turned to look at her but continued, her voice even. "Maybe she was nervous, being out there alone. She heard the guy's truck and pulled out her phone and pretended to be talking to someone so whoever was driving past would get the idea she could summon help if she needed to."

"Do women really do things like that?" Nate asked and wished he could take the words back as soon as he said them.

"Yeah, they do," she said, the expression in her eyes making him feel about three feet tall. "Because you know—men."

None of them had a good response to this. The silence stretched. Finally, Travis said, "Let's see if we can find anyone else who saw this woman. I also have a list of bank employees. Let's talk to them and see if any of them remember 'Al.' Jamie, I want you to help with that. Most of the employees are young women—they might be more willing to open up to you." He clicked a few keys on his laptop. "I just forwarded the list to you."

"I'll get right on it," she said, then slipped out the door.

"I'll see if I can find any campers or snowshoers or skiers or fishermen who might have seen a woman who fits the description Abel gave us," Nate said.

"Let's not drop the ball on his," Travis said.

"Right," Nate said. He wasn't going to drop the ball on Jamie, either. He'd do whatever it took to make her see he wasn't the boy who had hurt her seven years ago. She might never feel close to him again, but at least they could be friends.

Chapter Five

Jamie left the sheriff's department at nine o'clock, after working her way through half the bank employees on the list Travis had forwarded to her. So far, none of the people she'd spoken to remembered Michaela talking to anyone special, and they had no recollection of a single man who stood out for them.

She picked up a sleepy Donna from Mrs. Simmons's house. Donna had already taken a bath and changed into a pair of flannel pajamas with large, colorful dogs all over them. Jamie had a pair just like them. Over the past couple of years, Donna had gotten into the habit of keeping a number of clothes at the caregiver's house, which made things easier for everyone. As Jamie put an arm around Donna and escorted her into their house, she caught the smell of the coconut shampoo her sister used. The scent and the feel of the soft flannel beneath her hand transported her back to the days when Donna was little and Jamie, seven years older, often helped her get ready for bed. Once Donna was bathed and dressed in pajamas, the sisters would snuggle together in Donna's bed, and Jamie would read to her until she fell asleep.

Tonight, she led her upstairs to the room across the hall from Jamie's own and tucked her in. Donna turned on her side and studied the big whiteboard on her bedroom wall, where Jamie drew in a calendar every month and noted both sisters' schedules. Donna liked knowing what was supposed to happen each day. "Work tomorrow," she said. "I'll see Henry."

Right, Jamie thought as she kissed her sister, then switched out the light. Sometime tomorrow she'd have to find time to stop by the grocery store and check out Henry. He was probably harmless, but it didn't hurt to be careful.

She walked across the hall to her room and exchanged her uniform for yoga pants and an oversize sweatshirt. Taking off the heavy utility belt and body armor was the definite signal that she was off duty. Time to relax. Except she was too restless to settle. She went downstairs and wandered through the familiar rooms—the kitchen, with its white-painted cabinets and blue Formica countertops; the formal dining room she had turned into a home office; and the wood-paneled living room with its comfortable tweed-covered sofa and chairs and heavy wood tables. The house was out of style but comfortable and familiar.

She and Donna had grown up in this house and had lived here together until Jamie had gone off to college. She hadn't gone far—only across the mountains to Boulder, and the University of Colorado. She had studied business, thinking she would look for a job in Junction, so that she could be close to Donna and her parents. Then, her parents had been killed in a car accident, plowed into by a tourist who was texting while driving. The tourist had walked away with only a few bruises, while her parents had both been pronounced dead at the scene.

So much for a business career in Junction. Jamie needed to be in Eagle Mountain, with Donna. She might have sold the family home and moved with her sister to Junction or Denver or somewhere else, but the thought made her heart ache. Eagle Mountain was home. And Donna didn't do well with change. She needed familiar things—her home, the neighbors she knew, her job at the grocery store—to keep her firmly grounded.

Jamie had moved back to Eagle Mountain for good four years ago. After a series of low-paying clerical jobs, the opportunity at the sheriff's department had been a welcome relief—a way for Jamie to stay in Eagle Mountain and earn a living that would support her and her sister. But it had also been a lifesaver because it gave Jamie a focus and purpose. She had discovered, somewhat to her surprise, that she loved the work. She liked looking out for her hometown and the people in it, and she liked being part of a team that was trying to protect everyone here.

Oh, it wasn't all good feelings and easy times. She had been sworn at by people she stopped for traffic violations, kicked and punched by a shoplifter she had chased down on Main Street, with half a dozen locals and tourists standing around watching the battle and no one lifting a finger to help her. And she had looked on the bodies of those murdered women and felt a mixture of sickness and anger—and a fierce desire to stop the man before he hurt anyone else.

The loud trill of an old-fashioned phone startled her. She raced to grab her cell phone off the hall table, and frowned at the screen, which showed Unknown Number. A sales call? A scammer? Or maybe one of the bank employees, calling her back because he or she had remembered something. She answered, cautious. "Hello?"

"It's Nate. I called to see how you're doing."

The deep voice vibrated through her, making her heart flutter, but she steeled herself against the sensation. The question—coming from him—annoyed her. "I'm fine. Why wouldn't I be?"

"Finding a dead woman shakes up most people. It shook me up."

She settled onto the sofa, a pillow hugged to her stomach. "I'm fine," she said. "It's part of the job. I knew that going in."

"From what I saw today, you're good at your job."

Was he flattering her, trying to persuade her to forgive him? She sighed. "Nate, I don't want to do this."

"Do what?"

"I don't want to pretend we're friends. We're not. We can't be."

"Why not?"

"You know why not."

A long pause. She began to wonder if he had hung up on her. Then he said. "So, because we were once lovers—each other's first lovers—we can't be friends now? Jamie, that was seven years ago. We were kids."

"And now we're adults, and we don't have to pretend we're two old pals."

"I don't know why not," he said. "There was a time I knew you better than anyone—and you knew me better."

"Like you said, that was seven years ago." A lot had happened since then. She wasn't the same woman anymore.

"We're going to be working together on this case," he said. "We shouldn't be enemies."

"You're not my enemy." Did he really think that? "But we can't be…close…anymore."

"Why not?"

Because if she let him too close, she knew she would fall for him again. And she couldn't trust him to not leave her again—at the next promotion, or if someone better came along. He had proved before that he looked out for his own interests and he wasn't one to stick with a relationship if things got tough. "It would be too complicated," she said. "I know you don't like that." He had said that when he broke up with her before. *There's no sense us staying together. It would be too complicated.*

Was that sound him grinding his teeth together? "You've got a lot of wrong ideas about me," he said.

"You're the one who gave them to me."

"Fine. Have it your way. We won't be 'close'—whatever that means to you. But we can be civil. Don't make this more difficult than it has to be."

"I wouldn't dream of it. Now I'd better go. We'll have another long day tomorrow. Good night."

She didn't wait for him to answer but hung up. She'd handled that well, she thought. No sense starting something that was bound to end badly. She'd been very mature and matter-of-fact. She ought to be proud of herself.

She knew a lot about grief now. The pain never went away, but with time, it always got better.

NATE SCANNED THE sheltered meadow at the base of Mount Wilson with his binoculars, counting the number of elk in the small herd gathered there. Most of them still looked to be in good shape, but this would be a good place to put one of the feeding stations the Department of Wildlife had decided to set up starting this weekend. Local ranchers and hunters had volunteered to help distribute the hay and pellets to the three main feeding sites in the area. The supplies were being delivered by helicopter, which meant the project wouldn't be hampered by the still-closed highway.

He entered the information about the herd into a database on his phone, then snowshoed back to the trailhead where he had left his truck. Once inside the cab, with the heater turned up high, he headed down the road, his speed at a crawl, alert for signs of anything unusual. As he passed the turnout toward a closed campground, he caught a flash of color through the trees and stopped. The binoculars came out and he zeroed in on a dark gray SUV parked up against an icy expanse of exposed rock. He scanned the area and focused in on two climbers halfway up the ice.

He followed the SUV's tracks in the snow and parked behind the vehicle. By the time he got out of his truck, the two climbers were headed down. He walked over and met them when their feet hit the snow. No helmets, he noted, and no ropes or harnesses or other safety gear. Maybe they thought they didn't need it, that their spiked shoes and ice axes were enough.

The first man, about six feet tall, with a slight build and sandy hair cut short, eyed Nate suspiciously. "You need something?" he asked.

"You and your friend climb here often?" Nate asked as the other young man, who was a couple of inches taller than his companion and had a head of brown curls, joined them. Something about these two was familiar, but he couldn't place them. Maybe he had seen them around town somewhere.

"Sometimes," the first man said. "There's no law against it." He ran his thumb along the edge of the ice ax he hefted. It wasn't a threatening gesture, but it made Nate aware of the ax as a weapon.

"No, there's not." He addressed the second young man, who also had an ice ax, which he held down by his side. "Were the two of you around here yesterday?"

"Not yesterday," the dark-haired man said. "Why do you want to know?"

"I'm looking for anyone who might have seen a blonde woman in this area, alone, yesterday morning," Nate said. "What are your names?"

"I'm Lex." The blond offered his hand, and gave a firm shake. "This is Ty."

"Did the two of you see a woman around here yesterday morning—blond hair, walking alongside the road?"

The barest flicker of a glance passed between the two climbers. "We weren't here yesterday," Lex said.

"Right," Nate said. "What about the other times you've been out here? Have you ever seen a woman like that in this area?"

A longer exchange of glances, then Ty shook his head. "No. We've run into women climbing at the park in town but not out here."

"I wouldn't think any woman would risk walking along the road by herself around here," Lex said. "Not with that serial killer going around offing women." His expression became more animated. "Somebody at the restaurant last night said something about another woman being killed yesterday. Was this blonde the Ice Cold Killer's latest victim?"

"No," Nate said. "The sheriff would just like to talk to her."

"This guy's sure making the sheriff look like an idiot," Lex said. "Killing all these women practically under his nose."

"I heard one of the victims was even done in on the sheriff's family ranch," Ty said. "That's got to have him furious."

"The sheriff definitely isn't an idiot," Nate said. "Have you seen anyone else in the area—fishermen, hikers, other climbers? It's possible one of them was here yesterday and saw this woman."

"We see people all the time," Ty said. "But most of them we never know their names."

"You're kind of grasping at straws, aren't you?" Lex

asked. "Questioning random people in the woods isn't going to help you find this killer."

Three years on the job had given Nate plenty of experience dealing with the public. He'd gotten into the habit of identifying them as particular types. He'd learned to deal with each type a different way. Nate cataloged these two as civilian know-it-alls, always happy to tell him how to do his job. "Do either of you know a guy named Al?" he asked.

Lex laughed. "There was a guy named Al in my organic chemistry class last semester. Do you think he's your killer?"

"Have you met anyone named Al in Eagle Mountain?" Nate asked.

"Nope," Ty said. "But then, we don't know many people here."

"So you're students?"

"Graduated," Lex said.

"What do you do now?" Nate asked.

"Right now, we're going to try another route up this ice." He turned back toward the rock face. "Good luck with your search."

Not waiting for Nate to say anything else, Lex stepped up onto a small protrusion in the ice, swung his ax over his head and buried the tip with a heavy thud. Ty moved ten feet farther down the face and began to climb also. Nate might not even have been there, for all they were concerned.

Their disdain grated, but Nate knew he was better off ignoring them the same way they ignored him. They didn't have anything to tell him. But he made note of the license tag on their SUV as he walked back to his truck. When he had a better cell signal, he'd call it in.

From there, he drove past the spot where they had found

Michaela in her car. Crime scene tape still festooned the area, and someone had left a bouquet of flowers in the snow on the shoulder of the road, the blossoms of what might have been daisies and carnations wilting and turning brown in the cold.

He passed the parking area for the snowshoe trail and thought of Jamie, and the anger with which she had confronted him yesterday. He was aware she had been cool to him since his return to Eagle Mountain, but her coldness had surprised him. Her initial agitation over her runaway dogs had morphed into real ire—almost as if she was continuing the last conversation they had had, like it was the next day instead of seven years later. At one time, her reaction might have caused him to respond in anger, also. Now, with time and maturity, the fact that she still had such strong feelings intrigued him.

Jamie had been his best friend at one time, the one person in the world he knew he could always count on. Things had ended badly between them—and he was willing to take his share of responsibility for that. But life was too short to throw away a friendship like that.

He was close enough now to a group of private summer cabins that he decided to go a little out of his way and check them out. Though not strictly part of his duties, he liked to do a regular drive-by of the properties, to check for any vandalism, break-ins or maintenance issues. The cabins, a cluster of seven log structures of one or two rooms each, were privately owned, but on Forest Service land. Most of the cabins had been built eighty or a hundred years ago and the owners were allowed to continue to use them after the land was turned over to the Forest Service. They weren't allowed to enlarge the cabins or use them for any other purpose. Most of them weren't suitable for year-round living, anyway, being uninsulated and off-grid, and Nate had yet to encounter anyone out here after the first snow.

He turned onto the road leading up to the cabins and parked in front of the heavy chain that blocked the way. Half a dozen heavy locks hung from the chain. Cabin owners or friends would have combinations or keys that allowed them to open the chain and pass through. Nate studied the obviously fresh tire tracks on either side of the chain. Someone had entered and exited this way in the last day or so—maybe even this morning. Possibly one of the cabin owners had stopped by to check on his property.

Leaving his truck parked, Nate stepped over the chain and followed a winding track to the first cabin. Old wooden shutters covered the windows of the structure—protection against weather and both four-legged and two-legged animals. A hand-painted sign hung over the door, *Lazy Daze* burned into the wood.

Nate followed the tire tracks past four more cabins, all the way back to the most remote in the grouping, set a short distance from the others. No one was at the cabin now, but tracks in the snow showed where a vehicle had parked, and where at least two people had walked around. Like the first cabin, wooden shutters covered the windows and the door was padlocked. Nate studied the door, unable to shake the uneasiness that had his nerves on hyperalert. Something wasn't right here. He sniffed the air and caught the sharp tang of wood smoke, and shifted his gaze to the chimney of the cabin. No smoke emanated from it now, but someone might have had a fire in there recently.

He walked around the side of the cabin, hoping to find an uncovered window that would allow him to peek in. He spotted a door that provided access to a covered back porch and headed for it, intending to check if it was locked. But he hadn't gone far when something clamped onto his ankle, pain lancing through him, stealing his breath. Vision fogged with shock, he stared down at the jagged steel trap clamped around his foot.

Chapter Six

"We've had a garbled radio transmission from one of our officers." The woman from Colorado Parks and Wildlife who contacted dispatch spoke with a distinct Texas drawl. "All of the personnel in this area are involved in the supply delivery near County Road Two. I didn't get a reply when I tried to make contact again, but reception is very bad in that area. Could one of your officers check it out for us?"

"I can take that," Jamie said. "I'm headed out now." She had stopped by the dispatch center to say hello to her friend, Anong, who was on duty that afternoon.

Anong keyed her microphone. "I have a deputy here who can check out that call for you," she said. "What is the location?"

"We think it came from somewhere around Sundance cabins—the summer cabins off Forest Service Road 1410? Wildlife officer Nate Hall."

Jamie bit back a groan of annoyance. Was this some twisted way for Nate to make sure he saw her again? But she immediately dismissed that notion, and a tickle of fear replaced her irritation. Was Nate in some kind of trouble? "I'm on my way," she said.

"I'll let the sheriff's department know what's up," Anong said, her wide face soft with concern. "Is Officer Hall a friend of yours?"

"Not exactly."

Nate wasn't a friend, but he wasn't her enemy. She had meant that. And even if she had hated his guts, he was a fellow officer who might be in trouble. She was in her cruiser headed out of town when the sheriff called her. "I'm sending Gage out as backup," he said.

"Nate's going to be really embarrassed if this is the radio equivalent of a butt dial," she said.

"Better embarrassed than in real trouble," Travis said.

"Yes, sir."

She punched the accelerator, going as fast as she dared on the icy roads. She resisted the urge to switch on her lights and sirens. That was a sure way to draw a crowd. She wouldn't mind embarrassing Nate a little but no need to go overboard. And if he was in a dangerous situation, no sense putting other people at risk.

She spotted his truck parked at the entrance to the enclave of summer cabins. The chain over the road was in place, and nothing looked out of order. She got out of her cruiser and spotted tire tracks leading toward the cabins. Had Nate seen someone and followed them—or was he merely checking the cabins for signs of vandalism or break-ins? It was something they had had trouble with in the past—usually bored teens breaking into a cabin to have a party or mess things up.

She cupped her hands around her mouth. "Nate!"

Her voice echoed back to her, followed by ringing silence. A chill wind buffeted her, and she rubbed her shoulders against the cold. Better to get back in the cruiser and wait for Gage to arrive. She turned back toward her vehicle, then froze as a cry reached her—an animal sound that sent an icy jolt through her. Heart hammering, she raced toward the sound. "Nate!" she shouted again.

The reply was stronger now, a strangled cry for help.

She ran faster, slipping and falling on the ice, but picking herself up and charging on. She found him alongside a cabin, hunched over on the ground, his face as pale as the snow around him. "Jamie!"

"Nate, what happened?" She fell to her knees beside him, then recoiled in horror at the sight of the trap around his foot. The steel teeth had sliced through his thick pack boots and blood stained the snow around him. She swallowed hard. "Who would have something like that out here?"

"I think it was a booby trap," he said. "It was covered up pretty well, and it's attached to the cabin, so that anyone caught in it couldn't get away." He indicated the thick chain that ran between the trap and the cabin wall, where it was fastened to an iron ring sunk into one of the logs.

She forced herself to ignore the blood and her thoughts of what the trap must have done to Nate's leg, and bent to study the contraption itself. Then she grasped the sides of the trap and pulled hard, but barely managed to move them. "You can't open it that way," Nate said. "You have to stand on it. See these pieces?" He indicated ear-shaped metal pieces on either side of the trap's jaw. "Stand on them and your weight will force the trap open."

"All right." She stood and he scooted back, giving her room to position herself. She straddled the trap, facing him. "I don't want to hurt you," she said.

"It already hurts like the devil," he said. "You can't make it worse. Just do it and get it over with."

Right. She took a deep breath, then stepped down on first one ear, then the other. The jaws eased open. With a groan, Nate pulled his foot from the trap. Jamie shoved the trap aside and knelt beside him once more. "I should go call an ambulance," she said. "Will you be okay if I leave you?"

"I kept waiting for whoever did this to come back." He lifted a pistol from the ground beside him. "But they didn't show." He frowned. "How did you know I was here?"

"Someone from your office called and said they had had a garbled transmission from you and asked us to check it out."

"And you were the lucky one." His eyes met hers. She wanted to look away but couldn't, mesmerized by the tenderness behind the pain. She remembered other times when he had looked in her eyes that way, moments when they had trusted each other with secrets, turned to each other for comfort or united in lovemaking. She leaned toward him, drawn by the pull of memories and a longing she hadn't even realized was in her, to feel that close again.

"Jamie! Nate! What's going on?"

Gage's shouts yanked her back to the present and she pulled away, then stood and went to meet him. "Someone set a leghold trap beside this cabin and Nate stepped in it," she said.

Gage followed her to where Nate sat. He had dragged himself over to lean against the wall of the cabin, a thin trail of blood marking his path. "How are you doing?" Gage asked.

"The bleeding has almost stopped. My boot is ruined, but it probably kept the trap from destroying my leg." He grimaced at his mangled boot. "The ankle might be fractured, but it's not a bad break. It doesn't hurt as much, now that the pressure of the trap is off."

Gage squatted down to get a better look at the trap. "I hope you're up on your tetanus shots," he said. "This thing is pretty rusty."

"It's an old trap," Nate said. "An antique. New ones have smooth jaws, not toothed ones. I seem to remember one of these cabins had some old traps hanging up on the wall. Not this one, but another in this group. Take a look for me, will you?"

"I will, after we get an ambulance for you," Gage said.

"I don't need an ambulance," Nate said. "The two of you can get me to one of your vehicles. That will be a lot faster than waiting for an ambulance to come all the way out here—especially since you'll have to drive halfway back to town to get a cell signal."

Gage studied him a moment, then nodded. "All right. I guess we could do that." He looked around them. "What about whoever did this?"

"I'd like to get a look inside this cabin," Nate said. "The tracks in the snow indicate someone has been here recently. Maybe someone is squatting here and they set the trap to discourage anyone investigating too closely."

"Then they're not very bright," Gage said. "They had to know someone getting hurt in a trap like that would bring the law down on this place."

"Maybe they thought they could get to whoever was caught before anyone else found out," Nate said.

"We'll get someone out here to take a look," Gage said. "First, let's get you to the clinic in town." He offered his hand and Nate grasped it and heaved to his feet.

Jamie rushed in to steady him, and Gage moved in on the other side. "We could make a chair and carry you," Gage said.

"I've still got one good leg," Nate said. "I might as well use it."

Slowly, awkwardly, they made their way around the cabin and onto the road. Nate gritted his teeth and breathed hard but made no protest. After what seemed like an hour—but was probably only fifteen minutes—they reached Jamie's cruiser. Gage opened the door and helped Nate into the passenger seat. "You take him to the clinic," Gage said. "I'll stay here and make sure no one disturbs the crime scene. You phone for help when you get into cell range."

"All right."

Nate said nothing on the drive into town. Eyes closed, he rested his head against the window. Jamie wondered if he was asleep. When they reached the turnoff onto the county road, Jamie called Adelaide and told her what had happened. She promised to call ahead to the clinic and to send Dwight and another deputy to assist Gage.

Jamie ended the call and looked at Nate. His eyes were open and he was watching her. "You okay?" she asked, focusing on the road again.

"I'm okay."

At the clinic, Jamie insisted on fetching a wheelchair from inside to transport Nate inside. He didn't object. When questioned by the staff about how he ended up with his leg caught in a trap, he said, "I'm a wildlife officer," as if that explained everything.

X-rays revealed his ankle was badly bruised, the skin mangled and requiring stitches, but it wasn't broken. "Those pack boots have a lot of padding," the doctor said as Nate completed the final paperwork for his visit. "That probably saved you."

He left with his ankle in an air splint, hobbling on crutches. "I'll drive you home," Jamie said.

He directed her to a cabin on a ranch on the edge of town. "The original owner built it as an artist's studio," Nate said as he unlocked the door. "Come in and take a look."

She moved past him, into a room with blond wood floors and large windows that flooded the space with natural light. A galley kitchen filled the corner of the room, and doors opened onto a single bedroom and bath.

"How did you ever find this place?" she asked, not hiding her admiration.

Nate sank onto the leather sofa and leaned the crutches against the wall behind him. "The officer who had my job before me lived here," he said. "When he moved to Cortez, he worked out a deal with the landlord for me to take over his lease."

It felt awkward standing while he was sitting, so she sat on the other end of the sofa. "I guess your parents don't still have a place in town, do they?" she asked.

"No, they sold out and moved to Texas three years ago. My dad said he got tired of shoveling snow, and my brother and his kids are in Dallas and my mom wanted to be closer to the grandkids."

"I guess I lost track of them," she said. "I had a lot going on just then."

"Your parents' deaths," he said. "I remember. My mom told me." He leaned over and fiddled with the fastening on his Aircast. "I kept meaning to get in touch with you, to tell you how sorry I was." He glanced at her. "I guess I messed that up, too."

She shook her head. "It's all right." She had been so devastated at the time she couldn't even remember who had or hadn't expressed their sympathy.

"That must have been rough," he said. "Losing both of them at once. Mom said you were living in Boulder at the time."

"Yeah. I came home to take care of Donna. She was so upset. It took her a long time before she could accept that they weren't coming back."

"You could have taken her with you, gone back to the city."

"I didn't want to do that to her. She had already lost her parents—I couldn't have her lose her home and her friends, all the things that were familiar to her. Routine is really important to her."

"What about all you lost?" he said. "You must have had a job, friends, a home?"

She shifted to angle her body toward him. "Eagle Mountain is my home. And I had just graduated. It's not as if I had a career or anything. Besides, if I hadn't come back here, I never would have gotten into law enforcement. I'd have probably ended up in a cubicle somewhere, bored out of my mind, instead of doing something active that I'm good at. Besides, who are you to give me a hard time about coming back here to live? You did it."

"Yeah, I did. It was a good opportunity for me." He shrugged. "And I missed it. I missed a lot of things." His gaze zeroed in on her.

She stood. "I'd better go. Somebody will return your truck tomorrow, I imagine."

Before he could protest, his phone rang. She headed for the door. He answered the call and said, "Wait up a minute. It's Gage."

Hand on the doorknob, she paused. Nate listened a moment, then said, "Jamie is here. I'm going to put you on speaker. Tell her what you told me."

"We found evidence that someone was squatting in that cabin," Gage said. "Maybe more than one person. We've got a reserve deputy sitting on the place waiting for them to come back. We'll want to question them about that trap. How's the leg?"

"Bad bruise, no break, some stitches," Nate said. "I have to stay off it a few days."

"You got lucky," Gage said.

"I guess you could look at it that way."

"We found two more of those traps—one on the other side of the cabin, and one near the front steps," Gage said.

"Looks like you missed that second one by inches, judging by your prints in the snow. And you were right—the traps were taken off the wall of a nearby cabin."

"Is there anything in the cabin to tell you the identity of the squatter?"

"Not much—some blankets, dishes, canned food. We talked to the owner—he lives in Nebraska—and it sounds like everything we found was stuff that he keeps there."

"How did the squatter get in? I didn't see any sign of a break-in."

"The owner keeps the key under a flowerpot on the back porch. It's not there now."

Nate rolled his eyes. "Well, it'll be interesting to see if anyone shows up and who they are."

"I'm wondering if it might be our killer," Gage said.

"What makes you think that?" Nate asked.

"Just a hunch. I mean, if you wanted to stay off the radar, this would be a good place to hide, wouldn't it?"

Chapter Seven

"Henry and I have a date!" Donna announced at breakfast the next morning. Sunlight streamed from the window behind her, promising another beautiful day.

"Oh?" Jamie tried not to show too much curiosity. She still hadn't gotten by the store to meet Henry, though she needed to do so soon.

"He's going to take me to dinner and the movies." Donna spoke around a mouthful of half-chewed cereal.

"Don't talk with your mouth full," Jamie chided. "And we don't have a movie theatre in Eagle Mountain."

Donna chewed and swallowed. "I know that," she said. "We're going to watch a movie at his house."

"When are you planning to do this?"

"Soon."

Which could mean next month or this afternoon. "You can't go out with Henry until I meet him," Jamie said.

"Why do you have to meet him? He's *my* boyfriend."

"I still need to check him out and make sure he's a good person for you to date." That he wasn't someone who was trying to take advantage of Donna's vulnerability.

"I don't have to approve of your boyfriends."

"I don't have any boyfriends." She had had only a few casual dates since breaking up with Nate. Thinking about that now made her feel pathetic. But she was far too busy to have time for a relationship.

"But if you did, you wouldn't wait for my permission to date them," Donna said. "I shouldn't have to, either."

"I'm your big sister. It's my job to look after you."

"I'm nineteen. I don't need you to look after me."

But you do, Jamie thought. Donna knew it, too, even if she wouldn't admit it. Jamie could understand that her sister was frustrated that she wasn't able to do the things other people her age could do. She was high-functioning, but she had led a sheltered life. She didn't understand that there were people in the world who would take advantage of her. "I'm not saying you can't go out with Henry," she said. "I just want to meet him first." She leaned across the table and put her hand over Donna's. "I would say that even if we switched places and you were just like me." The words weren't a lie. If Michaela's family had insisted on meeting "Al" before Michaela went out with him, maybe the bank teller would be alive today.

But Donna was in a stubborn mood this morning. "What if I don't want you to meet him?"

"Donna, please. If he's your friend, of course I want to meet him."

"He's *my* friend. Can't I have anything that's just mine?" She shoved back her chair and stomped off.

Jamie sighed and resisted the urge to get up and follow Donna. It wouldn't hurt to let her sulk a little. And her bad moods rarely lasted long.

Ten minutes later, after Jamie had finished breakfast and cleared away the dishes, she found Donna waiting by the front door, her backpack in hand. "Time to go to work," she said.

"It is," Jamie said. "When you get off at three, you know to come straight to Mrs. Simmons's?"

"I know." She headed out the door to Jamie's cruiser.

The two sisters didn't speak on the short drive to the grocery store. Donna could walk the few blocks from their house to the store, but Jamie liked to drive her when she could. "Is Henry working today?" she asked as she pulled into the parking lot.

"He is." Donna opened the door. "'Bye." She hurried into the store, not looking back.

Jamie made a note to swing by later and find out exactly when Henry would be working, as well as his last name and more about him.

She parked behind the sheriff's department and entered through the back door. Adelaide waylaid her as she emerged from the locked room. "We're holding a masquerade ball at the community center Friday night, all proceeds to benefit folks in town for whom the road closures have caused a financial hardship. I hope you plan to be there."

"Oh." Jamie blinked. "A masquerade party?"

"Wear a costume and a mask." Adelaide looked her up and down. "I'm sure you're creative enough to come up with something. If you can't, the volunteers at the Humane Society thrift store have combed through donations and assembled a number of suitable disguises at very reasonable prices. And you're not on schedule to work that evening—I already checked."

"I don't know." Jamie searched for some excuse, but it was tough to think straight with Adelaide's steel gaze boring into her. Seventy-plus years, much of it spent bossing people around, had made the sheriff's department office manager a formidable force.

"It's for a good cause," Adelaide said. "People who work on the other side of the pass haven't been able to get to work, and store owners have suffered losses with fewer tourists visiting and the inability to replenish their stocks. People are really hurting and we want to help them."

"Of course," Jamie said. "I'll be there." Maybe she'd take Donna. Her sister liked dressing up, and she would enjoy seeing everyone's costumes.

Satisfied, Adelaide let her pass. Jamie made her way to the conference room, helped herself to a cup of coffee but bypassed the box of doughnuts. She settled at the table next to Dwight. A few moments later Nate clumped in on crutches and sank into the chair across from her. He looked better than he had yesterday. "How's the ankle?" she asked.

"It's there."

The sheriff entered the room and they all settled in to listen to the usual bulletins and updates, including a summary of the previous day's events at the summer cabins, for anyone who might not have gotten the full story yet. "No one showed up at the cabin while our officer was there," Travis said. "We can't afford to post someone there full-time, but if any of you are in the area, make it a point to swing by." He glanced down at his open laptop. "Did we get anything from Michaela Underwood's phone records?"

"There was one call at eight oh two the morning she was killed," Dwight said. "That could have been from Al. It came from a payphone at the Shell station. It's probably the only payphone in town. The phone box is around the side of the building, out of view of the road, and no one remembers seeing anyone using it that morning."

"Where are we on the search for the blonde woman Abel Crutchfield saw walking along Forest Service Road 1410?" Travis asked.

"Nowhere," Gage said. "We haven't found anyone else who saw her, or any blonde woman who lives out that way. In fact, no one lives out that way."

"What about the bank employees?" Travis asked.

"I interviewed all the employees," Jamie said. She checked her notes. "One woman, Janis Endicott, remembers Michaela talking about Al, but none of them remember seeing him or could give any new details."

"Anything else on this case?" Travis asked. "Any thoughts or insights any of you might have had about it?"

"I thought of one thing," Jamie said. When every head swiveled to look at her, she fought down a blush and forced herself to keep her voice steady. "While the other women who were killed seemed like crimes of opportunity, he apparently targeted Michaela."

"We could be dealing with a copycat," Dwight said.

"Maybe," Travis said. "Though nothing we've learned about Michaela points to her having an enemy who would want to kill her. And we can't be sure our killer didn't target and stalk any of the other women." He turned to Jamie. "That's good thinking, Deputy."

She swallowed, steeling herself for her next words. "I also thought maybe we should give the killer a target and see if he takes the bait."

"What are you talking about?" Nate hadn't said anything so far in the meeting, but he spoke up now.

Jamie shifted in her chair. She had lain awake a long time last night, thinking about this. "I could drive around, out of uniform and in my personal vehicle, in some of the areas we know he's killed other women and see if anyone behaves suspiciously."

"No." Nate spoke loudly and leaned across the table toward her.

She shrank back. "I'd be smart," she said. "And we could have other officers watching me."

"It might not be a bad idea," Travis said. "You wouldn't have to be alone. We could have another officer hidden in the car with you."

Nate leaned back in his chair, silent, though he continued to glare at Jamie. She ignored him. "I think it's worth a try," she said.

Travis nodded. "I think so, too. We'll set something up for this evening. Dwight, you can go with her."

"Yes, sir."

Jamie struggled to remain composed, even as an adrenaline rush at the thought of possibly facing down a killer—or helping to capture him—made it difficult to sit still.

The rest of the meeting was a blur of routine announcements about training, schedules and upcoming events—including the masquerade party on Friday. When the sheriff dismissed them, she rose and left the room, intending to head out on patrol. Nate followed on her heels. "Jamie, wait up."

She stopped and looked back at him as he limped down the hallway toward her. "If you're going to lecture me about how I shouldn't put myself out there as bait for a killer, don't waste your breath," she said. "I'll be perfectly safe."

"More like it will all be a waste of time," he said. "I think this guy is too smart to fall for a trap like that."

"It's worth a try," she said.

He nodded. "I wish I could go with you."

She looked down at the cast on his foot. "I suppose you could bash the killer over the head with your crutches."

He laughed. "Yeah, well, just be careful."

"I'm always careful," she said.

"Yeah, you are, aren't you?"

How was she supposed to interpret the look he gave her? Equal parts frustration and—was that pity? She shook her head. She was imagining things. Nate might still have a few feelings for the girl she had been, but he didn't know enough about her now to really care.

"OFFICER HALL, AREN'T you supposed to be home, resting?"

Nate did his best to stand up straight—despite his cast and crutches—as he swiveled to face Adelaide. The septuagenarian eyed him over the top of purple-framed bifocals, her gaze taking in his khaki uniform. "Surely you aren't on duty?"

"I came in to give the sheriff my formal statement about what happened yesterday," Nate said. "And I'm in uniform because I'm here in an official capacity, as an officer of Parks and Wildlife." That was what he had told himself, anyway. It didn't feel right to show up at the sheriff's department in civilian clothing. Whether it was the uniform or the sheriff feeling sorry for him, Travis had asked Nate to sit in on the morning meeting.

"How long are you going to be laid up with your injuries?" Adelaide asked.

"Six weeks. Maybe less." He was determined to get back to work as swiftly as possible. The idea of sitting around the house with his foot up for the next month and a half was beyond depressing.

"If you're determined to be up and about so soon, you should come to the masquerade ball this Friday night." Adelaide handed him a postcard. The front of the card showed an attractive woman with a black, feathered mask hiding her features. "Proceeds benefit the folks here in Eagle Mountain who have been hit hardest by the heavy snow and road closures. There will be food, music and dancing, and prizes for the best costumes."

"I don't think I'll be doing any dancing just yet," Nate said. He tried to hand the card back to Adelaide, but she refused to take it.

"You can sit, have a drink and something to eat, and enjoy seeing everyone's costumes."

"What are you coming as?" he asked Adelaide.

The devilish look that came into her fading blue eyes made him take a step back. "You'll just have to wait and see. One more reason for you to show up."

"I'll, uh, think about it." He retreated to the door, moving faster than he would have thought possible in his condition.

His next stop was the grocery store. If he was going to be sitting home for the next few weeks, he needed to stock up on snacks and easy meals. He made his way to the produce section and was sizing up the potatoes when a familiar voice hailed him. "Hello, Officer Nate."

Smiling, he turned to greet Donna Douglas. Jamie's sister wore one of the grocery's blue aprons over a green sweater and jeans, her curly brown hair pulled back in a ponytail. He had never paid much attention to her when he and Jamie were dating. He'd thought of her as just a kid, seeming younger than her years because of her mental disability. "Hello, Donna," he said.

"You're Jamie's friend." Donna grinned. "Her boyfriend."

How was he supposed to answer that? "Jamie and I are friends."

"What happened to your foot?" She stared at the blue Aircast encasing his left foot.

"I hurt it at work."

"What kind of work do you do?"

"I work for Parks and Wildlife."

"I remember now. We met you when we were snowshoeing. Did a big animal step on your foot?"

"Not exactly."

"Hey, Donna."

They turned to see a stocky, moon-faced young man wheeling a produce cart toward them. His blue eyes shone from behind his black-framed glasses as he grinned at

Donna. Donna grinned back. It made Nate think of cartoons he had seen as a child, where a pair of lovers looked at each other and hearts exploded in the air around them. He couldn't see any hearts around these two, but he had no doubt they were there.

"This is Henry." Donna took the young man's hand when he stopped beside them. "He's my boyfriend."

Henry nodded. "Donna's my girlfriend."

"You look like you make a good couple," Nate said.

"Thanks." Donna released Henry's hand. "I have to get back to work," she said. "We don't want to get in trouble." She waved to Nate and hurried back toward the register area.

"Me, too," Henry said. He began unloading apples from a box on a cart, arranging them in a neat pyramid. "You should buy an apple." He handed Nate a large red fruit. "They're very good, and good for you."

"I think I will." Nate pulled a plastic bag from the roll at one end of the bin and selected three more apples to go with the one Henry had given him.

"Are you a police officer?" Henry was staring at Nate's khaki uniform and gun.

"A kind of police officer, yes." He didn't mention Parks and Wildlife. When he named his employer, people invariably thought he was a park ranger, not a cop. Never mind that he had the same training as any other law enforcement officer. He wrote tickets, investigated crimes and made arrests all the time as part of his job. And most of the lawbreakers he faced met up with him when he was alone in the wilderness—and almost all of them carried guns.

"Do you know anything about all those women who died?"

Henry's question startled him, but he told himself it shouldn't have surprised him. The Ice Cold Killer was the number one topic of conversation in Eagle Mountain these days. Henry had probably heard his customers and his family talking about the case.

"I'm trying to help find the man who killed those women," Nate said.

"Michaela was my friend." Henry's mouth turned down, and his lip quivered. He sniffed. "She worked at the bank and she helped me with my account."

"I'm very sorry you lost your friend," Nate said.

"I saw her the day before she died. She came in here to the store. She did that sometimes. She would buy a salad or fruit for her lunch and say hello to me."

"That's good that you got to see her."

Henry was frowning—or maybe concentrating very hard. Nate couldn't tell. "She was with a man," Henry said. "They were laughing and she was smiling at him—different from the way she smiled at me."

The hair on the back of Nate's neck stood up. "Who was the man, do you know?"

Henry shook his head. "I didn't know him. But I think maybe he was her boyfriend."

Nate set the bag of apples in his cart and moved closer to Henry, the way he might approach a skittish deer. "Henry, do you think you would recognize that man if you saw him again?"

He nodded. "I think so. I'm pretty good at remembering people."

"Could you come to the sheriff's department with me and tell them what you told me, and maybe describe the man to them?"

Henry's frown deepened. "I can't come now. I have to work." His voice rose. A couple of shoppers turned to stare.

"What time do you get off work?" Nate asked.

Henry tilted his head to one side, thinking. "I get off today at three o'clock," he said.

"If I come back here at three, will you go to the sheriff's office with me?" Nate asked. "Just for a little bit?"

Henry shrugged. "I guess so. Is it important?"

"Yes. It's important."

"Okay." He turned back to arranging the apples. "See you at three."

Nate finished his shopping, his mind racing. If Henry was telling the truth—and he would have no reason to lie—then he might have seen Michaela with her killer. This might be the break they had been waiting for.

Chapter Eight

Jamie didn't make it back to the grocery store until three fifteen. Donna got off at three, so Jamie reasoned this would be a good opportunity for her to meet Henry without upsetting her sister if things didn't go well. "I'm looking for someone named Henry, who works in your produce department," she told the young woman at the office, whose name tag identified her as Veronique.

"Henry?" Veronique's eyebrows rose. "He's not in any kind of trouble, is he?"

"No, no. I just wanted to meet him. He's, uh, he's friends with my sister, Donna."

"Oh, Donna! Of course." Veronique brightened. "She and Henry left at three. He said something about walking her home." She giggled. "They're so cute together."

So much for Jamie's plan to meet Henry alone. "What is Henry like?" she asked.

"Oh, he's a good kid. Like Donna. He came to us from the same program."

"You mean, he's developmentally disabled, too."

"Yeah. Down syndrome, I think. But a good worker. Friendly. Customers like him. They like Donna, too."

"How old is he?"

"Early twenties. He lives with his mother, I think. Why do you want to know?"

"Donna says he's her boyfriend."

Veronique giggled again. "Yeah, those two are really sweet on each other. It's cute."

"Thanks." Jamie left the store and returned to her cruiser. Henry didn't sound like a serial killer who was going to lure her sister to a remote location and kill her. But she still wanted to meet him. She checked her watch. They might already be at Mrs. Simmons's, but since they were on foot, and Donna was never one to hurry, Jamie ought to be able to catch up with them en route and introduce herself.

She cruised slowly through the streets of Eagle Mountain, waving to people she passed and keeping an eye out for her sister and the mysterious Henry. She pulled into Mrs. Simmons's driveway, wondering if her sister had arrived ahead of her. She hoped Henry hadn't already left. Knowing Mrs. Simmons, she would have invited him in.

The sitter met Jamie on the front porch. "I was getting ready to call you," she said, before Jamie could speak. "Donna isn't here. It's not like her to be so late.'

Jamie tried to push back the fear that climbed in her throat and the painful drumming of her heart. "She left the store at three," she said. "And I didn't see her on the drive over. Maybe I misunderstood where she was going." She squeezed Mrs. Simmons's clasped hands. "I'll go back to the store and talk to them again. Call me right away if she shows up."

Mrs. Simmons nodded, her face creased with worry.

Before heading to the store, Jamie stopped at her house. Donna was always going on about wanting to stay by herself. Maybe when she said she was going home, she meant exactly that, and she had brought Henry here to the house.

But the house was locked up tight, and only the dogs responded to Jamie's calls.

Back at the store, Jamie had to hunt up Veronique in the bakery, where she was accepting an order from a vendor. "Are you sure Donna and Henry said they were headed home?" she asked.

"Yes." Veronique looked up from her clipboard. "I spoke to him myself when he was punching out."

"Maybe he meant his home. Can you give me his parents' number?"

Veronique's brow furrowed. "We're not supposed to give out personal information about our employees."

"I'm a sheriff's deputy. And I'm trying to make sure my sister is safe." Jamie couldn't rein in her impatience.

"Oh, uh, okay."

Jamie followed the woman to the front office, and a few moments later was dialing the number for Mrs. O'Keefe. While she listened to the phone ring, she thought about the approach she should take with these people. She didn't want to send them into a panic. "Hello?" a woman answered.

"Hello, Mrs. O'Keefe?"

"Yes."

"This is Jamie Douglas. I'm Donna Douglas's sister. She works with your son, Henry, at the grocery store."

"Oh, yes," the woman's voice softened. "We've met Donna before." She chuckled. "Henry is quite taken with her."

"Have you seen Henry, or talked to him, since he got off work at three?"

"No. He mentioned this morning that he was going to walk Donna to the house where she stays every afternoon while you work. It's only a few blocks, and we do like to encourage Henry to be as independent as possible. He's really very responsible."

Jamie took a deep breath. She hated worrying this

woman, who sounded very nice. But in Mrs. O'Keefe's position, she would want to know. "Donna and Henry never showed up at the sitter's," she said. "I'm trying to find them now."

"Oh, no! That doesn't sound like Henry at all." Her voice broke. "You don't think this horrible killer has decided to go after them, do you?"

"I'm sure that's not it," Jamie said, as much to reassure herself as to allay Mrs. O'Keefe's fears. "They probably decided to stop off at a restaurant or something. Donna mentioned this morning that she and Henry wanted to go on a date."

"Yes. Yes, that sounds reasonable." Mrs. O'Keefe was clearly trying to keep it together.

"I'm a sheriff's deputy," Jamie said. "We'll start looking for them right away. I'll call you as soon as I know anything."

"Please do. This is so unlike Henry. He's such a good boy. Well, he's a man now, of course, but he'll always be my boy."

"I understand." Jamie sometimes had to remind herself that, while Donna would always be her little sister, she was a grown woman.

"Is everything all right?" Veronique asked when Jamie ended the call.

"I'm sure they're fine," Jamie said. "I'm going to look for them."

She checked the most likely spots first—the Cakewalk Café, Peggy's Pizza and Kate's—but no one had seen Donna or Henry, together or alone. As Jamie cruised down Eagle Mountain's main drag, she scanned the sidewalks and shops for any sign of the two young people.

Tense with worry, she headed for the sheriff's department. She hated to involve the department in her family's business, but she needed her fellow officers' help in tracking down Donna and Henry before they got into trouble. Anyone could take advantage of two such trusting souls.

She parked on the street and entered through the front door. If Travis wasn't in his office, Adelaide would know where to find him.

But when Jamie approached Adelaide's desk, she discovered the office manager wasn't alone. "Hey, Jamie!" Donna stood and hurried around Adelaide's desk to hug her sister.

Jamie hugged her back and had to wait a few seconds before she felt safe speaking. "What are you doing here?" she asked Donna.

"I'm waiting for Henry," Donna said, as if this explained everything.

"Donna's friend is giving a statement to the sheriff," Adelaide said.

"A statement about what?"

"I don't know," Adelaide said. "Nate brought him in."

"Nate Hall?" How was Nate involved in any of this?

"He gave us a ride in his truck," Donna said. "He has a set of deer antlers and a shotgun in it."

"I don't understand," Jamie said. "Did something happen?" She addressed her sister. "Did someone try to hurt you and Henry while you were walking home?"

Donna looked puzzled. "No. We came here with Nate, in his truck."

"I'm sure he'll be finished in a few minutes," Adelaide said. "Then you can ask the sheriff what this is about."

Not knowing what else to do, Jamie sat, only half paying attention to the conversation Donna and Adelaide were having about the masquerade ball on Friday. After about five minutes, the door to the sheriff's office opened and Nate emerged with a stocky young man who wore black framed glasses. The young man—Henry—grinned as Donna rushed to meet him. "I still need to walk you home," he said.

"Hello, Henry. I'm Donna's sister, Jamie." Jamie offered her hand and Henry solemnly shook it.

"Nice to meet you," he said.

Jamie looked past him to address Nate, who supported himself with crutches. "What are Henry and my sister doing here at the sheriff's department?"

"Henry was friends with Michaela Underwood," Nate said. "He saw her in the store the day before she died, with a man he thought was her boyfriend."

"Al," Jamie said. The man who might have been her killer.

"He gave us a very good description of the man," Nate said. "He's been a big help to us."

"I need to walk Donna home now," Henry said.

"I'll drive Donna home," Jamie said. "And I need to call your mother, Henry. When you didn't come home, she was worried. The way Mrs. Simmons and I were worried about Donna when she didn't show up on time." She glared at Nate as she said the last words. He had the grace to look chagrined.

"I'll give you a ride to your place, Henry," Nate said. "After we call your mom."

Jamie already had her phone out and was dialing the O'Keefes' number. Mrs. O'Keefe answered after the first ring. "Henry is fine," Jamie said. "He and Donna are here at the sheriff's department. Everything is all right. They're not in trouble. Henry was able to give some evidence in a case we're working on. An officer is going to bring him home… Of course, if you would rather. I understand." She chatted with Mrs. O'Keefe for another minute and then ended the call. "Your mother is coming to get you," she told Henry.

"I'll wait with him, if you want to go," Nate said.

"No, I do not want to go." Jamie took Nate's arm and tugged him toward the hallway. Reluctantly, he hobbled after her.

She led the way into the empty conference room and shut the door behind him. He held up his hand to stop her speaking. "Before you lay into me, I realize I screwed up," he said. "I should have let you know what was going on and that your sister was safe. I didn't mean to worry you."

"You didn't mean to worry me? There is a killer out there who preys on women. My sister would be an easy target. I wasn't worried—I was petrified."

"I get that, and I'm sorry." He took her hand, his thumb tracing the contours of her knuckles, the touch reassuring—and unsettling. "I'm really sorry. I promise not to do that to you again."

She wanted to continue to rage at him but feared that if she opened her mouth again, she'd start crying. She forced back the tears and pulled her hand away from his. "How did you find out Henry knew Michaela?" she asked.

"I was buying groceries and we got to talking. He saw my uniform and asked if I knew about the murders—then he told me he had seen Michaela the day before she died, with a man he hadn't seen her with before."

"Then how did my sister get involved?"

"When I showed up at three to pick up Henry and bring him here to make his statement, Donna was with him. He said she needed to come with him and I didn't see any harm in it." He grimaced. "I should have realized you'd be worried."

"I know. And really, Donna should have called me herself. She knows she's supposed to."

"Am I forgiven?" he asked.

His contrite tone almost made her laugh. The tension of the afternoon had her emotions ricocheting all over the place. "I'll think about it," she said, moving past him.

Henry and Donna waited where Nate and Jamie had left them, seated in chairs by the door, holding hands. "I want to take Donna to the party Friday night," Henry said, standing as Nate and Jamie approached.

"We're supposed to wear costumes," Donna said, bouncing on her toes with excitement.

Jamie opened her mouth to say no. Donna needed to stay home, where she would be safe. But she couldn't keep her sister a prisoner. And Jamie had planned to attend the masquerade party anyway. "All right," she said.

Donna looked to Henry, who nodded. "Good," he said.

Jamie took her sister's hand. "Come on. I'll take you to Mrs. Simmons's," she said.

"See you tomorrow," Henry said. He stopped and blew Donna a kiss. She returned the gesture, blushing and giggling. Jamie couldn't help smiling. Veronique was right—Donna and Henry made a cute couple. She was happy Donna had found a friend, but her heart ached at the knowledge that no matter how hard she tried, she could never protect her sister from all the ways the world could hurt her.

NATE HAD JUST settled onto the sofa, feet up, a cup of cocoa in one hand, a suspense novel in the other, when someone rapped on his door. "Who is it?" he called. He could count on the fingers of one hand the number of people who had stopped by for a visit since he had moved in four months ago.

"It's Travis."

Intrigued, Nate levered himself to his feet and clomped

to the door with the aid of one crutch. He unlocked it and opened it to admit the sheriff. "I wanted to see how you're doing and check if you needed anything," Travis said.

"Thanks, but I'm okay." Nate dropped back onto the sofa. He doubted the sheriff had really come over to check on him. Travis had something on his mind. Even back in college, when they had roomed together, Travis had a tendency to brood. "Have a seat," Nate said.

Travis sat, elbows on his knees, hands clasped in front of his mouth, saying nothing.

"How are the wedding preparations going?" Nate asked. "It won't be long now."

"They're going okay. Lacy is a little anxious about the weather. Some of the guests won't be able to attend if the road doesn't open."

"You won't be able to get away for your honeymoon, either," Nate said.

"I'm not going anywhere until this killer is caught. Lacy knows that."

"You never were one to leave a job unfinished. What's the latest?"

"We can't get a police artist to come here, because of the road closures, but I've arranged for one to Skype with Henry O'Keefe. I'm hoping we can get an image we can publish in the paper and distribute around town. Someone knows this guy."

"He may not be the killer."

"Maybe not. But he might have seen something that morning that could help us find the killer." He sat up straight. "He's going to strike again, I'm sure."

"What about the plan to have Jamie drive around, trying to attract the killer's attention?" Nate didn't like the idea, but it wasn't his decision to make.

"We're going to do that tonight," Travis said. "I put it

off one night after we got the description from Henry. I wanted to see if that led to anyone obvious. It didn't, but maybe we'll have better luck with the drawing. Meanwhile, Dwight is going out with Jamie tonight. Gage and I will be on duty nearby, ready to close in."

"Jamie is pretty new to the force, isn't she?"

"She's been with us almost a year. She's been a good addition to the department."

"I knew her growing up," Nate said. "I never would have dreamed she'd go into law enforcement. It's not anything she ever talked about." Whereas he had decided to aim for a job with Parks and Wildlife when he was still in his teens. The idea of being able to study wildlife and actively protect it, while also helping to educate the public, had appealed to him, as had the freedom to spend lots of time outdoors.

"She's hardworking and good with people," Travis said. "She's smart. And we're working to diversify the force to better reflect the population we serve. We're hoping to recruit more women like her."

"She seems to really like the work. But are you sure she's up for this decoy exercise tonight? This killer—or killers—has made a habit of killing women very quickly." His stomach clenched as he spoke.

Travis's gaze met Nate's, unwavering. "I wouldn't ask Jamie to do this if I didn't believe she could handle it," he said. "So, what's going on between you two?"

Nate looked away. "Nothing is going on between us."

"I thought I sensed some...tension."

Nate laughed. "Oh, there's tension all right. She can't stand me."

"And why is that?"

He blew out a breath. Travis wasn't the type to press if Nate told him to mind his own business, but maybe getting his levelheaded friend's perspective would help. "Jamie and I dated during high school," he said. "We were really close. I guess you could say we were each other's first love. But then it was time to go to college and I was going away. I didn't think it was fair to ask her to wait for me, so I broke things off with her. I thought we could still be friends, but she didn't see it that way." His shoulders sagged. "I guess you could say things ended badly. Apparently, she's never forgiven me. Maybe because I wasn't around to support her after her parents died."

"It takes a lot of energy to hold on to anger that long," Travis said. "It makes me think there's more than animosity behind it."

"Think that if you like, but she's made it clear she doesn't want to have anything to do with me."

Travis's phone rang and he answered. He listened for a moment, frowning, then stood. "I'm on my way." He pocketed his phone again. "That was Adelaide," he said. "The Ice Cold Killer has struck again—only this time, the woman got away."

Chapter Nine

"You're going to be all right, Tammy. You're safe now."
Jamie handed the distraught young woman a cup of water,
then sat next to her, pulling the chair close. Tammy Patterson, reporter for the *Eagle Mountain Examiner*, had stumbled into the sheriff's department ten minutes before, her
clothes torn, her face bloodied, tears running down her
cheeks. She had sobbed incoherently, something about
the Ice Cold Killer coming after her. "You're safe now,"
Jamie murmured again and pressed a cold compress to the
swelling on the side of Tammy's face.

"The sheriff is on his way," Dwight Prentice said from
the doorway of the conference room. "The paramedics
are coming, too."

Jamie nodded. It wouldn't hurt to have Tammy's bruises
checked. "Drink some water," she urged. "When the sheriff gets here, we'll need you to tell us what happened, but
remember, you're safe and you're with friends."

Tammy nodded and drank. Her hands didn't shake as
badly now, and the flow of tears had subsided.

Dwight glanced over this shoulder. "Sheriff's here." A
moment later, Travis entered.

"Hello, Tammy," he said. "I understand you've had a
frightening time of it."

She drew in a deep, shuddering breath. "I was terrified. But I'm alive and safe now—that's what counts."

Travis pulled up a chair across from Tammy. "You may be able to help us catch this guy and stop him from hurting other women. So I need you to tell me everything you can remember about what happened—even if the detail seems too small to be important. Can you do that?"

She nodded, licked her lips and began speaking, hesitantly at first, then with more assurance. "I was out on County Road Two. Colorado Parks and Wildlife is going to start putting out food for the deer and elk who have been stressed by all this snow, and they have a staging area out there for the supplies and volunteers. I went out there to get photos for the paper."

She took a sip of water, then continued. "I was on my way back to town, maybe three miles from the staging area. It had started snowing, and visibility wasn't that good. Then all of a sudden, I saw a woman standing on the side of the road. She was waving her arms. I had to stop. I pulled over to the shoulder and she ran up to the passenger side of the car. I rolled down the window and she told me she had had a fight with her boyfriend, who was drunk. She needed to get to town—or at least to borrow a phone so she could call a friend to come get her. Of course I said I'd help her. She was so distressed—clearly, she had been crying, and her hair was all down in her eyes, and she sounded almost hysterical. I unlocked the car and leaned over to clear stuff off the passenger seat so she could get in."

She closed her eyes and a shudder went through her. "All of a sudden, the driver's-side door opened and someone grabbed me and started hauling me out of the car. I screamed and started trying to fight him off. I thought at first it was the woman's boyfriend, angry because I was getting involved. But then the woman came around to the side of the road. While he held my arms, she grabbed at my legs and started trying to wrap them with duct tape."

"The woman was helping him?" Jamie asked.

Tammy's eyes met hers. "Looking back now, I don't think it really was a woman," she said. "This person was really strong."

"Do you think it was a man, dressed up like a woman?" Travis asked.

"Maybe," Tammy said. "She was tall for a woman, and she had lots of blond hair, all falling in front of her face. She never really looked directly at me. I think the hair might have been a wig. And like I said, she was so strong."

Travis nodded. "All right. Tell us about the other man. The one who grabbed you."

Tammy shook her head. "There's not much to tell. He was behind me most of the time. I only saw him for a few seconds, from the side. He was dressed all in black, with a ski mask pulled down over his head."

"How tall do you think he was?" Travis asked. "How much taller than you?"

"He was taller than me—most men are. But he wasn't really tall, so I'd say, maybe five-ten. But the ground was really uneven there, and he was behind me, so he might have been six feet tall, just standing on lower ground."

"What about build?" Travis asked. "Was he stocky, or really muscular?"

She shook her head. "No, he was just, you know, average. I wish now I had paid more attention, but I was so scared. I was sure he was going to kill me."

"You got away," Jamie reminded her. "You're safe."

"What did you do?" Travis asked. "How did you get away?"

"I fought so hard. When he grabbed me, I had picked up

my notebook off the passenger seat so the woman could get in. It had a pen clipped to it. I grabbed the pen and stabbed at him—at his hands, his face. And I kicked at the woman. She dropped the duct tape and it rolled into the dirt." Tammy's eyes widened. "I remember now—she swore, and her voice was different—deeper. A man's voice."

"Did he say a name, or address the other man in any way?" Travis asked.

Tammy closed her eyes. Jamie imagined her putting herself back in that place. "No. They didn't say anything to each other. The man in the ski mask was angry that I fought, and he hit me—hard." She put a hand to her bruised face. "But I was so terrified. I knew if I didn't get away from them, I would die. So I did everything I could think of. I kept stabbing with the pen, and I spat at him and tried to bite him. When he dragged me from the car, I hooked one foot onto the bottom of the seat. It threw him off balance. The side of the road is really rough over there, and there's a lot of snow. He slid down into the ditch, away from me. I got up and crawled back into the car and slammed the door. The engine was still running, so I just floored it. I almost ran over the woman.

"I don't even remember getting here. I just drove, as fast as I could. I kept looking in the mirror, to see if they followed me, but they didn't."

"Where were you, exactly, when this happened?" Travis asked.

"On County Road Two. There's that little neighborhood of houses in there, then a stretch of woods, then a big curve. This was right after the big curve."

"You want me to go out and take a look?" Dwight spoke from the doorway.

"Take Gage with you. Find the scene and cordon it off. Do a search, then hit the houses around there. Talk to everyone you can. Find out if they know anything. Or saw or heard anything"

"That's only a few miles from where Michaela's body was found," Jamie said. "The killers might live in one of those houses."

"I want to go out there tonight, see if we can draw them out." Travis said. He turned to Jamie. "If you're still up for it, Deputy."

"I am."

"I'll call Gage," Dwight said, and left them as two paramedics entered. Travis and Jamie moved away to let them check out Tammy.

"You don't have to do this decoy op if you're uncomfortable with it," Travis told Jamie. "There's no doubt these two are dangerous."

"I want to, sir," she said. "This may be our best chance to catch them. They'll be frustrated that Tammy got away."

"I agree." He clapped her on the shoulder. "Go home now and change."

"Yes, sir." She glanced at Tammy. "What about her?"

"She lives with her parents here in town. I'll call them in a minute and they can come pick her up. She should be safe there, but I'll put a reserve deputy on the house tonight, just in case. Be back here at seven o'clock."

"Yes, sir." She hurried from the room, buzzing with excitement. She might be able to catch these killers—tonight.

"YOU'RE BEING AN IDIOT," Nate mumbled to himself as he grabbed his crutches and swung out of the cab of his truck. He had just pulled into Jamie's driveway. It was six thirty at night. Her car was in the driveway, and most of the windows of the house were lit up, so he was pretty sure she was home. She'd probably be furious to see him. He should leave her alone. But, knowing she was going out there tonight, possibly to face a serial killer—or more than one serial killer—he couldn't stay away.

He positioned the crutches under his arms and paused a moment to look up at the house. The place didn't look that much different than it had when he was in high school, at least in the dark. The same stone lions sat on either side of the steps leading up to the wide front porch, and the same wooden swing hung from the porch rafters. He and Jamie had spent many hours on that swing, sometimes making out, but mostly talking, about everything. He hadn't been able to talk to anyone like that since. Maybe it was only as a teenager that a man could be comfortable baring his soul that way. Or maybe he could only do it with Jamie.

He clumped his way up the walk, navigated the steps, crossed the porch and rang the doorbell. It echoed loudly through the house. "I'll get it!" a voice shouted, followed by the thunder of running feet on a hardwood floor.

The door opened and Donna peeked out. "Hello," she said, then held the door open wider. "Come in."

Jamie appeared behind her sister. She caught the door and held it. "What are you doing here?" she asked.

"I just wanted to talk, okay? Please?"

Reluctantly, she let him in. "I don't have much time," she said as he moved past her. "I have to be at the sheriff's department at seven."

"I know what you're going to do tonight," he said.

"I'm going to do my job."

"You're sure dressed up for work," Donna said.

Nate let his gaze slide over the short blue dress, with its low-cut neckline and full, swirly skirt. It was made of some soft fabric that hugged her curves, and the skirt stopped several inches above the tops of the tall black boots she wore. A sudden pull of attraction caught him off guard.

"Donna, I left my purse upstairs," Jamie said. "Could you get it for me, please?"

When Donna had left them, Jamie turned back to Nate. "Why are you staring at me that way?"

"Is that what you're wearing tonight?" he asked.

"Yes.'

"You'll have on a coat, right?"

"My car has a heater. I don't want these two to have any doubt that I'm a young woman."

Yeah, there was no doubt of that. "You should wear a vest," he said.

Her eyebrows rose. "You mean a tactical vest?"

"Yes."

"These two use a knife," she said. "They don't shoot people. And they slit throats. A tactical vest wouldn't be any help at all."

"You don't know they don't have a gun."

"They didn't use it on Tammy today. If they had one, you'd think they would have."

"Tammy? Is that the woman who got away from the killer? Travis got the call while he was at my house."

"Killers. There are two of them."

"What happened this afternoon?" he asked. "You can tell me—I'm part of the team and I'm going to hear about it in the briefing tomorrow morning anyway."

She crossed her arms over her chest. She probably didn't realize how much it enhanced her cleavage. Nate shifted, hoping she didn't notice the effect she was having on him. "Aren't you on medical leave?" she asked.

"From my Parks and Wildlife job—not from the team that's hunting this killer. I can sort data and do research with one foot in a cast. So what happened to Tammy? And Tammy who?"

Jamie glanced up the stairs, then lowered her voice.

"Tammy Patterson—the reporter for the paper? She stopped to help a woman who flagged her down. Only it wasn't a woman—it was a man in a wig. A second man came out of the woods and grabbed Tammy and he and the one dressed like a woman tried to wrap her up in duct tape. Tammy fought like a wildcat and managed to get away."

"She was lucky."

"Yes. And she may be our lucky break. I'm really hoping we catch these two tonight." She took a step back. "You still haven't told me why you're here."

"I just—" He shoved his hands in his pockets. He'd feel better if he could pace, but that was impossible on crutches. "I just wanted to tell you to be careful." He couldn't believe how lame he sounded, but he hadn't thought this out very well—he had just gotten in his truck and started to drive, and ended up here.

"I'm not an idiot," she said.

"I know that. But neither are these killers."

"Why do you care, anyway?" she asked.

"Because I do." Their eyes met and the heat in her gaze rocked him back. Jamie might *say* she couldn't stand him, but that was not what it felt like right now. He leaned toward her. Another half second and he would have to kiss her. She looked like she wanted to kiss him back. He just needed to be a little closer...

"Here's your purse. It wasn't upstairs, it was on the kitchen table." Donna came into the room, the purse dangling from her wrist. Jamie looked away and Nate suppressed a groan of disappointment. "Are you going to stay with me while Jamie goes out?" Donna asked.

"Nate isn't going to stay with you," Jamie said. "You're going to Mrs. Simmons's."

"I could stay with her," Nate said. "I don't mind." And

he'd be here when Jamie got home, to make sure she was all right.

"Yay!" Donna clapped her hands. "Do you like to play cards? We can play cards."

"Donna, I don't think—" Jamie began.

"Really, I don't mind," Nate said. "Let me stay."

"Pleeeease!" Donna put her hands together as if praying. "I don't want to go to Mrs. Simmons's all the time. I want to stay here."

Jamie blew out a breath. "Okay." She frowned at Nate. "I guess I will feel better, knowing she's with you."

"She'll be safe with me," Nate said. If he couldn't look after Jamie, at least he could look after her sister.

"This feels really weird," Jamie said, as she drove slowly along County Road Two, constantly scanning the side of the road for any sign of life. The afternoon's snow had stopped, and the plows had left fresh drifts on the roadside that reflected back the glow from her headlights.

"Imagine how I feel." Dwight Prentice spoke from his position on the floorboard of the back seat.

Jamie grimaced, remembering the awkward contortions required for the six-foot-three deputy to hide in her car. "We're passing that neighborhood Tammy mentioned," she said.

"The place where she pulled over is around the next big curve," Dwight said. "By the time we got there, the new snow had almost covered the area. By now the plows will have wiped out everything—not that there was anything to find. We didn't see so much as a hair or a button."

Jamie cruised slowly past the spot, where yellow crime scene tape fluttered from roadside brush. "We haven't even passed another car in ten minutes," she said.

"When you can find a place to turn around, go ahead

and do so," Dwight said. "We'll make one more pass past that neighborhood. Pretend you're looking for an address. If you don't attract any attention after that, we'll call it a night."

"Maybe Tammy getting away scared them off," Jamie said, as she pulled over onto the shoulder and prepared to turn around.

"They can't have gone far," Dwight said. "The highway out of town is still closed."

She swung the car around, then gasped and slammed on the brakes as her headlights lit up the figure of a man on the side of the road. He put up one hand to shield his eyes, then hunched over and turned back toward the woods. Jamie shoved open the door and bailed out of the car, her Glock already drawn. "Stop, police!"

Jamie heard Dwight move in behind her. The man, who wore a fur cap with earflaps and sported a full beard, dropped two items and raised his hands over his head. "Don't shoot," he pleaded.

"Get on your knees," Dwight ordered. "Hands behind your head."

The man did as asked and Dwight moved in closer, Jamie behind him. She nudged at the rifle the man had dropped and what she now recognized as a hand-held spotlight. The first rush of adrenaline was fading, leaving behind a sinking feeling. "Who are you, and what are you doing out here in the middle of the night?" he asked.

"It's only nine o'clock," he said.

"What's your name?" she asked.

The man—who up close looked to be at least seventy—looked away and didn't answer.

Dwight rummaged in the man's pocket and pulled out a wallet. He flipped it open and read. "Mitch Oliphant."

He looked at the man. "What were you doing out here, Mr. Oliphant?"

Again, no answer.

Jamie nudged the spotlight with her toe. "It looks to me like you were spotlighting deer," she said. "Which is against the law."

"You ain't no game warden," Oliphant said.

No. The local game warden was currently at Jamie's house, babysitting her sister.

"In fact, how do I know you're even a cop?" Oliphant continued. "You sure ain't dressed like one." He leered and she suppressed the urge to tug on her short skirt.

"We can still enforce the law," she said. "How long have you been out here tonight?"

"There's no law against being out at night. I was taking a walk."

"With your rifle and a spotlight?" Dwight asked.

"I couldn't find my flashlight. And a man's got a right to defend himself, with that crazy killer running around."

"What do you know about the killer?" Jamie asked.

Oliphant glared at her. "Nothing."

"Have you seen anyone else while you were taking your walk?" Jamie asked. "Anyone at all?"

"No. Can I get up now? Being down on the ground like this hurts my knees."

Jamie and Dwight exchanged glances. "You can get up," Jamie said. "Slowly."

"At my age, that's the only speed I got." Grunting, Oliphant rose to his feet. "Are you gonna keep me standing out here in the cold all night?" he asked.

"Where do you live?" Dwight asked.

"The address is on my license." Oliphant stared at Dwight, who didn't back down. Jamie focused on the two, trying to ignore her freezing feet and wishing she had thought to get her coat from the car. "I live out on Fish Camp Road," Oliphant finally said.

Jamie gaped. That had to be at least eight miles from where they were standing. "Did you walk all the way from there?"

"No. My truck is parked up the road about a quarter mile." He jerked his head toward town.

"We'll let you go if you promise to go home and stay there," Dwight said. "Don't be out here at night where you don't have any business."

Oliphant muttered something to the effect that it was a free country and turned away, but Jamie called after him. "Mr. Oliphant?"

He glanced back at her. "What?"

"Do you come out here often? Walking?"

"What's it to you?"

"You might be able to help us. We're looking for a woman—a tall blonde. A couple of people have seen her out here, walking along the road. She told one woman who stopped to help her that she had a boyfriend who beats her. We want to make sure she's all right." It was close enough to the truth.

The lines between Oliphant's brows deepened. "I think I saw her, once. But when she saw me, she took off—right into the woods, like a scared rabbit."

"Did you get a good look at her?" Dwight asked. "Do you think you'd recognize her again?"

The old man shook his head. "I only saw her for a few seconds. She was tall and thin, with a lot of blond hair, all hanging down in her face."

"Where were you when you saw her?" Jamie asked.

He looked around them. "I don't know. Somewhere around here. I can't remember."

"When did you see her?" Dwight asked.

"A week ago? Maybe more." He shrugged. "It was just a few seconds. I didn't mark it on my calendar or anything."

Jamie glanced at Dwight. He shook his head slightly, indicating he didn't have anything to add. "All right, Mr. Oliphant, you can go," Jamie said. "If we have any more questions, we'll be in touch."

He picked up his rifle and the spotlight, then shuffled away, down the shoulder of the road. Jamie got back into the car and turned the heat up to high. Dwight slid into the passenger seat. "What do you make of his story about the blonde?" he asked, as she turned onto the highway and headed for town.

"It sounds like these two troll for women pretty regularly," she said. "The guy dressed up in the wig is the bait to get the women to stop, then his friend comes out of the woods. Together, they subdue and kill the women." She shuddered. "Creepy."

"Travis is going to get a police artist with Tammy and see if we can get a portrait we can circulate," Dwight said.

"He probably only wears the disguise when they're out hunting," Jamie said.

"Maybe the artist can give us an idea of what the guy looks like without a wig."

"Maybe." She yawned. "I hate that we didn't lure them out tonight."

"You didn't hesitate when we saw Oliphant," Dwight said. "That was good."

"I knew you had my back."

She drove to the sheriff's department, where she and Dwight made their report to the sheriff, then she headed for home. It was all she could do to stay awake for the drive. The tension of the day had drained her. As she pulled into the driveway, she saw that someone had left the porch light on for her. The door opened while she was still standing on the porch, fumbling for her keys, and she walked in— right into Nate's arms.

Chapter Ten

The strength of Nate's embrace felt so familiar—so right. Jamie closed her eyes and rested her head on his shoulder, breathing in the clean, masculine scent of him, feeling as if she could let go completely, and he would continue to hold her up. "Tough night?" he asked after a moment, his voice low, his warm breath stirring her hair.

She lifted her head and looked up at him. "We didn't see the killers," she said. "We stopped and questioned an old man. I think he was spotlighting deer, but we couldn't prove it, so we had to let him go."

"Who was it?" Nate asked.

"Mitch Oliphant."

He nodded. "I know Mitch. And yeah, he was probably spotlighting deer." He frowned. "Did he do something to upset you?"

"No. I'm just tired. Seeing Tammy this afternoon and then going out there tonight—it's a lot to take in."

"You've had to be strong for a long time." He smoothed his hand down her arm. "You've carried a lot of weight on your shoulders for the past few years. I'm sorry I wasn't there for you then. But I'm here for you now."

His words—and the meaning behind them—were more seductive than any sexy love-words. She prided herself on standing on her own two feet, but sometimes—times like tonight—it was so hard. To be able to lean on someone else, just for a little while, was a luxury she craved the way some people wanted sex or money. She stared into his eyes, trying to figure out the catch to his words—to figure out what he expected from her in exchange for his help. But she saw nothing but tenderness, and allowed herself to let down her guard just a little.

Just long enough for one kiss. She closed her eyes as his lips met hers, letting her body soften and mold to his. They kissed as if they had been apart only a few hours instead of seven years. She tilted her head to deepen the kiss and he tasted both familiar and new. She had missed this—this closeness, this communicating without words, this swell of desire and need and the promise of fulfillment. She had been here before with him, and yet she wasn't kissing a boy this time but a man, with a man's power and knowledge and patience. The thought thrilled her and had her wondering if they could sneak upstairs to her bedroom without Donna hearing them.

She eased back slightly and opened her eyes. He was smiling—a look filled with triumph. That gleam of victory set her back on her heels. She shoved away from him and raked a hand through her hair, trying to think. "Hey." He reached for her. "It's okay."

"No, it is not okay," she said. Her heart hammered and her buzzing nerves left her feeling shaky and off-balance. "This is a mistake. A big mistake."

"YOU'VE GOT TO give me something to do." The next morning, Nate leaned on one crutch in front of the sheriff's desk and pleaded with Travis. "I'm going nuts sitting at the house staring at the walls." With nothing else to occupy his mind, he kept replaying that kiss with Jamie. He'd finally broken through the wall she had erected between

them, and she'd let him know she still cared for him—
and the next thing he knew, she'd been shoving him out
the door, muttering that she "couldn't do this," deaf to his
pleas for an explanation.

Travis shifted his gaze to the dark blue Aircast that
encased Nate's left ankle. "How long are you off duty?"
he asked.

"Until the doctor clears me to return. He says that could
be as long as six weeks, but I'm going to be back before
then."

Sure you are. Travis had the grace not to say the words
out loud, but Nate could read his friend well enough.
"Look," he said. "My ankle is busted, not my brain.
Haven't you got data that needs crunching, or investigation notes that need reviewing? You need help, don't you?"

"Yes." Travis shoved back his chair and stood. He motioned for Nate to follow him and led the way to a room
that was apparently dedicated to the investigation. Photographs of the victims and their crime scenes filled the
walls, two long tables contained tagged evidence, and another table held a computer terminal and stacks of paperwork.

Jamie looked up from her seat at this table. Her face
paled, then reddened as she stared at Nate. With her cheeks
flushed and several tendrils of hair escaping from the knot
at the base of her neck, she struck Nate as incredibly desirable—a thought he immediately shoved to the back of
his mind. "Nate's going to help you with that witness database," Travis said, then left them.

The sound of the door closing behind Travis echoed in
the still room. The plastic chair Nate grabbed from a row
against the wall protested loudly as he dragged it to the
table. He sat opposite Jamie, who focused on the computer screen. He waited, deciding he'd let her speak first.

"I'm compiling a database of every witness we've interviewed so far," she said after a long, uncomfortable moment. "We need to review their statements, look for similarities, or anything that stands out, and decide if we want to interview them again. You can start reading over their statements while I input the data." She nodded to the stack of file folders at her elbow.

"All right." He took a couple of inches of folders off the top of the pile and placed them in front of him but didn't open one, his eyes steady on her.

After another long moment, she looked over at him. "What?" she asked.

"We need to clear the air between us," he said.

She looked back at the computer, though her hands remained motionless on the keyboard. "I don't know what you're talking about."

"Yes, you do. Ever since I came back to town, you've been giving me the cold shoulder."

She started to shake her head, but he continued. He hadn't really planned to say all this, but now that he was talking, it felt good to get his feelings out in the open. "I get that you were hurt when I broke things off when I went to college," he said. "I'm sorry about that. I really am. But that was seven years ago. We're both adults now. I can't believe you're still holding a stupid thing I did back then over my head."

"I'm not!" She put both hands to her head, as if she wanted to yank out her hair, then lowered them to the table, fists clenched. Her eyes met his and he saw again the pain there, and felt the corresponding ache in his own chest. "You think because we were…involved before, we can be again," she said. "And that's not going to happen."

"You say that—but when you kissed me last night, I wasn't getting that message at all."

Now she looked as if she wanted to throw something at him. He prepared to duck. She glanced toward the door, as if to reassure herself they were still alone. She shifted her gaze back to him. "That kiss last night wasn't about any emotional attachment," she said. "You want me to admit I'm attracted to you—all right, I will. I'm sure that makes you very happy. But you were right when you said we're both adults now. I'm mature enough to know that a relationship between the two of us would be a bad idea."

"Why do you say that?" He leaned across the table toward her, his hands inches from hers, though not touching. "I was serious when I said I care about you," he said. "There was a time when you were the best friend I had. You probably know me better than most people. Why would it be so horrible if we got together?"

"It might be wonderful, for a while." She sounded wistful. "But it wouldn't last. There's no point putting myself through all that."

How do you know it won't last? he started to ask, but couldn't get the words out. Because really, she was right. He had dated at least a dozen women since he had moved away. None seriously. And he wasn't looking for serious with her. At least he didn't think so. She really did know him better than anyone else, didn't she?

He slid his hands away and sat back. "Then we don't have to be lovers," he said. "If I agree to respect that boundary, can we at least be friends? Can we work as a team on this case without this—this coldness between us?"

She hesitated, then looked him in the eye. "Yes. We can do that."

He was a little embarrassed at how much he wanted to whoop and celebrate over such a simple thing. He settled for nodding and opened the file folder on the top of his pile. "All right," he said. "Glad we got that settled. Let's get to work."

JAMIE WAS SURPRISED to find she missed Nate after he left at two for a doctor's appointment. After their awkward—but she could admit now, probably necessary—conversation, they had settled into an efficient and, yes, friendly, work pattern. She was reminded of how smart he was—organized and quick to winnow out nonessential information and grasp patterns, traits that probably helped him with wildlife research. She couldn't help but be reminded of all those afternoons they had spent studying together—he coaching her through chemistry and advanced algebra, she helping him with English and history. They each brought different strengths to the table, and it was the same this afternoon. With his help, she was able to get every witness into the database, and had almost completed summarizing what each one had to say by the time she clocked out at six. Tomorrow she'd finish up and begin indexing by keyword, and focus on people they needed to interview again.

Donna also worked until six today, so Jamie swung by the grocery store and picked her up. She was waiting out front with Henry, the two holding hands. Jamie smiled in spite of herself. They really were a cute couple, and they looked so happy. There was something to be said for the naivety of first love—before you knew how much it hurt when things turned sour.

Nate hadn't even tried to deny that he wasn't interested in a long-term romance. At least he'd been honest, and he had confirmed her instinct to avoid falling for him again. They would keep things friendly but platonic.

If Jamie had thought Donna would distract her from thoughts of the handsome wildlife officer, her hope was in vain. "Did you see Nate today?" Donna asked as Jamie drove toward home.

Jamie tightened her hands on the steering wheel. "Why would I see Nate?" she asked.

"You work together, don't you?"

Not exactly. Of course, they had worked together today. "I saw Nate at work today," she said.

"He's cuuuute," Donna said, using one of her favorite descriptions. "I like him. Is he going to come over again soon?"

"I don't think so," Jamie said.

"Why not? You like him, don't you?"

"I like Nate as a friend."

Donna giggled. "I think you like him more than that."

"No. I do not."

"Then why did you kiss him last night? You don't kiss friends like that."

"Donna!" She glanced at her sister. "What were you doing watching us?"

"I heard you come in last night. I wanted to say good-night. Then I saw you two kissing." She put a hand to her mouth, giggling again. "Is he a good kisser?"

Jamie groaned. She couldn't begin to explain her complicated feelings for Nate—and how much she regretted that kiss—to her sister. "You shouldn't spy on people," she said. "It isn't nice."

"Henry kissed me."

Jamie blinked and almost missed the turn into their driveway. At the last minute, she braked and steered the car up to the garage. She had talked to Donna about sex more than once over the years, and was confident her sister understood what was and wasn't appropriate behavior. But how much of a defense was that understanding when it came to overheated hormones? Jamie had all but thrown herself at Nate last night in a moment of weakness. She needed to know more about how Donna felt about this new relationship with Henry.

Jamie switched off the car, took a deep breath and

turned to her sister. "When did Henry kiss you?" she asked, sounding much calmer than she felt.

"In the break room last Friday. We had our break together, then he leaned over and kissed me on the cheek." She put a hand to her cheek, a dreamy look in her eyes. "He had really soft lips."

Jamie melted a little, from both relief and a rush of tenderness. "That's very sweet," she said. "Henry sounds like a real gentleman."

"He is," Donna said. "He said his mother told him he has to respect me."

Thank you, Mrs. O'Keefe, Jamie silently breathed. She opened her door. "Come on," she said. "Let's make dinner. How does ravioli sound?"

"Ravioli sounds great!" Donna jumped out of the car and raced up the walk, all thoughts of Nate and kissing gone.

Together, the sisters made dinner. Donna's job was to set the table and put ice in glasses, a job she did with minimal mess. When she dropped an ice cube, one of the dogs was happy to snatch it up and carry it off to chew. Over supper, Donna told Jamie about helping Mrs. Simmons fold laundry that morning, and a boy she had seen at the store who wore a knit cap made to look like a dinosaur. "I want a hat like that for Christmas," Donna declared.

They were doing dishes when the doorbell rang, sending the dogs into a barking frenzy, toenails scrabbling on the wood floors as they raced to hurl themselves at the intruder. Jamie shouted for them to quiet as she hurried to the front door, then peered out the sidelight at their visitor.

When she opened the door, Tammy Patterson gave her a faint smile. "Hi," she said. "Do you think I could talk to you for a minute?"

"Sure." Jamie's gaze shifted to the street, where a compact car idled, a man at the wheel.

"That's my brother," Tammy said. "He drove me over." She waved at him and he lifted his hand, then put the car in gear and drove away. "He'll pick me up when I call him."

"Come on in." Jamie held open the door. The dogs surged forward to inspect the new arrival, but Jamie shooed them away. Donna watched from the bottom of the stairs. "This is my sister, Donna," Jamie said. "Donna, this is my friend, Tammy."

"Hi, Donna," Tammy said.

"Hi." Donna nibbled her thumb. "Can I watch my show?" she asked.

"Sure. Tammy and I will talk in the kitchen."

Donna hurried off to the living room to insert the cartoon DVD she loved, while Jamie led the way to the kitchen. "Do you want some tea?" she asked, as she filled the kettle.

"Sure." Tammy sat at the table. "I hope you don't mind my coming by," she said. "I had some questions."

"Sure." Jamie put the kettle on, then took the chair opposite Tammy. The bruise on the reporter's cheek had turned a sickly yellow and purple, and there were gray shadows under her eyes. "What can I help you with?" Jamie asked.

"Do you know when I'll get my car back?" Tammy asked.

"I'm not sure. But I can check. You need your car for work, don't you?"

"My mom said I could borrow hers. I just wondered." She ran her thumb back and forth along the edge of the table. "Maybe it's better if I drive my mom's car for a while. The killers wouldn't recognize it."

"You're worried those two are going to come after you, aren't you?" Jamie asked.

Tammy raised her head, her expression bleak. "Shouldn't I be? I'm the only person who's seen them. Well, one of them. If they go ahead and finish the job they started, I won't be able to identify them."

Tammy had a legitimate concern. Under other circumstances, Jamie might have advised the reporter to take a vacation somewhere else until the killers were caught, but that wasn't possible with the roads closed. "I think the best thing you can do right now is to not go anywhere alone," Jamie said. "You were smart to have your brother drive you tonight."

"Yeah, well, that might make it tough to do my job. Of course, I haven't gone back to work yet, though I'll need to soon."

The teakettle whistled and Jamie got up and made the tea. As she poured the water, the smell of apples and cinnamon wafted up on the steam. She hoped the homey smell would help comfort Tammy.

"Do you have any leads in the case?" Tammy asked when Jamie joined her again. "I'm not asking as a reporter."

"You've given us our best lead so far," Jamie said. "But we haven't identified a suspect yet."

"The sheriff has set up a teleconference with a police artist tomorrow," Tammy said. She smoothed her hands down the thighs of her jeans. "I'm really nervous about getting it wrong. I mean, everything happened so fast."

"Police artists are used to working with nervous people," Jamie said. "He—or she—will help you provide the details they need. You probably remember more than you think."

"That's something else that worries me. I know you'll probably think I'm being stupid. I mean, of course I want to find out who is doing this and stop them from killing anyone else. But all along, I've told myself it had to be someone from outside—a stranger to Eagle Mountain who got trapped here by the weather and for whatever reason decided to go on a killing spree."

Jamie nodded. "I think that's a perfectly natural reaction. This seems like such a safe place."

"Right." She bit her lip and looked down at her lap.

"What is it?" Jamie leaned toward the other woman. "Do you know something—have you remembered something—about the killers that might help us catch them?"

Tammy shrugged. "It's nothing, really. Not anything helpful. It's just, well, ever since it happened, I can't shake the feeling that the man in that wig was someone I know. There was something familiar about him. I've tried and tried to think who it could be, but I can't even imagine. But I can't shake the idea that the killer really isn't a stranger. He's someone who lives here. Someone I might even be friends with."

Jamie nodded, an icy knot in the pit of her stomach. "It's always been a possibility—a probability, even. And it would be horrible to find out these two are people we all like, even admire. It's the kind of thing that makes you question your judgment about everyone."

Tammy sighed. "So you don't think I'm crazy?"

"Of course not."

"I promise, I'd tell you if I remembered anything definite," Tammy said.

"You may remember more when you talk to the artist," Jamie said. She pushed the tea toward Tammy. "Drink up."

Tammy took a long sip of tea, then set the cup down. "I already feel better, talking to you," she said. "Though I don't see how you do the job you do. I mean, I see enough nasty stuff as a reporter, but I only have to take pictures and report. I don't have to wade right into the awful, dangerous stuff or deal with truly horrible people."

"Most of the time the job isn't like that," Jamie said. "The work is interesting, and I believe it's important."

"Good for you." Tammy picked up her cup and smiled at Jamie over its rim. "When this is over, maybe I'll interview you for the paper."

"Why would you want to do that?"

"Eagle Mountain's first female deputy—that's newsworthy, don't you think?"

"Only if we were in the 1950s. I really don't want to call attention to myself."

"I'll keep asking, until you change your mind."

"Right. So what else can we talk about?"

Tammy laughed. "Fair enough. Are you going to the charity masquerade tomorrow night?"

Jamie had already forgotten about the party. "I promised I would. I have to figure out some kind of costume. Will you be there?"

"You bet. I'm even looking forward to it. I mean, if no one else can recognize me in my costume, that means the killers can't, either. I'm hoping I can relax and have a good time."

The two chatted about possible costumes and the weather forecast while they finished their tea, then Tammy phoned her brother. When he arrived, Jamie walked her to the door, but the gist of their conversation kept replaying in her mind. Jamie hadn't thought about the killers being at the party. But if they were locals, why wouldn't they attend and mingle?

And maybe even pick out their next victim.

Chapter Eleven

"Now you remember what I told you?" Jamie adjusted the cat ears atop Donna's head, then looked her sister in the eye. "Tell me."

"I'm to stay with Henry and his mom and not talk to strangers." Donna smoothed the end of the long tail attached to the back of her leggings. "But if everyone is in costume, how will I know if they're a stranger or not?"

Donna had a point. Jamie figured most people would recognize her and Donna, despite Donna's painted-on whiskers and pink nose, and the feathered mask Jamie had added to her own jester's getup. But if someone went all out with a full mask or a furry suit or something, identification might be difficult. "If you're not sure you know someone, ask their name," she said. "If they won't tell you, or you don't recognize the name, walk away. But the best thing is to stay with Henry and Mrs. O'Keefe." Henry's mom had volunteered to chaperone the couple, for which Jamie was deeply grateful. Though she and Donna were attending the charity ball to support those in need, Jamie planned on working, too, trying to spot a killer or killers among the partygoers.

To that end, she'd chosen a costume that allowed her to move, and run if necessary, and that made it easy to conceal her weapon. The multicolored satin tunic, black tights and flat shoes fit the bill perfectly, though she was sure she was in for a night of teasing from her fellow officers. She picked up the jester's hat from the table by the door and handed Donna her coat. "Come on. We don't want to be late."

Volunteers had transformed the Eagle Mountain Community Center into a ballroom that was one part Mardi Gras excess and one part high school prom sentiment. Swaths of black and purple fabric draped the walls and white twinkle lights glowed everywhere. A mirrored disco ball straight out of the 1980s cast spangled light across the dance floor, where a Tyrannosaurus Rex gyrated with a veiled belly dancer and a firefighter in full bunker gear swayed with a woman in a hot pink, retro ski suit.

"Wow!" Donna gasped as she and Jamie waited in line to surrender their tickets.

"Hello, ladies." Adelaide greeted Jamie and Donna when they reached the front of the line. "You both look very nice." Adelaide had teased and sprayed her hair into a 1960s-style beehive and wore oversize hoop earrings and a pink-and-orange paisley minidress.

"What are you supposed to be?" Donna asked.

"I'm a go-go dancer." She stood and lifted one leg to show off orange tights and white, knee-high boots. "Before your time, of course, but I remember those days fondly."

Jamie returned the older woman's grin. She could picture a younger Adelaide grooving to the beat in her psychedelic finery.

They moved farther into the room and surveyed the packed house. Most of the town must have turned out for the fund-raiser. "How are we ever going to find Henry?" Donna asked.

"We'll look for him," Jamie said. "If he's here, we'll find him."

She scanned the milling crowd and spotted Travis right away. No costume and mask could disguise the sheriff's erect form and focused expression. In any case, he was dressed as an Old West lawman, complete with a silver star pinned to a brocaded vest. Next to him his fiancée, Lacy Milligan, looked stunning in a short red-and-black flounced dress that pegged her as an old-time saloon girl.

Gage Walker continued the Old West theme with a mountain man getup, including a fringed buckskin shirt, coonskin cap and what might have been a coyote pelt thrown over one shoulder. The woman in the calico dress, her hair in a prim bun that effectively hid the blue dip-dyed ends, must be his wife, Maya. She was carrying an old-fashioned slate and chalk. Of course. Maya was a school-marm—fitting, since she taught at the local high school.

"There's Henry!" Donna jumped up and down and waved enthusiastically at a brown-clad figure hurrying toward them. As he drew nearer, Jamie realized Henry was dressed as a dog, with floppy ears, whiskers and a shiny black nose.

Mrs. O'Keefe followed him across the floor. A white wig and a cap covered her brown hair, and a dress so wide it must have been held out by a hoopskirt forced her to turn sideways as she maneuvered through the crowd. She held a large plush bone in one hand. "I'm Old Mother Hubbard," she said after they had exchanged greetings. She tapped Henry on the shoulder with the stuffed bone. "This is my poor dog."

Henry paused only a moment to grin at his mother before turning back to Donna. "We want to go get some food," he said.

"All right," Mrs. O'Keefe said. "I'll come with you." She picked up her skirts. "Do you want to come, too?" she asked Jamie.

"Thanks, but I need to check in with the sheriff."

Jamie worked her way through the crowd, past two superheroes, a soldier, three princesses, a witch and many other costumes she couldn't recognize. While she could guess the identity of almost everyone she passed, a knight in full armor and a six-foot rabbit confounded her.

Gage and Maya had moved on by the time Jamie reached Travis and Lacy, and the DJ had turned up the music, so that they had to lean close to hear each other. "Any instructions?" she asked.

"Mingle," Travis said. "Keep an eye on other single women to see if any strangers approach them."

"Stranger is a relative term," Lacy said, scanning the crowd. "There are some wild costumes. Did you see the guy dressed as an octopus?"

"Just keep your eyes open," Travis said. "And have fun."

Lacy linked her arm in his. "Speaking of fun, I want to check out the silent auction table."

The normally stern sheriff's face transformed as he smiled at Lacy—a smile so full of love and tenderness that it made Jamie's breath catch. What would it be like to have a man look at her that way?

"Hello, Deputy. That's a very amusing costume you have."

She whirled around to find herself face-to-face with a melodrama villain, complete with an outrageously curled black mustache, black suit with a black string tie and a dapper cane. Nate shook one pointed end of her collar, making the attached bell jingle. "Do you know how to juggle?" he asked.

"I do it every day," she deadpanned.

He nodded slowly. "Yes, I guess you do." Leaning on a polished black cane, he looked out at the crowded dance floor. "I'd ask you to dance, but this cast is seriously cramping my style."

She had a sudden memory of dancing with him in a crowded high school gym. They hadn't worried about style back then, content to hold each other close and sway in time to the music. She looked away, afraid the unexpected swell of longing for that time showed on her face. "Don't take this wrong," she said. "But I'm trying to look like I'm at this party alone. Nothing personal."

"Single and vulnerable," he said. "Still trying to lure the killer?"

She shrugged. "It's worth a try."

"What will you do if he takes the bait?"

"I won't let him reel me in, if that's what you're worried about. The idea is to string him along, and find out as much about him as I can."

"Of course, you might just end up with a perfectly innocent man who has a thing for women wearing bells."

She was pretty sure her mask diluted the effect of the scowl she aimed at him, but he got the message. "All right." He held up his hands and took a step back. "I'll see if I can find any tall, sort of masculine women with long blond hair."

He hobbled away into the crowd and Jamie moved toward the buffet table. She caught a glimpse of Donna and Henry on the edge of the dance floor, moving to an upbeat rock song. They made up for their awkwardness with enthusiasm and joy. Donna stood with her hands in the air, swiveling her hips, her tail switching from side to side, while Henry pumped his arms and bent his knees, his puppy-dog ears flopping as he nodded in time to the music. Jamie put a hand to her chest as if she could contain the sudden, fierce swell of love for her sister.

Jamie had been seven when Donna was born. Her parents had explained that Donna was different and would need Jamie's help growing up. But all Jamie had seen was her sister's perfection—her round, dimpled face and trusting brown eyes. As soon as she was able, Donna watched Jamie's every move and tried hard to imitate her big sister. Jamie cheered her on, helped with the exercises and therapy doctors prescribed, played games with her and read to her. Other little girls played with dolls, but Jamie had a real live doll in Donna.

In high school things had changed some, as Jamie grew more independent, working a job, dating, going out with friends and doing so many things that didn't include Donna. And Donna had her own friends, too. She participated in Special Olympics and worked part-time after school. But her sister was always important to her. One of the toughest things about leaving to go to college had been moving away from Donna. Jamie had told herself it would be good for her sister to not be as dependent on her, but she had never hesitated to come home after her parents had died. Donna needed her—and Jamie needed Donna, too. Caring for her sister had helped heal her grief. Donna had given her a purpose and a focus at a time when her life seemed so out of control.

She moved around the room, greeting people she knew, talking briefly, but always moving on. She wanted anyone watching to know that she was here alone, the kind of woman who might be easy prey. After an hour or so she moved on to the buffet table and began filling her plate with food contributed by restaurants in town. She leaned over to snag a mini kebab and jostled a man dressed as a pirate. "Sorry," she said, stepping back.

"Oh, no, ma *cher*. It is *moi* who should apologize." The French accent was cheesy and obviously fake, but it went with his over-the-top costume—satin-clad pirate, complete with dreadlocks, a fake beard and eye patch. A chill raced up Jamie's spine as she studied him. She was sure she didn't know this guy. She was also sure the costume—and the accent—were designed to hide his identity.

She shifted her plate to her left hand and stuck out her right. "I'm Jamie," she said.

"So charmed, I am sure," he oozed, then bent and kissed her hand. She had to restrain herself from snatching it back, and suppressed a silent *ew*.

Instead, she forced herself to smile and to look at him with what she hoped was a flirtatious expression. "Are you new in town?" she asked. "I don't think I recognize you."

"That is the idea, is it not?" He grinned, revealing a gold tooth—fake, she was sure. It was the kind of thing that might distract a person from looking too closely. But she wasn't distracted. She studied him, searching for any identifying marks. But the wig, beard and eye patch did a good job of hiding most of his features. The one eye that looked back at her was brown, but since that was the most common eye color, the detail might not be significant.

He noticed her studying him and looked away. "I have seen you around town, I think," he said. "Do you live here?"

"Yes. And you?"

"I am a pirate. I live a life of adventure on the high seas." He turned away and selected a cheese puff from a tray. "Have you tasted these?" he asked. "Delicious."

"Yeah. They look great." She added one to her plate and pretended to survey the rest of the offerings in front of him, while observing him out of the corner of her eye.

"You are here alone?" he asked after a moment.

"Yeah. Uh, my boyfriend and I just split and I've been

kind of bummed. But I figure it's time I got back out there and circulated, you know?" Maybe if he thought she was on the rebound, he'd mistake her for an easy mark.

"Ahhh." Hard to interpret that remark. And the fake beard was so full she couldn't tell much about his expression. Had the sheriff or one of her fellow deputies noticed her talking to this guy yet? It wouldn't hurt to have another person she could compare notes with later about his appearance. "Are you here alone?" she asked.

"Yes. Like you, I am all by myself." He set aside his half-eaten food. "Would you like to dance?"

"Sure."

They moved toward the dance floor. When he took her hand, she pretended to look eager, though she couldn't hide her shock when he pulled her so forcefully against him. Still smiling, she pushed back, putting a few inches between them, primarily because she didn't want him to discover that she was armed.

"You do not like me to take liberties," he said, in that same cheesy accent.

"Well, I hardly know you." She forced herself to smile into his eyes. "Though I wouldn't mind getting to know you better."

"That can be arranged." They swayed together until the song ended, then he led her from the dance floor. "Why don't we go outside, where it's quiet, so we can talk," he said, taking her hand and pulling her toward the door.

The last thing she intended to do was go out into the parking lot with him. She resisted. "I'm having fun," she said. "Let's have another dance." Maybe she could get some of his DNA under her fingernails—scratch him or something. She'd have to make it look like an accident...

"I want to talk, not dance." He pulled her toward the

door once more. He was really strong. He wouldn't have had much trouble overpowering the women who were killed, especially with another man helping him.

"Jamie! Jamie! Where are you going?"

Jamie stopped and spun around as Donna jogged up to her. "Where are you going?" Donna asked.

"Nowhere." She pulled free of the pirate's grasp and smoothed Donna's hair. "Are you having a good time?" she asked.

"Yes." Donna looked at the pirate. "Who is this?"

"A friend," the pirate said. He moved as if to take Donna's hand, but Jamie blocked him. The thought of this creep touching her sister made her skin crawl.

"Do you need something?" Jamie asked Donna, pulling her sister's attention away from the pirate.

"I want to go with Henry and his mom back to his place. She said we could watch a movie and make popcorn. All this noise makes my head hurt."

Jamie glanced over Donna's shoulder and saw Mrs. O'Keefe and Henry approaching. "If it's all right with you, I thought Donna could spend the night," Mrs. O'Keefe said. "We can swing by your house and get her things. She can sleep in the guest room, right across the hall from me. I'll take good care of her."

"Please, Jamie! Please let me go." Donna put her hands together, begging.

"All right," Jamie said. "That sounds like a good idea." A great one, really. Donna would be away from the pirate and his friend and safe, and Jamie would be free to focus on her work.

"Thanks!" Donna kissed Jamie's cheek, then hurried away.

Jamie turned back toward the pirate, but he was gone.

She scanned the crowd, searching for him, but he had vanished. Had he left the party—or only gone in search of his next victim?

AFTER MAKING A TOUR of the room and greeting a few people he knew, Nate made a few bids on silent auction items, then filled a plate with food from the buffet and found a chair against one wall. He would have preferred to spend the evening with Jamie. He had looked forward to catching up on all that had been happening in their lives the past four years. He wanted to prove to her that he could be her friend, without demanding more from her than she wanted to give.

Which meant he had to respect this crazy idea she had about putting herself out there as bait for the Ice Cold Killers. No doubt she was capable of looking out for herself, but it wouldn't hurt for him to act as backup, so he made sure to choose a chair that gave him a view of most of the room. He munched chicken wings and cheese balls as she made her way around the room, then stiffened and set aside his plate as a man in a pirate costume started hitting on her. Nate wasn't close enough to hear what the man was saying, but he could read the guy's body language well enough.

When the pirate grabbed Jamie's hand and kissed it, Nate gripped the curved handle of the cane until his knuckles ached. It was made of stout wood and could serve as an effective weapon if need be. He imagined breaking it over the head of this guy, who was standing much too close to Jamie. Who was this joker, to think he could get away with leering at her that way?

Was that the kind of man she wanted—one who leered and kissed her hand, and came on too strong? Was she falling for charm that was as fake as his dreadlocks?

"Do you know him?"

Nate turned to find Travis had taken the chair next to him. The sheriff nodded toward the man with Jamie. "Can you tell who he is under the wig and beard?"

"No." Nate went back to studying the man. The fake beard, mustache, dreadlocks and eye patch covered three-fourths of the man's face. "I don't think I've seen him before."

"Me, either," Travis said. "And Jamie doesn't act as if she recognizes him."

"What makes you think that?" Jamie was smiling at the man now.

"She's leaning away from him," Travis said. "And there's a lot of tension in her shoulders."

Nate saw what Travis meant and felt his own shoulders relax a little. Jamie was flirting with the man, but she wasn't truly attracted to him. She was interested in him as a suspect. "Do you think he's one of the guys you're looking for?" Nate asked, keeping his voice low.

"Maybe," Travis said.

Nate shifted his weight to one hip and slid his phone from his pocket. "Face me and pretend to be posing for a picture," he said. "I'll zoom in for a shot of the pirate."

"Good idea." Travis angled toward Nate, his back to Jamie and the buccaneer. Nate snapped a few photos, zooming in as far as the camera would go. He tucked the phone into his pocket and both men sat back in their chairs again. "I'll send you the files and maybe your tech people can do something with them."

"Thanks," Travis said.

The pirate led Jamie onto the dance floor, where he plastered himself to her. Nate had to grip the edge of his seat to keep from storming out there and prying the two apart. But Jamie put some distance between them and managed the rest of the dance with a pained expression on her face. The song ended and a tug-of-war between the two followed. "I think he's trying to get her to leave," Nate said. He shoved to his feet. "Maybe I need to go interrupt."

Travis put out a restraining hand. "Give it a minute."

Nate stilled but didn't sit back down. Jamie and the pirate continued to argue, and then Donna, Henry and Henry's mother hurried toward her. The pirate stepped back, then began to melt into the crowd.

"I'm going to follow him," Travis said and left.

Donna and the others exited the room and Jamie looked around. Nate hurried toward her, moving as fast as he could with the cane. "I watched the whole thing," he said by way of greeting. "Are you okay?"

"I'm fine." She searched the crowd. "I think he might have been one of the men we're looking for," she said, her voice tight with excitement.

"Travis is following him," Nate said. He touched her shoulder, forcing her to look at him. "What did he say to you?"

"He flirted in this horrible French accent," she said. "In fact, it was so bad, I think that was the point."

"He wanted to disguise his voice," Nate said.

"Yes, I think so."

"After you danced—was he trying to convince you to leave with him?" Nate asked.

"Yes," she said. "But when Donna and the O'Keefes interrupted, he slipped away."

"He didn't want anyone else to see him with you," Nate said.

"I tried to memorize everything I could about him," she said. "But his costume covered up everything. And he didn't have any really outstanding features—no visible moles or a crooked nose or anything."

"I took a few pictures of him with my phone," Nate

said. "Travis will have them analyzed. Maybe he can get something from that."

"That was a good idea," Jamie said.

Travis joined them once more, a little breathless. "I lost him," he said. "I saw him slip out the back door to the parking lot, but by the time I made it out there, he was gone."

"Did you get a look at his car?" Nate asked.

Travis shook his head, then turned to Jamie. "What information did he give you?" he asked.

"Not much," she said. "He avoided any of my questions about who he was or where he was from. The costume hid most of his face, and he spoke with a terrible French accent." She sighed. "About all I can tell you is that he has brown eyes, good teeth and is about six feet tall, average build. And he's strong. I think he probably works out. He could have easily overpowered those women."

"I think he's fairly young," Nate said. "He moved like a younger man."

Jamie nodded. "Yes. In his twenties, I think. Maybe early thirties."

"That doesn't give us much to go on," Nate said.

"Send me those photographs you took," Travis said. "We'll print them up and try to find out if anyone else talked to him tonight." He looked around the room. "We'll talk to as many women here as we can tonight. Let's find out if he approached any of them. Maybe they saw or heard something we didn't."

"Adelaide is taking tickets at the door," Jamie said. "She probably saw him when he came in, and she talks to everyone."

"I'll question her," Travis said. "We'll also compare the photograph to the sketches the police artist did from Henry and Tammy's descriptions."

"Were the sketches of the same man?" Nate asked.

"Two different men," Travis said. "If we're right, the man Henry saw with Michaela—the one who called himself Al—is the masked man who came up behind Tammy. The man she described to us is the decoy and accomplice."

They separated to question the other party guests. Though a couple of people Nate talked to had seen the pirate from a distance, none of them had spoken with him. By midnight, the party began breaking up. Nate met up with Travis and Jamie once more. "Adelaide remembers the guy," Travis said. "But she couldn't tell us anything we didn't already know."

"I found one woman he approached," Jamie said. "He asked her to dance, but then her boyfriend returned with a drink and he left in a hurry."

"He doesn't want any witnesses," Travis said. "I'm becoming more and more certain that this is one of the killers." He watched guests file toward the exit. "I don't think there's anything more we can do here tonight. Let's go home, and in the morning we can take a look at the photos Nate took."

He left them. "I'd better get my coat," Jamie said, heading for the cloakroom.

Nate limped alongside her. "Where's Donna?" he asked.

"She's going to spend the night at Henry's house."

"So you're going home alone?"

"I guess I am." A smile ghosted across her lips. "That's something I haven't done in a very long time."

"I'll follow you home," he said.

"You don't have to do that." She accepted her coat—the same down parka she had worn the day he met her and Donna snowshoeing—from the man behind the counter in the cloakroom.

"I know." Nate took the coat and held it for her. "But

there's a killer out there who may have been targeting you. I think it's safer if I follow you."

She slipped her arms into the coat, then glanced up at him. "Okay. Thanks."

They fed into the stream of vehicles leaving the community center parking lot, and he followed her to the bungalow on Oak Street. At one time he could have driven to this place blindfolded. He had spent as much time here back in high school as he had in his own house. He parked behind Jamie and followed her to the front door.

"I'll be all right now," she said, as she unlocked the door.

"Humor me and let me make sure," he said.

As soon as she opened the door, the three dogs galloped toward them, barking furiously when they saw Nate. "Quiet!" Jamie shouted. "It's only Nate."

He had removed the fake mustache in the truck on the way here, along with the hat, so that he hoped he looked more like himself. He bent and offered the back of his hand to the biggest dog—the husky—to sniff. The other dogs followed suit and soon he was patting all three while they jostled for attention.

"They're obviously fine," Jamie said. "They wouldn't act like this if someone had managed to break in."

Nate said nothing, but stumped through all the downstairs rooms, looking for signs of any disturbance. Though, since he didn't live here, how would he know if something was out of place or not, unless the intruder had done something obvious like leave a window open?

"Do you want to look under the bed, too?" she asked, when he returned to her in the foyer, at the bottom of the stairs leading to the second floor.

No, but he wouldn't mind looking *in* her bed. He didn't say the words out loud, but they must have shown on his face. She blushed. She looked so impossibly sweet and sexy. He reached out and removed the jester's hat, and smoothed back her hair.

"What?" she asked.

"Are you sure you'll be okay here tonight, by yourself?" he asked. "If you're nervous, I could stay. I'd sleep on the couch, I promise."

"I'll be fine." She took his arm and led him to the door. "Go home and I'll see you tomorrow at the sheriff's department."

"All right." Maybe he wouldn't go right home. Maybe he'd park his truck down the block and watch her place for a while, just to be sure. She didn't have to know.

He opened the door and started to step onto the porch, but the sight of a dark-colored SUV cruising slowly as it approached made him freeze. "Who's that?" he asked, nodding toward the vehicle.

Jamie peered past him, one hand on his shoulder. "I don't know."

He reached behind her and switched off the porch light, plunging them into shadow. He was aware of her labored breathing as the vehicle drove slowly past. Though the driver was hard to make out in the darkness, Nate was sure he turned his head to look at them.

"The license plate on the car is obscured," Jamie whispered.

Nate pulled her back into the house, and shut and locked the door. "Do you think that was him?" Jamie asked. "The man at the dance?"

"I don't know. It could have been." Nate pulled her close, his heart pounding. He needed to reassure himself that she was safe. She didn't fight him, but relaxed in his embrace, her head nestled in the hollow of his shoulder. "I'm not leaving you here alone," he said.

"No." She lifted her head, her eyes searching his. Then she rose up on tiptoe and pressed her lips to his, her eyes still open, still locked to his.

Chapter Twelve

Nate closed his eyes and gave himself up to the kiss, caressing her with lips and hands, welcoming the tangle of her tongue with his, the soft sweetness of her mouth, the dizzying *want* her touch sent blazing through him.

He didn't know how long it was before she pulled away. He was breathing hard, half wondering if he was dreaming, telling himself he had to keep it together. She had to set the pace here. He had promised himself he wouldn't take more than she would give, and it was a promise he was determined to keep.

"I don't think you should sleep on the couch," she said.

He released his hold on her and took a step back. He couldn't think clearly when she was so close. "Are you sure about this?" he asked, his voice hoarse, not sounding like his own.

She nodded. "I know if I turn my back on these feelings—if I don't give us this chance—then I'm going to regret it."

"Yeah." He raked one hand through his hair. "Yeah, I'll regret it, too." It felt big and important, a move that would change him—would change them. But it felt right, too.

She leaned past him and double-checked the door lock, then took his hand and led him up the stairs.

Jamie climbed the stairs, Nate's grip firm and reassuring in hers, helping to calm the butterflies going wild in her chest. She led him down the hall, but not to the room that had been hers growing up. Nate had sneaked up to that room one night, climbing the drainpipe and shimmying across the porch roof to climb into her window. They hadn't really done anything—too fearful of the consequences if they had been caught. But there had been something so thrilling about cuddling together on her bed—she in flannel pajamas decorated with pink hearts, he in jeans and a sweatshirt. They had kissed and whispered to each other until, hearing her father get up to go to the bathroom and sure his next stop would be her bedroom, he had slipped out the window and to the ground once more.

But she didn't take him to that room. About a year after her parents' death, she had moved into the master bedroom. She had given away their king-size bed and replaced it with an iron four-poster she had purchased from a local antique shop, making payments each pay period for three months until the bed was hers. She had stored the family photos that had adorned the walls and replaced them with black-and-white photos of Eagle Mountain landscapes, also purchased from a local shop.

Nate stopped in the doorway and surveyed the room. "What?" she asked. "Are you weirded out because this used to be my parents' room?"

"No. I'd forgotten this was theirs. I was just admiring it. Admiring you."

"You were looking at the walls—you weren't looking at me."

"I was admiring what the walls tell me about you."

She faced him, hands on his shoulders. "What do they tell you?"

His eyes met hers. "That you love beautiful things. Not

frilly or over the top, but beautiful." He tossed the cane aside and fit his hands to her waist. "That you love this place—you love Eagle Mountain."

"I do," she said. That was one of the things that made her so uneasy about him. Nate had come back to Eagle Mountain, but she didn't sense that it was home for him—not the way it was home for her.

But she didn't want to think about that now. And she didn't want to talk anymore. When he opened his mouth as if to speak, she put two fingers to his lips to silence him, then she began loosening the knot of his string tie.

Tie loosened, she began working her way down the buttons on his starched white shirt. He slid his hand around to lower the zipper on her tunic, the sudden rush of cool air on her back mitigated by his warm hand smoothing down her spine. Impatient to be closer still, she pushed his jacket off his shoulders, then his shirt, her heart thudding harder as she admired the defined muscles of his chest and shoulders. Stripped of camouflaging clothing, he resembled a Viking warrior.

"Your turn," he murmured and pushed the tunic over her shoulders and down to the floor, followed quickly by the tights, until she was standing before him in her bra and panties, goose bumps prickling her arms and shoulders. He stripped out of his trousers and stood before her in boxers—which did little to hide his desire. She was contemplating this, dry mouthed and breathless, when he forced her attention to more practical concerns. "What about protection?" he asked.

"In the drawer by the bed."

He moved the short distance to the bed, opened the drawer of the nightstand and took out a package of condoms, and gave her a questioning look.

"Don't flatter yourself," she said, her face burning.

"I didn't say anything."

"You didn't have to—I could see it in your eyes." She joined him by the bed. "You thought I bought these, planning to bring you up here."

"It's none of my business why you bought them," he said. "I'm just glad you have them." He sat on the side of the bed and began to open the package.

But she couldn't not tell him now. "There was this guy I went out with a few times. I thought maybe…" She shook her head. "Nothing came of it." She pressed her lips together. She had said enough. She didn't want him to know there hadn't been anyone else since him. She hadn't dated much, what with Donna and her job. And when she did go out with someone, she found it difficult to let down her guard with men.

He set aside the condom box and reached for her. "It's okay. Come here."

She crawled onto the bed next to him, nerves warring with excitement. She wanted this—needed this. But she was afraid of making a mistake.

Then he was kissing her, hands gently exploring, warm fingers coaxing delicious sensations from her. She began to relax and to make her own discoveries about his body. Everything about him—about being here with him—was both familiar and new. He was Nate—the first man and the only man she had ever made love with. The man she had trusted with all her secrets. He was the same—yet very different. He was bigger than she remembered. Broader and more muscular. A man, where he had been a boy.

"You've grown into a beautiful woman," he said, shaping his hand to one breast.

"I guess we've both changed," she said, breathless again as he dragged his thumb across her sensitive nipple.

"For the better." He kissed her fiercely, his hand moving

down to stroke her sex, until desire all but overwhelmed her. She felt impatient, desperate and a little out of control.

"I really don't want to wait anymore," she said, digging her fingers into the taut skin of his shoulders.

In answer, he held her close and plunged two fingers into her, then began to stroke more deftly. She came fast and hard, thrusting against him, crying out in relief. He held her a little while longer and then, smiling, he reached for the box of condoms.

When they came together again, she felt more in control, though no less eager for him. As he filled her she let out a long sigh that grew to a low moan as he began to move. Nervousness long vanquished, she matched his rhythm, every sense focused on the moment. Desire began to build once more, lifting her up, climbing with him to that wonderful height. When at last she could wait no longer and leaped, he followed, the two of them clinging tightly together for the glide back down to earth.

Neither of them said anything for long minutes. She rested her head on his chest and reveled in the strong, steady thud of his heartbeat, and the rise and fall of his body beneath hers with each breath. She felt so connected to him it took all her strength to shove off the bed and head to the bathroom.

When she returned a few moments later, she thought from the steady, deep rhythm of his breathing that he was asleep. She slid in next to him and he reached for her. "I was afraid for you tonight," he said.

It took her a moment to comprehend that he was talking about earlier in the evening, when the pirate had approached her. "I was never in any danger," she said.

"I know. But if that was one of the killers—he's murdered six women, seemingly at random. Someone with a mind like that—it's terrifying."

"Yes, it is." She propped herself on one elbow, wanting to see his face. "Thank you for following me home and for offering to stay."

"You would have sent me away, if we hadn't seen that car driving past."

"I would have regretted it. I might even have called you back before you got to your truck."

He laughed and pulled her close in a bear hug. "I was going to park my truck at the end of the block and watch your house all night, to make sure you were safe."

The words brought a lump to her throat. To think that he cared so much. Fearing losing control, she rolled onto her back and searched for a less emotional topic of conversation. "How is your ankle?" she asked.

"Sex is a terrific pain reliever." He lay back beside her. "I figure in another week or so I'll be able to ditch the cane."

"I'm glad it's not bothering you too much."

"The worst part is the boredom. I haven't been off work this long since I graduated college. I used to think I was lazy, but I've discovered I really hate being idle."

"Me, too." She laughed. "Though sometimes I think it might be nice to try out a life of leisure—for a few days, anyway."

He reached down and laced his fingers in her hand. "You've got a lot on your plate. Tell me about Donna."

The question surprised her. It wasn't as if Nate hadn't known Donna almost as long as he had known Jamie. "What about her?"

"She seems to have things together and is pretty smart. Will she ever be able to live on her own?"

Jamie tensed and took her hand from his. Why was he asking that question? Why now? "Maybe. But she'll always need help. The man I end up with has to take Donna as part of the bargain." Might as well be up-front about that now. She held her breath, waiting for his answer.

"Of course," he said. "I like Donna. I always have. It's good to see her so happy."

She relaxed again. He wasn't lying. His acceptance and even affection for Donna was one of the reasons she had fallen in love with him. "I hope she does okay tonight. She's never spent a night away from home before. She's never wanted to."

"And it feels strange to you," he said.

"Yes. But everything about this night is a little strange."

"You didn't think I'd be here with you."

"No. But I'm glad you are." She took his hand again.

He rolled over to face her and pulled her close once more. "I'm always here for you," he said. "I'm going to keep saying that until you believe it."

She believed he meant his words, but she didn't trust him not to break his own promise. She owed it to herself not to let him break her heart, too.

NATE LEFT JAMIE'S place after breakfast the next morning. She didn't come right out and say so, but he sensed she wanted him gone before her sister returned home. He could understand explaining his presence might be awkward, and he was willing to let her ease into the idea of the two of them being together again.

He headed toward the sheriff's department, and along the way found himself searching driveways and side streets for the dark SUV that had driven past Jamie's house the night before. Had the driver really been the man in the pirate costume—the murderer? Or had he and Jamie let paranoia and fear get the better of them? In broad daylight, it was easy to think the latter, but he decided to reserve judgment until after he talked to the sheriff.

Travis was at his desk and hard at work. Upcoming wedding or not, the sheriff was going to spend every spare hour on this case.

"Any luck getting an ID from the photo I sent, or the police artist sketches?" Nate asked, after Adelaide had escorted him to Travis's office.

"No." Travis passed a sheet of paper to Nate. "Take a look."

The paper featured side-by-side comparisons of the photograph Nate had taken of the pirate and two sketches of men. "Are these the police artist sketches from the information Henry and Tammy provided?" Nate asked.

"Yes. Do either of them look familiar to you?"

Nate studied the images, comparing each to the photograph of the pirate, and to his mental images of people he knew. "I don't recognize them," he said. "And neither of them looks like the pirate to me."

"The police artist thinks the guy in the pirate costume may have made his nose look larger with makeup, and the gold tooth is probably a fake," Travis said. "He suggested we look for someone with a theatrical background, so I asked the local theatre group to give me a list of any men who have been involved in their productions." He passed Nate a second sheet of paper. "I've highlighted the names of men who fall into the right age group. There are only half a dozen."

Nate's eyebrows rose. "Gage's name is on here."

"Yeah. He was in a comedy revue they did a couple of years ago. I left it on there to give him a hard time, but he was with me when several of the murders occurred, so we can safely rule him out."

Nate tossed the papers back onto the desk and lowered himself into the visitor's chair. "Last night, I followed Jamie home from the community center," he said.

"I was worried about her being alone. I know she's a cop, but these two killers seem to have a knack for eluding us."

"Never a bad idea to be safe," Travis said.

"Yeah, well, I was saying goodnight to her when a dark-colored SUV passed. It could have been dark gray or black, and I think it was a Toyota. It passed the house very slowly, and it seemed the driver was looking at the house—though it was dark, so I can't be sure." He gripped the arms of the chair and leaned toward Travis. "The license plate was obscured—the license plate light was out and it looked as if mud or something else had been smeared over most of the plate."

"Whoever was driving the car didn't want the plate read," Travis said. "What did you do?"

"We decided I should spend the night at her place, in case the guy came back." He kept his expression blank, letting Travis use his imagination to fill in any details on sleeping arrangements. No way was Nate going to elaborate. Travis was his friend, but he was also Jamie's boss, and there were some things he didn't need to know.

"I'll add your description of the vehicle to the other information we've collected," Travis said.

Nate sat back again, frustration churning his stomach. "What's your gut tell you on this?" he asked. Travis would have made it his business to know everything there was to know about this case, and he was good at spotting patterns and making connections.

Travis drew in a deep breath and waited a long beat before he spoke. "We're looking for two men—young and strong, from five-nine to, say, six-two," he said. "They're working together. One of them can pass as a woman while wearing a wig, and probably acted as a decoy to induce the victim to stop, so that the other man could overpower her. That decoy technique may be a new twist or something they've done all along."

"You know most of the people around here," Nate said. "Do you have any suspects in mind?"

"There were two men who were on my radar from the very first," he said. "College students who were here over winter break. My sister invited them to the scavenger hunt at the ranch where Fiona Winslow was killed."

"I think I remember them," Nate said. "Cocky young guys. They got in an argument with Fiona and Ken Rutledge."

"Right. They may have been the last to see Fiona before she left Ken and went looking for a couple of the other women."

"You said they were on your radar? But no longer?"

"They supposedly left town when the road reopened briefly earlier in the month. At least, I haven't seen them around, and they moved out of the cabin where they were staying."

"But they could still be here," Nate said. "Hiding."

"They could."

"I assume you contacted the school they attend?"

"I did. Neither of them reported for classes. But they could have decided to quit school."

"What about parents? Friends?"

"I don't have that information," Travis said. "The aunt who owns the cabin here where they were staying hasn't heard from them. If the roads were open, I'd send someone to Fort Collins to talk to people. I contacted a local investigator and asked him to do some checking, but we don't have much of a budget for that kind of thing, and so far he hasn't come up with anything significant. No one can say for sure these two are in Fort Collins—but no one is sure they aren't, either."

"I've got lots of time on my hands," Nate said. "I could drive around the county, do some checking. Tell me who I'm looking for. I sort of remember them from before, but not clearly."

"I'll print out their ID photos for you. Their names are Alex Woodruff and Tim Dawson."

"Alex. That could be the Al who was with Michaela," Nate said.

"Maybe. Tammy and Henry are coming in this morning to look at some photographs, including the one you took last night. We'll see if they can pick out Alex and Tim."

"I have a few ideas of places they might be staying," Nate said.

"Tell me, and I'll send a couple of deputies out to check," Travis said.

Nate shook his head. "I want to look around first before you waste any of your resources. I'll let you know if I see anything suspicious."

"If you find these two, call for backup," Travis said. "After what they did to these women, they won't think twice about killing you."

"I'm no hero," Nate said. "If we find them, we'll send in our own army to take them. They won't know what hit them."

"The women they killed probably didn't, either," Travis said. "I want to make it tougher for them to take anyone by surprise, so I'm holding a press conference at eleven. I'm going to let everyone know about the possible use of a decoy, as well as release the photograph of the pirate and the two police sketches. Maybe we'll get lucky and someone knows where these two are hiding."

"What about releasing the photos of Tim and Alex?" Nate asked. "That's probably your best bet of finding out if anyone around here has seen them lately."

"I may do that, too." The printer that sat on the credenza behind Travis whirred and he leaned back and plucked a sheet of paper from the tray. "These are Alex Woodruff and Tim Dawson's driver's license photos," he said as he handed the printout to Nate.

Nate studied the photos of the two young men—one with straight, sandy hair cut short, the other with a mop of brown curls. His eyes widened and his heart beat faster. "I know these guys." He looked up and met the sheriff's gaze. "They're definitely still in the area. I talked to them only four days ago."

Chapter Thirteen

Donna returned from her stay with the O'Keefes full of descriptions of what she saw, what they ate and everything she had done. Jamie listened to this nonstop narrative as she cleaned up the kitchen, delighted the evening had gone so well—and only a little guilty that she had scarcely missed her sister, focused as she was on Nate. Donna, so caught up in her own happy memories, never asked how Jamie had spent her evening.

At nine forty-five, she and Donna loaded all three dogs into the car for their annual checkups. Darcy Marsh was the newest veterinarian in town, a pleasant young woman who had a real rapport with animals. She greeted Donna, Jamie and the three dogs enthusiastically. "I saw you at the masquerade last night but never made my way around to you," she said, as she washed her hands before examining the dogs.

"I'm sorry I missed you," Jamie said.

"What was your costume?" Donna asked. "I was a cat."

"You were a very cute cat," Darcy said. "Ryder and I went as Roy Rogers and Dale Evans—complete with stick horses." She laughed. "At least they raised a lot of money to help people who have been hurt by the road closures. And we had a lot of fun."

"How is Ryder?" Jamie asked. Darcy's fiancé, Ryder Stewart, was a Colorado State Highway Patrol trooper.

"He's great." Darcy put her stethoscope to Targa's chest and for a few moments, the only sound in the room was the dogs panting loudly. "She sounds good," Darcy pronounced at last. "Now let's hear the rest of them."

Some fifteen minutes later, after Darcy had examined ears, teeth and every other accessible part of the three dogs, she pronounced all the canines in good health. While Jamie paid the bill, Donna and a vet tech took the dogs out to Jamie's SUV. "At the party last night, did either of you notice a guy dressed as a pirate?" Jamie asked Darcy and her receptionist, Stacy. "He had long dreadlocks, a beard and mustache and an eye patch, and he spoke with a cheesy French accent."

"I didn't see anybody like that," Stacy said as she accepted Jamie's credit card.

"Me, either." Darcy leaned toward Jamie. "Why do you ask?"

Jamie shook her head. "I was just wondering."

But Darcy wasn't going to be put off so easily. "Are you working on this Ice Cold Killer case?" she asked.

"I think it's safe to say every law enforcement officer in the county is working on this case," Jamie hedged.

"Yeah. But the sheriff's department would know more than anyone." Darcy rubbed her arms, as if she was chilled. "I just wondered if you're any closer to finding out who is killing all these women. I'm still trying to wrap my head around Kelly being gone."

Kelly Farrow had been Darcy's partner in the veterinary business—and the Ice Cold Killer's first victim. Had that really been less than a month ago?

"We have some leads," Jamie said. "I can't say anything more, but it feels like we're making progress."

"Thanks," Darcy said. "That helps a little, I guess."

It didn't really help, Jamie knew. Nothing would until the killings stopped. Even she, with all her law enforcement training, didn't feel safe alone anymore. She signed the credit card slip, said goodbye, then headed across the parking lot to where Donna and the dogs waited in the SUV. Jamie stopped short, her hand on the door handle, as a dark SUV pulled out of the lot. The hairs on the back of her neck stood up as she tried to read the vehicle's license plate and realized it was obscured.

Heart racing, she yanked open her car door and slid into the driver's seat. She started the engine with one hand and fastened her seat belt with the other, then took off out of the parking lot, tires squealing.

"Why are you driving so fast?" Donna asked, steadying herself with one hand on the dashboard.

"I thought I saw someone I know and I want to catch up with him," Jamie said. She scanned the road ahead and the driveways they passed, but there was no sign of the SUV.

"Who are you trying to find?" Donna asked.

"A man I met at the party last night."

"The pirate? Henry and I saw you talking to him." Donna shook her head. "He didn't look very nice to me."

For all her innocence and tendency to be too trusting, Donna sometimes had very good instincts about people. "I don't think he is very nice," Jamie said. "If you see him again, don't say anything to him, just come find me. If you're at work, you can call me."

"Is he a bad man?" Donna sank down in her seat, her face creased with worry.

"I don't know," Jamie said. "But you remember we talked about this before. It's good to be careful around people you don't know."

"I know."

Jamie pulled into the parking lot of the history museum and turned the SUV around. "Let's go home," she said. "We both need to get ready for work." She would tell the sheriff about the dark SUV with the obscured plate. They'd have a better chance of finding it if everyone in the department was looking. The killer had been able to hide from them so far, but as long as the roads stayed closed, he wouldn't be able to run far.

"I MET THESE two while I was on patrol Tuesday." Nate tapped the photos Travis had given him. "They were ice climbing that exposed rock face by Snowberry campground. I'm sure it was the same two, though they introduced themselves as Lex and Ty. I even thought they looked familiar, but I didn't connect them to the scavenger hunt at your ranch."

"Did they say anything to indicate where they were staying?" Travis grabbed a notepad and prepared to take notes.

"No. But they did tell me they were college graduates. They shut down my attempts to get any more information." Nate grimaced. "I stopped to ask them if they'd seen a woman with long blond hair in the area. They said no, but they mentioned the Ice Cold Killer. They seemed eager to talk about it, in fact."

"Oh? What did they say?"

"Mainly, they talked about how good the killer was at eluding you. Their exact words were that the killer was making you look like an idiot."

Travis nodded. "That fits with the suggestion we've had that the killer likes taunting law enforcement. He wants to prove he's smarter than the people who are pursuing him." He pushed his chair back. "I'm going to put out an APB on these guys, and I'll mention them at my press conference this morning. If they're in the area, someone will see them and we'll find them."

"Let me know if I can do anything to help," Nate said.

He left the sheriff's department, but instead of going home, he headed to the national forest, to the campground where he had encountered Alex and Tim. He parked at the entrance to the closed campground and walked over to the rock wall where the two had been climbing. A cold wind buffeted him as he got out of the truck. A low, gray sky promised more snow soon. The drifts at the foot of the wall lay undisturbed. Leaning heavily on his crutch, Nate scanned the area for any trace the two might have left behind. They had been meticulous about cleaning up their crime scenes, but they might not have been so careful here.

But any evidence they might have left had been buried by four inches of fresh snow. Nate returned to his truck and sat, thinking. The two young men had abandoned their aunt's cabin, perhaps because they sensed the sheriff was closing in on them. Though they had had a chance to leave town when the road opened briefly, they had elected to stick around and continue the killings. Three women had been murdered since the road had closed again. Alex and Tim had to be living somewhere. Somewhere without neighbors who might get suspicious and report them to the sheriff's department. Somewhere near here—the area where the murder of Michaela Underwood and the attack on Tammy Patterson had occurred.

Of course! He slapped the steering wheel, then started the truck. Why hadn't he seen it before? The squatters in the summer cabin—the ones who had set those animal traps around the hideout—they had to be Alex and Tim.

He drove to the cabin and parked past the cabins, at a trailhead that was little used this time of year, then hiked back to the cabins. At the chain across the road, he unholstered his weapon and took a firmer grip on his cane. He didn't intend to confront anyone who might be here, but he wanted to be prepared in case they spotted him first.

The snow on the road leading to the cabins had been packed down by the sheriff's department vehicles, making walking less arduous than the last time Nate was here. He paused halfway up to take in the scattering of cabins, each a short distance from its neighbor, with its own picnic table and outbuildings. In summer, these cabins would form a thriving community. The same families had owned these little getaways for generations, and each summer would be a reunion of old friends. Grandparents and grandchildren, parents who had come here as children themselves and new people who had married into the families would gather for barbecue and picnics, volleyball games and horseshoe competitions. With no cell phone or television service, and little space inside the small dwellings, they looked to each other and the outdoors for entertainment. Cherished memories and soul-deep relationships kept families returning year after year, and made them guard jealously what was, for many, a little piece of heaven.

In the cold of winter the cabins didn't look so inviting. They stood with shuttered windows and padlocked doors in the ringing silence of the forest, like a forgotten ghost town. Nate moved silently through the deep snow, a wraith himself, slipping between the trees.

Alert for any sign of more traps, he approached the cabins slowly, moving as stealthily as possible, hampered as he was by the crutch and the awkward air boot. He reached the cabin the traps had been taken from first. He could see them piled on the front porch, and the pale outlines where they had hung on the side of the building.

He passed the other six cabins, pausing to scan the snow around each one for any sign of activity before moving on to the cabin where he had been snared. There were more signs of activity here—depressions covered over by fresh snow that marked the path of law enforcement vehicles in and out, churned earth where he had sat waiting for rescue, and new, stout padlocks on the front and back doors.

Nate stood on the back porch of the cabin, searching through the trees. Though this cabin was the furthest back in the grouping, the forest road looped around behind it, so that anyone sitting on this porch, or looking out the back picture window, could hear approaching traffic, and even catch a glimpse of the vehicle through a gap in the trees.

Nate studied that gap, then started walking, making his way through the trees until he reached an opening that widened out to provide access to the road. Someone could park a vehicle here, access it via the path through the woods, and be gone before anyone driving on the road reached the cabin.

At the sound of an approaching vehicle, he shrank back into the trees, and watched as a Rayford County sheriff's department vehicle sped by. Grinning, Nate made his way back to the cabin.

He was waiting on the front porch when Travis and Gage pulled in. "Where's your truck?" Travis asked as he mounted the steps.

"I parked at a trailhead down the road," Nate said.

"That's a long way to walk with a busted ankle," Gage said.

"I didn't want anyone to see me."

"Whereas, we didn't care." Gage looked around them. "I guess you had the same idea we did."

"Alex and Tim must have been the squatters in this cabin," Nate said.

"It's a good place to hide," Gage said. "But they risked being trapped in here. There's only one entrance or exit."

"Not exactly." Nate stood. "Let me show you what I found." He led them back through the woods to the clearing next to the road. "If they kept a lookout, they could be out of the cabin and gone before law enforcement reached them," he said.

"They could even set up an alarm to warn them when someone was coming," Gage said as the three of them walked back to the cabin. "One of those cables you drive over and it rings a bell or something. Or a camera focused on the drive."

"We didn't find anything like that when we searched the place," Travis said.

"It's like the crime scenes," Gage said. "They know how to clean up after themselves."

"We're going to look again." Travis paused at the door and pulled on a pair of gloves. "You can help if you want, Nate."

"Sure." He accepted a pair of gloves. "It's not as if I have anything better to do."

An hour later they had combed every inch of the small cabin and come up with nothing to link Alex and Tim to either the cabin or the murders.

"They've cleared out of here," Travis said. "We'll check the other cabins, but I don't think we'll find anything."

"I walked around all of them when I arrived today," Nate said. "I didn't find any sign of activity at any of them."

"There are more of these summer cabins, aren't there?" Gage asked.

"There's one more grouping like this, with six cabins, on the other side of the county," Nate said.

"Then that's where we look next," Travis said.

"Let me go with you," Nate said.

Travis looked at the cast boot on his leg.

"I'll stay out of the action," Nate said. "I won't get in your way. But you need me there."

"Why is that?" Gage asked.

"Because I have a key to the gate," Nate said. "I can get you in there without anyone else knowing."

Chapter Fourteen

When Jamie arrived for her shift Saturday afternoon, Nate met her in the hallway. He had shed the cast boot and traded the crutch for a cane, which recalled the costume he had worn last night—and everything else about last night. But Jamie was pretty sure he could have greeted her dressed as a clown and she would have still thought about last night. "Hello," he said, the warmth in his smile making her heart beat a little faster.

"Hi." She nodded and started to move past him, determined to remain professional while she was on the job.

He turned and walked alongside her. "Busy morning?" he asked.

"Uh, yeah. We took the dogs to the vet." Should she mention the dark SUV she had seen pulling out of the lot?

"Did you catch the sheriff's press conference this morning?" Nate asked.

"No. I didn't know there was one." Was she supposed to have been there? No one had notified her. "What was it about?"

"He'll fill you in. There's a meeting in five minutes."

"I saw the notice in the locker room." Maybe she would bring up the SUV in the meeting.

Jamie and Nate were the last to enter the situation room, where Travis stood at the end of the conference table, beside a large poster on an easel. The poster featured the enlarged photos of two young men, two sketches of men and a photograph of the man dressed in the pirate costume.

"For those of you who might not have heard the press conference this morning, these are two men we want to question regarding the Ice Cold Killer murders." Travis indicated the left photo, of a slender young man with light brown hair. "This is Alex Woodruff, also known as Al, also known as Lex. He may be using other names." Travis consulted his notes. "He's twenty-two years old, until recently an undergraduate at Colorado State University, where he was studying psychology. He was also involved in the university's theatrical company, where he met Tim Dawson."

Travis indicated the second photograph, of a young man with dark, curly hair. "Tim, also known as Ty, is twenty-one, also a psych major, also active in the theatre company. As far as I have been able to determine, the two did not return to classes when they started up again last week. Previously they were staying in a cabin belonging to Tim's aunt, on County Road Five. They left there some time before last week and may have broken into and been living at Sundance cabins, though they are no longer there."

Jamie and several others at the table looked at Nate. "Yeah, that's the cabin where I was hurt," he said.

"Alex and Tim may have set those traps to slow down anyone who came after them," Travis said. "Nate talked to them that morning near Snowberry campground. They were climbing, and introduced themselves as Lex and Ty."

"They're not very creative with their aliases," Gage observed.

"They were driving a dark gray Toyota Highlander," Nate said. "I made note of the license plate and the vehicle is registered to Timothy Dawson."

"Alex Woodruff and Tim Dawson were suspects for the first three murders," Travis said. "We ruled them out after they supposedly left town. Now that we know they're back in town, we need to bring them in and question them."

He tapped the drawings in the middle of the poster. "These are drawings the police artist from Denver made after Skype sessions with Henry O'Keefe and Tammy Patterson. As you can see, they bear some resemblance to Alex and Tim, though nothing definitive. We brought Henry and Tammy back in this morning, and Henry picked out Alex's photo from a selection of photos we gave him, and identified him as the man he saw with Michaela Underwood the day before she was murdered. Tomorrow we'll take the photo to the bank and see if any of Michaela's co-workers recognize him. Tammy wasn't able to identify the man who was posing as a woman who lured her to stop, probably because of his disguise."

Travis moved on to the photograph at the bottom of the poster. "This man was at the masquerade party at the community center last night," he said. "He approached Deputy Douglas and tried to persuade her to come into the parking lot with him. When they were interrupted, he fled. He could be Alex or Tim in disguise, but we can't be sure."

He laid aside the pointer and faced them. "I've released these images to the media, and I've issued a BOLO for Alex, Tim and their vehicle. We're hoping someone will spot them and report the sighting."

"In the meantime, we're going to keep hunting for them. Dwight, I want you and Jamie to come with me and Gage this afternoon. We're going to check another set of summer cabins. These two have to be living somewhere, and since they broke into one cabin, they might try another."

He looked around the table. "Does anyone else have any questions, or anything to add?"

Jamie raised her hand.

"Yes, Deputy?"

"This morning, as I was leaving Darcy Marsh's veterinarian office, I saw a dark gray SUV, with the license plate obscured, exiting the parking lot."

"Do you think this was the same vehicle that drove by your house last night?" Travis asked.

Jamie stared. How had Travis known about that vehicle?

He must have read the question on her face. "Nate mentioned a vehicle fitting that description drove slowly past your house late last night," he said.

Nate! What else had he told his buddy, Travis, about last night? She tried hard to fight back a blush but wasn't sure she succeeded. "Yes, I think it was the same vehicle," she said. "A dark gray SUV—it could have been a Highlander—with the license plate obscured."

"We'll add that information to what we already know," Travis said.

She sat back, avoiding looking at Nate—or at anyone else. If the sheriff knew about her and Nate, how long would it be before everyone knew? Not that she was ashamed of having him spend the night, but she liked to keep her private life private. She didn't want to be the subject of gossip.

As soon as the meeting was over, she stood and made for the door. But Nate waylaid her in the hallway. "Jamie, wait up!" he called. "I'll ride with you to the cabins."

She pretended she hadn't heard, but that only made Nate raise his voice. "Jamie!"

She whirled to face him. "What?"

The word came out louder than she had intended. Now everyone was staring. She wished a hole would open in the floor and she could drop down into it.

Nate clomped up to her. "What's wrong?" he asked. "You look upset."

Aware of the others around them, she made for an empty office. Nate followed and shut the door behind him. If any of the others had seen them come in here—and they probably had, because cops didn't miss much—they'd talk. But at least what they said would only be speculation. "Did you tell Travis you were at my house last night?" she asked.

"Yes," Nate said. "He needed to know about the SUV we saw. It could be important to the case."

"Did you tell him you spent the night?"

"Yes."

She wanted to shake him but settled for clenching her hands. "Nate, how could you? He's my boss."

"I told him I stayed in case the guy in the pirate costume decided to pay you a visit. For all he knows, I slept on the couch." He put his hands on her shoulders. "I respect your privacy," he said. "And I'm not the kind of guy who shares private details like that with anyone else."

"Travis is your friend."

"Yes, but like you said, he's your boss. I'm not going to talk about you with him. It wouldn't be right."

She had never known Nate to lie to her before. Some of the tension in her shoulders eased. "Thank you. I'm sorry I overreacted. I just…" She shook her head.

"You want to take things slow," he said. "I understand. But remember—we're both single. We don't work for the same department. There's nothing wrong with us having a relationship."

"I know." She reached up and caressed his forearm. "But this is all so new…"

He kissed her forehead. "I know. You want to be sure this is going to work for you before you say anything. I get that. And I can be patient."

"Thanks for understanding." She wanted to melt into his arms and enjoy more than that gentle peck on the forehead. But she was on the clock, and they both had work to do. "Come on," she said. "We'd better get going."

The Juniper Creek cabins were tucked alongside a frozen creek in a section of national forest up against the base of Dakota Ridge. Since Nate was riding with her, Jamie ended up leading the convoy of sheriff's office vehicles. She stopped at the pipe gate that blocked the entrance to the cabins and Nate got out and post-holed through the snow to unlock one of half a dozen padlocks affixed to the chain around the gatepost.

"Why do you have a key?" she asked, when he returned to the cruiser.

"A buddy of mine owns one of the cabins. He lives in Denver now, so he gave me a key so I could check on the place for him."

As Travis had instructed, Jamie parked in the road at the bottom of a hill that led up to the cabins. The other deputies and the sheriff arranged their vehicles around hers to form a barricade across the road. Then they got out and gathered around the sheriff.

"We'll pair up and search every cabin for any signs of recent occupation," Travis said. "Nate will wait here and radio if anyone approaches. If you see anyone, or anything that raises concern, radio for backup. And be very cautious. They set a booby trap at the other cabin, so it's likely, if they've moved here, they've done the same."

Jamie and Deputy Dwight Prentice were tasked with searching the first three cabins. Six little residences formed a semicircle at the top of a rise, identical square cottages with front and back porches, metal roofs and board-and-batten siding painted forest service green. Heavy wooden shutters covered the windows, and stovepipes protruded from most of the roofs.

They approached up the road. As Jamie followed Dwight, trying to walk in the tracks he left in the deep snow, she was uncomfortably aware that anyone at the top of that hill would be able to see them coming. Though they all wore ballistic vests, a shooter could still do a lot of damage, and even kill them.

But no one fired on them, and the only sounds were the movements of the other members of the sheriff's department. "It doesn't look like anyone has come this way in a while," Dwight said when they reached the first cabin. A set of elk antlers hung over the front door, and a breeze stirred wind chimes that hung from one corner of the eaves.

Dwight tried the door, then knocked. "Sheriff's department!" he called loudly. "Open up!"

No one answered. She and Dwight hadn't expected them to. A stout padlock secured the front door. But they had to follow procedure.

Jamie peered through a gap in the shutters over the big front window, but could make out nothing in the darkness. "Let's check the perimeter," Dwight said.

They each circled around one side of the structure and met at the steps leading up to the rear porch, which had been screened in. The screen door was open, revealing a patio table and a stack of lawn chairs. The back door into the house was locked.

"Let's check the other cabins," Jamie said.

She led the way this time to the second cabin in the circle. The front door of this one featured a hand-carved wooden sign identifying it as McBride's Place. Snow had drifted around the foundation and buried the back steps.

As with the first cabin, Dwight and Jamie found no sign that anyone had been here in weeks.

They had the same results at the third cabin. To Jamie, the whole enclave felt deserted, preserved under a blanket of snow, waiting for spring. If Alex and Tim had ever been here, they had moved on before the last big snow.

They met Gage and Travis in front of the sixth cabin, and walked together back along the road toward the vehicles. "We didn't see any sign that anyone has been here," Dwight reported.

"Some here," Gage said. He scanned the thick woods around them. "It's a good hiding place, but maybe too remote for our killers. The other cabins were closer to town and other people."

"None of the murders have occurred near here," Travis said. "But they have to have shelter. We chased them out of the other cabin, so where did they go?"

"Maybe they have a friend who's putting them up," Jamie said.

"Or they broke into a summer home," Dwight said. "There are plenty of those in the area."

Travis nodded, but said nothing.

Nate met them at the gate. "Did you find anything?" he asked.

"Nothing," Travis said. "You should have waited in the cruiser. It would have been warmer."

"I've been doing some investigating of my own," Nate said. "I can't let you have all the fun."

"What did you find?" Travis asked.

"It might be nothing. Then again, it might be something." He led them back through the gate, up the Forest Service road about fifty feet to a trailhead. "I started thinking," Nate said. "This trail runs along behind the cabins, on the other side of the creek. It might be a back way in.

And someone's used it recently." He indicated tracks from snowshoes. "Two people, as close as I can figure."

"But we didn't find any tracks by the cabins," Gage said. "Unless someone is flying in through a window, we'd have seen signs of their passage in the snow."

"It could just be recreational snowshoers," Dwight said.

"It could," Nate agreed. "I still think it's worth following them, at least until you're past the cabins."

"Dwight and I can check them out," Jamie said.

"All right," Travis said. "We'll wait at the vehicles."

Jamie and Dwight headed up the trail. The snow was soft, which made the going slow. Deeper in the woods, the snowshoe tracks were more clearly visible, oval outlines in the snow. "I'd guess two men, from the size of the tracks," Dwight said.

"Yeah," Jamie said. "And it probably is just a couple of guys out for the day. We know no one went near the cabins."

"The killers have done a pretty good job of staying one step ahead of us," Dwight said. "If they were the ones at the Sundance cabins, they might have figured we'd look here next—it's a similar setup."

"Maybe," Jamie said. "But it doesn't hurt to check." When they had traveled about a quarter of a mile up the trail, she glimpsed one of the cabins through the trees. "If someone was going to cut over to the cabins, they'd do it somewhere in here," she said.

"Right here." Dwight stopped and indicated where the tracks turned off.

Picking up their pace, Dwight and Jamie followed the tracks to the edge of the icy creek, where they lost them in the deep snow along the creek bank. A bitter wind rattled the branches of the scrub oak that crowded the creek bank. Jamie hugged her arms across her chest against the cold.

"Did they wade across the creek?" she asked. "I don't see any tracks on the other side." Across the creek, the snow covered the open expanse between the creek and the cabins in a smooth white blanket.

"Me, either," Dwight said. "Let's see if we can pick up the tracks somewhere on this side of the creek." He headed one direction, while Jamie started off in the opposite direction. Carefully picking her way around the scrub oak and deadfall, she searched for some sign of the snowshoe tracks they had been following.

After about two minutes, she came upon a place where snow had been cleared away to reveal a stone campfire ring, logs drawn up on three sides for seating. Smoke curled up from the blackened contents of the ring, the scent of wet ash leaving a bitter taste in her mouth. "Dwight!" she called. "I've found something." She leaned over for a closer look and her heart hammered in her throat as she spotted what looked like blond hair.

Crashing sounds heralded Dwight's approach. He jogged up to her. "What is it?" he asked.

She pointed to the fire ring. "The ashes are still hot."

He found a tree branch and used it to poke at the smoldering fire. "There's some cloth in here," he said.

"And what looks like hair," she said. She put a hand to her mouth, fighting a wave of nausea. "You don't think it's a body, do you?"

"It's not real hair, I don't think." He fished a mane of yellow hair, half-melted and streaked black with ash, and held it up. "It's a wig," he said. "A woman's blond wig."

Chapter Fifteen

Nate stood in the situation room at the sheriff's department, trying to ignore the throbbing in his ankle. His doctor probably wouldn't approve of him having ditched the cast boot so soon, but he was sick of hobbling around on it. And he had plenty to distract him from the pain. The evidence collected from the fire pit had been arranged on the table in front of him. In addition to the half-burned blond wig, Jamie and Dwight had retrieved the remains of a wig of black dreadlocks, a fake beard and mustache, and black fabric garments that may have been the pirate costume. Before removing the items, they had photographed and measured the scene, and these photographs were also part of the evidence now.

"Do you think you can get DNA from the wigs?" Nate asked Travis.

"Maybe," the sheriff said. "If they aren't too badly burned. But that doesn't do us any good right now, since we can't get the wigs to the lab to test for DNA."

"I'll get to work adding all of this to our database," Jamie said, moving to the computer in the corner of the room.

"Lacy and I are supposed to have dinner with our officiate," Travis said. "But if you need me for anything…"

"You'll be the first to hear if there's a new development," Jamie said.

Travis left and she looked at Nate. "You might as well go home, too."

"I was thinking I could go and get us some dinner," he said.

"I packed a sandwich," she said. "It's in my locker."

"Doesn't something hot from Moe's Pub sound better? My treat." It wasn't the most romantic date he could think of, but it would give them a little time alone to talk.

"All right," she relented. "I guess I could go for a burger."

"No cheese, no onions, right?"

She smiled. "You remember."

"Some things you don't forget." And some people. Even in the years they had been apart, he hadn't forgotten about her. For a long time, she had been his fondest memory from his past. Returning to Eagle Mountain had made him wonder if they could make new memories together in the future.

Go slow, he reminded himself as he headed for his truck. Jamie had made it clear she wouldn't be rushed.

When he returned with their food half an hour later, she was bent over the computer. She looked up when he deposited the brown paper bag containing their burgers on the desk beside her. "Good timing," she said. "I was just finishing up."

He pulled a chair up across from her and handed her the diet soda he knew she preferred, then began distributing the food. "Thanks," she said, unwrapping her burger. "I really am starved."

"Tromping around in the woods in the cold burns a lot of calories," he said.

She nodded as she chewed, then swallowed. "How is your ankle?"

"It's there." He sipped his iced tea. "I guess Donna got home okay this morning?"

"Yes. She had a great time. Mrs. O'Keefe is so nice to take her."

"Are things serious between her and Henry?" he asked. "I mean, are they in love?"

Jamie frowned. "I don't know. They really like each other, but it's hard to say. I mean, Donna loves a lot of things. She loves her favorite TV shows and her stuffed cat and our three dogs. And she loves me. If I asked her, she would probably say she loves Henry, but I'm not sure if she knows what romantic love means."

"We all talk about loving lots of different things," he said. "Donna might not have the vocabulary to describe how her feelings for those things are different, but I'll bet down inside she knows the difference. I think that's part of being human." She stared at him a long moment, until he began to feel uncomfortable. "Did I say something wrong?" he asked.

"No. I think you said something very wise. I have to remind myself sometimes that my sister is her own person. I'm so used to looking after her and making decisions for her that I forget that sometimes. Her feelings and thoughts are real and valid even if I don't understand them. She's growing and changing all the time, though I don't always remember that."

"What does she do while you're working late like this?" he asked.

"She stays with our neighbor, Mrs. Simmons. She's a retired nurse and she and Donna really get along great. I was lucky to find her."

"I don't imagine that's cheap."

"No. But Donna gets some disability income that helps pay for it, and it's not like I spend my money on much else."

She said this as a kind of a joke, but he knew it was true. Jamie had never been one for fancy clothes or expensive hobbies and as far as he could tell, that hadn't changed. He had dated women who spent more on clothes and shoes and hair care, or cars and theatre tickets and furniture, than Jamie probably made in a year. It wasn't that she didn't care about her appearance or her surroundings, but she considered other things more important. She had dealt with more challenges than most women her age and had had to grow up much faster.

She finished her burger and stuffed the wrapper in the bag, then glanced up at the wall clock. "I should call Donna and tell her goodnight," she said. "I try to do that whenever I'm working late."

While she made the call, he stood and wandered over to the evidence table. The items they had pulled from the fire ring still reeked of smoke, along with the burnt-plastic smell of the singed artificial hair from the wigs. He picked up the evidence bag that contained the blond wig and examined it more closely.

Jamie joined him at the table. "Where in Eagle Mountain would someone get a wig like this?" he asked.

"The volunteers at the Humane Society thrift store put together a bunch of costumes for the masquerade ball," Jamie said. "When they open Monday morning I thought I'd go over there and ask if they had a blond wig, and if they remember who they sold it to. And the pirate costume. There couldn't have been too many like that, so I'm hoping they'll remember selling it."

Nate laid the wig back on the table. "I don't think it was an accident that they left this stuff near those cabins," he said.

"I don't, either," she said. "They guessed we would look or them there, because they had used that other cabin."

"They're taunting us," Nate said.

"Yes. They've done it before. They killed Fiona Win-low at the scavenger hunt, when there were off-duty of-icers all around them. They got a charge out of getting way with murder right under our noses."

"That's why the pirate focused on you at the party last night," Nate said. "It's why he drove by your house, and why he was hanging out at the vet's office this afternoon. Your spotting him wasn't an accident. He wanted you to see him and to know he's keeping tabs on you."

She shrugged. "It's creepy, but he's not going to do anything to me. I'm not going to let him trick me into coming with him somewhere. And I'm not going to mistake either Alex or Tim for innocent college students who need a lift somewhere, or a woman who needs help. I know better."

"You need to be careful," he said. "And you shouldn't go out alone."

"I'm alone in my patrol cruiser every time I work a shift," she said. "I know how to handle myself."

"There are two of them and only one of you," Nate said. "Maybe you should partner with another officer until this is over. Talk to Travis."

"No!" Her eyes flashed with anger. "You wouldn't suggest something like that to a male deputy."

"These two aren't killing men," he said.

"And they aren't going to kill me." She sat in front of the computer once more. "I appreciate your concern, but I can look after myself. I've been doing it a long time."

"I know." He shoved his hands in his pockets and stared at the floor, trying to rein in his emotions. "But that doesn't stop me from worrying."

"Nate." Her voice held a note of warning.

"What?"

"If we're going to be a…a couple, then you can't d
this."

"I can't worry about you? I don't know how to stop it. O
is it that you don't want me to talk about being worried?"

"You can worry—just don't try to stop me from doin;
my job."

If the shoe was on the other foot—if she objected to hin
going to work every day because it was dangerous—h
would hate it. And they would probably fight about it. H
wasn't going to let that happen. "I don't want you to give uj
your job," he said. "And I was out of line, suggesting yo
partner up with another deputy. I shouldn't have said that."

"Apology accepted." She hesitated, then added. "And
it's nice to know someone is concerned about me. It mean;
a lot."

He nodded. What he really wanted was to pull her to
him and kiss her, but now wasn't the time or place. "I'
better go," he said. "You've got work to do and I shoul
probably put this ankle up and slap an ice pack on it o
something."

"You do that," she said. "I'll see you tomorrow."

He left, leaning more heavily on his cane as he crosse
the parking lot to his truck. A thin sliver of moon shon
overhead, amidst about a million diamond-bright stars
With few streetlights and most of the businesses shut dow
for the evening, there was little to compete with the nightly
show in the heavens.

Nate drove slowly down Main, past silent storefront;
and empty curbs. Moe's Pub, with its single lit sign, wa
the only business open, and only half a dozen cars and
trucks remained in the gravel lot next to the tavern. A mai
emerged from Moe's front door and waved as Nate drov
past, and Nate lifted one finger in salute. When Nate wa;

teenager, he had hated how quiet things were here after six or seven o'clock. The nearest movie theatre was an hour away and there had been nothing to do and nowhere to hang out with friends, away from the scrutiny of parents and teachers.

Now that he was older, he appreciated the peace and quiet. After a couple of years of partying in college he had had his fill, and these days he would rather watch a movie from the comfort of his couch, or visit with friends in their homes. He chuckled. Was this a sign of maturity—that he had no desire to hang out all night?

He approached the turnoff toward his house but instead of taking it, he drove half a mile farther and made the turn onto Jamie's street. He would just cruise by and make sure everything was all right. Just to help him sleep easier.

He slowed as he neared her house, and tightened his hands on the steering wheel as he took in the dark shape of an SUV in her driveway. Jamie's SUV was parked at the sheriff's department. So who was this? He flicked on his brights, trying to make out the figure in the driver's seat.

Just then, the vehicle in Jamie's driveway roared to life. The SUV reversed out of the driveway and barreled straight at Nate, who only had time to brace himself for the crash.

Chapter Sixteen

"Officer, please respond to MVA, Oak Street."

Jamie keyed her mike and responded. "Unit five responding."

"Copy that, unit five. EMS and fire are also on the way."

Jamie switched on her lights and siren and punched the accelerator. Oak was her street, with little traffic during daylight. Had one of her neighbors come home after too much to drink and clipped another car? Or had the deer who liked to wander into town and eat people's landscaping leaped out in front of a motorist?

As she turned onto the street, her headlights illuminated a pickup truck in front of the house. With a start, she realized it was Nate's truck. He stood beside it, head in his hands. She braked to a stop and, leaving the cruiser running, jumped out of the car and raced to his side. "Nate, what happened?" she asked. "Are you all right?"

"I'm fine. But my truck..." He pointed to the front of the truck. Jamie took a few steps forward and stared at the pile of bricks that had once been her mailbox surround and at the crushed front end of Nate's pickup, steam hissing from the radiator.

"What happened?" she asked again, but before he could answer, an ambulance approached and parked across the street, followed by a fire truck. Merrily Rayford and Em nett Baxter climbed out of the ambulance and headed for Nate and Jamie, while a trio of firefighters in yellow bunker gear surrounded the truck.

"Is this our victim?" Merrily, a wiry blonde, set down a plastic tote and swept the beam of a flashlight over Nate's face. "That's quite a knot you have there. Did you hit your head on the dash?"

Nate put up a hand to shield his eyes as the EMT spotlighted a golf-ball-sized knot near his right temple. "It was a pretty hard impact. The air bags exploded and I couldn't really see anything for a few seconds." He brushed at the front of his jacket, which was coated in fine white dust. "What a mess."

"Lower your hand so I can see your eyes, please." He did as instructed and Merrily finished her examination. "Are you experiencing any pain?" she asked. "Neck, back, ribs, chest?"

"Just my head."

Merrily flicked a glance at Jamie. "How much did you have to drink tonight?" she asked.

"Nothing," Nate said.

"He hasn't been drinking," Jamie affirmed. "He and I were working at the sheriff's department until twenty minutes ago."

"Then how did you end up taking out this mailbox?" Emmett asked.

"Another vehicle ran me off the road," he said.

Merrily nodded and pressed a gauze square to the knot on Nate's head, which was seeping a little blood. "I don't see any sign of a concussion," she said. "But you ought to have someone with you tonight. And you could have whiplash or other injuries. Sometimes the shock of the accident masks pain. If you start experiencing any other symptoms, you should see a doctor right away."

"All right," he said. "Thanks."

While Merrily and Emmett packed up their gear and returned to the ambulance, Jamie pulled Nate aside. "Who forced you off the road?" she asked.

"That dark gray SUV that's been following you around was parked in your driveway," he said. "I slowed down to get a better look and hit my brights. The vehicle came barreling out the drive and headed right toward me. I had to wrench the wheel over to avoid being hit head-on." He frowned at the pile of crumbled brick in front of his bumper. "Sorry about your mailbox."

"Who was it?" she asked. "Did you get a good look at the driver?"

"No. Whoever it was had a knit cap pulled down low over his forehead, and a scarf wrapped around the lower half of his face."

She stared, trying to take in all he had said. "Are you sure it was the same SUV?" she asked.

"Yes. A Toyota Highlander. He was parked in your driveway, lights out." She could feel his eyes on her, and she could feel the anger and concern radiating from him, though it was too dark for her to read his expression. "He was waiting for you."

She gripped his arm, as much to steady herself as to command his attention. "What were you doing here?"

He hesitated, then said, "I was headed home and decided to drive by, just to check on the place. I'm not sure why—maybe I had an idea he would try something like this. I don't think it was a coincidence that he drove by here last night, and that he was waiting when you came out of the vet's office this afternoon."

Jamie didn't want to believe that this killer had targeted her. But she had been trained to draw conclusions based on evidence, and the evidence—as well as intuition—told her Nate was right.

"Jamie!"

She turned at the sound of her name. Donna, her puffy purple coat pulled on over pink flannel pajamas, jogged across the lawn toward her. Mrs. Simmons, swathed in a drab car coat, followed at a more sedate pace. "Jamie, what is going on?" Donna asked, throwing her arms around her sister.

"It's okay," Jamie said, hugging Donna to her. Feeling her sister's bulk calmed her. Donna was safe. Nate was going to be all right. That was all that mattered right now. "Just a little accident."

Donna turned to look at Nate. "Nate, are you hurt?" she asked.

His smile was more of a grimace, but Jamie was touched by the effort. "Just a bump on the head," he said. "I'll be fine."

"Your poor truck!" Donna pointed at the crumpled vehicle. "And the mailbox. How will we get the mail?"

"We can get a new mailbox," Jamie said.

"Such a commotion." Huffing a little, Mrs. Simmons joined them. "We heard the sirens and saw the lights and Donna insisted on coming out to see," she said. Her eyes shone and she kept darting glances at Nate and the wrecked truck, and the firefighters, who had retreated to the fire engine. Jamie suspected the caregiver had been as eager as Donna to be a part of the excitement.

"Did you see what happened?" Jamie asked.

Mrs. Simmons shook her head. "We were watching TV in the back of the house."

"We were watching Bollywood," Donna said. "And I had it turned up loud. I love the music and the dancing."

"But then we heard sirens and I looked out and saw the

flashing lights," Mrs. Simmons said. She leaned in closer and lowered her voice to a whisper. "Was it drunk driving, do you think?"

"No," Jamie said. "What about earlier? Did you see anyone over here at my house—another car in the driveway?"

"No." Mrs. Simmons's eyes widened and she put a hand to her mouth. "Someone was at your house? Who?"

"I don't know." Jamie didn't want to frighten the older woman. "It was probably someone with the wrong address. They weren't looking where they were going when they backed out of the driveway and hit Nate who had to swerve to avoid them."

She jumped as the fire truck's siren bleated. The firefighters waved as they pulled away from the curb. Merrily and Emmett jogged toward the ambulance. "Another call just came in," Emmett said.

The street seemed eerily silent after the emergency vehicles had left them. Jamie's feet and fingers ached with cold. "You need to get inside before you freeze," she told Donna.

"When will you be home?" Donna asked.

"When my shift is over." Jamie patted Donna's shoulder. "You go on back with Mrs. Simmons and I'll see you after eleven." She hoped it wouldn't be much later than that.

"Are you sure everything is all right?" Mrs. Simmons asked.

"It will be fine." She smiled in a way that she hoped was reassuring.

Donna and Mrs. Simmons returned to the caregiver's house and Jamie took out her phone. "I'm going to take some photographs and then I'll call a wrecker for your car."

"I'll get the wrecker driver to take me home," Nate said. "I guess there's nothing else I can do tonight."

"You heard Merrily," Jamie said. "You shouldn't be alone tonight."

"It's just a bump on the head," he said. "I'll be fine."

She dug her house keys from her pocket and pressed them into his hands. "You can stay with me tonight. I'll make up the couch." She wasn't ready to deal with awkward questions from Donna just yet.

He looked at the keys. "Are you sure?"

"I'm sure. Make yourself at home. I'll see to your truck, file my report, then I'll pick up Donna and be home before midnight."

She started to turn away, but he touched her arm. "You know what this means, him parked in your driveway?" he asked. "He's decided to go after you."

Her stomach knotted, but she refused to acknowledge the truth of his words. "He may be going after me," she said. "But you're the one who keeps getting hurt."

"I'm tough," he said. "I can take it."

"You don't think I can?"

"You're the strongest woman I know," he said. "But I don't want to have to find out what it would be like to not have you around."

He turned and strode toward the house, with only a trace of a limp. Jamie's chest hurt as she watched him mount the steps to the porch and let himself inside her house, but she didn't know whether the fear that threatened to strangle her was because someone might be trying to kill her—or because Nate cared so much.

NATE WOKE TO a throbbing head, in a room where the light didn't feel quite right. As sleep fled and his vision cleared, he looked up at the woman leaning over him. Donna, a pink knit hat pulled down over her brown hair, a fuzzy pink robe over pink pajamas, looked at him with an expression of great concern. "Hello," she said. "Why are you sleeping on our couch?"

After confirming that he was still dressed, Nate threw off the quilt he'd been sleeping under and shoved into a sitting position. "Jamie thought it would be better if I stayed here instead of going home alone after I was hurt last night," he said.

Donna nodded. "Good idea. Do you want some breakfast? We have cereal, or toaster waffles."

"What kind of cereal?" Nate asked.

Donna scrunched up her nose. "The healthy kind."

He suppressed a laugh. "Then maybe waffles?"

"Good choice!" She whirled and skipped away.

Nate made his way to the bathroom, where he rinsed his mouth and washed his face, and grimaced at the haggard, bruised visage that stared back at him. He ran a hand over his chin, the sandpaper rasp of a day's growth of beard making him wince. Nothing he could do about that now.

The smell of coffee drew him to the kitchen, where Jamie stood before the toaster, an empty plate in one hand, a coffee mug in the other. "Nate's here," Donna announced, unnecessarily, as Jamie had already turned to greet him.

"How are you feeling?" she asked, as he took a mug from the cabinet and filled it from the coffee maker beside the sink.

"I've got a headache, but nothing two aspirin and a little caffeine won't cure." He sipped the coffee and closed his eyes, savoring the sensation of its warmth spreading through him.

"Waffles will make you feel better," Donna said.

"Sit down and I'll fix you some waffles," Jamie said.

"I can look after myself," he said.

"It's not like I'm slaving over a hot stove." She set aside her coffee and pushed him toward the table. The toaster dinged and she plucked two waffles from the slots, dropped them on the plate, then set the plate in front of him. Donna pushed the syrup toward him.

He started to protest that he hadn't meant to take her waffles, but she had already inserted two more frozen discs into the toaster and pulled another plate from the cabinet. Three minutes later, she sat across from him. "I have to take Donna to work at eight, so I can give you a ride to your place," she said.

"Drop me off at the station," he said. "I want to talk to Travis about what happened last night."

"All right." She turned to Donna. "When you get off work this afternoon, wait for Mrs. Simmons to pick you up," she said. "I don't want you walking by yourself today."

"I can walk." Donna mopped up syrup with a forkful of waffle. "I like to walk."

"I know you do, but it's safer right now for you to wait for Mrs. Simmons."

Nate waited for Donna to protest, or to ask why, but she only mumbled "All right," and remained focused on finishing her breakfast. Was she as aware as they were of the danger the Ice Cold Killers posed to a young woman walking by herself? Or had experience taught her she wouldn't win an argument with her sister?

"Remember to wait for Mrs. Simmons," Jamie said. "Don't leave the store on your own."

"I'd rather go home with Henry." Donna looked up from her plate. "His mom said I could come over any time."

"We don't want to take advantage of Mrs. O'Keefe's hospitality," Jamie said. "Besides, if you go over to Henry's house all the time, he might get tired of you."

"He won't get tired of me," she said. "He loves me."

The expression in Jamie's eyes softened, though her mouth was still tight with worry. Nate wondered if he would ever tire of watching her this way—he was beginning to think not.

"Henry asked me to a birthday party tomorrow night," she said. "His cousin's birthday. She lives in a big house and has a hot tub and a snowmobile. She's going to have music and cake, and at midnight, they're going to shoot off fireworks."

"How long have you known about this?" Jamie asked.

Donna stuck out her lower lip. "I forgot to tell you. But Henry's mom is supposed to call you."

"I really don't want you out so late," Jamie said. "Especially with people I don't know. Maybe some other time."

"But I want to go!" Donna stood, her chair skidding backward. "You can't tell me what to do all the time. I'm old enough to decide for myself." Tears streamed down her face as she stared at Jamie. "I want to decide for myself," she sobbed, then whirled and ran from the room.

Jamie stared after her, then laid down her fork and pushed back her chair. She started to rise, then sank back down and turned to Nate. "Do you think I'm wrong?" she asked. "I'm only trying to protect her."

Nate clamped his mouth shut. Getting involved in a dispute between two sisters sounded like a bad idea any time. "You know your sister better than I do," he said.

"She wants to be independent," Jamie said. "She wants to be like other young women her age and it hurts her that she isn't. She doesn't show it, but I know it hurts. It's so unfair—she never did anything to deserve this."

"Neither did you," he said.

The look she gave him was so full of anguish he ached for her. "I want her to be happy," she said. "But most of all, I want her to be safe. Especially now. Especially with this killer preying on local women." She leaned across the table and took his hand. "What do you think I should do? Please tell me."

He took a sip of coffee, buying time. "Why not wait and talk to Mrs. O'Keefe?" he said. "Find out more about this party—where it is and who else will be there. Then you'll have a better idea of the risk involved."

She nodded. "All right. That makes sense." She sat back and let out a breath. "Thanks."

She stood and began gathering dishes. He rose and helped. They worked silently. She filled the dishwasher, while he put away the waffles and syrup—as he had done after other meals he had eaten here when they were in high school.

She had just closed the dishwasher when the doorbell rang. The dogs erupted into barking, a mad scrabble of toe-nails on the wood floor as they raced for the door. "Company!" Donna called, stomping down the stairs.

By the time Nate and Jamie reached the foyer, Donna was peering out the side window. "It's the sheriff," she announced.

Jamie shushed the dogs and ordered them back, then opened the door for Travis. He had his back to them, surveying the ruined mailbox. When he turned around, he didn't seem surprised to see Nate standing with Jamie. "I heard about what happened here last night," he said. "Jamie's report said something about a dark gray Highlander?"

"Come in." Jamie stepped back and held the door open wider. "Donna, you'd better go upstairs and get dressed or you'll be late."

Nate braced himself for another protest, but Donna merely turned and headed upstairs again. "Would you like some coffee?" Jamie asked. "I can make a fresh pot."

"No, thanks." He turned to Nate. "Tell me what happened."

Nate repeated his story about seeing the SUV in Jamie's driveway and gave his description of the driver.

"To anyone passing, he'd look like someone bundled up against the cold," Travis said. "But he made sure you wouldn't be able to give a description of him."

"I'm sure it's Alex or Tim," Nate said. "Everything points to it. I'd recognize the vehicle again. If we can find it, maybe we can find them."

"That's another reason I stopped by this morning," Travis said. "We found the Highlander. The VIN matches the one owned by Tim Dawson."

"That's great," Jamie said. "If they've been using it all this time, there's bound to be evidence—hairs, fibers, DNA."

Travis didn't seem nearly as excited as Jamie about the find. Then again, the sheriff was not the most emotional person around. "Where did you find it?" Nate asked.

"Out on Forest Service Road 1410, near the Sundance cabins," Travis said. "A call came in about eleven last night that someone had seen a fire in that area. By the time the first pumper truck got there, it was burned down to the frame."

"Accident or arson?" Nate asked.

"Oh, it was deliberate," Travis said. "The fire crew said they could smell the diesel fuel before they even got out of their truck."

"They were destroying evidence," Jamie said.

"Yes," Travis said. "And destroying our best link to them."

Chapter Seventeen

"Some folks nicknamed it the green monster." Bud O'Brien slapped his gloved hand on the hood of a mostly-green vintage pickup truck with oversize tires. "It looks like crap, but it will get you where you want to go."

"I guess I don't have much choice," Nate said, accepting the keys from the garage owner. His own truck was awaiting an assessment by an insurance appraiser—something that wouldn't happen until the highway reopened. Estimates on when that would be varied from tomorrow to next week, or next month. It all depended on how fast a road crew could clear away the many avalanches that had covered the pavement and how long fresh snows held off.

Today was sunny, the glittering white of the landscape blinding, the sky the blue of lake ice, the air bitterly cold and sharp enough that a deep breath was painful. The green monster's tires crunched over the snow-packed road as Nate headed out of town. Though he had discarded the air boot on his ankle and managed to walk without limping at least half the time, he hadn't been cleared to return to work, and Travis had nothing new for him to do. He'd decided to check out the site where Alex and Tim had burned their truck, more out of curiosity than from any hope of finding a real clue.

Bud O'Brien had hauled away what was left of the vehicle that morning, but a blackened patch of earth and soot-stained snow marked the spot, at the entrance to the summer cabins. Nate parked his truck well past the site and walked back along the road, then circled the patch of melted snow and ash that formed a muddy slurry. The smell of burned rubber and diesel fuel lingered in the air, and bits of broken glass and melted rubber littered the area. The deep tracks of Bud's wrecker led from the site to the road.

Nate's examination offered no new insight, so he walked back up toward the cabins, retracing the path he'd taken the day he was injured, wondering if any evidence lay buried under the thick snow, and trying to piece together the events of the last twelve hours. Alex and Tim must have driven out here last night immediately after one of them tried to run him down. The other would have followed in whatever vehicle they were using now—a stolen car? Travis would have zeroed in on any recently stolen vehicles, but he hadn't mentioned anything in the briefing at the sheriff's department that morning.

He had almost reached the cabin where he had been injured when movement in the underbrush caught his attention. At first he thought he had startled a deer, but a flash of red and blue made him reject that notion. Someone—no, two people—were running away from the cabin.

He started after then, but the deep snow and his still-tender ankle brought him to a quick halt. He'd never catch those two this way. He held his breath and listened as his quarry moved away, thrashing and cursing marking their progress. They were headed toward the road that ran behind the cabins, but thick brush and snow impeded their progress. If Nate hurried, he might be able to head them off.

Ignoring the pain in his ankle, he took off running

again, this time along the road, the snow there still packed down from sheriff's department vehicles, making movement easier. When he reached his truck, he gunned the engine. For all its dilapidated appearance, the vehicle had plenty of power. He raced around the hairpin curve where the road wound behind the cabins. He spotted the truck, and two figures emerging from the woods and climbing the snow-covered embankment toward a dirty brown Jeep Wrangler.

Nate braked hard and angled the truck in front of the Jeep. They wouldn't be able to move forward without hitting him, and backing up would send them perilously close to the embankment. As the two suspects reached the Jeep, Nate emerged from his truck, his Glock drawn. "Stop, and put your hands up where I can see them," he ordered.

The two young men—teenagers, he guessed—inched their hands into the air. This wasn't Alex and Tim. So why had they run from him? "Don't shoot," the slighter of the two said, staring out from beneath a red knit beanie and a fringe of blond bangs with frightened blue eyes.

"Who are you?" His companion, a handsome, broad-shouldered kid dressed all in black, demanded.

"Officer Nate Hall," he said. "Who are you?"

The teens looked at each other. "We haven't done anything wrong," the blond said.

"You were trespassing on private property," Nate said. Technically, the land on which the cabins sat belonged to the Forest Service, but the cabins themselves were private. "What were you doing at the cabins?"

"We were just looking for a friend," the blond said. His voice wavered and his hands shook.

"Who were you looking for?"

"We don't know their names," the boy dressed darker said. His expression wasn't exactly a sneer, but he showed none of his friend's nervousness. "They're just a couple of climbers we met. We followed them here and figured they were staying at the cabins."

"When did you meet them?" Nate asked.

The darker boy shrugged. "I don't know. A week ago?"

"It was last Monday," his friend said.

"Turn around and place your hands against the vehicle." Nate motioned with the Glock.

"You don't have any right—" the dark-haired boy said.

"He's got a gun," the other boy said. "Just do what he says."

Nate frisked each of them. They weren't armed, but he extracted their wallets and flipped them open. "Giuseppe Calendri and Greg Eicklebaum," he said, examining the driver's license photos, which gave local addresses. He holstered the Glock and returned the wallets, then took out the flyer with the pictures of Alex and Tim and held it out to them. "Are these the two climbers you met?" he asked.

The darker boy—Giuseppe—stuck out his lower lip. "I don't know."

"They had on stocking caps and sunglasses," the blond, Greg, said. "These look like driver's license photos. Nobody really looks like their driver's license photo, do they?"

Nate folded the flyer and stuck it back in his pocket. "Why did you run from me just now?" he asked.

"We didn't know you were a cop," Greg said. "You could have been anybody. I mean, there's a guy running around killing people. For all we knew, that was you."

"The Ice Cold Killer only kills women," Nate said.

"So far," Greg said. "But what if he changes his mind?"

"And it's not like you're in uniform, or even in a cop car." Giuseppe frowned. "You didn't show us a badge, either."

Nate pulled out his ID and flipped it open.

The boys leaned over to study it. "Aww, man," Greg said. "You're not even a real cop."

"I'm a real cop." Nate returned his credentials to his pocket.

"Well, we aren't fishing without a license or hunting out of season," Giuseppe said, his cockiness back. "And we didn't do anything to those cabins. Maybe we just got lost while we were out hiking and decided to cut through there to our car."

Nate didn't waste time arguing with him. "You can go," he said. "For now."

He waited until the boys were in their vehicle before he got into his own and pulled up far enough to let them out. Then he fell in behind them and followed them all the way to town. They turned off toward the gated neighborhood where they both lived, and Nate headed to the sheriff's department, to find out more about Giuseppe Calendri and Greg Eicklebaum.

JAMIE AND TRAVIS were going over the evidence database she had compiled when Nate walked into the office. How long was it going to be before this goofy, lightheaded feeling stopped sweeping over her every time she saw him? She had to fight to keep a sappy smile from her face, though there was no way she couldn't look at him. If nothing else, she wanted to see if she could detect whatever Donna had seen that convinced her sister that Nate was in love with her.

Okay, so maybe there was a little extra warmth in his eyes. And he really looked at her, his gaze lingering, instead of just sweeping over her. But that didn't really mean he was in love—did it?

"What can you tell me about Giuseppe Calendri and

Greg Eicklebaum?" Nate asked, sinking into the chair Travis offered him.

"Where did you run into those two?" Travis asked.

"At Sundance cabins," Nate said. "I wanted to see where Alex and Tim burned the Highlander, then I walked up to the cabins. Those two took off through the woods like a couple of startled deer."

"Giuseppe goes by Pi," Travis said. "He and Greg and a third boy, Gus Elcott, got in a little trouble a couple of weeks ago. They had some kind of competition going, racking up points for whoever could do the most outrageous dare. I had them do community service, shoveling snow, as punishment."

"I think they know something about Alex and Tim," Nate said. "When I asked them what they were doing at the cabins, they said they met a couple of climbers last Monday. They thought they were staying at the cabins and were looking for them. I showed them the pictures of Alex and Tim and they said they didn't recognize them, but I think they're lying."

"Do you know Pi and Greg?" Travis asked Jamie.

She shook her head. "I remember seeing their names as possible witnesses for Christy O'Brien's murder."

"They were spotted near the site of the murder that night," Travis said. "But they swore they didn't see a thing." He stood. "I think you and I should have a talk with Pi. He's the ringleader of that group."

"He struck me as a smug brat," Nate said.

"He's smart," Travis said. "He'll make a good witness if we can get him to tell us what he knows."

"Why did you want to take me to question this boy, instead of Nate?" Jamie asked when she and Travis were in the sheriff's cruiser, headed toward the exclusive neighborhood where the Calendris lived.

"I could say I want to give you more experience questioning suspects," Travis said. "That's true, and it would be the politically correct answer. But also, Nate already struck out questioning the boys. He cornered them and they dug in their heels. Pi strikes me as the type who likes to be the star of the show. You're closer to his age, and a woman, so I think he'll want to impress you."

Jamie smiled. She could always count on the sheriff to be honest. "I'll do my best to appear to hang on his every word," she said.

Chapter Eighteen

The Calendris lived in an impressive stone-and-cedar home with views of the snow-capped mountains. The young man who answered Travis's knock was handsome as any teen heartthrob, with thick dark hair flopping over his brow and deep-set, intense brown eyes. "Hello, Sheriff," he said, showing no surprise at the lawman's appearance. He nodded to Jamie as she walked past. "Hello, Deputy."

He closed the door and led them into an expansive great room, with soaring fir-plank ceilings and a massive stone fireplace in which a fire crackled. "I suppose you're here to ask me more about the two climbers we told Officer Hall about," he said, taking a seat on an oversize leather ottoman. "I'm sorry, I really don't know anything else to tell you."

"Where did you meet them?" Travis asked.

"Those ice falls by the national forest campground," Pi said. "It's not an official climbing area, but with all the snow and cold we've had this winter, there are some impressive features there. We wanted to give it a try and they were just finishing up a climb, but they gave us some good route-finding tips."

"Who is we?" Travis asked.

"Gus Elcott and Greg Eicklebaum were with me." Pi flashed a smile at Jamie. "They were busy unloading our climbing gear, so I did most of the talking with the two climbers."

"Did they tell you their names?" Jamie asked.

Pi shook his head. "No."

"Did they say where they were from? Where they were staying?" Travis asked.

"No."

"You told Officer Hall that you had followed them to the cabins," Travis said. "When was that?"

Pi waved a hand. "Oh, after we finished climbing I thought I spotted the guys' truck on the side of the road. I slowed down, thinking I'd stop and thank them for their help, and ask if they knew other good climbing areas around there. But as I slowed down, they pulled out in front of me. So I followed them until they pulled into the cabins. When they saw me, though, they pulled out and left."

"If they left, what made you think they were staying there?" Jamie asked.

Pi shrugged. "Just a hunch I had. I believe in following hunches."

"Have you seen either of these two since that day?" Travis asked.

"No." He leaned forward, elbows on his knees. "Why are you so interested in them? Have they done something wrong?"

"We'd like to question them in connection with a case," Travis said.

Pi sat back and nodded. "You think they have something to do with those women who were murdered," Pi said. "Maybe they're the Ice Cold Killer. I'm right, aren't I?"

"Describe these two," Travis said, ignoring Pi's suspicions. "How old do you think they were? What did they look like?"

"They were in their twenties, I think," Pi said. "One

was about my height—six feet—and the other was an inch or two taller."

"What color hair?" Travis prompted.

Pi shook his head. "They were wearing knit caps and those face things—balaclavas? It was really cold out, and when you're climbing ice, it gets even colder."

"What color eyes?"

"They had on sunglasses."

"Anything else?" Travis asked. "Did they have accents? Say where they were from?"

"No. We just talked about climbing."

Travis frowned, but closed his notebook and stood. Jamie and Pi rose also. "What are you and Greg and Gus up to these days, besides climbing?" Travis asked.

"We're staying out of trouble," Pi said.

"No more dares?"

Pi laughed. "No more dares. Thought it was fun while it lasted. Gus ended up with the most points, though we never declared an official winner."

"Points?" Jamie asked.

Pi flashed his movie-star smile again—a smile that had probably left more than one teenage girl weak at the knees, Jamie thought. "We had a little competition going where we accumulated points for different accomplishments. Some of them were a little risky, but we didn't mean any harm." He glanced at Travis. "Though I guess things were getting a little out of hand there at the end. It was probably just as well that we stopped."

"Don't start up again," Travis said. "Someone might get hurt."

"We won't," Pi said as he walked them to the door. "Although I think about it sometimes, things I might have done to earn more points. Just as a mental exercise, of course." He opened the door and Travis and Jamie exited.

Pi followed them onto the steps. "I hope you catch your killers," he said. "That's something that would have been worth a lot of points when we were playing our game. Someone who caught a serial killer would have been the ultimate winner."

"This isn't a game," Travis said. "If you know something that would help us, you need to tell us."

"I don't know anything," Pi said, his expression remaining pleasant. "Just another mental exercise." He returned to the house and closed the door behind him.

"There's something he's not telling us," Jamie said as she buckled her seat belt. "We need to talk to Greg and see what he says."

"We'll talk to Greg." Travis started the cruiser. "And maybe Pi is hiding something. Or maybe he just wants us to think he's smarter than he is."

"He probably isn't smarter than the killers," Jamie said.

"They're making mistakes," Travis said. "Leaving behind more evidence. We're going to find them."

"That would be a nice wedding present, wouldn't it?" Jamie said. "Closing this case before you leave on your honeymoon."

"Yeah," Travis agreed. "I know Lacy would appreciate it if we could start our marriage without this hanging over us."

"They haven't killed anyone in six days," Jamie said. "Maybe because we're closing in on them, forcing them to spend more time running."

"I wish I could think that's a good thing," he said. "But everything I've read says serial killers feel compelled to chase the high they get from killing. It's like a drug and the longer they go without it, the more the craving builds."

She bit the inside of her cheek, trying to create some

saliva for her suddenly dry mouth. "Nate thinks the killers have targeted me," she said.

"I don't think he's wrong," Travis said. He glanced at
her, then refocused his attention on the road. "That's another reason I wanted you with me this afternoon. I don't
want you patrolling alone until this is settled. And before
you say anything, I would do the same if a killer appeared
to be stalking a male deputy."

"Yes, sir." As much as she wanted to protest that her
training enabled her to look after herself, the truth was,
these two killers frightened her. She never wanted to be
in the position where she had to face them down alone.

MONDAY AFTERNOON, JAMIE devoted herself to helping
Donna get ready for the party. Henry's mom had answered
all her questions and reassured her that the birthday party
would be well supervised and safe. Donna could enjoy
the party and Jamie didn't have to feel like a terrible person for keeping her home. Donna had been ecstatic at the
news and had spent hours going through her clothes, deciding what to wear

Though her sister had attended homecoming dances and
senior prom with groups of friends, and she had met Henry
and his mother at the masquerade ball, this was her first
real date, and she threw herself into it with all the fanfare
of a Hollywood actress preparing for her first red carpet
premiere. A long bubble bath was followed by a session
with blow dryer and curling iron. She sat in a kitchen chair
before her dresser mirror and fidgeted while Jamie shaped
her hair into dozens of short ringlets all over her head.

"Close your eyes," Jamie ordered before she sprayed
a liberal application of hair spray. A sparkly pink bow
carefully clipped over one ear formed the finishing touch.
Though Jamie had feared the final effect would be more

French poodle than *femme fatale*, Donna ended up looking perfectly lovely.

"I need perfume," Donna said, jumping up from her chair. "Something that smells really good."

Jamie didn't normally wear perfume, but she unearthed a bottle of her mother's favorite scent in the back of a closet. She dabbed some on Donna's wrist and her sister sniffed appreciatively. "It smells pretty," she said. "Like Mom, when she dressed up to go out."

Jamie had a sudden memory of watching her mother put on her makeup before going out to dinner with their father. When she was done, she would call both girls to her and give them a little spritz of her perfume "to have a little bit of me with you while I'm away." Now it felt like she was here again with them. "Mama would be so proud of you now," Jamie said, then turned away before she started crying and Donna, always so sympathetic to others' emotions, joined in. "Let's finish getting you ready."

Half an hour before Henry and his mother were due to arrive, Donna stood before Jamie. The orange ribbed tights she had chosen to go with her pink party dress—because orange was Henry's favorite color—made her look like a sherbet dessert—but a charming one. Henry would no doubt be delighted. Jamie's gaze shifted to the silver high heels Donna had borrowed from Jamie's closet. "Are you sure you don't want your pink flats?" she asked. "They'll be more comfortable for dancing."

"I don't want to be comfortable," Donna said. "I want to be pretty."

"Your flats are very pretty," Jamie said, resisting the impulse to rant about a culture that made women believe beauty was something they had to suffer for. Donna didn't care about any of that—she just wanted to be like the other young women she saw, with their high heels and fancy dresses.

"Is my face okay?" Donna turned and peered anxiously into the mirror. With Jamie's help, she wore not only powder and lip gloss, but eye shadow and mascara, which made her look older and, yes, more sophisticated.

"You look beautiful," Jamie said, hugging her gently, so as not to muss her hair.

The doorbell rang and the dogs began to bark. The sisters raced downstairs to answer it, but instead of Henry and his mother, Nate stood on the doorstep, his arms full of flowers. "Hello," he said. He offered a bouquet to Donna. "These are for you."

"Flowers!" Donna buried her nose in the blossoms—a handful of pink and white carnations and a single overblown rose.

"And these are for you." Nate extended a second bouquet—more carnations and alstroemeria—to Jamie.

"Where did you find flowers?" she asked. "I'm sure the florist hasn't had a delivery in weeks."

"They had a few blooms left," he said. He turned back to Donna. "You look beautiful."

She blushed and giggled, and teetered on her heels, so that Jamie reached out to steady her. She should find a way to pull Mrs. O'Keefe aside and give her the pink flats, in case Donna wanted to change later.

"What should I do with my flowers?" Donna asked.

"I'll put them in a vase," Jamie said. She took her sister's bouquet along with her own to the kitchen, glad for a few moments alone to organize her thoughts. Nate's arrival was a surprise, but it didn't feel wrong to have him here for this milestone. She wondered if he understood how important this was for her and for Donna, too, and wanted to celebrate with them. Maybe he did, since he had brought the flowers.

Voices drew her back to the foyer, where Henry stood, dressed in black jeans and boots, a Western-cut white shirt, black leather jacket and a string tie. "Henry, you look so handsome," Donna cooed.

"And you look beautiful," he said, eyes shining.

Donna turned to Jamie. "And look—he brought me a corsage."

Jamie duly admired the corsage—made of pink silk roses and silk ferns—and slid it onto Donna's wrist. "Before you go, I have to get a picture," Jamie said, rushing to retrieve her phone.

The resulting photos showed the couple arm in arm, grinning at the camera, then at each other. Donna had never looked happier, Jamie thought.

"We have to go," Henry said.

Nate helped Donna with her coat. He and Jamie followed the couple onto the front porch and waved to Mrs. O'Keefe, who waited in the car.

Back inside, Jamie stood for a moment with her head down, one knuckle pressed hard above her upper lip, determined to hold back tears. Nate put his arm around her. "I can't believe I'm being so silly," she said. "You'd think I was sending my only kid to war or something. It's just a dance."

"I'm wondering if it's because she's doing something you thought she might never do," Nate said. "She's going on a real date with a young man she loves. She's doing something other girls her age do all the time, but that not every girl with her disability gets to do or is able to do."

Jamie looked up at him, blinking hard and somehow managing to keep the tears from overflowing. "I never thought of that," she said. "I… I think you might be right."

He took her hand in his. "I figured you might appreciate a little distraction tonight, so I thought I'd take you out."

"A real date?" she asked.

"A real date." He surveyed the yoga pants and sweatshirt she wore. "I can wait while you change."

She laughed and punched his chest. Unlike her casual clothes, he wore pressed jeans, a dark blue dress shirt and sports coat. "What makes you think I need to change?"

He grinned and waggled his eyebrows. "I can help you, if you like."

"Then we might never leave the house."

"I'm liking this idea better and better." He lunged toward her and she danced out of his reach and raced up the stairs.

"I'll be down in ten minutes," she called over her shoulder.

A pleasant thrill of excitement hummed through her as she rifled through her closet, trying to choose the right outfit. She settled on a pale blue cashmere sweater, black tights, a short black skirt and tall leather boots. Warm, easy to move in, but still sexy.

She was leaning over the bathroom sink, finishing her makeup, when Nate entered, a glass of wine in each hand. "I thought you might like this." He handed her a glass.

She sipped, her eyes locked to his. Despite the fading black eye and bruised temple, he had never looked more handsome to her. Maturity sat well on him, and though she still recognized the boy he had been, she appreciated more the man he had become.

She set aside the wine glass and wrapped her arms around him. "This was a good idea," she said.

"The wine? Or the date."

"The date."

He set his own glass beside hers, then drew her close for

a kiss—not the eager kiss of an impatient lover or the perfunctory embrace of a man doing what was expected, but a deep, tender caress that invited lingering and exploration.

She arched her body to his and angled her mouth to draw even closer, sinking into the sensation of his body wrapped around her and the response of her own. Her pulse thrummed in her ears and all thought of anything or anyone fled, and with it every bit of tension that had lately strained her nerves and disturbed her sleep.

She moaned in protest when Nate pulled away, and opened her eyes to stare at him accusingly. "Your phone," he said, gesturing toward the bedroom.

Then she realized a tinny reproduction of an old-fashioned phone ring was echoing from the bedroom. She pushed past him and retrieved the phone from the dresser. When she saw Mrs. O'Keefe's name her relaxed happiness vanished. "Hello? Mrs. O'Keefe, is everything all right?"

"Oh, Jamie!" Mrs. O'Keefe's voice broke in what sounded like a sob. "I'm so sorry. I don't know what to do."

"What is it? What happened?" Nate moved in behind her and she glanced back at him, sure her eyes reflected her sense of panic, then held the phone a little away from her ear so that he could hear, too.

"I stopped to get gas and went inside to pay," Mrs. O'Keefe said, the words pouring out in a rush. "I was sure Henry and Donna would be fine while I was away, but when I came out, she was gone."

"Gone? Donna is gone?" Jamie's voice rose, on the edge of hysteria. Nate's arm encircled her, holding her up as her knees threatened to buckle. "Where is she?"

"I don't know!" Mrs. O'Keefe wailed. "Henry said two men in masks grabbed her and dragged her from the car. One of them hit him—he's bleeding, and when I got there he was hysterical. A sheriff's deputy is here, but I knew I needed to call you."

"We're on our way." Jamie ended the call and grabbed her keys from the dresser. "We have to go," she said, already running for the stairs. "Someone's taken Donna."

Chapter Nineteen

Nate drove as fast as he dared from Jamie's house to the corner where Eagle Mountain's two gas stations stood opposite each other. It had started to snow again, and the streets were mostly empty. Mrs. O'Keefe's Honda sat beside the end gas pump, a sheriff's department cruiser behind it. Jamie was out of the truck before Nate had come to a complete stop, hurrying to where Gage stood with Mrs. O'Keefe beside her vehicle. When Mrs. O'Keefe saw Jamie approaching, she burst into sobs.

Gage moved to one side while Jamie embraced the older woman. Nate approached him. "What have you got?" Nate asked.

"Two men in a white soft-top Jeep pulled up. One got out, jerked open the back door of the O'Keefe car and slashed the seat belt. He clamped one hand over Donna's mouth and dragged her out of the vehicle. When Henry tried to go after them, he punched him—hard. I think the poor kid's nose is probably broken."

"Did anyone see what happened?"

Gage shook his head. "Mrs. O'Keefe was the only customer and the clerk was busy with her."

Nate nodded toward a camera mounted above the gas pumps. "Maybe we'll get something from that."

"Maybe," Gage said. "But the camera is focused next to

the pumps, to catch people who drive off without paying for their gas. The kidnappers pulled up on the far side of the O'Keefe car. Henry says they wore masks."

"We don't need to see them to know who did this," Nate said.

The ambulance pulled in on the other side of the gas pumps, followed by the sheriff's cruiser.

EMT Emmett Baxter climbed out and approached the car. Mrs. O'Keefe and Travis met him. Jamie walked over to stand with Gage and Nate, her arms hugged tightly across her chest. The lighting under the gas pump canopy cast a sickly yellow glow, and snow blew around them in dizzying swirls.

Nate went to his truck and retrieved his coat and put it around her shoulders. "It's freezing out here," he said.

"I don't even feel it," she said. "I don't feel anything." Her eyes met his, red-rimmed and bleak. "What if they kill her?"

"You can't think that," he said.

She glanced over toward the car, where Henry sat in the back seat. "Go see about Henry," she said. "He had to see it happen, and he tried to protect her." She covered her mouth with her hand. He started to reach for her, but she pulled away. "Go make sure Henry is okay."

Henry sat between Emmett and his mother in the back seat of the Honda. Nate opened the passenger door and leaned in. "How's it going?" he asked.

"His nose is broken," Emmett said. "We'll have to splint it." He turned back to Mrs. O'Keefe. "We can give him something for the pain first, if you think that's all right."

"Of course." Mrs. O'Keefe squeezed her son's hand. "It's going to be all right," she said.

"It won't be all right without Donna," he moaned.

"Give me your other hand," Mrs. O'Keefe said. "And look at me."

Henry opened his hand and stared at the crumpled rectangle of white pasteboard in it.

"What have you got there?" Mrs. O'Keefe asked.

Nate leaned in past her. "Let me see," he said.

Henry held out his hand and Nate stared at the crumpled business card. "Ice cold," he read.

"He shoved this into my hand before he took Donna away," Henry said.

Nate took the card carefully, holding it by the edges, and walked over to where Travis stood with Jamie. When she saw what he held, her face blanched white, but she said nothing.

Travis frowned at the card. "This doesn't fit the pattern for the other women," he said.

"No, it doesn't," Nate said. "The others were all alone, taken when no one else was around."

Travis turned to Jamie. "Did you see any strange cars around your house when the O'Keefes and Donna left there this evening?"

"No." She bit her lip. "But I wasn't really looking."

"I didn't see anyone, either," Nate said. He had been focused on Jamie. Still, if Alex and Tim had been there, wouldn't he have known?

"I think they were watching your house and followed Mrs. O'Keefe to the gas station," Travis said. "They saw their chance to grab Donna and took it."

"But why Donna?" Jamie asked. "She never hurt anyone!"

It was the question everyone left behind when a loved one senselessly died asked—the question the families of Kelly Farrow and Christy O'Brien and Michaela Underwood and all the other murder victims had asked. Usually, there was no explanation for a crime like this.

"I don't think they were really after Donna," Travis said.

"Then why?" Jamie looked dazed.

"I think they were after you," Travis said. "This was a way to get to you. To get to a cop. It's what they've wanted all along."

"They can have me," she said. "As long as they don't hurt Donna."

"They're not going to have either of you," Travis said.

"We have to figure out where they've taken her," Nate said. "They have to be holed up somewhere."

Gage emerged from the gas station office. "The security camera at the pump picked up a partial plate number for the vehicle the kidnappers were in," he said. He handed Travis a slip of paper.

"It's the last two numbers of a Colorado plate," Travis said. "That will help—the first three letters are the same for half the cars registered in the county, but the last three are different." He returned the paper to Gage. "Call this in to Dwight. Tell him to do a search for every white Jeep Wrangler in the county and see if he can match this."

"I'm on it," Gage said.

"Let me help," Jamie said. "I'm good on the computer and focusing on the search will help keep me from going crazy."

Travis looked at her a long moment, as if trying to decide if she was going to crack up. "All right," he said. "Go help Dwight."

"I'll take you," Nate said.

They drove to the station in silence. There was no sense trying to comfort Jamie with words. The only thing that counted was action. He parked in front of the sheriff's department and came around to open the door for her. She slipped off his jacket and pressed it on him. "Are you coming in?" she asked.

He shook his head. "No. I'm going to talk to Pi and Greg again. Neither were very forthcoming when we interviewed them earlier, but Travis thinks they know something they aren't telling us, and I'm going to find out what that is."

But when Mrs. Calendri answered the door and Nate showed her his ID, she told him her son wasn't at home. "He's with Greg and Gus," she said.

"Could you call him for me?" Nate shoved his hands in the pocket of his jacket, which still carried a faint whiff of the lotion Jamie used. "It's important."

She retreated into the house and returned with a phone in her hand. She held it to her ear for a moment, then shook her head. "He isn't answering." Another pause, then she said, "Pi, please call your mother as soon as you can. It's important." She ended the call.

"Do you know Greg and Gus's numbers?" Nate asked.

"No. I don't. What is this about? Is Pi in some kind of trouble?"

"I hope not, Mrs. Calendri. We're trying to find someone who may be involved in a crime, and we think your son might be able to help us."

The lines around her eyes tightened. "I don't have Greg and Gus's numbers, but I can tell you where they live."

Greg Eicklebaum lived only two blocks away. Nate drove there and found him and Gus playing video games in a den off the garage. "We don't know where Pi is," Greg said after Nate explained his mission. "He was supposed to come over this afternoon, then said he had something else to do."

Nate sat and faced the boys, so close to them their knees almost touched. "You've got to tell me everything you know about those two climbers you saw out near the campground that day," he said. "We think they kidnapped a young disabled woman this evening. Her life may depend on us finding them." His throat tightened as he said the words, but he pushed the image of Donna, helpless and afraid, away. He had a job to do, and that meant staying focused on facts, not emotions.

The two boys exchanged glances, then Gus said, "We saw one of them this morning."

"Where?"

"We were walking over to the park to shoot hoops." He gestured to the north. "This white Jeep pulled up to the stop sign and we looked over and it was one of the guys—the taller one, with the lighter hair. I remembered his sunglasses—really sharp Oakleys. We waved, but I don't think he saw us."

"You don't know where he was driving from—or where he went?" Nate asked.

"No," Gus said. "But Pi figured he must live near here, because nobody else really drives around here. I mean, there aren't any through streets or anything."

"Can you think of anything else that could help us find this guy?" Nate asked.

They both shook their heads. "I wish we could," Greg said. "Really."

"If you think of anything, call the sheriff's office," Nate said.

He returned to the sheriff's department and found Gage and the sheriff huddled with Dwight and Jamie in the situation room. "We think we've got something," Gage said when Nate joined them.

"There are a lot of white Jeeps registered in the county," Dwight said, tapping the keys of a laptop open on the desk before him. "But only two with the two numbers the security camera caught. One is registered to Amber Perry of 161 Maple Court, the other to Jonathan Dirkson of 17 Trapper Lane."

"Trapper Lane," Nate said.

The others stared at him. "Trapper Lane is in the same neighborhood as Pi Calendri and Greg Eicklebaum," he said. "I just talked to Greg and Gus Elcott, and Greg said they saw one of the climbers they had run into earlier, driving a white Jeep in their neighborhood this morning."

"What's the contact information for Dirkson?" Travis said.

"I'm on it," Jamie said, furiously typing at a second laptop. "Jonathan Dirkson's contact information is in Phoenix," she said.

"That's it!" Nate said. "The house on Trapper Lane is probably a vacation home. Alex and Tim broke into an unoccupied home and made use of the vehicle that was probably in the garage."

"A lot of houses in that neighborhood are second homes," Gage said. "And a lot of people rent them out short-term. Alex and Tim could tell anyone who asked they were vacationing here and the chances of anyone checking with the house's owner are slim to none."

"Let's go," Travis said.

Jamie shoved back her chair. "I'm coming with you," she said. "And don't tell me to stay here. If I'm really the one they want, then maybe I can help to trap them."

"All right." Travis turned to Nate. "I suppose you're going to come, too."

"You could use another trained officer."

"Go with Jamie, in her cruiser," Travis said. "And try not to get hurt. I don't want to have to explain to your boss how you were injured yet again when you aren't even officially on duty."

FOUR SHERIFF'S DEPARTMENT CRUISERS—and most of the sheriff's department, plus Nate—blockaded both ends of Trapper Lane. They surrounded the house, and the sheriff used a bullhorn to demand that Tim and Alex release Donna and come out with their hands up. But the only reaction they received was silence, and furtive looks through the curtains from the neighbors.

Dwight approached the house from the side, then returned to the others. "The Jeep isn't in the garage," he said. "Maybe they aren't here."

"Then we search the house," Travis said.

While the others hung back to provide cover, he and Gage approached the front door. Travis knocked, then tried the knob, and the door swung open. They disappeared into the house and emerged a long five minutes later. "It's clear," Travis called.

The others entered the empty, though orderly, house. Dust covers draped the furniture in every room but the kitchen and a small den where Tim and Alex had apparently established themselves. A couple of sleeping bags were rolled up on the floor of the den, and a few empty cans in the kitchen garbage can were the only evidence of occupation.

"Search every room," Travis said. "I want anything that might be tied to them, or that might tell us where they are now."

Dwight found Donna's corsage on the floor of the mudroom, the flowers crushed. Jamie stared at the forlorn flowers, then turned away, breathing hard.

"I noticed a shed out back," Dwight said. "Someone should check that."

"I will," Jamie said. She needed to get out of this house where her sister had been held.

The shed was a prefab wooden structure, about five feet

by seven feet, with a single door. The door wasn't locked, but Jamie had to force it open. When she finally stepped inside, she saw the reason for her difficulty as she shone her flashlight over the body of Pi Calendri. Her heart sank as she passed the light over the wound in his shoulder and the pool of blood on the concrete floor.

"Somebody help me," he moaned, and Jamie dropped to her knees beside him.

"Pi, what happened?" she asked, feeling for his pulse.

But she never heard his answer, as her head exploded in pain, and the world went black.

Chapter Twenty

Jamie came to in a fog of pain. Her head pounded and her arms ached, and the smell of dust and old wood smoke mingled with the haunting scent of her mother's perfume. As her head cleared, she realized she was lying on a bed, her hands bound beneath her back. Dusty wood beams stretched overhead and nothing looked familiar. She turned her head to the side and relief surged through when she saw a teary-eyed Donna staring back at her, and the memory of being with Pi in the garden shed returned. Someone must have attacked her and brought her to this place. "Are you all right?" Jamie whispered.

"I tore my tights," Donna said. "And I lost my flowers."

Before they could talk more, the door opened and a young man in a blue beanie and parka shuffled in. "Who are you and what are you doing with us?" Jamie asked.

"You don't know who I am?" He chuckled. "I'm the Ice Cold Killer."

Jamie recognized him now, from the flyer Travis had printed. Tim Dawson. "There are two of you," Jamie said. "Where's your friend?"

"So you figured that out, did you?" He stripped off his coat to reveal a faded red sweatshirt over jeans, then dropped into a straight-backed wooden chair. "He had some things he had to take care of."

"What are you going to do with us?" she asked.

"What do you think?" He clasped his hands behind his head. "The same thing we did to the others. My friend is out there now, looking for a good place to dump your bodies."

Donna began to cry. Though her hands were bound, Jamie shifted her body toward her sister, trying to comfort her. "Why are you doing this?" she asked.

"You haven't figured that out?" He leaned toward her. "Cops are so clueless. The Ice Cold Killer kills women, right? So killing a cop would be the ultimate. Your sister was just a way to get to you."

Jamie lay back on the bed, trying to memorize the details of her surroundings, searching for a way out. The room they were in wasn't very big, and seemed to be a combination kitchen, dining, living room and bedroom. A cabin, then. One of those Forest Service cabins where Alex and Tim had hidden before? Presumably when the second killer returned, they would kill Donna and Jamie, and transport them to the dump site. Or would they transport them first and kill them there? The latter provided more opportunities for escape, but she couldn't rely on that.

She would probably only have one chance to save her sister. She would have to be ready to take it, with no hesitation.

"WHERE'S JAMIE?" NATE ASKED, when he had finished searching the upstairs bedroom of the house, which had yielded no evidence that the two killers had ever been in there.

Dwight looked up from pulling books from the bookcase. "She went out to check the shed."

"You let her go out there alone?" Nate asked.

"I'd let you go out there alone," Dwight said.

Nate didn't bother answering but raced outside. The

door of the shed stood open, and as he approached, he heard moaning.

Pi Calendri lay in a pool of blood on the floor of the garden shed, his head resting on the deck of a lawnmower, his feet on a sack of mulch. Nate pulled out a phone and called for an ambulance, then knelt beside the young man and tried to rouse him.

Pi's eyes flickered open. "It hurts bad," he said, his voice faint.

"Hang in there, buddy," Nate said. "Help is on the way." He examined the injury to the boy's shoulder. Pi had lost a lot of blood and he might be in shock, but the wound was a clean one. "Tell me what happened, so I can find out who did this."

"Those two climbers? I saw one this morning and figured they were in the neighborhood. I knew you were looking for them. I figured maybe they were the Ice Cold Killers. I figured I'd find them—you know, be a hero." He closed his eyes. "Guess I was really stupid."

"Stay with me," Nate said. "The ambulance will be here soon."

Pi moaned.

"Pi!" Nate patted his cheek and the young man opened his eyes. "Did you see a woman come in here? Just a little while ago."

"No, I haven't seen anything. Just help me, man, I'm scared."

"I'll help you, I promise," Nate said. "What did you see before you were shot?"

"I found the house. I knew it was the right one because I saw the Jeep in the garage. I looked through the back window and saw one of the guys with this chubby girl dressed all in pink. I was looking for a way into the garage. I thought maybe I'd disable the Jeep so they couldn't leave, you know? But when I got back here, the other one stepped out from the shed and just shot me."

"Did you overhear any conversation? Did they say where they were headed from here?"

Pi shook his head and closed his eyes again. "I didn't hear anything. It really hurts. Where's that ambulance?"

"It will be here soon."

The light changed and Nate turned to see Dwight in the doorway. "What happened to him?" he asked.

"Gunshot wound. The ambulance is on its way."

"Where's Jamie?"

"I don't know." Nate rose. "Stay with Pi, will you? I've got to go look for her."

He found Travis in the living room, on the phone. The sheriff ended the call. "I put out a BOLO on the Jeep, and there's already an Amber Alert for Donna."

"With the roads closed, we know they can't go far," Nate said.

"It's still a big county," Travis said.

"I think they'll go somewhere familiar," Nate said. "Some place they don't think we'll look, because we've looked there before."

"You think they'll go back to the summer cabins?" Travis asked.

"It makes the most sense," Nate said. "It's easy to get to, but away from other houses and people."

"Which cabins?" Travis asked.

"Sundance," Nate said. "They stayed there at least a few days, and the back way to the road makes it easier for them to get away. And they burned the Toyota there. They keep coming back to that location."

"Then let's go."

JAMIE FOCUSED ON keeping Tim talking. As long as she was talking, she and Donna were still alive. "What made you come to Eagle Mountain?" she asked. "You'd have a lot more targets in a big city like Denver."

"More cops, too," Tim said. "But coming here was my partner's idea. Some woman he knew was here and he wanted to see her. Then he realized how easy it would be to fool a little sheriff's department like this one. It was kind of an experiment, I guess."

"And you just went along with the idea of killing a bunch of women?" Jamie wasn't sure she did a good job of masking her disgust.

"Yeah, well, I was a little freaked out with the first one, but then, it was kind of a thrill, you know? Getting away with something, right under the cops' noses." He stood and walked over to the bed. "And now there'll be one less cop to follow us around."

Donna whimpered and pressed closer against Jamie, who could feel her shaking. "Is this really your sister?" Tim asked. "She doesn't look like you. Must be a drag, having to look after her."

"It's not a drag," Jamie said. "Donna is the most wonderful sister in the world. I'm very lucky to have her."

"Well, you won't have anything much longer. As soon as my friend gets back—" He made a slashing motion across his throat.

Donna began to sob again.

A phone rang and Tim answered. "Yeah? Where are you, man? I'm waiting… What? You're gonna make me deal with both of them?… No, I'm not saying I can't do it, just that that's not how this works. We're a team, aren't we?… All right, all right. I'll bring them and we can do them there. Where are you?" He glanced toward the window. "It's really coming down out there, isn't it?… Yeah,

I know you like the snow 'cause it covers our tracks. It's still cold… All right. Be there in a few." He replaced the phone in his pocket. "Change of plans, ladies. We're gonna go for a little ride." He reached for Donna but as soon as he touched her, she screamed.

"Shut up!" He slapped her across the face, then pulled a bandanna from his pocket and stuffed it in her mouth. "You cooperate or I'll slit your throat right here." He shifted his gaze to Jamie. "And if you give me any trouble, I'll kill her first—slowly."

Jamie suppressed a shudder. For whatever reason, Alex had left Tim to deal with her and Donna on his own. That upped the odds in her favor. "Donna, honey, you do what he says," she said.

Tim hauled Donna to her feet. "That's better," he said. "Now I'm gonna put you in this chair by the door, then I'll get your sister. I'll tie the two of you together and cut loose your feet, then we'll all go out to the car. And remember, don't try anything." He pulled a small pistol from beneath his sweatshirt. "I can't miss from this close range."

Jamie's stomach clenched as she stared at the pistol, then she forced herself to look away. Even if he fired on her, he might not kill her. Some chance of staying alive was better than none. She braced herself and when he bent over to pull her to her feet, she resisted. "I'm caught on something," she said, pretending to try to raise up. "I think the tape on my wrists is hung up on a spring or something."

"What?" He bent over to take a closer look and she brought her knees up and hit him hard in the nose. A sickening crunch, and blood spurted across her. Tim screamed and dropped the pistol, clutching at his nose. He stumbled backward and Jamie struggled upright. She dived for the gun even as he reached for it, and then he was standing over her, kicking her and cursing. She dodged his blows and kicked out at the pistol, sending it skittering under the bed. Tim struck her hard on the side of the head. Her vision blurred and her stomach heaved. "Donna, run!" she shouted. "Hop or crawl if you have to, just leave."

Donna remained in her chair, tears streaming down her face. "Jamie, I can't leave you!"

"Donna, go!"

"Neither one of you are going anywhere." Tim had retrieved the gun and stood over her, the barrel of the pistol inches from her forehead. Jamie closed her eyes and thought of Nate—how she would never see him again, or get to tell him that she loved him. She'd been so foolish, wasting time being afraid of what might happen, instead of enjoying the time they had together.

The door to the cabin burst open and gunfire exploded. Jamie braced herself against the pain she was sure would come, but instead only felt hands reaching for her. She opened her eyes to find Nate beside her, slashing through the tape at her wrists and ankles. She threw her arms around him and he gathered her close. "Donna?" she asked.

"She's fine. Travis is helping her."

The tears she had been holding back for the last few hours burst forth. "I love you," she sobbed. "I'm sorry I didn't tell you before."

"Shhh." He patted her back, soothing her. "You didn't have to tell me," he said. "I knew."

"How did you know?" She stared at him through the tears.

"That day I saw you at the scavenger hunt on Travis's ranch, when you wouldn't even look at me. I knew I'd never stopped loving you—and that you wouldn't avoid me like that unless there were still some strong feelings buried somewhere."

"You were awfully sure of yourself," she said.

"I was sure you were the only woman for me," he said. had to go away to figure that out, but now I'm back to ay."

Jamie clutched his shoulder. "I come with a lot of bag- ige, you know."

He hugged her close. "Donna isn't baggage," he whis- ered. "She's an extra bonus. I never had a sister, you now."

"Am I gonna be your sister?" Donna knelt beside them.

"If you'll have me for a brother," Nate said.

"I think you'd better ask Jamie if she'll have you for a usband," Donna said. "That's the way it's supposed to ork, you know. You propose to your girlfriend, not her ster."

Jamie almost laughed out loud at the expression on ate's face, but he recovered quickly and took her hand. What about it, Jamie?" he asked. "Will you marry me?"

"Yes." She kissed him.

"Yes!" Donna said and kissed him, too.

Someone cleared his throat, and Jamie looked up to see le sheriff standing over them. "Tim Dawson is dead," he iid. "Do you know where Alex Woodruff is?"

"He called and told Tim to meet him somewhere, and to ring us with him," Jamie said. "But I don't know where." he looked at Nate. "Did you shoot Tim?"

"If I hadn't, he would have killed you," he said.

She nodded. "Yes."

"Maybe we can trace Alex through Tim's phone," Tra- is said. "We'll gather what evidence we can here. In the leantime, Nate, will you take Jamie and her sister home?"

"I should stay and help," Jamie said, trying to scram- le to her feet.

"Take care of your sister first," Travis said. "That's an rder, Deputy."

"Yes, sir." She would take care of Donna. She and Na~~
together. They would be a family. Amazing how wonde~~
ful that sounded.

Ice Cold Killer Claims Another Victim

A twenty-three-year-old local woman is the Ice Cold Killer's latest victim, after her body was found in her vehicle on County Road Seven early Tuesday morning. Her identity has not been released, pending notification of her next of kin.

Sheriff Travis Walker announced Monday evening that Timothy Dawson, 21, who was one of the chief suspects in the string of murders that have shocked Rayford County over the past few weeks, was killed during a confrontation with law enforcement officers. Dawson's accomplice remains at large and, as the latest murder seems to indicate, intends to continue his killing spree.

* * * * *

LET'S TALK
Romance

For exclusive extracts, competitions
and special offers, find us online:

MILLS & BOON
A ROMANCE FOR EVERY READER

- **FREE** delivery direct to your door
- **EXCLUSIVE** offers every month
- **SAVE** up to 25% on pre-paid subscriptior

SUBSCRIBE AND SAVE

millsandboon.co.uk/Subscribe

MILLS & BOON

THE HEART OF ROMANCE

A ROMANCE FOR EVERY READER

ODERN
Prepare to be swept off your feet by sophisticated, sexy and seductive heroes, in some of the world's most glamourous and romantic locations, where power and passion collide.

TORICAL
Escape with historical heroes from time gone by. Whether your passion is for wicked Regency Rakes, muscled Vikings or rugged Highlanders, awaken the romance of the past.

EDICAL
Set your pulse racing with dedicated, delectable doctors in the high-pressure world of medicine, where emotions run high and passion, comfort and love are the best medicine.

ue Love
Celebrate true love with tender stories of heartfelt romance, from the rush of falling in love to the joy a new baby can bring, and a focus on the emotional heart of a relationship.

Desire
Indulge in secrets and scandal, intense drama and plenty of sizzling hot action with powerful and passionate heroes who have it all: wealth, status, good looks…everything but the right woman.

EROES
Experience all the excitement of a gripping thriller, with an intense romance at its heart. Resourceful, true-to-life women and strong, fearless men face danger and desire - a killer combination!

To see which titles are coming soon, please visit

millsandboon.co.uk/nextmonth

JOIN US ON SOCIAL MEDIA!

Stay up to date with our latest releases, author news and gossip, special offers and discounts, and all the behind-the-scenes action from Mills & Boon...

 @millsandboon

 @millsandboonuk

 facebook.com/millsandboon

 @millsandboonuk

It might just be true love...

GET YOUR ROMANCE FIX!

Get the latest romance news,
exclusive author interviews, story
extracts and much more!

MILLS & BOON

MODERN

Power and Passion

Prepare to be swept off your feet by sophisticated, sexy and seductive heroes, in some of the world's most glamourous and romantic locations, where power and passion collide.

MILLS & BOON
True Love
Romance from the Heart

Celebrate true love with tender stories of heartfelt romance, from the rush of falling in love to the joy a new baby can bring, and a focus on the emotional heart of a relationship.